# VELOCITY

Dean Koontz was born and raised in Pennsylvania. He is the author of many number one bestsellers. He lives with his wife Gerda and their dog Trixie in southern California.

ALSO BY DEAN KOONTZ

*The Taking*
*Odd Thomas*
*The Face*
*By the Light of the Moon*
*One Door Away From Heaven*
*From the Corner of His Eye*
*False Memory*
*Seize the Night*
*Fear Nothing*
*Mr. Murder*
*Dragon Tears*
*Hideaway*
*Cold Fire*
*The Bad Place*
*Midnight*
*Lightning*
*Watchers*
*Strangers*
*Twilight Eyes*
*Darkfall*
*Phantoms*
*Whispers*
*Forever Odd*
*Brother Odd*
*The Mask*
*The Vision*
*The Face of Fear*
*Night Chills*
*Shattered*
*The Voice of the Night*
*The Servants of Twilight*
*The House of Thunder*
*The Key to Midnight*
*The Eyes of Darkness*
*Shadowfires*
*Winter Moon*
*The Door to December*
*Dark Rivers of the Heart*
*Icebound*
*Strange Highways*
*Intensity*
*Sole Survivor*
*Ticktock*
*The Funhouse*
*Demon Seed*
*Life Expectancy*
*The Husband*

DEAN KOONTZ

# *Velocity*

HARPER

HarperCollins*Publishers*
77–85 Fulham Palace Road,
Hammersmith, London W6 8JB

www.harpercollins.co.uk

Special overseas edition 2006
15

First published in Great Britain by
HarperCollins*Publishers* 2005



ISBN-13: 978-0-00-719697-5
ISBN-10: 0-00-719697-0

Typeset in Meridien by Palimpsest Book Production Limited,
Polmont, Stirlingshire
Printed and bound in Great Britain by
Clays Ltd, St Ives plc

This book is dedicated to Donna and Steve Dunio,
Vito and Lynn Cerra, Ross and Rosemary Cerra.
I'll never figure out why Gerda said yes to me.
But now your family has a crazy wing.

*A man can be destroyed but not defeated.*

—Ernest Hemingway,
The Old Man and the Sea

*And now you live dispersed on ribbon roads,*
*And no man knows or cares who is his neighbour*
*Unless his neighbour makes too much disturbance,*
*But all dash to and fro in motor cars,*
*Familiar with the roads and settled nowhere.*

—T. S. Eliot,
Choruses from "The Rock"

# VELOCITY

# PART ONE

# The Choice is Yours

# 1

With draft beer and a smile, Ned Pearsall raised a toast to his deceased neighbor, Henry Friddle, whose death greatly pleased him.

Henry had been killed by a garden gnome. He had fallen off the roof of his two-story house, onto that cheerful-looking figure. The gnome was made of concrete. Henry wasn't.

A broken neck, a cracked skull: Henry perished on impact.

This death-by-gnome had occurred four years previously. Ned Pearsall still toasted Henry's passing at least once a week.

Now, from a stool near the curve of the polished mahogany bar, an out-of-towner, the only other customer, expressed curiosity at the enduring nature of Ned's animosity.

"How bad a neighbor could the poor guy have been that you're still so juiced about him?"

Ordinarily, Ned might have ignored the question.

He had even less use for tourists than he did for pretzels.

The tavern offered free bowls of pretzels because they were cheap. Ned preferred to sustain his thirst with well-salted peanuts.

To keep Ned tipping, Billy Wiles, tending bar, occasionally gave him a bag of Planters.

Most of the time Ned had to pay for his nuts. This rankled him either because he could not grasp the economic realities of tavern operation or because he enjoyed being rankled, probably the latter.

Although he had a head reminiscent of a squash ball and the heavy rounded shoulders of a sumo wrestler, Ned was an athletic man only if you thought barroom jabber and grudge-holding qualified as sports. In those events, he was an Olympian.

Regarding the late Henry Friddle, Ned could be as talkative with outsiders as with lifelong residents of Vineyard Hills. When, as now, the only other customer was a stranger, Ned found silence even less congenial than conversation with a "foreign devil."

Billy himself had never been much of a talker, never one of those barkeeps who considered the bar a stage. He was a listener.

To the out-of-towner, Ned declared, "Henry Friddle was a pig."

The stranger had hair as black as coal dust with traces of ash at the temples, gray eyes bright with dry amusement, and a softly resonant voice. "That's a strong word—*pig.*"

"You know what the pervert was doing on his roof? He was trying to piss on my dining-room windows."

Wiping the bar, Billy Wiles didn't even glance at the tourist. He'd heard this story so often that he knew all the reactions to it.

"Friddle, the pig, figured the altitude would give his stream more distance," Ned explained.

The stranger said, "What was he—an aeronautical engineer?"

"He was a college professor. He taught contemporary literature."

"Maybe reading that stuff drove him to suicide," the tourist said, which made him more interesting than Billy had first thought.

"No, no," Ned said impatiently. "The fall was accidental."

"Was he drunk?"

"Why would you think he was drunk?" Ned wondered.

The stranger shrugged. "He climbed on a roof to urinate on your windows."

"He was a sick man," Ned explained, plinking one finger against his empty glass to indicate the desire for another round.

Drawing Budweiser from the tap, Billy said, "Henry Friddle was consumed by vengeance."

After silent communion with his brew, the

tourist asked Ned Pearsall, "Vengeance? So you urinated on Friddle's windows first?"

"It wasn't the same thing at all," Ned warned in a rough tone that advised the outsider to avoid being judgmental.

"Ned didn't do it from his roof," Billy said.

"That's right. I walked up to his house, like a man, stood on his lawn, and aimed at his dining-room windows."

"Henry and his wife were having dinner at the time," Billy said.

Before the tourist might express revulsion at the timing of this assault, Ned said, "They were eating quail, for God's sake."

"You showered their windows because they were eating quail?"

Ned sputtered with exasperation. "No, of course not. Do I look insane to you?" He rolled his eyes at Billy.

Billy raised his eyebrows as though to say *What do you expect of a tourist?*

"I'm just trying to convey how pretentious they were," Ned clarified, "always eating quail or snails, or Swiss chard."

"Phony bastards," the tourist said with such a light seasoning of mockery that Ned Pearsall didn't detect it, although Billy did.

"Exactly," Ned confirmed. "Henry Friddle drove a Jaguar, and his wife drove a car—you won't believe this—a car made in *Sweden*."

"Detroit was too common for them," said the tourist.

"Exactly. How much of a snob do you have to be to bring a car all the way from Sweden?"

The tourist said, "I'll wager they were wine connoisseurs."

"Big time! Did you know them or something?"

"I just know the type. They had a lot of books."

"You've got 'em nailed," Ned declared. "They'd sit on the front porch, *sniffing* their wine, reading books."

"Right out in public. Imagine that. But if you didn't pee on their dining-room windows because they were snobs, why *did* you?"

"A thousand reasons," Ned assured him. "The incident of the skunk. The incident of the lawn fertilizer. The dead petunias."

"And the garden gnome," Billy added as he rinsed glasses in the bar sink.

"The garden gnome was the last straw," Ned agreed.

"I can understand being driven to aggressive urination by pink plastic flamingos," said the tourist, "but, frankly, not by a gnome."

Ned scowled, remembering the affront. "Ariadne gave it my face."

"Ariadne who?"

"Henry Friddle's wife. You ever heard a more pretentious name?"

"Well, the Friddle part brings it down to earth."

"She was an art professor at the same college. She sculpted the gnome, created the mold, poured the concrete, painted it herself."

"Having a sculpture modeled after you can be an honor."

The beer foam on Ned's upper lip gave him a rabid appearance as he protested: "It was a *gnome,* pal. A *drunken* gnome. The nose was as red as an apple. It was carrying a beer bottle in each hand."

"And its fly was unzipped," Billy added.

"Thanks *so* much for reminding me," Ned grumbled. "Worse, hanging out of its pants was the head and neck of a dead goose."

"How creative," said the tourist.

"At first I didn't know what the hell *that* meant—"

"Symbolism. Metaphor."

"Yeah, yeah. I figured it out. Everybody who walked past their place saw it, and got a laugh at my expense."

"Wouldn't need to see the gnome for that," said the tourist.

Misunderstanding, Ned agreed: "Right. Just *hearing* about it, people were laughing. So I busted up the gnome with a sledgehammer."

"And they sued you."

"Worse. They set out another gnome. Figuring I'd bust up the first, Ariadne had cast and painted a second."

"I thought life was mellow here in the wine country."

"Then they tell me," Ned continued, "if I bust up the second one, they'll put a third on the lawn, *plus* they'll manufacture a bunch and sell 'em at cost to anyone who wants a Ned Pearsall gnome."

"Sounds like an empty threat," said the tourist. "Would there really be people who'd want such a thing?"

"Dozens," Billy assured him.

"This town's become a mean place since the pâté-and-brie crowd started moving in from San Francisco," Ned said sullenly.

"So when you didn't dare take a sledgehammer to the second gnome, you were left with no choice but to pee on their windows."

"Exactly. But I didn't just go off half-cocked. I thought about the situation for a week. *Then* I hosed them."

"After which, Henry Friddle climbed on his roof with a full bladder, looking for justice."

"Yeah. But he waited till I had a birthday dinner for my mom."

"Unforgivable," Billy judged.

"Does the Mafia attack innocent members of a man's family?" Ned asked indignantly.

Although the question had been rhetorical, Billy played for his tip: "No. The Mafia's got *class*."

"Which is a word these professor types can't

even spell," Ned said. "Mom was seventy-six. She could have had a heart attack."

"So," the tourist said, "while trying to urinate on your dining-room windows, Friddle fell off his roof and broke his neck on the Ned Pearsall gnome. Pretty ironic."

"I don't know ironic," Ned replied. "But it sure was *sweet.*"

"Tell him what your mom said," Billy urged.

Following a sip of beer, Ned obliged: "My mom told me, 'Honey, praise the Lord, this proves there's a God.'"

After taking a moment to absorb those words, the tourist said, "She sounds like quite a religious woman."

"She wasn't always. But at seventy-two, she caught pneumonia."

"It's sure convenient to have God at a time like that."

"She figured if God existed, maybe He'd save her. If He didn't exist, she wouldn't be out nothing but some time wasted on prayer."

"Time," the tourist advised, "is our most precious possession."

"True," Ned agreed. "But Mom wouldn't have wasted much because mostly she could pray while she watched TV."

"What an inspiring story," said the tourist, and ordered a beer.

Billy opened a pretentious bottle of Heineken,

provided a fresh chilled glass, and whispered, "This one's on the house."

"That's nice of you. Thanks. I'd been thinking you're quiet and soft-spoken for a bartender, but now maybe I understand why."

From his lonely outpost farther along the bar, Ned Pearsall raised his glass in a toast. "To Ariadne. May she rest in peace."

Although it might have been against his will, the tourist was engaged again. Of Ned, he asked, "Not another gnome tragedy?"

"Cancer. Two years after Henry fell off the roof. I sure wish it hadn't happened."

Pouring the fresh Heineken down the side of his tilted glass, the stranger said, "Death has a way of putting our petty squabbles in perspective."

"I miss her," Ned said. "She had the most spectacular rack, and she didn't always wear a bra."

The tourist twitched.

"She'd be working in the yard," Ned remembered almost dreamily, "or walking the dog, and that fine pair would be bouncing and swaying so sweet you couldn't catch your breath."

The tourist checked his face in the back-bar mirror, perhaps to see if he looked as appalled as he felt.

"Billy," Ned asked, "didn't she have the finest set of mamas you could hope to see?"

"She did," Billy agreed.

Ned slid off his stool, shambled toward the men's room, paused at the tourist. "Even when cancer withered her, those mamas didn't shrink. The leaner she got, the bigger they were in proportion. Almost to the end, she looked *hot.* What a waste, huh, Billy?"

"What a waste," Billy echoed as Ned continued to the men's room.

After a shared silence, the tourist said, "You're an interesting guy, Billy Barkeep."

"*Me?* I've never hosed anyone's windows."

"You're like a sponge, I think. You take everything in."

Billy picked up a dishcloth and polished some pilsner glasses that had previously been washed and dried.

"But then you're a stone too," the tourist said, "because if you're squeezed, you give nothing back."

Billy continued polishing the glasses.

The gray eyes, bright with amusement, brightened further. "You're a man with a philosophy, which is unusual these days, when most people don't know who they are or what they believe, or why."

This, too, was a style of barroom jabber with which Billy was familiar, though he didn't hear it often. Compared to Ned Pearsall's rants, such boozy observations could seem erudite; but it was all just beer-based psychoanalysis.

He was disappointed. Briefly, the tourist had

seemed different from the usual two-cheeked heaters who warmed the barstool vinyl.

Smiling, shaking his head, Billy said, "Philosophy. You give me too much credit."

The tourist sipped his Heineken.

Although Billy had not intended to say more, he heard himself continue: "Stay low, stay quiet, keep it simple, don't expect much, enjoy what you have."

The stranger smiled. "Be self-sufficient, don't get involved, let the world go to Hell if it wants."

"Maybe," Billy conceded.

"Admittedly, it's not Plato," said the tourist, "but it *is* a philosophy."

"You have one of your own?" Billy asked.

"Right now, I believe that my life will be better and more meaningful if I can just avoid any further conversation with Ned."

"That's not a philosophy," Billy told him. "That's a fact."

At ten minutes past four, Ivy Elgin came to work. She was a waitress as good as any and an object of desire without equal.

Billy liked her but didn't long for her. His lack of lust made him unique among the men who worked or drank in the tavern.

Ivy had mahogany hair, limpid eyes the color of brandy, and the body for which Hugh Hefner had spent his life searching.

Although twenty-four, she seemed genuinely unaware that she was the essential male fantasy in the flesh. She was never seductive. At times she could be flirtatious, but only in a winsome way.

Her beauty and choirgirl wholesomeness were a combination so erotic that her smile alone could melt the average man's earwax.

"Hi, Billy," Ivy said, coming directly to the bar. "I saw a dead possum along Old Mill Road, about a quarter mile from Kornell Lane."

"Naturally dead or road kill?" he asked.

"Fully road kill."

"What do you think it means?"

"Nothing specific yet," she said, handing her purse to him so he could store it behind the bar. "It's the first dead thing I've seen in a week, so it depends on what other bodies show up, if any."

Ivy believed that she was a haruspex. Haruspices, a class of priests in ancient Rome, divined the future from the entrails of animals killed in sacrifices.

They had been respected, even revered, by other Romans, but most likely they had not received a lot of party invitations.

Ivy wasn't morbid. Haruspicy did not occupy the center of her life. She seldom talked to customers about it.

Neither did she have the stomach to stir through entrails. For a haruspex, she was squeamish.

Instead, she found meaning in the species of the cadaver, in the circumstances of its discovery, in its position related to the points of the compass, and in other arcane aspects of its condition.

Her predictions seldom if ever came true, but Ivy persisted.

"Whatever it turns out to mean," she told Billy as she picked up her order pad and a pencil, "it's a bad sign. A dead possum never indicates good fortune."

"I've noticed that myself."

"Especially not when its nose is pointing north and its tail is pointing east."

Thirsty men trailed through the door soon after Ivy, as if she were a mirage of an oasis that they had been pursuing all day. Only a few sat at the bar; the others kept her bustling table to table.

Although the tavern's middle-class clientele were not high rollers, Ivy's income from tips exceeded what she might have earned had she attained a doctoral degree in economics.

An hour later, at five o'clock, Shirley Trueblood, the second evening waitress, came on duty. Fifty-six, stout, wearing jasmine perfume, Shirley had her own following. Certain men in barrooms always wanted mothering. Some women, too.

The day-shift short-order cook, Ben Vernon, went home. The evening cook, Ramon Padillo, came aboard. The tavern offered only bar food:

cheeseburgers, fries, Buffalo wings, quesadillas, nachos . . .

Ramon had noticed that on the nights Ivy Elgin worked, the spicy dishes sold in greater numbers than when she wasn't waitressing. Guys ordered more things in tomatillo sauce, went through a lot of little bottles of Tabasco, and asked for sliced jalapeños on their burgers.

"I think," Ramon once told Billy, "they're unconsciously packing heat into their gonads to be ready if she comes on to them."

"No one in this joint has a chance at Ivy," Billy assured him.

"You never know," Ramon had said coyly.

"Don't tell me you're packing in the peppers, too."

"So many I have killer heartburn some nights," Ramon had said. "But I'm *ready.*"

With Ramon came the evening bartender, Steve Zillis, whose shift overlapped Billy's by an hour. At twenty-four, he was ten years younger than Billy but twenty years less mature.

For Steve, the height of sophisticated humor was any limerick sufficiently obscene to cause grown men to blush.

He could tie knots in a cherry stem with just his tongue, load his right nostril with peanuts and fire them accurately into a target glass, and blow cigarette smoke out of his right ear.

As usual, Steve vaulted over the end gate in

the bar instead of pushing through it. "How're they hangin', Kemosabe?"

"One hour to go," Billy said, "and I get my life back."

"*This* is life," Steve protested. "The center of the action."

The tragedy of Steve Zillis was that he meant what he said. To him, this common tavern was a glamorous cabaret.

After tying on an apron, he snatched three olives from a bowl, juggled them with dazzling speed, and then caught them one at a time in his mouth.

When two drunks at the bar clapped loudly, Steve basked in their applause as if he were the star tenor at the Metropolitan Opera and had earned the adulation of a refined and knowledgeable audience.

In spite of the affliction of Steve Zillis's company, this final hour of Billy's shift passed quickly. The tavern was busy enough to keep two bartenders occupied as the late-afternoon tipplers delayed going home and the evening drinkers arrived.

As much as he ever could, Billy liked the place during this transitional time. The customers were at peak coherency and happier than they would be later, when alcohol washed them toward melancholy.

Because the windows faced east and the sun lay west, softest daylight painted the panes. The ceiling fixtures layered a coppery glow over the burnt-red mahogany paneling and booths.

The fragrant air was savory with the scents of wood flooring pickled in stale beer, candle wax, cheeseburgers, fried onion rings.

Billy didn't like the place enough, however, to linger past the end of his shift. He left promptly at seven.

If he'd been Steve Zillis, he would have made a production of his exit. Instead, he departed as quietly as a ghost dematerializing from its haunt.

Outside, less than two hours of summer daylight remained. The sky was an electric Maxfield Parrish blue in the east, a paler blue in the west, where the sun still bleached it.

As he approached his Ford Explorer, he noticed a rectangle of white paper under the driver's-side windshield wiper.

Behind the steering wheel, with his door still open, he unfolded the paper, expecting to find a handbill of some kind, advertising a car wash or a maid service. He discovered a neatly typed message:

*If you don't take this note to the police and get them involved, I will kill a lovely blond schoolteacher somewhere in Napa County.*

*If you do take this note to the police, I will instead kill an elderly woman active in charity work.*

*You have six hours to decide. The choice is yours.*

Billy didn't at that instant feel the world tilt under him, but it did. The plunge had not yet begun, but it would. Soon.

# 2

Mickey Mouse took a bullet in the throat.

The 9-mm pistol cracked three more times in rapid succession, shredding Donald Duck's face.

Lanny Olsen, the shooter, lived at the end of a fissured blacktop lane, against a stony hillside where grapes would never grow. He had no view of the fabled Napa Valley.

As compensation for his unfashionable address, the property was shaded by beautiful plum trees and towering elms, brightened by wild azaleas. And it was private.

The nearest neighbor lived at such a distance that Lanny could have partied 24/7 without disturbing anyone. This offered no benefit to Lanny because he usually went to bed at nine-thirty; his idea of a party was a case of beer, a bag of chips, and a poker game.

The location of his property, however, was

conducive to target shooting. He was the most practiced shot in the sheriff's department.

As a boy, he'd wanted to be a cartoonist. He had talent. The Disney-perfect portraits of Mickey Mouse and Donald Duck, fixed to the hay-bale backstop, were Lanny's work.

Ejecting the spent magazine from his pistol, Lanny said, "You should have been here yesterday. I head-shot twelve Road Runners in a row, not a wasted round."

Billy said, "Wile E. Coyote would've been thrilled. You ever shoot at ordinary targets?"

"What would be the fun in that?"

"You ever shoot the Simpsons?"

"Homer, Bart—all of them but Marge," Lanny said. "Never Marge."

Lanny might have gone to art school if his domineering father, Ansel, had not been determined that his son would follow him into law enforcement as Ansel himself had followed *his* father.

Pearl, Lanny's mother, had been as supportive as her illness allowed. When Lanny was sixteen, Pearl had been diagnosed with non-Hodgkin's lymphoma.

Radiation therapy and drugs sapped her. Even in periods when the lymphoma was controlled, she did not fully regain her strength.

Concerned that his father would be a useless nurse, Lanny never went away to art school. He remained at home, took up a career in law enforcement, and looked after his mother.

Unexpectedly, Ansel was first to die. He stopped a motorist for speeding, and the motorist stopped *him* with a .38 fired point-blank.

Having contracted lymphoma at an atypically young age, Pearl lived with it for a surprisingly long time. She had died ten years previously, when Lanny was thirty-six.

He'd still been young enough for a career switch and art school. Inertia, however, proved stronger than the desire for a new life.

He inherited the house, a handsome Victorian with elaborate millwork and an encircling veranda, which he maintained in pristine condition. With a career that was a job but not a passion, and with no family of his own, he had plenty of spare time for the house.

As Lanny shoved a fresh magazine in the pistol, Billy took the typewritten message from a pocket. "What do you make of this?"

Lanny read the two paragraphs while, in the lull of gunfire, blackbirds returned to the high bowers of nearby elms.

The message evoked neither a frown nor a smile from Lanny, though Billy had expected one or the other. "Where'd you get this?"

"Somebody left it under my windshield wiper."

"Where were you parked?"

"At the tavern."

"An envelope?"

"No."

"You see anyone watching you? I mean, when you took it out from under the wiper and read it."

"Nobody."

"What do you make of it?"

"That was my question to you," Billy reminded him.

"A prank. A sick joke."

Staring at the ominous lines of type, Billy said, "That was my first reaction, but then . . ."

Lanny stepped sideways, aligning himself with new hay bales faced with full-figure drawings of Elmer Fudd and Bugs Bunny. "But then you ask yourself *What if . . . ?*"

"Don't you?"

"Sure. Every cop does, all the time, otherwise he ends up dead sooner than he should. Or shoots when he shouldn't."

Not long ago, Lanny had wounded a belligerent drunk who he thought had been armed. Instead of a gun, the guy had a cell phone.

"But you can't keep what-ifing yourself forever," he continued. "You've got to go with instinct. And your instinct is the same as mine. It's a prank. Besides, you've got a hunch who did it."

"Steve Zillis," said Billy.

"Bingo."

Lanny assumed an isosceles shooting stance, right leg quartered back for balance, left knee flexed, two hands on the pistol. He took a deep breath and popped Elmer five times as a shrapnel of blackbirds exploded from the elms and tore into the sky.

Counting four mortal hits and one wound, Billy said, "The thing is . . . this doesn't seem like something Steve would do—or could."

"Why not?"

"He's a guy who carries a small rubber bladder in his pocket so he can make a loud farting sound when he thinks that might be funny."

"Meaning?"

Billy folded the typewritten message and tucked it in his shirt pocket. "This seems too complex for Steve, too . . . subtle."

"Young Steve is about as subtle as the green-apple nasties," Lanny agreed.

Resuming his stance, he spent the second half of the magazine on Bugs, scoring five mortal hits.

"What if it's real?" Billy asked.

"It's not."

"But what if it is?"

"Homicidal lunatics only play games like that in movies. In real life, killers just kill. Power is what it's about for them, the power and sometimes violent sex—not teasing you with puzzles and riddles."

Ejected shell casings littered the grass. The

# Odd Thomas

## Dean Koontz

He's Odd. Odd Thomas, to be precise. Genius fry-cook at the Pico Mundo Grill; boyfriend to the gorgeous Stormy Llewellyn – and possibly the only person with a chance of stopping one of the worst crimes in the bloody history of murder . . .

Something evil has come to the desert town that Odd and Stormy call home. It comes in the form of a mysterious man with a macabre appetite, a filing cabinet full of information on the world's worst killers, and strange, hyena-like shadows following him wherever he goes. Odd is worried. He knows things, sees things – about the living, the dead and the soon to be dead. Things that he has to act on. Now he's terrified for Stormy, himself and Pico Mundo. Because he knows that on Wednesday August 15, a savage, blood-soaked whirlwind of violence and murder will devastate the town.

Today is August 14.
And Odd is far from sure he can stop the coming storm . . .

'This is a read-at-a-sitting novel with a terrific final twist'
*Observer*

ISBN 0 00 713074 0
£6.99

# The Face

## Dean Koontz

THE FACE. As Hollywood's most dazzling star he has the love of millions – but the hatred of one deeply twisted soul. Just before Christmas, the star has received six messages promising a very nasty surprise.

The Face's security chief is Ethan Truman, an ex-cop with a troubled past. He's found the messenger but not the source of the threat, and he's worried. But not half as worried as he would be if he knew that Fric, the Face's ten-year-old son, was home alone and getting calls from 'Moloch, devourer of children'. The terrified boy is planning to go into hiding in his father's vast mansion – putting himself beyond Ethan's protection.

And Ethan may be all that stands between Fric and an almost unimaginable evil . . .

'The master of our darkest dreams' *The Times*

ISBN 0 00 713071 6
£6.99

westering sun polished the tubes of brass to a bloody gold.

Aware that he hadn't quelled Billy's doubt, Lanny continued: "Even if it were real—and it's not—what is there to act upon in that note?"

"Blond schoolteachers, elderly women."

"Somewhere in Napa County."

"Yeah."

"Napa County isn't San Francisco," Lanny said, "but it's not unpopulated barrens, either. Lots of people in lots of towns. The sheriff's department plus every police force in the county together don't have enough men to cover all those bases."

"You don't need to cover them all. He qualifies his targets—a *lovely* blond schoolteacher."

"That's a judgment," Lanny objected. "Some blond schoolteacher you find lovely might be a hag to me."

"I didn't realize you had such high standards in women."

Lanny smiled. "I'm picky."

"Anyway there's also the elderly woman *active in charity work.*"

Jamming a third magazine in the pistol, Lanny said, "A lot of elderly women are active in charities. They come from a generation that cared about their neighbors."

"So you aren't going to do anything?"

"What do you want me to do?"

Billy had no suggestion, only an observation: "It seems like we ought to do something."

"By nature, police are reactive, not proactive."

"So he has to murder somebody first?"

"He isn't going to murder anyone."

"He says he will," Billy protested.

"It's a prank. Steve Zillis has finally graduated from the squirting-flowers-and-plastic-vomit school of humor."

Billy nodded. "You're probably right."

"I'm for sure right." Indicating the remaining colorful figures fixed to the triple-thick wall of hay bales, Lanny said, "Now before twilight spoils my aim, I want to kill the cast of *Shrek*."

"I thought they were good movies."

"I'm not a critic," Lanny said impatiently, "just a guy having some fun and sharpening his work skills."

"Okay, all right, I'm out of here. See you Friday for poker."

"Bring something," Lanny said.

"Like what?"

"Jose's bringing his pork-and-rice casserole. Leroy's bringing five kinds of salsa and lots of corn chips. Why don't you make your tamale pie?"

As Lanny spoke, Billy winced. "We sound like a group of old maids planning a quilting party."

"We're pathetic," Lanny said, "but we're not dead yet."

"How would we know?"

"If I were dead and in Hell," Lanny said, "they wouldn't let me have the pleasure of drawing cartoons. And this sure isn't Heaven."

By the time Billy reached his Explorer in the driveway, Lanny Olsen had begun to blast away at Shrek, Princess Fiona, Donkey, and their friends.

The eastern sky was sapphire. In the western vault, the blue had begun to wear off, revealing gold beneath, and the hint of red gesso under the gilt.

Standing by his SUV in the lengthening shadows, Billy watched for a moment as Lanny honed his marksmanship and, for the thousandth time, tried to kill off his unfulfilled dream of being a cartoonist.

# 3

An enchanted princess, recumbent in a castle tower, dreaming the years away until awakened by a kiss, could not have been lovelier than Barbara Mandel abed at the Whispering Pines.

In the caress of lamplight, her golden hair spilled across the pillow, as lustrous as bullion poured from a smelter's cauldron.

Standing at her bedside, Billy Wiles had never seen a bisque doll with a complexion as pale or as flawless as Barbara's. Her skin appeared translucent, as though the light penetrated the surface and then brightened her face from within.

If he were to lift aside the thin blanket and sheet, he would expose an indignity not visited on enchanted princesses. An enteral-nutrition tube had been inserted surgically into her stomach.

The doctor had ordered a slow continuous feeding. The drip pump purred softly as it supplied a perpetual dinner.

She had been in a coma for almost four years.

Hers was not the most severe of comas. Sometimes she yawned, sighed, moved her right hand to her face, her throat, her breast.

Occasionally she spoke, though never more than a few cryptic words, not to anyone in the room but to some phantom of the mind.

Even when she spoke or moved her hand, she remained unaware of everything around her. She was unconscious, unresponsive to external stimulation.

At the moment she lay quiet, brow as smooth as milk in a pail, eyes unmoving behind their lids, lips slightly parted. No ghost breathed with less sound.

From a jacket pocket, Billy took a small wire-bound notebook. Clipped to it was a half-size ball-point pen. He put them on the nightstand.

The small room was simply furnished: one hospital bed, one nightstand, one chair. Long ago Billy had added a barstool that allowed him to sit high enough to watch over Barbara.

Whispering Pines Convalescent Home provided good care but an austere environment. Half the patients were convalescing; the other half were merely being warehoused.

Perched on the stool beside the bed, he told her about his day. He began with a description of the sunrise and ended with Lanny's shooting gallery of cartoon celebrities.

Although she had never responded to anything he'd said, Billy suspected that in her deep redoubt, Barbara could hear him. He needed to believe that his presence, his voice, his affection comforted her.

When he had no more to say, he continued to gaze at her. He did not always see her as she was now. He saw her as she'd once been—vivid, vivacious—and as she might be today if fate had been kinder.

After a while he extracted the folded message from his shirt pocket and read it again.

He had just finished when Barbara spoke in murmurs from which meaning melted almost faster than the ear could hear: "I want to know what it says. . . ."

Electrified, he rose from the stool. He leaned over the bed rail to stare more closely at her.

Never before had anything she'd said, in her coma, seemed to relate to anything that *he* said or did while visiting. "Barbara?"

She remained still, eyes closed, lips parted, apparently no more alive than the object of mourning on a catafalque.

"Can you hear me?"

With trembling fingertips, he touched her face. She did not respond.

He had already told her what the strange message said, but now he read it to her just in case her murmured words had referred to it.

When he finished, she did not react. He spoke her name without effect.

Sitting on the stool once more, he plucked the little notebook from the nightstand. With the small pen, he recorded her seven words and the date that she had spoken them.

He had a notebook for each year of her unnatural sleep. Although each contained only a hundred three-by-four-inch pages, none had been filled, as she did not speak on every—or even most—visits.

*I want to know what it says*

After dating that unusually complete statement, he flipped pages, looking back through the notebook, reading not the dates but just some of her words.

*lambs could not forgive*

*beef-faced boys*

*my infant tongue*

*the authority of his tombstone*

*Papa, potatoes, poultry, prunes, prism*

*season of darkness*

*it swells forward*

*one great heave*

*all flashes away*

*twenty-three, twenty-three*

In her words, Billy could find neither coherence nor a clue to any.

From time to time through the weeks, the months, she smiled faintly. Twice in his experience she had laughed softly.

On other occasions, however, her whispered words disturbed him, sometimes chilled him.

*torn, bruised, panting, bleeding*

*gore and fire*

*hatchets, knives, bayonets*

*red in their eyes, their frenzied eyes*

These dismaying utterances were not delivered in a tone of distress. They came in the same uninflected murmur with which she spoke less troubling words.

Nevertheless, they concerned Billy. He worried that at the bottom of her coma, she occupied a dark and fearsome place, that she felt trapped and threatened, and alone.

Now her brow furrowed and she spoke again, "The sea . . ."

When he wrote this down, she gave him more: "What it is . . ."

The stillness in the room grew more profound, as if countless fathoms of thickening atmosphere pressed all currents from the air, so that her soft voice carried to Billy.

To her lips, her right hand rose as though to feel the texture of her words. "What it is that it keeps on saying."

This was the most coherent she had been, in coma, and seldom had she said as much in a single visit.

"Barbara?"

"I want to know what it says . . . the sea."

She lowered her hand to her breast. The furrows faded from her brow. Her eyes, which as she spoke had roved beneath their lids, grew fixed once more.

Pen poised over paper, Billy waited, but Barbara matched the silence of the room. And the silence deepened, and the stillness, until he felt that he must go or meet a fate similar to that of a prehistoric fly preserved in amber.

She would lie in this hush for hours or for days, or forever.

He kissed her but not on the mouth. That would feel like a violation. Her cheek was soft and cool against his lips.

Three years, ten months, four days, she had been in this coma, into which she had fallen only a month after accepting an engagement ring from Billy.

# 4

Billy did not have the isolation that Lanny enjoyed, but he lived on an acre shrouded by alders and deodar cedars, along a lane with few residences.

He didn't know his neighbors. He might not have known them even if they had lived closer. He was grateful for their disinterest.

The original owner of the house and the architect had evidently negotiated each other into a hybrid structure, half bungalow, half upscale cabin. The lines were those of a bungalow. The cedar siding, silvered by the weather, belonged on a cabin, as did the front porch with rough-hewn posts supporting the roof.

Unlike most bipolar houses, this one appeared cozy. Diamond-pane, beveled-glass windows—pure bungalow—looked bejeweled when the lights were on. In daylight the leaping-deer weather vane on the roof turned with lazy grace

even in turbulent scrambles of wind.

The detached garage, which also contained his woodworking shop, stood behind the house.

After Billy parked the Explorer and closed the big door behind it, as he walked across the backyard toward the house, an owl hooted from its perch on the ridge line of the garage roof.

No other owls answered. But Billy thought he heard mice squeak, and he could almost feel them shivering in the shrubbery, yearning for the tall grass beyond the yard.

His mind felt swampy, his thoughts muddy. He paused and took a deep breath, savoring air redolent of the fragrant bark and needles of the deodars. The astringent scent cleared his head.

Clarity proved undesirable. He wasn't much of a drinker, but now he wanted a beer and a shot.

The stars looked hard. They were bright, too, in the cloudless sky, but the feeling he got from them was hardness.

Neither the back steps nor the floorboards of the porch creaked. He had plenty of time to keep the place in good, tight condition.

After gutting the kitchen, he himself had built the cabinets. They were cherry wood with a dark stain.

He had laid the tile floor: black-granite squares. The granite countertops matched the floor.

Clean and simple. He had intended to do the

whole house in that style, but then he had lost his way.

He poured a cold bottle of Guinness stout into a mug, spiked it with bourbon. When he *did* drink, he wanted punch in both the texture and the taste.

He was making a pastrami sandwich when the phone rang. "Hello?"

The caller did not respond even when Billy said hello again.

Ordinarily, he would have thought the line was dead. Not this evening.

Listening, he fished the typewritten message from his pocket. He unfolded it and smoothed it flat on the black-granite counter.

Hollow as a bell, but a bell without a clapper, the open line carried no fizz of static. Billy couldn't hear the caller inhale or exhale, as if the guy were dead, and done with breathing.

Whether prankster or killer, the man's purpose was to taunt, intimidate. Billy didn't give him the satisfaction of a third hello.

They listened to each other's silence, as if something could be learned from nothing.

After perhaps a minute, Billy began to wonder if he might be imagining a presence on the far end of the line.

If he was in fact ear-to-ear with the author of the note, hanging up first would be a mistake. His disconnection would be taken as a sign of fear or at least of weakness.

Life had taught him patience. Besides, his self-image included the possibility that he could be fatuous, so he didn't worry about looking foolish. He waited.

When the caller hung up, the distinct sound of the disconnect proved that he had been there, and then the dial tone.

Before continuing to make his sandwich, Billy walked the four rooms and bath. He lowered the pleated shades over all the windows.

At the dinette table in the kitchen, he ate the sandwich and two dill pickles. He drank a second stout, this time without the added bourbon.

He had no TV. The entertainment shows bored him, and he didn't need the news.

His thoughts were his only company at dinner. He did not linger over the pastrami sandwich.

Books lined one wall of the living room from floor to ceiling. For most of his life, Billy had been a voracious reader.

He had lost interest in reading three years, ten months, and four days previously. A mutual love of books, of fiction in all genres, had brought him and Barbara together.

On one shelf stood a set of Dickens in matched bindings, which Barbara had given him for Christmas. She'd had a passion for Dickens.

These days, he needed to keep busy. Just sitting in a chair with a book made him restless. He felt

vulnerable somehow.

Besides, some books contained disturbing ideas. They started you thinking about things you wanted to forget, and though your thoughts became intolerable, you could not put them to rest.

The coffered ceiling of the living room was a consequence of his need to remain busy. Every coffer was trimmed with dentil molding. The center of each featured a cluster of acanthus leaves hand-carved from white oak, stained to match the surrounding mahogany.

The style of this ceiling suited neither a cabin nor a bungalow. He didn't care. The project had kept him occupied for months.

In his study, the coffered ceiling was even more ornate than the ceiling in the living room.

He did not go to the desk, where the unused computer mocked him. Instead, he sat at a worktable arrayed with his carving tools.

Here also were stacks of white-oak blocks. They had a sweet wood smell. The blocks were raw material for the ornamentations that would decorate the bedroom ceiling, which was currently bare plaster.

On the table stood a CD player and two small speakers. The disc deck was loaded with zydeco music. He switched it on.

He carved until his hands ached and his vision blurred. Then he turned off the music and went to bed.

Lying on his back in the dark, staring at a ceiling that he could not see, he waited for his eyes to fall shut. He waited.

He heard something on the roof. Something scratching at the cedar-shake shingles. The owl, no doubt.

The owl did not hoot. Perhaps it was a raccoon. Or something.

He glanced at the digital clock on the nightstand. Twenty minutes past midnight.

*You have six hours to decide. The choice is yours.*

Everything would be all right in the morning. Everything always was. Well, not all right, but good enough to encourage perseverance.

*I want to know what it says, the sea. What it is that it keeps on saying.*

A few times, he closed his eyes, but that was no good. They had to fall shut on their own for sleep to follow.

He looked at the clock as it changed from 12:59 to 1:00.

The note had been under the windshield wiper when he had come out of the tavern at seven o'clock. Six hours had passed.

Someone had been murdered. Or not. Surely not.

Below the scratching talons of the owl, if it was an owl, he slept.

# 5

The tavern had no name. Or, rather, its function was its name. The sign at the top of the pole, as you turned from the state highway into the elm-encircled parking lot, said only TAVERN.

Jackie O'Hara owned the place. Fat, freckled, kind, he was to everyone a friend or honorary uncle.

He had no desire to see his name on the sign.

As a boy, Jackie had wanted to be a priest. He wanted to help people. He wanted to lead them to God.

Time had taught him that he might not be able to master his appetites. While still young, he had arrived at the conclusion that he would be a bad priest, which hadn't been the nature of his dream.

He found self-respect in running a clean and friendly taproom, but it seemed to him that simple satisfaction in his accomplishments would sour into vanity if he named the tavern after himself.

In Billy Wiles's opinion, Jackie would have made a fine priest. Every human being has appetites difficult to control, but far fewer have humility, gentleness, and an awareness of their weaknesses.

Vineyard Hills Tavern. Shady Elm Tavern. Candlelight Tavern. Wayside Tavern.

Patrons regularly offered names for the place. Jackie found their suggestions to be either awkward or inappropriate, or twee.

When Billy arrived at 10:45 Tuesday morning, fifteen minutes before the tavern opened, the only cars in the lot were Jackie's and Ben Vernon's. Ben was the day cook.

Standing beside his Explorer, he studied the low serried hills in the distance, on the far side of the highway. They were dark brown where scalped by earthmovers, pale brown where the wild grass had been faded from green by the arid summer heat.

Peerless Properties, an international corporation, was building a world-class resort, to be called Vineland, on nine hundred acres. In addition to a hotel with golf course, three pools, tennis club, and other amenities, the project included 190 multimillion-dollar getaway homes for sale to those who took their leisure seriously.

Foundations had been poured in early spring. Walls were rising.

Much closer than the palatial structures on the

higher hills, less than a hundred feet from the highway, a dramatic mural neared completion in a meadow. Seventy feet high, 150 feet long, three-dimensional, it was of wood, painted gray with black shadowing.

In the Art Deco tradition, the mural presented a stylized image of powerful machinery, including the drive wheels and connecting rods of a locomotive. There also were huge gears, strange armatures, and arcane mechanical forms that had nothing to do with a train.

A giant, stylized figure of a man in work clothes was featured in the section that suggested a locomotive. Body angled left to right as if leaning into a stiff wind, he appeared to be pushing one of the enormous drive wheels, as if caught up in the machine and pressing forward with as much panic as determination, as though if he rested for an instant he would slip out of sync and be torn to pieces.

None of the animated mural's moving parts was yet operational; nevertheless, it fostered a convincing illusion of movement, speed.

On commission, a famous artist with a single name—Valis—had designed the thing and had built it with a crew of sixteen.

The mural was meant to symbolize the hectic pace of modern life, the harried individual overwhelmed by the forces of society.

On the day when the resort opened for busi-

ness, Valis himself would set the thing afire and burn it to the ground to symbolize the freedom from the mad pace of life that the new resort represented.

Most locals in Vineyard Hills and the surrounding territory mocked the mural, and when they called it *art*, they pronounced the word with quotation marks.

Billy rather liked the hulking thing, but burning it down didn't make sense to him.

The same artist had once fixed twenty thousand helium-filled red balloons to a bridge in Australia, so it appeared to be supported by them. With a remote control, he popped all twenty thousand at once.

In that case, Billy didn't understand either the "art" *or* the point of popping it.

Although not a critic, he felt this mural was either low art or high craftsmanship. Burning it made no more sense to him than would a museum tossing Rembrandt's paintings on a bonfire.

So many things about contemporary society dismayed him that he wouldn't lose sleep over this small issue. But on the night of burning, he wouldn't come to watch the fire, either.

He went into the tavern.

The air carried such a rich scent that it almost seemed to have flavor. Ben Vernon was cooking a pot of chili.

Behind the bar, Jackie O'Hara conducted an

inventory of the liquor supply. "Billy, did you see that special on Channel Six last night?"

"No."

"You didn't see that special about UFOs, alien abduction?"

"I was carving to zydeco."

"This guy says he was taken up to a mother-ship orbiting the earth."

"What's new about that? You hear that stuff all the time."

"He says he was given a proctological exam by a bunch of space aliens."

Billy pushed through the bar gate. "That's what they all say."

"I know. You're right. But I don't get it." Jackie frowned. "Why would a superior alien race, a thousand times more intelligent than we are, come trillions of miles across the universe just to look up our butts? What are they—perverts?"

"They never looked up mine," Billy assured him. "And I doubt they looked up this guy's, either."

"He's got a lot of credibility. He's a book author. I mean, even before this book, he published a bunch of others."

Taking an apron from a drawer, tying it on, Billy said, "Just publishing a book doesn't give anyone credibility. Hitler published books."

"He did?" Jackie asked.

"Yeah."

"*The* Hitler?"

"Well, it wasn't *Bob* Hitler."

"You're jerking my chain."

"Look it up."

"What did he write—like spy stories or something?"

"Something," Billy said.

"This guy wrote science fiction."

"Surprise."

"*Science* fiction," Jackie emphasized. "The program was really disturbing." Picking up a small white dish from the work bar, he made a sound of impatience and disgust. "What—am I gonna have to start docking Steve for condiments?"

In the dish were fifteen to twenty maraschino-cherry stems. Each had been tied in a knot.

"The customers find him amusing," Billy said.

"Because they're half blitzed. Anyway, he pretends to be a funny type of guy, but he's not."

"Everyone has his own idea of what's funny."

"No, I mean, he pretends to be lighthearted, happy-go-lucky, but he's not."

"That's the only way I've ever seen him," Billy said.

"Ask Celia Reynolds."

"Who's she?"

"Lives next door to Steve."

"Neighbors can have grudges," Billy suggested. "Can't always believe what they say."

"Celia says he has rages in the backyard."

"What's that mean—rages?"

"He goes like nuts, she says. He chops up stuff."

"What stuff?"

"Like a dining-room chair."

"Whose?"

"His. He chopped it until there wasn't anything but splinters."

"Why?"

"He's cursing and angry when he's at it. He seems to be working off anger."

"On a chair."

"Yeah. And he does watermelons with an ax."

"Maybe he likes watermelon," Billy said.

"He doesn't *eat* them. He just chops and chops till nothing's left but mush."

"Cursing all the time."

"That's right. Cursing, grunting, snarling like an animal. Whole watermelons. A couple of times he's done dummies."

"What dummies?"

"You know, like those store-window women."

"Mannequins?"

"Yeah. He goes at them with an ax and a sledgehammer."

"Where would he get mannequins?"

"Beats me."

"This doesn't sound right."

"Talk to Celia. She'll tell you."

"Has she asked Steve why he does it?"

"No. She's afraid to."

"You believe her?"

"Celia isn't a liar."

"You think Steve's dangerous?" Billy asked.

"Probably not, but who knows."

"Maybe you should fire him."

Jackie raised his eyebrows. "And then he turns out to be one of those guys you see on TV news? He comes in *here* with an ax?"

"Anyway," Billy said, "it doesn't sound right. You don't really believe it yourself."

"Yeah, I do. Celia goes to Mass three mornings a week."

"Jackie, you joke around with Steve. You're relaxed with him."

"I'm always a little watchful."

"I never noticed it."

"Well, I am. But I don't want to be unfair to him."

"Unfair?"

"He's a good bartender, does his job." A shame-faced expression overcame Jackie O'Hara. His plump cheeks reddened. "I shouldn't have been talking about him like this. It was just all those cherry stems. That ticked me off a little."

"Twenty cherries," Billy said. "What can they cost?"

"It's not about the money. It's that trick with his tongue—it's semi-obscene."

"I never heard anyone complain about it. A lot

of the women customers particularly like to watch him do it."

"And the gays," Jackie said. "I don't want this being a singles bar, either gay or straight. I want this to be a *family* bar."

"*Is* there such a thing as a family bar?"

"Absolutely." Jackie looked hurt. In spite of its generic name, the tavern wasn't a dive. "We offer kid portions of French fries and onion rings, don't we?"

Before Billy could reply, the first customer of the day came through the door. It was 11:04. The guy wanted brunch: a Bloody Mary with a celery stick.

Jackie and Billy tended bar together through the lunchtime traffic, and Jackie served food to the tables as Ben plated it from the grill.

They were busier than usual because Tuesday was chili day, but they still didn't need a first-shift waitress. A third of the customers had lunch in a glass, and another third were satisfied with peanuts or with sausages from the brine jar on the bar, or with free pretzels.

Mixing drinks and pouring beers, Billy Wiles was troubled by a persistent image in his mind's eye: Steve Zillis chopping a mannequin to pieces, chopping, chopping.

As his shift wore on, and as no one brought word of a gunshot schoolteacher or a bludgeoned elderly philanthropist, Billy's nerves quieted. In

sleepy Vineyard Hills, in peaceful Napa Valley, news of a brutal murder would travel fast. The note must have been a prank.

After a slow afternoon, Ivy Elgin arrived for work at four o'clock, and at her heels thirsty men followed in such a state that they would have wagged their tails if they'd had them.

"Anything dead today?" Billy asked her, and found himself wincing at the question.

"A praying mantis on my back porch, right at my doorstep," Ivy said.

"What do you think that means?"

"What prays has died."

"I don't follow."

"I'm still trying to figure it."

Shirley Trueblood arrived at five o'clock, matronly in a pale-yellow uniform with white lapels and cuffs.

After her came Ramon Padillo, who sniffed the aroma of chili and grumbled, "Needs a pinch of cumin."

When Steve Zillis breezed in at six, smelling of a verbena-scented after-shave and wintermint mouthwash, he said, "How're they hangin', Kemosabe?"

"Did you call me last night?" Billy asked.

"Who, me? Why would I?"

"I don't know. I got a call, a bad connection, but I thought maybe it was you."

"Did you call me back?"

"No. I could hardly hear the voice. I just had a hunch it might be you."

Selecting three plump olives from the condiment tray, Steve said, "Anyway, I was out last night with a friend."

"You get off work at two o'clock in the morning and then you *go out*?"

Steve grinned and winked. "There was a moon, and I'm a *dog*." He pronounced it *dawg*.

"If I got off at two A.M., I'd be straight to bed."

"No offense, pilgrim, but you don't exactly ring the bell on the *zing* meter."

"What's that mean?"

Steve shrugged, then began to juggle the slippery olives with impressive dexterity. "People wonder why a good-lookin' guy like you lives like an old maid."

Surveying the customers, Billy said, "What people?"

"Lots of people." Steve caught the first olive in his mouth, the second, the third, and chewed vigorously to applause from the barstool gallery.

During the last hour of his shift, Billy was markedly more observant of Steve Zillis than usual. Yet he saw nothing suspicious.

Either the guy wasn't the prankster or he was immeasurably more cunning and deceitful than he appeared to be.

Well, it didn't matter. No one had been murdered. The note had been a joke; and sooner

or later the punch line would be delivered.

As Billy was leaving the tavern at seven o'clock, Ivy Elgin came to him, restrained excitement in her brandy-colored eyes. "Somebody's going to die in a church."

"How do you figure?"

"The mantis. What prays has died."

"Which church?" he asked.

"We'll have to wait and see."

"Maybe it won't be in church. Maybe it's just that a local minister or a priest is going to die."

Her intoxicating gaze held his. "I didn't think of that. You might be right. But how does the possum fit in?"

"I don't have a clue, Ivy. I don't have a talent for haruspicy, like you do."

"I know, but you're nice. You're always interested, and you never make fun of me."

Although he worked with Ivy five days a week, the impact of her extraordinary beauty and sexuality could make him forget, at times, that she was in some ways more girl than woman, sweet and guileless, virtuous even if not pure.

Billy said, "I'll think about the possum. Maybe there's a little bit of a seer in me that I don't know about."

Her smile could knock you off balance. "Thanks, Billy. Sometimes this gift . . . it's a burden. I could use a little help with it."

Outside, the summer-evening air was lemon

yellow with oblique sunshine, and the eastward-crawling shadows of the elms were one shade of purple short of black.

As he approached his Ford Explorer, he saw a note under the windshield wiper.

# 6

Although neither a dead blonde nor an elderly cadaver had been reported, Billy halted short of the Explorer, hesitant to proceed, reluctant to read this second message.

He wanted nothing more than to sit with Barbara for a while and then to go home. He didn't see her seven times a week, but he visited more days than not.

His stops at Whispering Pines were one of the blocks with which the foundation of his simple life had been built. He looked forward to them as he looked forward to quitting-time and carving.

He was not a stupid man, however, and not even merely smart. He knew that his life of seclusion might easily deteriorate into one of solitude.

A fine line separates the weary recluse from the fearful hermit. Finer still is the line between hermit and bitter misanthrope.

Slipping the note from under the wiper, crumpling it in his fist, and tossing it aside unread would surely constitute the crossing of the first of those lines. And perhaps there would be no going back.

He did not have much of what he wanted in life. But by nature he was prudent enough to recognize that if he threw away the note, he would also be throwing away everything that now sustained him. His life would be not merely different but worse.

In his trance of decision, he had not heard the patrol car enter the lot. As he plucked the note off the windshield, he was surprised by Lanny Olsen's sudden appearance at his side, in uniform.

"Another one," Lanny declared, as though he had been expecting the second note.

His voice had a broken edge. His face was lined with dread. His eyes were windows to a haunted place.

Billy's fate was to live in a time that denied the existence of abominations, that gave the lesser name *horror* to every abomination, that redefined every horror as a crime, every crime as an offense, every offense as a mere annoyance. Nevertheless, abhorrence rose in him before he knew exactly what had brought Lanny Olsen here.

"Billy. Dear sweet Jesus, Billy."

"What?"

"I'm sweating. Look at me sweating."

"What? What is it?"

"I can't stop sweating. It's not that hot."

Suddenly Billy felt greasy. He wiped one hand across his face and looked at the palm, expecting filth. To the eye, it appeared to be clean.

"I need a beer," Lanny said. "Two beers. I need to sit down. I need to think."

"Look at me."

Lanny wouldn't meet his eyes. His attention was fixed on the note in Billy's hand.

That paper remained folded, but something unfolded in Billy's gut, blossomed like a lubricious flower, oily and many-petaled. Nausea born of intuition.

The right question wasn't *what.* The right question was *who,* and Billy asked it.

Lanny licked his lips. "Giselle Winslow."

"I don't know her."

"Neither do I."

"Where?"

"She taught English down in Napa."

"Blond?"

"Yeah."

"And lovely," Billy guessed.

"She once was. Somebody beat her nearly to death. She was messed up really bad by someone who knew how to draw it out, how to make it last."

"*Nearly* to death."

"He finished by strangling her with a pair of her pantyhose."

Billy's legs felt weak. He leaned against the Explorer. He could not speak.

"Her sister found her just two hours ago."

Lanny's gaze remained fixed on the folded sheet of paper in Billy's hand.

"The sheriff's department doesn't have jurisdiction down there," Lanny continued. "So it's in the lap of the Napa police. That's something, anyway. That gives me breathing space."

Billy found his voice, but it was rough and not as he usually sounded to himself. "The note said he'd kill a schoolteacher if I didn't go to the police, but I went to you."

"He said he'd kill her if you didn't go to the police *and get them involved.*"

"But I went to you, I tried. I mean, for God's sake, I tried, didn't I?"

Lanny met his eyes at last. "You came to me informally. You didn't actually go to the police. You went to a friend who happened to be a cop."

"But I *went* to you," Billy protested, and cringed at the denial in his voice, at the self-justification.

Nausea crawled the walls of his stomach, but he clenched his teeth and strove for control.

"Nothing smelled real about it," Lanny said.

"About what?"

"The first note. It was a joke. It was a lame joke. There isn't a cop alive with the instinct to smell anything real in it."

"Was she married?" Billy asked.

A Toyota drove into the lot and parked seventy or eighty feet from the Explorer.

In silence they watched the driver get out of the car and go into the tavern. At such a distance, their conversation couldn't have been overheard. Nevertheless, they were circumspect.

Country music drifted out of the tavern while the door was open. On the jukebox, Alan Jackson was singing about heartbreak.

"Was she married?" Billy asked again.

"Who?"

"The woman. The schoolteacher. Giselle Winslow."

"I don't think so, no. At least there's no husband in the picture at the moment. Let me see the note."

Withholding the folded paper, Billy said, "Did she have any children?"

"What does it matter?"

"It matters," Billy said.

He realized that his empty hand had tightened into a fist. This was a friend standing before him, such as he allowed himself friends. Yet he relaxed his fist only with effort.

"It matters to me, Lanny."

"Kids? I don't know. Probably not. From what I heard, she must have lived alone."

Two bursts of traffic passed on the state highway: paradiddles of engines, the soft percussion of displaced air.

In the ensuing quiet, Lanny said plaintively, "Listen, Billy, potentially, I'm in trouble here."

"Potentially?" He found humor in that choice of words, but not the kind to make him laugh.

"No one else in the department would have taken that damn note seriously. But they'll say I should have."

"Maybe *I* should have," Billy said.

Agitated, Lanny disagreed: "That's hindsight. Bullshit. Don't talk like that. We need a mutual defense."

"Defense against what?"

"Whatever. Billy, listen, I don't have a perfect ten card."

"What's a ten card?"

"My force record card, my performance file. I've gotten a couple negative reports."

"What'd you do?"

Lanny's eyes squinted when he took offense. "Damn it, I'm not a crooked cop."

"I didn't say you were."

"I'm forty-six, never taken a dime of dirty money, and I never will."

"All right. Okay."

"I didn't *do* anything."

Lanny's pique might have been pretense; he couldn't sustain it. Or perhaps some grim mind's-eye image scared him, for his pinched eyes widened. He chewed on his lower lip as if gnawing on a disturbing thought that he wanted to bite

up, spit out, and never again consider.

Although he glanced at his wristwatch, Billy waited.

"What's true enough," Lanny said, "is I'm sometimes a lazy cop. Out of boredom, you know. And maybe because . . . I never really wanted this life."

"You don't owe me any explanations," Billy assured him.

"I know. But the thing is . . . whether I wanted this life or not, it's what I've got now. It's all I have. I want a chance to keep it. I gotta read that new note, Billy. Please give me the note."

Sympathetic but unwilling to yield the paper, which was now damp with his own perspiration, Billy unfolded and read it.

*If you don't go to the police and get them involved, I will kill an unmarried man who won't much be missed by the world.*

*If you do go to the police, I will kill a young mother of two.*

*You have five hours to decide. The choice is yours.*

On the first reading, Billy comprehended every terrible detail of the note, yet he read it again. Then he relinquished it.

Anxiety, the rust of life, corroded Lanny Olsen's face as he scanned the lines. "This is one sick son of a bitch."

"I've got to go down to Napa."

"Why?"

"To give both these notes to the police."

"Wait, wait, wait," Lanny said. "You don't know that the second victim's going to be in Napa. Could be in St. Helena or Rutherford—"

"Or in Angwin," Billy interrupted, "or Calistoga."

Eager to press the point, Lanny said, "Or Yountville or Circle Oaks, or Oakville. You don't know where. You don't know anything."

"I know some things," Billy said. "I know what's right."

Blinking at the note, flicking sweat off his eyelashes, Lanny said, "Real killers don't play these games."

"This one does."

Folding the note and tucking it in the breast pocket of his uniform shirt, Lanny pleaded, "Let me think a minute."

Immediately retrieving the paper from Lanny's pocket, Billy said, "Think all you want. I'm driving down to Napa."

"Oh, man, this is bad. This is wrong. Don't be stupid."

"It's the end of his game if I won't play it."

"So you're just going to kill a young mother of two. Just like that, are you?"

"I'll pretend you didn't say that."

"Then I'll say it again. You're going to kill a young mother of two."

Billy shook his head. "I'm not killing anyone."

"'The choice is yours,'" Lanny quoted. "Are you going to choose to make two orphans?"

What Billy saw now in his friend's face, in his eyes, was not anything that he had seen before across a poker table or anywhere else. He seemed to be confronted by a stranger.

"The choice is yours," Lanny repeated.

Billy didn't want a falling-out between them. He lived on the more companionable side of the line between recluse and hermit, and he did not want to find himself straddling that divide.

Perhaps sensing his friend's concern, Lanny took a softer tack: "All I'm asking is throw me a line. I'm in quicksand here."

"For God's sake, Lanny."

"I know. It sucks. There's no way it doesn't."

"Don't try to manipulate me like that again. Don't hammer me."

"I won't. I'm sorry. It's just, the sheriff's a hardass. You know he is. With my ten card, this is all he needs to take my badge, and I'm still six years short of a full pension."

As long as he met Lanny's eyes and saw the desperation in them, and saw something worse than desperation that he didn't want to name, he couldn't compromise with him. He had to look away and pretend to be speaking to the Lanny he'd known before this encounter.

"What are you asking me to do?"

Reading capitulation in the question, Lanny spoke in a still more conciliatory voice. "You won't regret this, Billy. It's going to be all right."

"I didn't say I'd do whatever you want. I just need to know what it is."

"I understand. I appreciate it. You're a true friend. All I'm asking is an hour, one hour to *think*."

Shifting his gaze from the tavern to the cracked blacktop at his feet, Billy said, "There's not much time. With the first message, it was six hours. Now it's five."

"I'm only asking for *one*. One hour."

"He must know I get off work at seven, so that's probably when the clock starts ticking. Midnight. Then before dawn he kills one or the other, and by action or inaction, I've made a choice. He'll do what he'll do, but I don't want to think I decided it for him."

"One hour," Lanny promised, "and then I'll go to Sheriff Palmer. I just have to figure the approach, the angle that'll save my ass."

A familiar shriek, but seldom heard in this territory, raised Billy's attention from the blacktop to the sky.

White on sapphire, three sea gulls kited against the eastern heavens. They rarely ventured this far north from San Pablo Bay.

"Billy, I need those notes for Sheriff Palmer."

Watching the sea gulls, Billy said, "I'd rather keep them."

"The notes are evidence," Lanny said plaintively. "That bastard Palmer will rip me a new one if I don't take custody of the evidence and protect it."

As the summer evening waned toward the darkness that always drove gulls to seaside roosts, these birds were so out of place that they seemed to be an omen. Their piercing, cold cries brought a creeping chill to the nape of Billy's neck.

He said, "I only have the note I just found."

"Where's the first one?" Lanny asked.

"I left it in my kitchen, by the phone."

Billy considered going into the tavern to ask Ivy Elgin the meaning of the birds.

"All right. Okay," Lanny said. "Just give me the one you've got. Palmer's gonna want to come talk to you. We can get the first note then."

The problem was, Ivy claimed to be able to read portents only in the details of *dead* things.

When Billy hesitated, Lanny grew insistent: "For God's sake, look at me. What is it with the birds?"

"I don't know," Billy replied.

"You don't know what?"

"I don't know what it is with the birds." Reluctantly, Billy fished the note from his pocket and gave it to Lanny. "One hour."

"That's all I need. I'll call you."

As Lanny turned away, Billy put a hand on his

shoulder, halting him. "What do you mean you'll call? You said you'd bring Palmer."

"I'll call you first, as soon as I've figured out how to tweak the story to give myself cover."

"'Tweak,'" Billy said, loathing the word.

Falling silent, the circling sea gulls wheeled away toward the westering sun.

"When I call," Lanny said, "I'll tell you what I'm gonna tell Palmer, so we'll be on the same page. *Then* I'll go to him."

Billy wished that he had never surrendered the note. But it *was* evidence, and logic dictated that Lanny should have it.

"Where are you going to be in an hour—at Whispering Pines?"

Billy shook his head. "I'm stopping there, but only for fifteen minutes. Then I'm going home. Call me at my place. But there's one more thing."

Impatiently, Lanny said, "Midnight, Billy. Remember?"

"How does this psycho know what choice I make? How did he know I went to you and not to the police? How will he know what I do in the next four and a half hours?"

No answer but a frown occurred to Lanny.

"Unless," Billy said, "he's watching me."

Surveying the vehicles in the parking lot, the tavern, and the arc of embracing elms, Lanny said, "Everything was going so smooth."

"Was it?"

"Like a river. Now this rock."

"Always a rock."

"That's true enough," Lanny said, and walked away toward his patrol car.

Mother Olsen's only child appeared defeated, slump-shouldered and baggy-assed.

Billy wanted to ask if everything was all right between them, but that was too direct. He couldn't think of another way to phrase the question.

Then he heard himself say, "Something I've never told you and should have."

Lanny stopped, looked back, regarding him warily.

"All those years your mom was sick and you looked after her, gave up what you wanted . . . that took more of the right stuff than cop work does."

As though embarrassed, Lanny looked at the trees again and said almost as if discomfited, "Thanks, Billy." He seemed genuinely touched to hear his sacrifice acknowledged.

Then as if a perverse sense of shame compelled him to discount, if not mock, his virtue, Lanny added, "But all of that doesn't leave me with a pension."

Billy watched him get in the car and drive away.

In a silence of vanished sea gulls, the breathless day waned, while the hills and the meadows and the trees gradually drew more shadows over themselves.

On the farther side of the highway, the forty-foot wooden man strove to save himself from the great grinding wheels of industry or brutal ideology, or modern art.

# 7

Barbara's face against the dimpled background of the pillow was Billy's despair and his hope, his loss and his expectation.

She was an anchor in two senses, the first beneficial. The sight of her held Billy fast and stable whatever the currents of a day.

Less mercifully, every memory of her from the time when she had been not just in the quick of life, but also vivacious, was a link of chain enwrapping him. If she sank from coma into full oblivion, the chain would pull taut, and he would sink with her into the darkest waters.

He came here not only to keep her company in the hope that she would recognize his presence even in her internal prison, but also to be taught how to care and not to care, how to sit still, and perhaps to find elusive peace.

This evening, peace was more elusive than usual.

His attention shifted often from her face to his

watch, and to the window beyond which the acid-yellow day soured slowly toward a bitter twilight.

He held his little notebook. He paged through it, reading the mysterious words that she had spoken.

When he found a sequence that particularly intrigued him, he read it aloud:

"—soft black drizzle—"

"—death of the sun—"

"—the scarecrow of a suit—"

"—livers of fat geese—"

"—narrow street, high houses—"

"—a cistern to hold the fog—"

"—strange forms . . . ghostly motion—"

"—clear-sounding bells—"

His hope was that, hearing her enigmatic coma-talk read back to her, she would be spurred to speak, perhaps to expand upon those utterances and make more sense of them.

On other nights his performance had sometimes drawn a reply from her. But never did she clarify what previously she had said. Instead she delivered a new and different sequence of equally inscrutable words.

This evening she responded with silence, and occasionally with a sigh uncolored by emotion, as if she were a machine that breathed in a shallow rhythm with louder exhalations caused by random power surges.

After reading aloud two sequences, Billy returned the notebook to his pocket.

Agitated, he had read her words with too much force, too much haste. At one point he'd heard himself and thought he sounded angry, which would do Barbara no good.

He paced the room. The window drew him.

Whispering Pines stood adjacent to a gently sloping vineyard. Beyond the window lay regimented vines with emerald-green leaves that would be crimson come autumn, with small hard grapes still many weeks from maturity.

The work lanes between the vine rows were mottled black with the shadows of the day's last hour, purple with grape pomace that had been spread as fertilizer.

Seventy or eighty feet from the window, a man alone stood in one of those lanes. He had no tools with him and did not appear to be at work.

If he was a grower or a vintner out for a walk, he must not be in a hurry. He stood in one place, feet planted wide apart, hands in his trouser pockets.

He seemed to be studying the convalescent home.

From this distance and in this light, no details of the man's appearance could be discerned. He stood in the lane between vines with his back to the declining sun, which revealed him only as a silhouette.

Listening to running feet on hollow stairs, which was in fact the thunder of his heart, Billy warned himself against paranoia. Whatever trouble might come, he would need calm nerves and a clear mind to cope.

He turned away from the window. He went to the bed.

Barbara's eyes moved under her lids. The specialists said this indicated a dream state.

Considering that any coma was a far deeper sleep than mere sleep itself, Billy wondered if hers were more intense than ordinary dreams—full of fevered action, crashing with a thunderstorm of sound, drenched in color.

He worried that her dreams were nightmares, vivid and perpetual.

When he kissed her forehead, she murmured, "The wind is in the east. . . ."

He waited, but she said no more, though her eyes darted and rolled from phantom to phantom under her closed lids.

Because those words contained no menace and because no sense of peril darkened her voice, he chose to believe that her current dream, at least, must be benign.

Although he didn't want it, he took from the nightstand a square cream-colored envelope on which his name had been written in flowing script. He tucked it in a pocket, unread, for he knew that it had been left by Barbara's doctor, Jordan Ferrier.

When medical issues of substance needed to be discussed, the physician always used the telephone. He resorted to written messages only when he had turned from medicine to the devil's work.

At the window again, Billy discovered that the watcher in the vineyard had gone.

Moments later, when he left Whispering Pines, he half expected to find a third note on his windshield. He was spared that discovery.

Most likely the man among the vines had been an ordinary man engaged in honest business. Nothing more. Nothing less.

Billy drove directly home, parked in the detached garage, climbed the back-porch steps, and found his kitchen door unlocked, ajar.

# 8

Billy had not been threatened in either of the notes. The danger confronting him was not to life and limb. He would have *preferred* physical peril to the moral jeopardy that he faced.

Nevertheless, when he found the back door of the house ajar, he considered waiting in the yard until Lanny arrived with Sheriff Palmer.

That option occupied his consideration only for a moment. He didn't care if Lanny and Palmer thought he was gutless, but he didn't want to think it of himself.

He went inside. No one waited in the kitchen.

The draining daylight drizzled down the windows more than it penetrated them. Warily, he turned on lights as he went through the house.

He found no intruder in any room or closet. Curiously, he saw no signs of intrusion, either.

By the time that he returned to the kitchen, he had begun to wonder if he might have failed

to close and lock the door when he had left the house earlier in the day.

That possibility had to be discounted when he found the spare key on a kitchen counter, near the phone. It should have been taped to the bottom of one of twenty cans of wood stain and varnish stored on a shelf in the garage.

Billy had last used the spare key five or six months previously. He could not possibly have been under surveillance that long.

Suspecting the existence of a key, the killer must have intuited that the garage was the most likely place in which it would have been hidden.

Billy's professionally equipped woodworking shop occupied two-thirds of that space, presenting numerous drawers and cabinets and shelves where such a small item could have been hidden. The search for it might have taken hours.

If the killer, after visiting the house, intended to announce his intrusion by leaving the spare key in the kitchen, logic argued that he would have saved himself the time and trouble of the search. Instead, why wouldn't he have broken one of the four panes of glass in the back door?

As Billy puzzled over this conundrum, he suddenly realized that the key lay at the very spot on the black-granite counter where he had left the first typewritten message from the killer. It was gone.

Turning in a full circle, he saw the note neither

on the floor nor on another counter. He pulled open the nearest drawers, but it was not in this one or in this one, or in this one. . . .

Abruptly he realized that Giselle Winslow's killer had not been here, after all. The intruder had been Lanny Olsen.

Lanny knew where the spare key was kept. When he had asked for the first note, as evidence, Billy had told him that it was here, in the kitchen.

Lanny had also asked where to find him in an hour, whether he would be going directly home or to Whispering Pines.

A sense of deep misgiving overcame Billy, a general uneasiness and doubt that began to curdle his trust.

If Lanny had all along intended to come here and collect the note as essential evidence, not later with Sheriff Palmer but right away, he should have said so. His deception suggested that he was not in a mood to serve and protect the public, or even to back up a friend, but was focused first on saving his own skin.

Billy didn't want to believe such a thing. He sought excuses for Lanny.

Maybe after driving away from the tavern in his patrol car, he had decided that, after all, he must have both of the notes before he approached Sheriff Palmer. And maybe he didn't want to make a call to Whispering Pines because he knew how important those visits were to Billy.

In that case, however, he would have written a brief explanation to leave in place of the killer's note when he took it.

Unless . . . If his intention was to destroy both notes instead of going to Palmer, and later to claim that Billy had never come to him prior to the Winslow murder, such a replacement note would have been evidence to refute him.

Always, Lanny Olsen had seemed to be a good man, not free of faults, but basically good and fair and decent. He'd sacrificed his dreams to stand by his ailing mother for so many years.

Billy dropped the spare key in his pants pocket. He did not intend to tape it again to the bottom of the can in the workshop.

He wondered just how many bad reports were on Lanny's ten card, exactly how lazy he had been.

In retrospect, Billy heard markedly greater desperation in his friend's voice than he had heard at the time:

*I never really wanted this life . . . but the thing is . . . whether I wanted it or not, it's what I've got now. It's all I have. I want a chance to keep it.*

Even most good men had a breaking point. Lanny might have been closer to his than Billy could have known.

The wall clock showed 8:09.

In less than four hours, regardless of the choice that Billy made, someone would die. He wanted this responsibility off his shoulders.

Lanny was supposed to call him by 8:30.

Billy had no intention of waiting. He snatched the handset from the wall phone and keyed in Lanny's personal cell-phone number.

After five rings, he was switched to voice mail. He said, "This is Billy. I'm at home. What the hell? What've you done? Call me *now.*"

Instinct told him not to attempt to reach Lanny through the sheriff's-department dispatcher. He would be leaving a trail that might have consequences he could not foresee.

His friend's betrayal, if that's what it was, had reduced Billy to the cautious calculations of a guilty man, although he had done nothing wrong.

A transient sting of mingled pain and anger would have been understandable. Instead, resentment swelled in him so thick, so quick, that his chest grew tight and he had difficulty swallowing.

Destroying the notes and lying about them might spare Lanny dismissal from the force, but Billy's situation would be made worse. Lacking evidence, he would find it more difficult to convince the authorities that his story was true and that it might shed light on the killer's psychology.

If he approached them now, he risked looking like a publicity seeker or like a bartender who sampled too much of his wares. Or like a suspect.

Riveted by that thought, he stood very still for a minute, exploring it. *Suspect.*

His mouth had gone dry. His tongue cleaved to his palate.

He went to the kitchen sink and drew a glass of cold water from the tap. At first he could barely choke down a mouthful, but then he drained the glass in three long swallows.

Too cold, drunk too fast, the water wrung a brief sharp pain from his chest, and washed nausea through his gut. He put the glass on the drainboard. He leaned over the sink until the queasiness passed.

He splashed his greasy face with cold water, washed his hands in hot.

He paced the kitchen. He sat briefly at the table, then paced some more.

At 8:30, he stood by the telephone, staring at it, although he had every reason to believe that it would not ring.

At 8:40, he used his cell phone to call Lanny's cellular number, leaving the house phone open. He got voice mail again.

The kitchen was too warm. He felt stifled.

At 8:45, Billy stepped outside, onto the back porch. He needed fresh air.

With the door wide open behind him, he could hear the telephone if it rang.

Indigo in the east, the sky overhead and to the west trembled faintly with the iridescent vibrations of an orange-and-green sunset.

The encircling woods bristled dark, growing

darker. If a hostile observer had taken up position in that timber, crouching in ferns and philodendrons, none but a sharp-nosed dog could have known that he was out there.

A hundred toads, all unseen, had begun to sing in the descending gloom, but in the kitchen, past the open door, all was silent.

Perhaps Lanny just needed a little more time to find a way to tweak the truth.

Surely he cared about more than himself. He could not have been reduced so totally, so quickly, to the most base self-interest.

He was still a cop, lazy or not, desperate or not. Sooner than later he would realize that he couldn't live with himself if, by obstructing the investigation, he contributed to more deaths.

The ink-spill in the east soon saturated the sky overhead, while in the west, all was fire and blood.

# 9

At 9:00, Billy left the back porch and went inside. He closed the door and locked it.

In just three hours, a fate would be decided, a death ordained, and if the killer followed a pattern, someone would be murdered before dawn.

The key to the SUV lay on the dinette table. Billy picked it up.

He considered setting out in search of Lanny Olsen. What he had thought was resentment, earlier, had been mere exasperation. Now he knew real resentment, a dark and bitter brooding. He badly wanted confrontation.

*Preserve me from the enemy who has something to gain, and from the friend who has something to lose.*

Lanny had been on day shift. He was off duty now.

Most likely he would be holed up at home. If he was not at home, there were only a handful of restaurants, bars, and friends' houses where he

might be found.

A sense of responsibility and a strange despairing kind of hope held Billy prisoner in his kitchen, by his telephone. He no longer expected Lanny to call; but the killer might.

The mute listener on the line the previous night had been Giselle Winslow's murderer. Billy had no proof, but no doubt, either.

Maybe he would call this evening, too. If Billy could speak to him, something might be accomplished, something learned.

Billy was under no illusion that such a monster could be charmed into chattiness. Neither could a homicidal sociopath be debated, nor persuaded by reason to spare a life.

Hearing the man speak a few words, however, might prove valuable. Ethnicity, region of origin, education, approximate age, and more could be inferred from a voice.

With luck, the killer might also unwittingly reveal some salient fact about himself. One clue, one small bud of information that blossomed under determined analysis, could provide Billy with something credible to take to the police.

Confronting Lanny Olsen might be emotionally satisfying, but it would not get Billy out of the box in which the killer had put him.

He hung the key to the SUV on a pegboard.

The previous evening, in a nervous moment, he had lowered the shades at all the windows.

This morning, before breakfast, he had raised those in the kitchen. Now he lowered them again.

He stood in the center of the kitchen.

He glanced at the phone.

Intending to sit at the table, he put his right hand on the back of a chair, but he didn't move it.

He just stood there, studying the polished black-granite floor at his feet.

He kept an immaculate house. The granite was glossy, spotless.

The blackness under his feet appeared to have no substance, as if he were standing on air, high in the night itself, with five miles of atmosphere yawning below, wingless.

He pulled the chair out from the table. He sat. Less than a minute passed before he got to his feet.

Under these circumstances, Billy Wiles had no idea how to act, what to *do.* The simple task of passing time defeated him, although he had not been doing much else for years.

Because he hadn't eaten dinner, he went to the refrigerator. He had no appetite. Nothing on those cold shelves appealed to him.

He glanced at the SUV key dangling on the pegboard.

He went to the phone and stood staring at it.

He sat at the table.

*Teach us to care and not to care. Teach us to sit still.*

After a while, he went to the study, where he spent so many evenings carving architectural ornaments at a corner worktable.

He collected several tools and a chunk of white oak from which he had only half finished carving a cluster of acanthus leaves. He returned with them to the kitchen.

The study had a telephone, but Billy preferred the kitchen this evening. The study also had a comfortable couch, and he worried that he would be tempted to lie down, that he would fall asleep and not be awakened by the killer's call, or by anything, ever.

Whether or not this concern was realistic, he settled at the dinette table with the wood and the tools.

Without a carver's vise, he could work only on the finer details of the leaves, which was engraving work akin to scrimshaw. The blade scraped a hollow sound from the oak, as if this were bone, not wood.

At ten minutes past ten o'clock, less than two hours before the deadline, he abruptly decided that he would go to the sheriff.

His house was not in any township; the sheriff had jurisdiction here. The tavern lay in Vineyard Hills, but the town was too small to have its own police force; Sheriff Palmer was the law there, too.

Billy snared the key from the pegboard, opened

the door, stepped onto the back porch—and halted.

*If you do go to the police, I will kill a young mother of two.*

He didn't want to choose. He didn't want *anyone* to die.

In all of Napa County, there might be dozens of young mothers with two children. Maybe a hundred, two hundred, maybe more.

Even with five hours, they couldn't have identified and alerted all the possible targets. They would have to use the media to warn the public. That might take days.

Now, with less than two hours, nothing substantive would be done. They might spend longer than that just questioning Billy.

The young mother, obviously preselected by the killer, would be murdered.

What if the children awakened? As witnesses, they might be eliminated.

The madman had not promised to kill *only* the mother.

On damp night air, a musky smell wafted from the rich layers of mast on the woodland floor and drifted from the trees to the porch.

Billy returned to the kitchen and closed the door.

Later, whittling leaf details, he pricked a thumb. He didn't get a Band-Aid. The puncture was small; it should close quickly.

When he nicked a knuckle, he remained too

intensely involved with the carving to bother attending to it. He worked faster, and didn't notice when he sustained a third tiny cut.

To an observer, had there been one, it might have seemed as though Billy *wanted* to bleed.

Because his hands remained busy, the wounds kept weeping. The wood soaked up the blood.

In time, he realized that the oak had completely discolored. He dropped the carving and put aside the blade.

He sat for a while, staring at his hands, breathing hard for no reason. In time, the bleeding stopped, and it didn't start up again when he washed his hands at the sink.

At 11:45, after patting his hands dry on a dish-towel, he got a cold Guinness and drank it from the bottle. He finished it too fast.

Five minutes after the first beer, he opened a second. He poured it in a glass to encourage himself to sip it and make it last.

He stood with the Guinness in front of the wall clock.

Eleven-fifty. Countdown.

As much as Billy wanted to lie to himself, he couldn't be fooled. He had made a choice, all right. *The choice is yours.* Even inaction is a choice.

The mother who had two children—she wouldn't die tonight. If the homicidal freak kept his end of the bargain, the mother would sleep the night and see the dawn.

Billy was part of it now. He could deny, he could run, he could leave his window shades down for the rest of his life and cross the line from recluse to hermit, but he could not escape the fundamental fact that he was part of it.

The killer had offered him a partnership. He had wanted no part of it. But now it turned out to be like one of those business deals, one of those aggressive stock offers, that writers in the financial pages called a *hostile takeover.*

He finished the second Guinness as midnight arrived. He wanted a third. And a fourth.

He told himself he needed to keep a clear head. He asked himself why, and he had no credible answer.

His part of the business was done for the night. He had made the choice. The freak would do the deed.

Nothing more would happen tonight, except that without the beer, Billy wouldn't be able to sleep. He might find himself carving again.

His hands ached. Not from his three insignificant wounds. From having clutched the tools too tightly. From having held the chunk of oak in a death grip.

Without sleep, he wouldn't be ready for the day ahead. With morning would come news of another corpse. He would learn whom he had chosen for death.

Billy put his glass in the sink. He didn't need

a glass anymore because he didn't care about making the beer last. Each bottle was a punch, and he wanted nothing more than to knock himself out.

He took a third beer to the living room and sat in his recliner. He drank in the dark.

Emotional fatigue can be as debilitating as physical exhaustion. All strength had fled him.

At 1:44, the telephone woke him. He flew up from the chair as if from a catapult. The empty beer bottle rolled across the floor.

Hoping to hear Lanny, he snared the handset from the kitchen phone on the fourth ring. "Hello" earned no reply.

The listener. The freak.

Billy knew from experience that a strategy of silence would get him nowhere. "What do you want from me? Why me?"

The caller did not respond.

"I'm not going to play your game," Billy said, but that was lame because they both knew that he had already been co-opted.

He would have been pleased if the killer had replied with even a soft laugh of derision, but he got nothing.

"You're sick, you're twisted." When that didn't inspire a response, Billy added, "You're human debris."

He thought he sounded weak and ineffective, and for the times in which he lived, the insults

were far from inflammatory. Some heavy-metal rock band probably called itself Sick and Twisted, and surely another was named Human Debris.

The freak would not be baited. He disconnected.

Billy hung up and realized that his hands were trembling. His palms were damp, too, and he blotted them on his shirt.

He was struck by a thought that should have but hadn't occurred to him when the killer had called the previous night. He returned to the phone, picked up the handset, listened to the dial tone for a moment, and then keyed in *69, instigating an automatic call-back.

At the farther end of the line, the phone rang, rang, rang, but nobody answered it.

The number in the digital display on Billy's phone, however, was familiar to him. It was Lanny's.

# 10

Graceful in starlight with oaks, the church stood along the main highway, a quarter of a mile from the turnoff to Lanny Olsen's house.

Billy drove to the southwest corner of the parking lot. Under the cloaking gloom of a massive California live oak, he doused the headlights and switched off the engine.

Picturesque chalk-white stucco walls with decorative buttresses rose to burnt-orange tile roofs. In a belfry niche stood a statue of the Holy Mother with her arms open to welcome suffering humanity.

Here, every baptized baby would seem to be a potential saint. Here, every marriage would appear to have the promise of lifelong happiness regardless of the natures of the bride and groom.

Billy had a gun, of course.

Although it was an old weapon, not one of recent purchase, it remained in working order. He had cleaned and stored it properly.

Packed away with the revolver had been a box of .38 cartridges. They showed no signs of corrosion.

When he had taken the weapon from its storage case, it felt heavier than he remembered. Now as he picked it off the passenger's seat, it still felt heavy.

This particular Smith & Wesson tipped the scale at only thirty-six ounces, but maybe the extra weight that he felt was its history.

He got out of the Explorer and locked the doors.

A lone car passed on the highway. The sidewash of the headlights reached no closer than thirty yards from Billy.

The rectory lay on the farther side of the church. Even if the priest was an insomniac, he would not have heard the SUV.

Billy walked farther under the oak, out from its canopy, into a meadow. Wild grass rose to his knees.

In the spring, cascades of poppies had spilled down this sloped field, as orange-red as a lava flow. They were dead now, and gone.

He halted to let his eyes grow accustomed to the moonless dark.

Motionless, he listened. The air was still. No traffic moved on the distant highway. His presence had silenced the cicadas and the toads. He could almost hear the stars.

Confident of his dark-adapted vision though of nothing else, he set out across the gently rising meadow, angling toward the fissured and potholed blacktop lane that led to Lanny Olsen's place.

He worried about rattlesnakes. On summer nights as warm as this, they hunted field mice and younger rabbits. Unbitten, he reached the lane and turned uphill, passing two houses, both dark and silent.

At the second house, a dog ran loose in the fenced yard. It did not bark, but raced back and forth along the high pickets, whimpering for Billy's attention.

Lanny's place lay a third of a mile past the house with the dog. At every window, light of one quality or another fired the glass or gilded the curtains.

In the yard, Billy crouched beside a plum tree. He could see the west face of the house, which was the front, and the north flank.

The possibility existed that this entire thing had in fact been a hoax and that Lanny was the hoaxer.

Billy did not know for a fact that a blond schoolteacher had been murdered in the city of Napa. He had taken Lanny's word for it.

He had not seen a report of the homicide in the newspaper. The killing supposedly had been discovered too late in the day to make the most recent edition. Besides, he rarely read a newspaper.

Likewise, he never watched TV. Occasionally he listened for weather reports on the radio, while driving, but mostly he relied on a CD player loaded with zydeco or Western swing.

A cartoonist might be expected also to be a prankster. The funny streak in Lanny had been repressed for so long, however, that it was less of a streak than a thread. He made reasonably good company, but he wasn't a load of laughs.

Billy didn't intend to wager his life—or a nickel—that Lanny Olsen had hoaxed him.

He remembered how sweaty and anxious and distressed his friend had been in the tavern parking lot, the previous evening. In Lanny, what you saw was what he was. If he'd wanted to be an actor instead of a cartoonist, and if his mother had never gotten cancer, he would still have wound up as a cop with a problematic ten card.

After studying the place, certain that no one was watching from a window, Billy crossed the lawn, passed the front porch, and had a look at the south flank of the house. There, too, every window glowed softly.

He circled to the rear, staying at a distance, and saw that the back door stood open. A wedge of light lay like a carpet on the dark porch floor, welcoming visitors across the kitchen threshold.

An invitation this bold seemed to suggest a trap.

Billy expected to find Lanny Olsen dead inside.

*If you don't go to the police and get them involved, I will kill an unmarried man who won't much be missed by the world.*

Lanny's funeral would not be attended by thousands of mourners, perhaps not even by as many as a hundred, though some would miss him. Not the world, but some.

When Billy had made his choice to spare the mother of two, he had not realized that he had doomed Lanny.

If he had known, perhaps he would have made a different choice. Choosing the death of a friend would be harder than dropping the dime on a nameless stranger. Even if the stranger was a mother of two.

He didn't want to think about that.

Toward the end of the backyard stood the stump of a diseased oak that had been cut down long ago. Four feet across, two feet high.

On the east side of the stump was a hole worn by weather and rot. In the hole had been tucked a One Zip plastic bag. The bag contained a spare house key.

After retrieving the key, Billy circled cautiously to the front of the house. He returned to the concealment of the plum tree.

No one had turned off any lights. No face could be seen at any window; and none of the curtains moved suspiciously.

A part of him wanted to phone 911, get help

here fast, and spill the story. He suspected that would be a reckless move.

He didn't understand the rules of this bizarre game and could not know how the killer defined *winning*. Perhaps the freak would find it amusing to frame an innocent bartender for both murders.

Billy had survived being a suspect once. The experience reshaped him. Profoundly.

He would resist being reshaped again. He had lost too much of himself the first time.

He left the cover of the plum tree. He quietly climbed the front-porch steps and went directly to the door.

The key worked. The hardware didn't rattle, the hinges didn't squeak, and the door opened silently.

# 11

This Victorian house had a Victorian foyer with a dark wood floor. A wood-paneled hall led toward the back of the house, and a staircase offered the upstairs.

On one wall had been taped an eight-by-ten sheet of paper on which had been drawn a hand. It looked like Mickey Mouse's hand: a plump thumb, three fingers, and a wrist roll suggestive of a glove.

Two fingers were folded back against the palm. The thumb and forefinger formed a cocked gun that pointed to the stairs.

Billy got the message, all right, but he chose to ignore it for the time being.

He left the front door open in case he needed to make a quick exit.

Holding the revolver with the muzzle pointed at the ceiling, he stepped through an archway to the left of the foyer. The living room looked as it

had when Mrs. Olsen had been alive, ten years ago. Lanny didn't use it much.

The same was true of the dining room. Lanny ate most of his meals in the kitchen or in the den while watching TV.

In the hallway, taped to the wall, another cartoon hand pointed toward the foyer and the stairs, opposite from the direction in which he was proceeding.

Although the TV was dark in the den, flames fluttered in the gas-log fireplace, and in a bed of faux ashes, false embers glowed as if real.

On the kitchen table stood a bottle of Bacardi, a double-liter plastic jug of Coca-Cola, and an ice bucket. On a plate beside the Coke gleamed a small knife with a serrated blade and a lime from which a few slices had been carved.

Beside the plate stood a tall, sweating glass half full of a dark concoction. In the glass floated a slice of lime and a few thin slivers of melting ice.

After stealing the killer's first note from Billy's kitchen and destroying it with the second to save his job and his hope of a pension, Lanny had tried to drown his guilt with a series of rum and Cokes.

If the jug of Coca-Cola and the bottle of Bacardi had been full when he sat down to the task, he had made considerable progress toward a state of drunkenness sufficient to shroud memory and numb the conscience until morning.

The pantry door was closed. Although Billy

doubted that the freak lurked in there among the canned goods, he wouldn't feel comfortable turning his back on it until he investigated.

With his right arm tucked close to his side and the revolver aimed in front of him, he turned the knob fast and pulled the door with his left hand. No one waited in the pantry.

From a kitchen drawer, Billy removed a clean dishtowel. After wiping the metal drawer-pull and the knob on the pantry door, he tucked one end of the cloth under his belt and let it hang from his side in the manner of a bar rag.

On a counter near the cooktop lay Lanny's wallet, car keys, pocket change, and cell phone. Here, too, was his 9-mm service pistol with the Wilson Combat holster in which he carried it.

Billy picked up the cell phone, switched it on, and summoned voice mail. The only message in storage was the one that he himself had left for Lanny earlier in the evening.

*This is Billy. I'm at home. What the hell? What've you done? Call me now.*

After listening to his own voice, he deleted the message.

Maybe that was a mistake, but he didn't see any way that it could prove his innocence. On the contrary, it would establish that he had expected to see Lanny during the evening just past and that he had been angry with him.

Which would make him a suspect.

He had brooded about the voice mail during the drive to the church parking lot and during the walk through the meadow. Deleting it seemed the wisest course if he found what he expected to find on the second floor.

He switched off the cell phone and used the dishtowel to wipe it clean of prints. He returned it to the counter where he had found it.

If someone had been watching right then, he would have figured Billy for a calm, cool piece of work. In truth, he was half sick with dread and anxiety.

An observer might also have thought that Billy, judging by his meticulous attention to detail, had covered up crimes before. That wasn't the case, but brutal experience had sharpened his imagination and had taught him the dangers of circumstantial evidence.

An hour previously, at 1:44, the killer had rung Billy from this house. The phone company would have a record of that brief call.

Perhaps the police would think it proved Billy couldn't have been here at the time of the murder.

More likely, they would suspect that Billy himself had placed the call to an accomplice at his house for the misguided purpose of trying to establish his presence elsewhere at the time of the murder.

Cops always suspected the worst of everyone. *Their* experience had taught them to do so.

At the moment, he couldn't think of anything to be done about the phone-company records. He put it out of his mind.

More urgent matters required his attention. Like finding the corpse, if one existed.

He didn't think he should waste time searching for the killer's two notes. If they were still intact, he would most likely have found them on the table at which Lanny had been drinking or on the counter with his wallet, pocket change, and cell phone.

The flames in the den fireplace, on this warm summer night, led to a logical conclusion about the notes.

Taped to the side of a kitchen cabinet was a cartoon hand that pointed to the swinging door and the downstairs hallway.

At last Billy was willing to take direction, but a shrinking, anxious fear immobilized him.

Possession of a firearm and the will to use it did not give him sufficient courage to proceed at once. He did not expect to encounter the freak. In some ways the killer would have been less intimidating than what he *did* expect to find.

The bottle of rum tempted him. He had felt no effect from the three bottles of Guinness. His heart had been thundering for most of an hour, his metabolism racing.

For a man who was not much of a drinker, he'd recently had to remind himself of that fact

often enough to suggest that a potential rummy lived inside him, yearning to be free.

The courage to proceed came from a fear of *failing* to proceed and from an acute awareness of the consequences of surrendering this hand of cards to the freak.

He left the kitchen and followed the hall to the foyer. At least the stairs were not dark; there was light here below, at the landing, and at the top.

Ascending, he did not bother calling Lanny's name. He knew that he would receive no answer, and he doubted that he could have found his voice anyway.

# 12

Opening off the upper hallway were three bedrooms, a bathroom, and a closet. Four of those five doors were closed.

On both sides of the entrance to the master bedroom were cartoon hands pointing to that open door.

Reluctant to be herded, thinking of animals driven up a ramp at a slaughterhouse, Billy left the master bedroom for last. He first checked the hall bath. Then the closet and the two other bedrooms, in one of which Lanny kept a drawing table.

Using the dishtowel, he wiped all the door-knobs after he touched them.

With only the one space remaining to be searched, he stood in the hall, listening. No pin dropped.

Something had stuck in his throat, and he couldn't swallow it. He couldn't swallow it because

it was no more real than the sliver of ice sliding down the small of his back.

He entered the master bedroom, where two lamps glowed.

The rose-patterned wallpaper chosen by Lanny's mother had not been removed after she died and not even, a few years later, after Lanny moved out of his old room into this one. Age had darkened the background to a pleasing shade reminiscent of a light tea stain.

The bedspread had been one of Pearl Olsen's favorites: rose in color overall, with embroidered flowers along the borders.

Often during Mrs. Olsen's illness, following chemotherapy sessions, and after her debilitating radiation treatments, Billy had sat with her in this room. Sometimes he just talked to her or watched her sleep. Often he read to her.

She had liked swashbuckling adventure stories. Stories set during the Raj in India. Stories with geishas and samurai and Chinese warlords and Caribbean pirates.

Pearl was gone, and now so was Lanny. Dressed in his uniform, he sat in an armchair, legs propped on a footstool, but he was gone just the same.

He had been shot in the forehead.

Billy didn't want to see this. He dreaded having this image in his memory. He wanted to leave.

Running, however, was not an option. It never had been, neither twenty years ago nor now, nor

any time between. If he ran, he would be chased down and destroyed.

The hunt was on, and for reasons he didn't understand, he was the ultimate game. Speed of flight would not save him. Speed never saved the fox. To escape the hounds and the hunters, the fox needed cunning and a taste for risk.

Billy didn't feel like a fox. He felt like a rabbit, but he would not run like one.

The lack of blood on Lanny's face, the lack of leakage from the wound suggested two things: that death had been instantaneous and that the back of his skull had been blown out.

No bloodstains or brain matter soiled the wallpaper behind the chair. Lanny had not been drilled as he sat there, had not been shot anywhere in this room.

As Billy had not found blood elsewhere in the house, he assumed that the killing occurred outside.

Perhaps Lanny had gotten up from the kitchen table, from his rum and Coke, half drunk or drunk, needing fresh air, and had stepped outside. Maybe he realized that his aim wouldn't be neat enough for the bathroom and therefore went into the backyard to relieve himself.

The freak must have used a plastic tarp or something to move the corpse through the house without making a mess.

Even if the killer was strong, getting the dead

man from the backyard to the master bedroom, considering the stairs, would have been a hard job. Hard and seemingly unnecessary.

To have done it, however, he must have had a reason that was important to him.

Lanny's eyes were open. Both bulged slightly in their sockets. The left one was askew, as if he'd had a cast eye in life.

Pressure. For the instant during which the bullet had transited the brain, pressure inside the skull soared before being relieved.

A book-club novel lay in Lanny's lap, a smaller and more cheaply produced volume than the handsome edition of the same title that had been available in bookstores. At least two hundred similar books were shelved at one end of the bedroom.

Billy could see the title, the author's name, and the jacket illustration. The story was about a search for treasure and true love in the South Pacific.

A long time ago, he had read this novel to Pearl Olsen. She had liked it, but then she had liked them all.

Lanny's slack right hand rested on the book. He appeared to have marked his place with a photograph, a small portion of which protruded from the pages.

The psychopath had *arranged* all of this. The tableau satisfied him and had emotional meaning to him, or it was a message—a riddle, a taunt.

Before disturbing the scene, Billy studied it. Nothing about it seemed compelling or clever, nothing that might have excited the murderer enough to motivate him to put forth such effort in its creation.

Billy mourned Lanny; but with a greater passion, he *hated* that Lanny had been afforded no dignity even in death. The freak dragged him around and staged him as if he were a mannequin, a doll, as if he had existed only for the creep's amusement and manipulation.

Lanny had betrayed Billy; but that didn't matter anymore. On the edge of the Dark, on the brink of the Void, few offenses were worth remembering. The only things worth recalling were the moments of friendship and laughter.

If they had been at odds on Lanny's last day, they were on the same team now, with the same and singular adversary.

Billy thought he heard a noise in the hall.

Without hesitation, holding the revolver in both hands, he left the master bedroom, clearing the doorway fast, sweeping the .38 left to right, seeking a target. No one.

The bathroom, closet, and other bedroom doors were closed, as he had left them.

He didn't feel a pressing need to search those rooms again. He might have heard nothing but an ordinary settling noise as the old house protested the weight of time, but it almost certainly

had not been the sound of a door opening or closing.

He blotted the damp palm of his left hand on his shirt, switched the gun to it, blotted his right hand, returned the gun to it, and went to the head of the stairs.

From the lower floor, from the porch beyond the open front door, came nothing but a summer-night silence, a dead-of-night hush.

# 13

As he stood at the head of the stairs, listening, pain had begun to throb in Billy's temples. He realized that his teeth were clenched tighter than the jaws of a vise.

He tried to relax and breathe through his mouth. He rolled his head from side to side, working the stiffening muscles of his neck.

Stress could be beneficial if you used it to stay focused and alert. Fear could paralyze, but also sharpen the survival instinct.

He returned to the master bedroom.

Approaching the door, he suddenly thought body and book would be gone. But Lanny still sat in the armchair.

From a tissue box on one of the nightstands, Billy plucked two Kleenex. Using them as an impromptu glove, he moved the dead man's hand off the book.

Leaving the book on the cadaver's lap, he

opened it to the place that had been marked by the photograph.

He expected sentences or paragraphs to have been highlighted in some fashion: a further message. But the text was pristine.

Still using the Kleenex, he picked up the photo, a snapshot.

She was young and blond and pretty. Nothing in the picture gave a clue to her profession, but Billy knew that she had been a teacher.

Her killer must have found this snapshot in her house, down in Napa. Before or after finding it, he brutally beat the beauty out of her.

No doubt the freak had left the photograph in the book to confirm for the authorities that the two murders had been the work of the same man. He was bragging. He wanted the credit that he had earned.

*The only wisdom we can hope to acquire is the wisdom of humility. . . .*

The freak hadn't learned that lesson. Perhaps his failure to learn it would lead to his fall.

If it was possible to feel genuinely heartbroken over the fate of a stranger, the photo of this young woman would have done the job had Billy stared at it too long. He returned it to the book and closed it in the yellowing pages.

After putting the dead man's hand atop the book, as it had been, he wadded the two Kleenex in his fist. He went into the bathroom that was

part of the master suite, pushed the plunger with the Kleenex, and then dropped them into the whirling water in the toilet bowl.

In the bedroom, he stood beside the armchair, not sure what he should do.

Lanny did not deserve to be left here alone without benefit of prayer or justice. If not a *close* friend, he had nevertheless been a friend. Besides, he was Pearl Olsen's son, and that ought to count for a lot.

Yet to phone the sheriff's department, even anonymously, and report the crime might be a mistake. They would want an explanation for the call that had been placed from this house to Billy's place soon after the murder; and he still had not decided what to tell them.

Other issues, things he didn't know about, might point the finger of suspicion at him. Circumstantial evidence.

Perhaps the ultimate intention of the killer was to frame Billy for these murders and for others.

Undeniably, the freak saw this as a game. The rules, if any, were known only to him.

Likewise, the definition of *victory* was known only to him. Winning the pot, capturing the king, scoring the final touchdown might mean, in this case, sending Billy to prison for life not for any rational reason, not so the freak himself could escape justice, but for the sheer *fun* of it.

Considering that he could not even discern the

shape of the playing field, Billy didn't relish being interrogated by Sheriff John Palmer.

He needed time to think. A few hours at least. Until dawn.

"I'm sorry," he told Lanny.

He switched off one of the bedside lamps and then the other.

If the house glowed like a centenarian's birthday cake through the night, someone might notice. And wonder. Everyone knew Lanny Olsen was an early-to-bed guy.

The house stood at the highest and loneliest point of the dead-end lane. Virtually no one drove up here unless they were coming to see Lanny, and no one was likely to visit during the next eight or ten hours.

Midnight had turned Tuesday to Wednesday. Wednesday and Thursday were Lanny's days off. No one would miss him at work until Friday.

Nevertheless, one by one, Billy returned to the other upstairs rooms and switched off those lights as well.

He doused the hall lights and went down the stairs, uneasy about all the darkness at his back.

In the kitchen, he closed the door to the porch and locked it.

He intended to take Lanny's spare key with him.

As he went forward once more through the first floor, he turned off all the lights, including

the ceramic gas-fueled logs in the den fireplace, using the barrel of the handgun to flip the switches.

Standing on the front porch, he locked that door as well, and wiped the knob.

He felt watched as he descended the steps. He surveyed the lawn, the trees, glanced back at the house.

All the windows were black, and the night was black, and Billy walked away from that closed darkness into an open darkness under an India-ink sky in which stars seemed to float, seemed to tremble.

# 14

He walked briskly downhill along the shoulder of the lane, ready to take cover in the roadside brush if headlights appeared.

Frequently, he glanced back. As far as he could tell, no one followed him.

Moonless, the night favored a stalker. It should have favored Billy, too, but he felt exposed by the stars.

At the house with the chest-high fence, the half-seen dog once more raced back and forth along the pickets, beseeching Billy with a whimper. It sounded desperate.

He sympathized with the animal and understood its condition. His plight, however, and his need to plan left him no time to stop and console the beast.

Besides, every expression of desired friendship has potential bite. Every smile reveals the teeth.

So he continued down the lane, and glanced

behind, and held tight to the revolver, and then turned left into the meadow where he waded through the grass in a fear of snakes.

One question pressed upon him more urgently than others: Was the killer someone he knew or a stranger?

If the freak had been in Billy's life well prior to the first note, a secret sociopath who could no longer keep his homicidal urges bottled up, identifying him might be difficult but possible. Analysis of relationships and a search of memory with an eye for anomaly might unearth clues. Deductive reasoning and imagination would likely paint a face, spell out a twisted motive.

In the event that the freak was a stranger who selected Billy at random for torment and eventual destruction, detective work would be more difficult. Imagining a face never seen and sounding for a motive in a vacuum would not prove easy.

Not long ago in the history of the world, routine daily violence—excluding the ravages of nations at war—had been largely personal in nature. Grudges, slights to honor, adultery, disputes over money triggered the murderous impulse.

In the modern world, more in the postmodern, most of all in the post-postmodern, much violence had become impersonal. Terrorists, street gangs, lone sociopaths, sociopaths in groups and pledged to a utopian vision killed people they did not know, against whom they had no realistic

complaint, for the purpose of attracting attention, making a statement, intimidation, or even just for the thrill of it.

The freak, whether known or unknown to Billy, was a daunting adversary. Judging by all evidence, he was bold but not reckless, psychopathic but self-controlled, clever, ingenious, cunning, with a baroque and Machiavellian mind.

By contrast, Billy Wiles made his way in the world as plainly and directly as he could. His mind was not baroque. His desires were not complex. He only hoped to live, and lived on guarded hope.

Hurrying through tall pale grass that lashed against his legs and seemed to pass conspiratorial whispers blade to blade, he felt that he had more in common with a field mouse than with a sharp-beaked owl.

The great spreading oak tree loomed. As Billy passed under it, unseen presences stirred in the boughs overhead, testing pinions, but no wings took flight.

Beyond the Ford Explorer, the church looked like an ice carving made of water with a trace of phosphorus.

Approaching, he unlocked the SUV with the remote key, and was acknowledged by two electronic chirps and a double flash of the parking lights.

He got in, closed the door, and locked up again.

He dropped the revolver on the passenger's seat.

When he attempted to insert the key in the ignition, something foiled him. A folded piece of paper had been fixed to the steering column with a short length of tape.

A note.

The third note.

The killer must have been stationed along the highway, observing the turnoff to Lanny Olsen's place, to see if Billy would take the bait. He must have noticed the Explorer pull into this parking lot.

The vehicle had been locked. The freak could have gotten into it only by breaking a window; but none was broken. The car alarm had not been triggered.

Thus far, every moment of this waking nightmare had felt keenly real, as veritable as fire to a testing hand. But the discovery of this third note seemed to thrust Billy through a membrane from the true world into one of fantasy.

With a dreamlike dread, Billy peeled the note off the steering column. He unfolded it.

The interior lights, activated automatically when he boarded the SUV, were still on, for he had so recently shut and locked the door. The message—a question—was clearly visible and succinct.

*Are you prepared for your first wound?*

# 15

*Are you prepared for your first wound?*

As though an Einsteinian switch had thrown time into slo-mo, the note slipped out of his fingers and seemed to float, float like a feather into his lap. The light went out.

In a trance of terror, reaching with his right hand for the revolver on the passenger's seat, Billy turned slowly to the right as well, intending to look over his shoulder and into the dark backseat.

There would seem to be too little room back there for a man to have hidden; however, Billy had gotten into the Explorer hastily, heedlessly.

He groped for the elusive gun, his fingertips brushed the checked grip of the weapon—and the window in the driver's door imploded.

As safety glass collapsed in a prickly mass across his chest and thighs, the revolver slipped out of his grasping fingers and tumbled onto the floor.

Even as the glass was falling, before Billy could turn to face the assault, the freak reached into the SUV and seized a handful of his hair, at the crown of his head, twisted it and pulled hard.

Trapped by the steering wheel and the console, pulled ruthlessly by the hair, unable to scramble into the passenger's seat and search for the gun, he clawed at the hand that held him, but ineffectively because a leather glove protected it.

The freak was strong, vicious, relentless.

Billy's hair should already have come out by the roots. The pain was excruciating. His vision blurred.

The killer wanted to pull him headfirst and backward through the broken-out window.

The back of Billy's skull rapped hard against the window sill. Another solid rap snapped his teeth together and knocked a hoarse cry from him.

He clutched at the steering wheel with his left hand, at the headrest on the driver's seat with his right, resisting. The hair would come out in a great handful. The hair would come out, and he would be free.

But the hair didn't, and he wasn't, and he thought of the horn. If he blew the horn, pounded the horn, help would come, and the freak would run.

At once he realized that only the priest in the rectory would hear, and if the priest came, the

killer wouldn't flee. No, he would shoot the priest in the face just as he had shot Lanny.

Maybe ten seconds had elapsed since the window had shattered, and the back of Billy's head was being drawn inexorably across the window sill.

The pain had quickly grown so intense that the roots of his hair seemed to extend through the flesh of his face—for his face hurt as well, stung as if flame had seared it—and seemed to extend also into his shoulders and arms, for as the tenacious roots came free, so did the strength in those muscles.

The nape of his neck chilled on contact with the window sill. Crumbles of gummy safety glass jagged his skin.

His head was being bent backward now. How quickly his exposed throat could be slit, how easily his spine might be snapped.

He let go of the steering wheel. He reached behind his back, fumbling for the door handle.

If he could open the door and thrust with sufficient force, he might unbalance his assailant, knock him down, and either break his grip or lose the hair at last.

To reach the handle—slippery in his sweaty fingers—he had to twist his arm behind himself so torturously and bend his hand at such a severe angle that he didn't have the range of movement to work the lever action.

As if sensing Billy's intent, the freak leaned all his weight against the door.

Billy's head was largely out of the car now, and a face suddenly appeared above him, upside-down to his face. A countenance without features. A hooded phantom.

He blinked to clear his vision.

Not a hood. A dark ski mask.

Even in this poor light, Billy could see the fevered gaze that glistered from the eyeholes.

Something sprayed the lower half of his face, from the nose down. Wet, cold, pungent yet sweet, a medicinal reek.

He gasped in shock, then tried to hold his breath, but the single gasp had undone him. Astringent fumes burned in his nostrils. His mouth flooded with saliva.

The masked face seemed to lower toward his, like a dark moon coming down, the cratered eyes.

# 16

The sedative wore off. Like a winch line turning on a drum, pain gradually hoisted Billy from unconsciousness.

His mouth tasted as if he'd drunk waffle syrup and chased it with bleach. Sweet and bitter. Life itself.

For a while he didn't know where he was. Initially he did not care. Raised from a sea of torpor, he felt saturated with unnatural sleep and yearned to return to it.

Eventually the unrelenting pain forced him to care, to keep his eyes open, to analyze sensation and to orient himself. He was lying on his back on a hard surface—the church parking lot.

He could smell the faint scents of tar, oil, gasoline. The vague nutty, musty fragrance of the oak tree spreading overhead in the darkness. His own sour perspiration.

Licking his lips, he tasted blood.

When he wiped his face, Billy found it slick with a viscous substance that was most likely a mixture of sweat and blood. In the dark, he could not see what had been transferred to his hand.

The pain was mostly in his scalp. He first assumed that it was a lingering effect of having had his hair nearly pulled out.

A slow pulsing ache, punctuated by a series of sharper pangs, radiated across his head, not from the crown, however, where his hair had been severely tested, but from his brow.

When he raised one hand and hesitantly explored the source, he found something stiff and wiry bristling from his forehead, an inch below the hairline. Although his touch was gentle, it triggered a spasm of sharper pain that made him cry out.

*Are you prepared for your first wound?*

He left the exploration of the injury for later, until he could see the damage.

The wound would not be mortal. The freak had not intended to kill him, only to hurt him, perhaps to scar him.

Billy's grudging respect for his adversary had grown to the point that he did not expect the man to make mistakes, at least not major ones.

Billy sat up. Pain swelled across his brow, and again when he got to his feet.

He stood swaying, surveying the parking lot. His assailant was gone.

High in the night, a cluster of moving stars, the running lights of a jet, growled westward. On this route, it was probably a military transport headed for a war zone. Another war zone different from the one down here.

He opened the driver's door of the Explorer.

Crumbled safety glass littered the seat. He plucked a Kleenex box from the console and used it to scrape the prickly debris off the upholstery.

He searched for the note that had been taped over the ignition. Evidently the killer had taken it.

He found the dropped key under the brake pedal. From the floor in front of the passenger's seat, he retrieved the revolver.

He had been allowed to keep the gun for the game ahead. The freak didn't fear it.

The substance with which Billy had been sprayed—chloroform or some other anesthetic—had a lingering effect. When he bent over, he grew dizzy.

Behind the wheel, with the door closed, with the engine running, he worried that he might not be fit to drive.

He turned on the air conditioner, angled two vents at his face.

As he assessed his transient dizziness, the interior lights went off automatically. Billy turned them on once more.

He tilted the rearview mirror to inspect his

face. He looked like a painted devil: dark red, but the teeth bright; dark red, and the whites of the eyes unnaturally white.

When he adjusted the mirror again, he saw at once the source of his pain.

Seeing did not immediately mean believing. He preferred to think that the residual dizziness from the anesthetic might be accompanied by hallucination.

He closed his eyes and took a few deep breaths. He strove to clear the image in the mirror from his mind, and hoped that when he looked again he would not see the same.

Nothing had changed. Across his forehead, an inch below the hairline, three large fishhooks pierced his flesh.

The point and the barb of each hook protruded from the skin. The shank also protruded. The bend of each hook lay under the thin meat of his brow.

He shuddered and looked away from the mirror.

There are days of doubt, more often lonely nights, when even the devout wonder if they are heirs to a greater kingdom than this earth and if they will know mercy—or if instead they are only animals like any other, with no inheritance except the wind and the dark.

This was such a night for Billy. He had known others like it. Always the doubt had receded. He

told himself that it would recede again, though this time it was colder and seemed certain to leave a higher water mark.

The freak had at first seemed to be a player to whom murder was a sport. The fishhooks in the forehead, however, had not been intended as merely a game move; and this was no game.

To the freak, these killings were something more than murder, but the something more was not a form of chess or the equivalent of poker. Homicide had symbolic meaning for him, and he pursued it with a purpose more serious than amusement. He had some mysterious goal beyond the killing itself, an aim for which he sought completion.

If *game* was the wrong word, Billy needed to find the right one. Until he knew the correct word, he would never understand the killer, and would not find him.

With Kleenex, he gently swabbed the clotted blood from his eyebrows, wiped most of it off his lids and lashes.

The sight of the fishhooks had clarified his mind. He wasn't dizzy anymore.

His wounds needed attention. He switched on the headlights and drove out of the church parking lot.

Whatever ultimate goal the freak might have, whatever symbolism he intended with the fish-hooks, he must also have hoped to send Billy to

a doctor. The physician would require an explanation of the hooks, and any response Billy made would complicate his predicament.

If he told the truth, he would tie himself to the murders of Giselle Winslow and Lanny Olsen. He would be the primary suspect.

Without the three notes, he could offer no evidence that the freak existed.

The authorities would not regard the hooks as credible evidence, for they would wonder if this was a case of self-mutilation. A self-inflicted wound was a ploy that murderers sometimes used to cast themselves as victims and thereby to deflect suspicion.

He knew the cynicism with which some cops would look upon his dramatic, bizarre, but superficial wounds. He knew it precisely.

Furthermore, Billy was a fresh-water angler. He fished for trout and bass. These substantial hooks were the size needed to land large bass if you were using live bait instead of lures. In his tackle box at home were hooks identical to those that now drew his blood.

He dared not go to a doctor. He'd have to be his own physician.

At 3:30 in the morning, he had the rural roadways to himself. The night was still, but the SUV made its own wind, which blustered at the broken-out window. In the halogen headlights, flat vineyards, hillside vineyards, and wooded

heights remained familiar to his eye but, mile by mile, became as alien to his heart as any foreign barrens.

# PART TWO

# Are You Prepared for Your Second Wound?

# 17

In February, after the extraction of a molar with roots fused to his jawbone, Billy had been given a prescription for a painkiller, Vicodin, by his periodontist. He had used only two of ten tablets.

The pharmacy label specified that the medication should be taken with food. He had not eaten dinner, and he still had no appetite.

He needed the medication to be effective. From the refrigerator, he got a baking dish of leftover homemade lasagna.

Although the punctures in his brow were plugged with clots and the bleeding had stopped, the pain continued unrelenting and made coherent thought increasingly difficult. He chose not to delay the few minutes necessary to zap the dish in the microwave. He put it cold on the kitchen table.

A pink sticker on the pill bottle counseled against consuming alcoholic beverages while

taking the painkiller. Screw that. He had no intention of driving a car or operating heavy machinery in the next several hours.

He popped the tablet and forked lasagna into his mouth, washing everything down with Elephant beer, a Danish brew boasting a higher alcohol content than other beers.

As he ate, he thought about the dead schoolteacher, about Lanny sitting in the bedroom armchair, about what the killer might do next.

Those lines of thought were not conducive to appetite or to digestion. The teacher and Lanny were beyond rescue, and there was no way to foretell the freak's next move.

Instead, he thought about Barbara Mandel, mostly about Barbara as she had been, not as she was now in Whispering Pines. Inevitably, these reminiscences led forward to the moment, and he began to worry about what would happen to her if he died.

He remembered the small square envelope from her physician. He fished it out of his pocket and tore it open.

The name DR. JORDAN FERRIER was blind embossed on the face of the cream-colored note card. He had precise handwriting: *Dear Billy, When you start timing your visits to Barbara in order to avoid me during my regular rounds, I know the time has come for our semiannual review of her condition. Please call my office to schedule an appointment.*

Sweat beaded the bottle of Elephant beer. He used Dr. Ferrier's note card as a coaster to protect the table.

"Why don't *you* call *my* office for an appointment," Billy said.

The baking dish was half full of lasagna. Although he had no appetite, he ate everything, shoving food into his mouth and chewing vigorously, ate as if eating could satiate anger as easily as it could hunger.

Eventually the pain in his forehead substantially subsided.

He went to his fishing gear in the garage. From his angler's kit, he retrieved needle-nose pliers with a wire-cutting edge.

In the house again, after locking the back door, he went to the bathroom, where he examined his face in the mirror. The mask of blood had dried. He looked like an aboriginal resident of Hell.

The freak had inserted the three hooks with care. Apparently, he had tried to do as little damage as possible.

To suspicious police, that tenderness would have supported the theory that these wounds were self-inflicted.

One end of the hook featured the bend and the barb. At the other end was an eye to which a snap and leader could be attached. Pulling either the barb or the eye through the puncture would further rip the flesh.

He used the pliers to snip off the eye from one hook. Between thumb and forefinger, he pinched the barbed end and extracted the cut shank.

When he had removed all three hooks, he took a shower as hot as he could tolerate.

After the shower, he sterilized the punctures as best he could with rubbing alcohol and then hydrogen peroxide. He applied Neosporin and covered the wounds with gauze pads fixed with adhesive tape.

At 4:27 A.M., according to the nightstand clock, Billy went to bed. A double bed, two sets of pillows. His head on one soft pillow, the hard revolver under the other.

*May the judgment not be too heavy upon us. . . .*

As his eyelids fell shut of their own weight, he saw Barbara in his mind's eye, her pale lips forming inscrutable statements.

*I want to know what it says, the sea. What it is that it keeps on saying.*

He was asleep before the clock counted the half hour.

In his dream, he lay in a coma, unable to move or to speak, but nonetheless aware of the world around him. Doctors in white lab coats and black ski masks loomed, working on his flesh with steel scalpels, carving clusters of bloody acanthus leaves.

Resurgent pain, dull but persistent, woke him at 8:40 Wednesday morning.

At first, he could not remember which of his

recent nightmarish experiences had been dreamed, which real. Then he could.

He wanted another Vicodin. Instead, in the bathroom, he shook two aspirin from a bottle.

Intending to take the aspirins with orange juice, he went into the kitchen. He had neglected to put the baking pan, crusted with the residue of lasagna, in the dishwasher. The empty bottle of Elephant beer stood on Dr. Ferrier's stationery.

Morning light flooded the room. The blinds had been raised. The windows had been covered when he'd gone to bed.

Taped to the refrigerator was a folded sheet of paper, the fourth message from the killer.

# 18

He knew beyond doubt that he had engaged the deadbolt in the back door when he had returned from the garage with the needle-nose pliers. Now it was unlocked.

Stepping onto the porch, he surveyed the western woods. A few elms in the foreground, pines beyond.

The morning sun bent all tree shadows in upon the grove and probed those dusky reaches without much illuminating them.

As his gaze traveled the greenwood, seeking the telltale flare of sunlight off the lenses of binoculars, he saw movement. Mysterious forms whidded among the trees, as fluid as the shadows of birds in flight, flickering palely when sunlight dappled them.

A sense of the uncanny overcame Billy. Then the forms broke from the trees, and they were only deer: a buck, two does, a fawn.

He thought that something must have spooked them in the woods, but they gamboled only a few yards onto the lawn before coming to a halt. As serene as deer in Eden, they grazed upon the tender grass.

Returning to the house, leaving the deer to their breakfast, Billy locked the back door even though he gained no safety from the deadbolt. If the killer didn't possess a key, then he owned lock picks and was experienced in their use.

Leaving the note undisturbed, Billy opened the fridge. He took out a quart of orange juice.

As he drank juice from the carton, washing down the aspirins, he stared at the note taped to the refrigerator. He did not touch it.

He put two English muffins in the toaster. When they were crisp, he spread peanut butter on them and ate at the kitchen table.

If he never read the note, if he burned it in the sink and washed the ashes down the drain, he would be removing himself from the game.

The first problem with that idea was the same that had pricked his conscience before: Inaction counted as a choice.

The second problem was that he himself had become a victim of assault. And he had been promised more.

*Are you prepared for your* first *wound?*

The freak had not underlined or italicized *first,* but Billy understood where the emphasis belonged.

Although he had his faults, self-delusion wasn't one of them.

If he didn't read the note, if he tried to opt out, he would be even less able to imagine what might be coming than he was now. When the ax fell on him, he would not even hear the blade cutting the air above his head.

Besides, this was in no way a game to the killer, which Billy had realized the previous night. Denied a playmate, the freak would not simply pick up his ball and go home. He would see this through to whatever end he had in mind.

Billy would have liked to carve acanthus leaves.

He wanted to work a crossword puzzle. He was good at them.

Laundry, yard work, cleaning out the rain gutters, painting the mailbox: He could lose himself in the mundane chores of daily life, and take solace in them.

He wanted to work at the tavern and let the hours pass in a blur of repetitive tasks and inane conversations.

All the mystery he needed—and all the drama—was to be found in his visits to Whispering Pines, in the puzzling words that Barbara sometimes spoke and in his persistent belief that there was hope for her. He needed nothing more. He had nothing more.

He had nothing more until *this,* which he didn't need and didn't want—but could not escape.

Finished with the muffins, he took the plate and knife to the sink. He washed them, dried them, and put them away.

In the bathroom, he peeled the bandage off his forehead. Each hook had torn him twice. The six punctures looked red and raw.

Gently he washed the wounds, then reapplied alcohol, hydrogen peroxide, and Neosporin. He fashioned a fresh bandage.

His brow was cool to the touch. If the hook had been dirty, an infection might not be prevented by his precautions, especially if the points and barbs had scored the bone.

He was safe from tetanus. Four years previously, renovating the garage to accommodate a woodworking shop, he'd sustained a deep cut in his left hand, from a hinge that corrosion had made brittle and sharp. He'd gotten a booster shot of DPT vaccine. Tetanus didn't worry him. He would not die of tetanus.

Neither would he die of infected hook wounds. This was a false worry to give his mind a rest from real and greater threats.

In the kitchen, he peeled the note off the refrigerator. He wadded it in his fist and took it to the waste can.

Instead of throwing the note away, he smoothed it on the table and read it.

*Stay home this morning. An associate of mine*

*will come to see you at 11:00. Wait for him on the front porch.*

*If you don't stay home, I will kill a child.*

*If you inform the police, I will kill a child.*

*You seem so angry. Have I not extended to you the hand of friendship? Yes, I have.*

*Associate.* The word troubled Billy. He did not like that word at all.

In rare cases, homicidal sociopaths worked in pairs. The cops called them *kill buddies.* The Hillside Strangler in Los Angeles had proved to be a pair of cousins. The D.C. Sniper had been two men.

The Manson Family numbered more than two.

A simple bartender might rationally hope to get the best of one ruthless psychopath. Not two.

Billy did not consider going to the police. The freak had twice proved his sincerity; if disobeyed, he would kill a child.

In this instance, at least, a choice was open to him that did not entail selecting anyone for death.

Although the first four lines of the note were straightforward, the meaning of the last two lines could not be easily interpreted.

*Have I not extended to you the hand of friendship?*

The mockery was evident. Billy also detected a taunting quality suggesting that information had been offered here that would prove helpful to him if only he could understand it.

Rereading the message six times—eight, even ten—did not bring clarity. Only frustration.

With this note, Billy had evidence again. Although it did not amount to much and would not itself impress the police, he intended to keep it safe.

In the living room, he surveyed the book collection. In recent years, it had been nothing to him except something to be dusted.

He selected *In Our Time.* He tucked the killer's note between the copyright page and the dedication page, and he returned the volume to the shelf.

He thought of Lanny Olsen sitting dead in an armchair with an adventure novel in his lap.

In the bedroom, he fetched the .38 Smith & Wesson from under the pillow.

As he handled the revolver, he remembered how it felt when it discharged. The barrel wanted to rake up. The backstrap hardened against the meat of the palm, and the recoil traveled the bones of the hand and arm, seeming to churn the marrow as a school of fish churned water.

In a dresser drawer was an open box of ammunition. He put three spare cartridges in each of the front pockets of his chinos.

That seemed to be enough insurance. Whatever might be coming, it would not be a war. It would be violent and vicious, but brief.

He smoothed the night out of the bedclothes.

Although he didn't use a spread, he plumped the pillows and tucked in the sheets so they were as taut as a drum skin.

When he picked up the gun from the nightstand, he remembered not only the recoil but also what it felt like to kill a man.

# 19

Jackie O'Hara answered his cell phone with a line he sometimes used when he worked behind the bar. "What can I do ya for?"

"Boss, it's Billy."

"Hey, Billy, you know what they were talking about in the tavern last night?"

"Sports?"

"The hell they were. We're not a damn sports bar."

Looking out a kitchen window toward the lawn from which the deer had vanished, Billy said, "Sorry."

"The guys in sports bars—the drinking doesn't mean anything to them."

"It's just a way to get high."

"That's right. They'd as soon smoke a little pot or even get a Starbucks buzz. We're not a damn sports bar."

Having heard this before, Billy tried to move

the discussion along: "To our customers, the drinking is a kind of ceremony."

"Beyond ceremony. It's an observance, a solemnity, almost a kind of sacrament. Not to all of them, but to most. *It's communion.*"

"All right. So were they talking about Big Foot?"

"I wish. The best, the really intense barroom talk used to be about Big Foot, flying saucers, the lost continent of Atlantis, what happened to the dinosaurs—"

"—what's on the dark side of the moon," Billy interjected, "the Loch Ness monster, the Shroud of Turin—"

"—ghosts, the Bermuda Triangle, all that classic stuff," Jackie continued. "But it's not like that so much anymore."

"I know," Billy acknowledged.

"They were talking about these professors at Harvard and Yale and Princeton, these scientists who say they're going to use cloning and stem cells and genetic engineering to create a superior race."

"Smarter and faster and better than we are," Billy said.

"So much better than we are," Jackie said, "they won't be human at all. It's in *Time* or maybe *Newsweek,* these scientists smiling and proud of themselves right in a *magazine.*"

"They call it the posthuman future," Billy said.

"What happens to us when we're *post?*" Jackie

wondered. "Post is toast. A *master race*? Haven't these guys heard of Hitler?"

"They think they're different," Billy said.

"Don't they have mirrors? Some idiots are crossing human and animal genes to create new . . . new *things*. One of them wants to create a pig that's got a human brain."

"How about that."

"The magazine doesn't say why a pig, like it should be obvious why a pig instead of a cat or a cow or a chipmunk. For God's sake, Billy, isn't it hard enough being a human brain in a human body? What kind of hell would it be, a human brain in a pig body?"

"Maybe we won't live to see it," Billy said.

"Unless you're planning to die tomorrow, you will. I liked Big Foot better. I liked the Bermuda Triangle and ghosts a lot better. Now all the crazy shit is *real*."

"Why I called," Billy said, "is to let you know I can't make it to work today."

With genuine concern, Jackie said, "Hey, what, are you sick?"

"I'm kind of queasy."

"You don't sound like you have a cold."

"I don't think it's a cold. It's like a stomach thing."

"Sometimes a summer cold starts that way. Better take zinc. They've got this zinc gel you squeeze up your nose. It really works. It stops a cold dead."

"I'll get some."

"Too late for vitamin C. You gotta be taking that all along."

"I'll get some zinc. Did I call too early, did you close up the tavern last night?"

"No. I went home at ten o'clock. All that talk about pigs with human brains, I just wanted to go home."

"So Steve Zillis closed up?"

"Yeah. He's a reliable boy. That stuff I told you, I wish now I hadn't. If he wants to chop up mannequins and watermelons in his backyard, that's his business, as long as he does his job."

Tuesday night was often slow in the bar business. If the traffic grew light, Jackie preferred to lock the tavern before the usual 2:00 A.M. closing time. An open bar with few or no customers in the wee hours is a temptation to a stickup artist, putting employees at risk.

"Busy night?" Billy asked.

"Steve said after eleven it was like the world ended. He had to open the front door and look outside to be sure the tavern hadn't been teleported to the moon or somewhere. He turned off the lights before midnight. Thank God there aren't two Tuesdays in a week."

Billy said, "People like to spend *some* time with their families. That's the curse of a family bar."

"You're a funny guy, aren't you?"

"Not usually."

"If you put that zinc gel up your nose and you don't feel any better," Jackie said, "call me back, and I'll tell you somewhere else you can stuff it."

"I think you'd have made a fine priest. I really do."

"Get well, okay? The customers miss you when you're off."

"Do they?"

"Not really. But at least they don't say they're glad you're gone."

Under the circumstances, perhaps only Jackie O'Hara could have made Billy Wiles crack a smile.

He hung up. He looked at his watch. Ten-thirty-one.

The "associate" would be here in less than half an hour.

If Steve Zillis had left the tavern shortly before midnight, he would have had plenty of time to go to Lanny's place, kill him, and move the body to the armchair in the master bedroom.

If Billy had been handicapping suspects, he would have given long odds on Steve. But once in a while, a long shot won the race.

# 20

On the front porch were two teak rocking chairs with dark-green cushions. Billy seldom needed the second chair.

This morning, wearing a white T-shirt and chinos, he occupied the one farthest from the porch steps. He didn't rock. He sat quite still.

Beside him stood a teak cocktail table. On the table, on a cork coaster, was a glass of cola.

He hadn't drunk any of the cola. He had prepared it as a prop, to distract the eye from consideration of the box of Ritz crackers.

The box contained nothing but the snub-nosed revolver. The only crackers were a stack of three on the table, beside the box.

Bright and clear and hot, the day was too dry to please the grape growers, but it was all right with Billy.

From the porch, between deodar cedars, he could see a long way down the rural road that

sloped up toward his house and far beyond.

Not much traffic passed. He recognized some of the vehicles, but he didn't know to whom they belonged.

Rising off the sun-scorched blacktop, shimmering heat ghosts haunted the morning.

At 10:53, a figure appeared in the distance, on foot. Billy did not expect the associate to hike in for the meeting. He assumed this was not the man.

At first the figure might have been a mirage. The furnace heat distorted him, made him ripple as if he were a reflection on water. Once he seemed to evaporate, then reappeared.

In the hard light, he looked tall and thin, unnaturally thin, as if he had recently hung on a cross in a cornfield, glaring the birds away with his button eyes.

He turned off the county road and followed the driveway. He left the driveway for the grass and, at 10:58, arrived at the bottom of the porch steps.

"Mr. Wiles?" he asked.

"Yes."

"I believe you're expecting me."

He had the raw, rough voice of one who had marinated his larynx in whiskey and slow-cooked it in years of cigarette smoke.

"What's your name?" Billy asked.

"I'm Ralph Cottle, sir."

Billy had thought the question would be ignored. If the man were hiding behind a false name, *John Smith* would have been good enough. *Ralph Cottle* sounded real.

Cottle was as thin as the distorting heat had made him appear to be from a distance, but not as tall. His scrawny neck looked as if it might snap with the weight of his head.

He wore white tennis shoes dark with age and filth. Shiny in spots and frayed at the cuffs, the cocoa-brown, summer-weight suit hung on him with no more grace than it would have hung from a coat rack. His polyester shirt was limp, stained, and missing a button.

These were thrift-shop clothes from the cheapest bin; and he had gotten long wear out of them.

"Mr. Wiles, may I come in the shade?"

Standing at the bottom of the steps, Cottle looked as if the weight of the sunlight might collapse him. He seemed too frail to be a threat, but you never could tell.

"There's a chair for you," Billy said.

"Thank you, sir. I appreciate the kindness."

Billy tensed as Cottle ascended the stairs but relaxed a little when the man had settled into the other rocker.

Cottle didn't rock, either, as if getting the chair moving was a more strenuous task than he cared to contemplate.

"Sir, do you mind if I smoke?" he asked.

"Yes. I do mind."

"I understand. It's a filthy habit."

From an inner coat pocket, Cottle produced a pint of Seagram's and unscrewed the cap. His bony hands trembled. He didn't ask if it was all right to drink. He just took a swig.

Apparently, he had sufficient control of his nicotine jones to be polite about it. The hooch, on the other hand, told him when he needed it, and he could not disobey its liquid voice.

Billy suspected that other pints were tucked in other pockets, plus cigarettes and matches, and possibly a couple of hand-rolled joints. This explained why a suit in summer heat: It was not only clothing but also a portmanteau for his various vices.

The booze didn't heighten the color of his face. His skin was already dark from much sun and red from an intricate web of burst capillaries.

"How far did you walk?" Billy asked.

"Only from the junction. I hitched a ride that far." Billy must have looked skeptical, for Cottle added, "A lot of people know me around these parts. They know I'm harmless, unkempt but not dirty."

Indeed, his blond hair looked clean, though uncombed. He had shaved, too, his leathery face tough enough to resist nicking even with the razor wielded by such an unsteady hand.

His age was difficult to determine. He might have been forty or sixty, but not thirty or seventy.

"He's a very bad man, Mr. Wiles."

"Who?"

"The one who sent me."

"You're his associate."

"No more than I'm a monkey."

"Associate—that's what he called you."

"Do I look like a monkey, either?"

"What's his name?"

"I don't know. I don't want to know."

"What's he look like?"

"I haven't seen his face. I hope I never do."

"A ski mask?" Billy guessed.

"Yes, sir. And eyes looking out of it cold as snake eyes." His voice quavered in sympathy with his hands, and he tipped the bottle to his mouth again.

"What color were his eyes?" Billy asked.

"They looked yellow as egg yolks to me, but that was just the lamplight in them."

Remembering the encounter in the church parking lot, Billy said, "There was too little light for me to see color . . . just a hot shine."

"I'm not such a bad man, Mr. Wiles. Not like him. What I am is weak."

"Why've you come here?"

"Money, for one thing. He paid me one hundred forty dollars, all in ten-dollar bills."

"One-forty? What—did you bargain him up from a hundred?"

"No, sir. That's the precise sum he offered. He said it's ten dollars for each year of your innocence, Mr. Wiles."

In silence, Billy stared at him.

Ralph Cottle's eyes might once have been a vibrant blue. Maybe all the alcohol had faded them, for they were the palest blue eyes that Billy had ever seen, the faint blue of the sky at high altitude where there is too little atmosphere to provide rich color and where the void beyond is barely concealed.

After a moment, Cottle broke eye contact, looked out at the yard, the trees, the road.

"Do you know what that means?" Billy asked. "My fourteen years of innocence?"

"No, sir. And it's none of my business. He just wanted me to make a point of telling you that."

"You said money was one thing. What was the other?"

"He'd kill me if I didn't come see you."

"That's what he threatened to do?"

"He doesn't make threats, Mr. Wiles."

"Sounds like one."

"He just says what is, and you know it's true. I come see you or I'm dead. And not dead easy, either, but very hard."

"Do you know what he's done?" Billy asked.

"No, sir. And don't you tell me."

"There's two of us now who know he's real. We can corroborate each other's story."

"Don't even talk that way."

"Don't you see, he's made a mistake."

"I wish I could be his mistake," Cottle said, "but I'm not. You think too much of me, and shouldn't."

"But he's got to be stopped," Billy said.

"Not by me. I'm nobody's hero. Don't you tell me what he's done. Don't you dare."

"Why shouldn't I tell you?"

"That's your world. It isn't mine."

"There's just one world."

"No, sir. There's a billion of them. Mine's different from yours, and that's the way it's gonna stay."

"We're sitting here on the same porch."

"No, sir. It looks like one porch, but it's two, all right. You know that's true. I see it in you."

"See what?"

"I see the way you're a little like me."

Chilled, Billy said, "You can't see anything. You won't even look at me."

Ralph Cottle met Billy's eyes again. "Have you seen the woman's face in the jar like a jellyfish?"

The conversation had suddenly switched from the main track to a strange spur line.

"What woman?" Billy asked.

Cottle knocked back another slug from the pint. "He says he's had her in the jar three years."

"Jar? Better stop pouring down that nose paint, Ralph. You're not making much sense."

Cottle closed his eyes and grimaced, as if he could see what he now described. "It's a two-quart jar, maybe bigger, with a wide-mouth lid. He changes the formaldehyde regularly to keep it from clouding."

Beyond the porch, the sky was crystalline. High in the clear light, a lone hawk circled, as clean as a shadow.

"The face tends to fold into itself," Cottle continued, "so you don't at first see a face. It's like something from the sea, clenched yet billowy. So he gently shakes the jar, gently swirls the contents, and the face . . . it blossoms."

The grass is sweet and green across the lawn, then taller and golden where nature alone tends to it. The two grasses produce distinct fragrances, each crisp and pleasant in its own way.

"You recognize an ear first," said Ralph Cottle. "The ears are attached, and the cartilage gives them shape. There's cartilage in the nose, too, but it hasn't held its shape very well. The nose is just a lump."

From the shining heights, the hawk descended in a narrowing gyre, describing silent and harmonious curves.

"The lips are full, but the mouth is just a hole, and the eyes are holes. There's no hair, 'cause he cut only from one ear to the other, from the top of the brow to the bottom of the chin. You can't tell it's a woman's face, and not a man's. He says

she was beautiful, but there's no beauty in the jar."

Billy said, "It's just a mask, latex, a trick."

"Oh, it's real. It's as real as terminal cancer. He says it was the second act in one of his best performances."

"Performances?"

"He has four photos of her face. In the first, she's alive. Then dead. In the third, the face is partly peeled back. In the fourth, her head is there, her hair, but the soft tissue of her face is gone, nothing but bone, the grinning skull."

From graceful gyre to sudden plunge, the hawk knifed toward the tall grass.

The pint told Ralph Cottle that he needed fortification, and he drank a new foundation for his crumbling courage.

Following a fumy exhalation, he said, "The first photo, when she was alive, maybe she was pretty like he says. You can't tell because . . . she's all terror. She's ugly with terror."

The tall grass, previously motionless in the fixative heat, stirred briefly in a single place, where feathers thrashed the stalks.

"The face in that first picture," Cottle said, "is worse than the one in the jar. It's a lot worse."

The hawk burst from the grass and soared. Its talons clutched something small, perhaps a field mouse, which struggled in terror, or didn't. At this distance, you couldn't be sure.

Cottle's voice was a file rasping on ancient wood. "If I don't do exactly what he wants me to, he promises to put *my* face in a jar. And while he harvests it, he'll keep me alive, and conscious."

In the bright pellucid sky, the rising hawk was as black and clean as a shadow once more. Its wings cleaved the shining air, and the high thermals were the pristine currents of a river through which it swam, and dwindled, and vanished, having killed only what it needed to survive.

# 21

Rockless in the rocking chair, Ralph Cottle said that he lived in a ramshackle cottage by the river. Two rooms and a porch with a view, the place had been hammered together in the 1930s and had been falling apart ever since.

Long ago, unknown rugged individuals had used the cottage for fishing vacations. It had no electric service. An outhouse served as the toilet. The only running water was what passed in the river.

"I think mainly it was a place for them to get away from their wives," Cottle said. "A place to drink and get drunk. It still is."

A fireplace provided heat and allowed simple cooking. What meals Cottle ate were spooned from hot cans.

Once the property had been privately owned. Now it belonged to the county, perhaps seized for back taxes. Like much government land, it was

poorly managed. No bureaucrats or game wardens had bothered Ralph Cottle since the day, eleven years ago, when he had cleaned out the cottage, put down his bedroll, and settled in as a squatter.

No neighbors lived within sight or within shouting distance. The cottage was a secluded outpost, which suited Cottle just fine.

Until 3:45 the previous morning, when he had been prodded awake by a visitor in a ski mask: *Then* what had seemed like cozy privacy had become a terrifying isolation.

Cottle had fallen asleep without extinguishing the oil lamp by which he read Western novels and drank himself to sleep. In spite of that light, he hadn't absorbed any useful details about the killer's appearance. He couldn't estimate the man's height or weight.

He claimed the madman's voice had no memorable characteristics.

Billy figured Cottle knew more but feared to tell. The anxiety that now simmered in his faded blue eyes was as pure and intense, if not as immediate, as the terror he described in the photograph of the unknown woman from whom the freak had "harvested" a face.

Judging by the length of his skeletal fingers and the formidable bones in his knobby wrists, Cottle had once been equipped to fight back. Now, by his own admission, he was weak, not just emotionally and morally, but physically.

Nevertheless, Billy leaned forward in his chair and tried again to enlist him: "Back me up with the police. Help me—"

"I can't even help myself, Mr. Wiles."

"You must've once known how."

"I don't want to remember."

"Remember what?"

"Anything. I told you—I'm weak."

"Sounds like you want to be."

Raising the pint to his lips, Cottle smiled thinly and, before taking a drink, said, "Haven't you heard—the meek shall inherit the earth."

"If you won't do it for yourself, do it for me."

Licking his lips, which were badly chapped by the heat and by the dehydrating effect of the whiskey, Cottle said, "Why would I?"

"The meek don't stand by and watch another man destroyed. The meek aren't the same as cowards. They're two different breeds."

"You can't insult me into cooperation. I don't insult. I don't care. I know I'm nothing, and that's all right with me."

"Just because you've come here to do what he wants, you won't be safe out there in your cottage."

Screwing the cap on the bottle, Cottle said, "Safer than you."

"Not at all. You're a loose end. Listen, the police will give you protection."

A dry laugh escaped the stewbum. "Is that why

you've been so quick to run to them—for their *protection*?"

Billy said nothing.

Emboldened by Billy's silence, Cottle found a sharper voice that was less mean than smug: "Just like me, you're nothing, but you don't know it yet. You're nothing, I'm nothing, we're all nothing, and as far as I care, if he leaves me alone, that psycho shithead can do what he wants to anybody because he's nothing, too."

Watching Cottle screw open the pint-bottle cap that he had just screwed shut, Billy said, "What if I throw your ass down those stairs and kick you off my land? He calls me sometimes just to wear on my nerves. What if when he calls I tell him you were drunk, incoherent, I couldn't understand a thing you said?"

Cottle's sunburned and blood-fused face could not turn pale, but his small purse of a mouth, snugged tight with self-satisfaction after his rant, now loosened and poured forth the dull coins of a counterfeit apology. "Mr. Wiles, sir, please don't take offense at my bad mouth. I can't control what comes out of it any more than I can control what I pour into it."

"He wanted to be sure you told me about the face in the jar, didn't he?"

"Yes, sir."

"Why?"

"I don't know. He didn't *consult* with me, sir.

He just put words in my mouth to bring to you, and here I am because I want to live."

"Why?"

"Sir?"

"Look at me, Ralph."

Cottle met his eyes.

Billy said, "Why do you want to live?"

As though Cottle had never considered it before, the question seemed to pin down some fluttering thing in his mind, like a rare moth to a specimen board, some ever-restless and ever-contentious and ever-bitter aspect of himself that for a moment he seemed at last disposed to consider. Then his eyes became evasive, and he clasped both hands, not just one, around the pint of whiskey.

"Why do you want to live?" Billy persisted.

"What else is there?" Avoiding Billy's eyes, Cottle raised the bottle in both hands, as if it were a chalice. "I could use just a taste," he said, as though asking for permission.

"Go ahead."

He took a small sip, but then at once took another.

"The freak made you tell me about the face in the jar because he wants that image in my head."

"If you say so."

"It's about intimidation, about keeping me off balance."

"Are you?"

Instead of answering the question, Billy said, "What else did he send you here to tell me?"

As if getting down to business, Cottle screwed the cap on the bottle again and this time returned the pint to his coat pocket. "You'll have five minutes to make a decision."

"What decision?"

"Take off your wristwatch and prop it on the porch railing."

"Why?"

"To count off the five minutes."

"I can count them with the watch on my wrist."

"Putting it on the railing is a signal to him that the countdown has started."

Woods to the north, shadowy and cool in the hot day. Green lawn, then tall golden grass, then a few well-crowned oaks, then a couple of houses down-slope and to the east. To the west lay the county road, trees and fields beyond it.

"He's watching now?" Billy asked.

"He promised he would be, Mr. Wiles."

"From where?"

"I don't know, sir. Just please, please take off your watch and prop it on the railing."

"And if I won't?"

"Mr. Wiles, don't talk that way."

"But if I won't?" Billy pressed.

His baritone rasp thinned to a higher register as Cottle said, "I told you, he'll take my face, and me awake when he does. *I told you.*"

Billy got up, removed his Timex, and propped it on the railing so that the watch face could be seen from both of the rocking chairs.

As the sun approached the zenith of its arc, it penetrated the landscape and melted shadows everywhere but in the woods. The green-cloaked conspiratorial trees revealed no secrets.

"Mr. Wiles, you've got to sit down."

Brightness fell from the air, and a chrome-yellow glare hazed the fields and furrows, forcing Billy to squint at numberless places where a man could lie in the open, effectively camouflaged by nothing more than spangled sunlight.

"You won't spot him," Cottle said, "and he won't like it that you're trying. Come back, sit down."

Billy remained on his feet at the railing.

"You've wasted half a minute, Mr. Wiles, forty seconds."

Billy didn't move.

"You don't know what a box you're in," Cottle said anxiously. "You're gonna need every minute he's given you to *think.*"

"So tell me about the box."

"You have to be sitting down. For God's sake, Mr. Wiles." Cottle wrung his voice as a worried old woman might wring her hands. "He wants you sitting *in the chair.*"

Billy returned to the rocking chair.

"I just want to be done with this," Cottle said.

"I just want to do what he told me and get out of here."

"Now you're the one wasting time."

One of the five minutes had passed.

"All right, okay," Cottle said. "This is him talking now. You understand? This is him."

"Get on with it."

Cottle nervously licked his lips. He slipped the pint from his coat, not seeking a taste at the moment, instead clutching it with both hands, as if it were a talisman with the occult power to lift the fog of whiskey that blurred his memory, ensuring that he would deliver the message clearly enough to save his face from being pickled in a jar.

"'I will kill someone you know. You will select the target for me from people in your life,'" Cottle quoted. "'This is your chance to rid the world of some hopeless asshole.'"

"The twisted sonofabitch," Billy said, and discovered that both of his hands were fisted, with nothing to punch.

"'If you don't select the target for me,'" Cottle continued quoting, "'*I* will choose someone in your life to kill. You have five minutes to decide. The choice is yours, if you have the balls to make it.'"

# 22

The effort to recall the precise wording of the message reduced Ralph Cottle to a hive of buzzing nerves. Countless anxieties swarmed through him and were glimpsed in his darting eyes, in his twitching face, in his trembling hands; Billy could almost hear the thrumming wings of dread.

While Cottle had recited the freak's challenge and conditions, with the penalty of death hanging over him if he got them wrong, the pint bottle had been a talisman with the power to inspire, but now he needed the contents.

Staring at the wristwatch on the porch railing, Billy said, "I don't need five minutes. Hell, I don't even need the three that're left."

Without intention, by not going to the police and getting them involved, he had already contributed to the death of one person in his life: Lanny Olsen. By his inaction, he had spared

the mother of two, but he had doomed his friend.

Lanny himself had been partly if not largely responsible for his own death. He had taken the killer's notes and had destroyed them to save his job and his pension, at the cost of his life.

Nevertheless, some of the blame lay with Billy. He could feel the weight; and always would.

What the freak demanded of him now was something new and more terrible than anything heretofore. Not by inaction this time, not by inadvertence, but by conscious intent, Billy was expected to mark someone he knew for death.

"I won't do it," he said.

Having guzzled a dram or two, Cottle was sliding the wet mouth of the bottle back and forth across his lips, as if he might French kiss it instead of drinking any more. Through his nose, he noisily inhaled the rising fumes.

"If you won't do it, he will," said Cottle.

"Why *would* I choose? I'm screwed either way, aren't I?"

"I don't know. I don't want to know. It's not my business."

"The hell it's not."

"It's not my business," Cottle insisted. "I've got to sit here till you give me your decision, then I give it to him, and I'm not a part of it anymore. You've got just more than two minutes left."

"I'm going to the cops."

"It's too late for that."

"I'm in shit to my hips," Billy admitted, "but I'll only be deeper later."

When Billy rose from his rocking chair, Cottle said sharply, *"Sit down!* If you try to leave this porch before I do, you'll be shot in the head."

The stewbum stowed bottles in his pockets, not weapons. Even if Cottle had a gun, Billy was confident about taking it from him.

"Not me," Cottle said. *"Him.* How he's watching us right now is through the scope of a high-powered rifle."

The gloom of the woods to the north, the dazzle of sun on the slope to the east, the rock formations and swales of the fields on the south side of the county road . . .

"He can just about read our lips," Cottle said. "It's the finest marksman's gun, and he's qualified for it. He can nail you at a thousand yards."

"Maybe that's what I want."

"He's willing to oblige. But he doesn't think you're ready. He says you will be eventually. In the end, he says, you'll ask him to kill you. But not yet."

Even with his weight of guilt, Billy Wiles suddenly felt like a feather, and he feared a sudden wind. He settled into the rocking chair.

"Why it's too late to go to the cops," Cottle said, "is because he planted evidence in her place, on her body."

The day remained still, but here came the wind. "What evidence?"

"For one thing, some of your hairs in her fist and under her fingernails."

Billy's mouth felt numb. "How would he get my hairs?"

"From your shower drain."

Before the nightmare had begun, when Giselle Winslow had still been alive, the freak had already been in this house.

The shade on the porch no longer held the summer heat at bay. Billy might as well have been standing on blacktop in the sun. "What else besides hairs?"

"He didn't say. But it's nothing the police will tie to you . . . unless for some reason you come under suspicion."

"Which he can make happen."

"If the cops start thinking maybe they should ask you for a DNA sample, you're finished."

Cottle glanced at the wristwatch.

So did Billy.

"One minute left," Cottle advised.

# 23

One minute. Billy Wiles stared at his wristwatch as if it were a bomb clock counting down to detonation.

He wasn't thinking about the fleeting seconds or the evidence planted at the scene of Giselle Winslow's murder, or about being in the sights of a high-powered rifle.

Instead, he was composing a mental directory of people in his life. Faces flickered rapidly through his mind. Those he liked. Those toward whom he was indifferent. Those he disliked.

These were dark shoals. He could founder on them. Yet turning his mind away from such thoughts proved as difficult as ignoring a knife held to his throat.

A knife of another kind, a knife of guilt cut him loose from these considerations at last. Realizing how seriously he had been calculating the comparative value of the people in his life, assessing which

of them had a lesser right to life than others, he could not repress a shudder of disgust.

"No," he said, seconds before his time ran out. "No, I'll never choose. He can go to Hell."

"Then he'll choose for you," Cottle reminded Billy.

"He can go to Hell."

"All right. It's your call. It's on your shoulders, Mr. Wiles. It's none of my business."

"Now what?"

"You stay in the chair, sir, right where you are. I'm supposed to go inside to the kitchen phone, wait for his call, and tell him your decision."

"I'll go inside," Billy said. "I'll take the call."

"You're making me crazy," Cottle said, "you're gonna get us both killed."

"It's my house."

When he raised the bottle to his mouth, Cottle's hands shook so badly that the glass rattled against his teeth. Whiskey dribbled down his chin.

Without wiping the spill off his face, he said, "He wants you in that chair. You try to go inside, he'll blow your brains out before you reach the door."

"What sense does that make?"

"Then he'll blow my brains out, too, because I couldn't make you listen to me."

"He won't," Billy disagreed, beginning to intuit something of the freak's perspective. "He's not ready to end it, not this way."

"What do *you* know? You don't know. You don't know squat."

"He's got a plan, a purpose, something that might not make sense to you or me, but it makes sense to him."

"I'm just a useless damn drunk, but even *I* know you're full of crap."

"He wants to work it all out the way he conceived it," Billy said more to himself than to Cottle, "not just end it in the middle with two head shots."

Anxiously surveying the sun-dazzled day beyond the front porch, spraying spittle as he spoke, Ralph Cottle said, "You bullheaded sonofabitch, will you *listen* to me! You don't *listen*!"

"I'm listening."

"More than anything, he wants things done *his* way. He doesn't want to talk to you. Get it? Maybe he doesn't want you to hear his voice."

That made sense if the freak was someone whom Billy knew.

Cottle said, "Or maybe he just doesn't want to listen to your bullshit any more than I do. I don't know. If you want to answer the phone to show him who's boss, just to piss him off, and he blows your brains out, I don't give a rat's ass. But then he'll kill me, too, and you can't choose for me. *You can't choose for me!*"

Billy knew that his instincts were right: The freak wouldn't shoot them.

"Your five minutes are up," Cottle said worriedly, gesturing toward the watch on the railing. "*Six* minutes. You're past six minutes. He won't like this."

In truth, Billy didn't *know* the freak would hold his fire. He suspected that would be the case, intuited it, but he didn't *know.*

"Your time is up. Going on seven minutes. *Seven minutes.* He expects me to leave the porch, go inside."

Cottle's faded blue eyes were boiled in fear. He had so little to live for, yet he was desperate to live.

*What else is there?* he had said.

"Go," Billy told him.

"What?"

"Go inside. Go to the phone."

Bolting up from his rocking chair, Cottle dropped the open pint. Several ounces of whiskey spilled from the uncapped mouth.

Cottle didn't stoop to retrieve his treasure. In fact, in his haste to get to the front door, he kicked the bottle and sent it spinning across the porch floor.

At the threshold to the house, he looked back and said, "I'm not sure how quick he'll call."

"You just remember every word he says," Billy instructed. "You remember every word *exactly.*"

"All right, sir. I will."

"And every inflection. You remember every word and *how he says it,* and you come tell me."

"I will, Mr. Wiles. Every word," Cottle promised, and he went into the house.

Billy remained alone on the porch. Perhaps still in the crosshairs of a telescopic sight.

# 24

Three butterflies, aerial geishas, danced out of the sunshine, into the porch shadows. Their silken kimonos flaring and folding and flaring in graceful swirls of color, as bashful as faces hidden behind the pleats of hand-painted fans, they fled, quick, into the brightness from which they had come.

*Performance.*

Perhaps this was the word that defined the killer, that would lead to an explanation of his actions, and that if understood would reveal his Achilles' heel.

According to Ralph Cottle, the freak had referred to the murder of a woman and to the peeling away of her face as "the second act" in one of his "best performances."

In assuming that the psychopath considered murder to be largely a thrilling game, Billy had been wrong. Sport might be part of it, but this

man wasn't entirely or even primarily motivated by a perverse sense of fun.

Billy didn't quite know what to make of the word *performance.* Maybe to his nemesis, the world was a stage, reality was a fraud, and all was artifice.

How that view could explain this homicidal behavior—or predict it—Billy didn't know, couldn't guess.

*Nemesis* represented wrong thinking. A nemesis was an enemy who could not be defeated. The better word was *adversary.* Billy had not given up hope.

With the front door standing open, the ring of the telephone would carry to the front porch. He had not heard it yet.

Lazily rocking the chair, not to make a harder target of himself, but to disguise his anxiety and thus rob the killer of the chance to take any satisfaction from it, Billy studied the nearest California live oak and then the next to the nearest.

They were huge old trees with broad canopies. Their trunks and branches looked black in the bright sun.

In those shadowy arbors, a sniper might find a crook of branches to serve as a platform to accommodate him and a tripod for his rifle.

The two nearest houses down-slope, one on this side of the road, one on the farther side, were well within the thousand-yard range. If nobody

had been home, the freak could have broken into one of those places; he might now be at an upstairs window.

*Performance.*

Billy was not able to think of any person in his life to whom that word had greater relevance than it did to Steve Zillis. The tavern was a stage to Steve.

Was it logical, however, that the freak, a vicious serial killer with a taste for mutilation, would have a sense of humor so simple and a concept of theater so puerile that he got a kick out of nose-shot peanuts, tongue-tied cherry stems, and jokes about dumb blondes?

Repeatedly Billy glanced at the wristwatch on the porch railing.

Three minutes was a reasonable wait, even four. But when five passed, that seemed to be too many.

He started to get up from the chair, but he heard Cottle's voice in memory—*You can't choose for me!*—and a weight of responsibility pressed him back into the rocker.

Because Billy had kept Cottle on the porch past the five-minute deadline, the freak might be playing payback, making them wait so their nerves would fray a little, to teach them not to screw with the big dog.

That thought comforted Billy for a minute. Then a more ominous possibility occurred to him.

When Cottle hadn't gone into the house promptly at the five-minute mark, when Billy had delayed two or three minutes, maybe the killer had taken the lack of punctuality to mean that Billy refused to choose a victim, which was indeed the case.

Having made that assumption, the freak might have decided that he had no reason to call Ralph Cottle. At that moment he could have picked up his rifle and walked out of the woods or away from one of the houses down-slope.

If he'd selected a victim in advance of hearing Billy's answer, which surely he had done, he might be eager to get on with his plans.

One of the people in Billy's life, the most important person, was of course Barbara, helpless in Whispering Pines.

Independent of any experience or knowledge that would justify his confidence, Billy sensed that this bizarre drama was still in the first act of three. His wretched antagonist was far from ready to conclude this performance; therefore, Barbara was not in imminent jeopardy.

If the freak knew anything about the subject of his torment—and he seemed to know a lot—he would realize that Barbara's death would instantly take all the fight out of Billy. Resistance was essential to drama. Conflict. Without Billy, there would be no act two.

He must take steps to protect Barbara. But he

needed to think hard about *how*, and he had time to do so.

If he was wrong about that, if Barbara was next, then this world was about to become a brief and bitter purgatory before he quickly moved on to a room in Hell.

Seven minutes had passed since Cottle had gone inside, seven and counting.

Billy got up from the rocker. His legs felt weak.

He pulled the revolver from the box of Ritz crackers. He didn't care if the drunkard saw it.

At the threshold of the open door, he called out, "Cottle?" and received no reply, and said, "Cottle, damn it."

He went into the house, crossed the living room, and stepped into the kitchen.

Ralph Cottle wasn't there. The back door stood open, and Billy knew that he had left it closed, locked.

He went out onto the back porch. Cottle wasn't there, either, nor was he in the yard. He had gone.

The phone hadn't rung, yet Cottle had gone. Maybe when the call hadn't come in, Cottle had taken the silence to be a sign that the killer judged him a failure. He could have panicked and fled.

Returning to the house, closing the door behind himself, Billy swept the kitchen with his gaze, looking for something amiss. He had no idea what that might be.

Everything seemed to be as it had been, as it should be.

Uncertainty gave way to misgiving, however, and misgiving became suspicion. Cottle must have taken something, brought something, *done* something.

From the kitchen to the living room, to the study, Billy found nothing out of the ordinary, but in the bathroom he discovered Ralph Cottle. Dead.

# 25

Hard fluorescent light painted a film of faux frost on Cottle's open eyes.

Having passed on rather than out, the drunk sat on the lidded seat of the toilet, leaning against the tank, head tipped back, mouth slack. Yellow rotten teeth framed a tongue that appeared milky pink and vaguely fissured from the dehydration of perpetual inebriation.

Billy stood breathless, stunned stupid, then backed out of the bathroom into the hall, staring at the corpse through the doorway.

He didn't retreat because of any stench. Cottle had not voided bowels or bladder in his death throes. He remained unkempt but not filthy—the only thing about which he had seemed to have any pride.

Billy just couldn't breathe in the bathroom, as though all the air had been sucked out of that space, as though the dead man had been killed

by a sudden vacuum that now threatened to suffocate Billy himself.

In the hallway, he could draw breath again. He could begin to think.

For the first time, he noticed the handle of the knife, which pinned Cottle's rumpled suit coat to him. A bright-yellow handle.

The blade had been thrust at an upward angle between the ribs on the left side, buried to the hilt. The heart had been pierced, and stopped.

Billy knew that the embedded blade measured six inches. The yellow knife belonged to him. He kept it in his angler's kit in the garage. It was a fishing knife, honed sharp to gut bass and fillet trout.

The killer had not been in the woods or in a meadow swale, or in a neighbor's house watching them through a telescopic rifle sight. That was a lie, and the drunkard had believed it.

As Cottle had approached the front porch, the freak must have entered by the back door. While Billy and his visitor had sat in the rockers, their adversary had been in the house, a few feet from them.

Billy had refused to choose someone in his life to be the next victim. As promised, the killer then made the choice with startling swiftness.

Although Cottle had been the next thing to a stranger, he was undeniably in Billy's life. And now in his house. Dead.

In less than a day and a half, in just forty-one hours, three people had been murdered. Yet this still felt to Billy like act one; perhaps it was the *end* of act one, but his gut instinct told him that significant developments lay ahead.

At every turn of events, he had done what seemed to be the most sensible and cautious thing, especially given his personal history.

His common sense and caution, however, played into the killer's hands. Hour by hour, Billy Wiles was drifting farther from any safe shore.

Down in Napa, evidence that might incriminate him had been planted in the house where Giselle Winslow had been murdered. Hairs from his shower drain. He didn't know what else.

No doubt evidence had been salted in Lanny Olsen's house, as well. For one thing, the place marker in the book under Lanny's dead hand was all but certainly a photo of Winslow, linking the crimes.

Now in his bathroom slumped a corpse from which bristled a knife that belonged to him.

Here in summer, Billy felt as if he were on an icy slope, the bottom invisible beyond a cold mist, still on his feet in a wild glissade, but gaining speed that, second by second, threatened his balance.

Initially the discovery of Cottle's corpse had shocked Billy into mental and physical immobility. Now several courses of action occurred to him, and he stood hobbled by indecision.

The worst thing he could do was act precipitately. He needed to think this through, attempt to foresee the consequences of each of his options.

He could afford no more mistakes. His freedom depended on his wits and courage. So did his survival.

Stepping into the bathroom again, he noticed no gore. Maybe this meant Cottle hadn't been killed in the bath.

Billy hadn't seen evidence of violence elsewhere in the house, either.

This realization focused him on the handle of the knife. Around the point of penetration, dark blood soaked the lightweight summer suit jacket, but the stain wasn't as large as he would have expected.

The killer had finished Cottle with a single thrust. He'd known precisely where and how to slip the thin blade between the ribs. The heart had stopped within a beat or two of being punctured, which minimized the bleeding.

Cottle's hands lay in his lap, one upturned and the other cupped against it, as if he'd died while applauding his killer. Mostly concealed, something was captured between the hands.

When Billy pinched a corner of the object and pulled it free of the dead man's grasp, he discovered a computer diskette: red, high density, the same brand that he had used in the days when he had worked at his computer.

He studied the body from different angles. He turned slowly in a full circle, surveying the bathroom for any clues the killer might have left either intentionally or inadvertently.

Sooner than later, he should probably go through Cottle's coat and pants pockets. The diskette gave him an excuse to postpone that unpleasant task.

In the study, after putting the revolver and the diskette on the desk, he removed the vinyl cover from his shrouded computer. He had not used the machine in almost four years.

Curiously, he had never unplugged it. He supposed this might be an unconscious expression of his stubborn—if fragile—hope that Barbara Mandel might one day recover.

In his second year of college, when he realized that not much of what he learned there would help him become the writer he wanted to be, he had dropped out. He had done manual labor of various kinds, writing diligently in his spare time.

At twenty-one, he had taken his first bartending job. The work had seemed ideal for a writer. He saw story material in every barfly.

Patiently developing his talent, he sold more than a score of well-received short stories to a variety of magazines. When he was twenty-five, a major publisher had wanted to collect them in a book.

The book sold modestly but earned critical

praise, suggesting that bartending would not forever be his primary occupation.

When Barbara came into Billy's life, she provided not merely encouragement but also inspiration. Just by knowing her, by loving her, he found a truer and clearer voice in his prose.

He wrote his first novel, and his publisher responded to it with excitement. The revisions suggested by the editor were minor, a month's work.

Then he lost Barbara to the coma.

The truer and clearer voice in his prose had not been lost with her. He could still write.

The desire to write, however, slipped away from him, and the will to write, and all interest in storytelling. He no longer wanted to explore the human condition in fiction, for he had too much hard experience of it in reality.

For two years, his publisher and editor were patient. But the month's work on his manuscript had become to him more than a lifetime of labor. He could not do it. He repaid the advance and canceled the contract.

Switching on this computer, even just to review what the killer had left in Ralph Cottle's hands, felt like a betrayal of Barbara, although she would have disapproved of—even mocked—such thinking.

He was a little surprised when the machine, so long unused, at once came to life. The screen

brightened, and the operating-system logo appeared as the simulated harp strings of the signature music issued from the speakers.

The computer might have been used more recently than he thought. The fact that the diskette was the same brand as the unused diskettes in one of his desk drawers suggested that it was in fact one of his and that the freak had composed his latest message at this keyboard.

Oddly enough, he was creeped out by this realization even more than he had been when he'd found the corpse in his bathroom.

Long unseen yet familiar, the software menu appeared. Because he had written his fiction in Microsoft Word, he tried it first.

That choice proved correct. The killer had written his message in Word, as well; and it loaded at once.

The diskette contained three documents. Before Billy could review the text, the telephone rang.

He figured it must be the freak.

# 26

Billy picked up the phone. "Hello?"

Not the freak. A woman said, "To whom am I speaking?"

"To whom am *I* speaking? You called me."

"Billy, that sounds like you. This is Rosalyn Chan."

Rosalyn was a friend of Lanny Olsen. She worked for the Napa County Sheriff's Department. She came into the tavern now and then.

Before Billy had been able to decide what to do about Lanny's body, it must have been found.

The instant that he realized he hadn't responded to her, Rosalyn said probingly, "Are you all right?"

"Me? I'm fine. Doin' okay. This heat's making me crazy, though."

"Is something wrong there?"

He flashed on a mental image of Cottle's corpse in the bathroom, and guilt rolled his mind into angles of disorientation. "Wrong? No. Why would there be?"

"Did you just call here and hang up without saying anything?"

Clouds of mystification thickened for a moment, then abruptly evaporated. For a moment he had forgotten what Rosalyn did in the sheriff's department. She was a 911 operator.

The name and address of every 911 caller appeared on her monitor as soon as she picked up the phone at her end.

"That was just—what?—was that even a minute ago?" he asked, thinking fast, or trying to.

"A minute ten now," Rosalyn said. "Did you—"

"What I did," he said, "is I keyed in 911 when I meant to call information."

"You meant to call 411?"

"I meant to call 411, but I pressed 911. I realized right away what I'd done, so I hung up."

The freak was still in the house. The freak had called 911. Why he had done this, what he hoped to achieve, Billy couldn't figure, at least not under this pressure.

"Why didn't you stay on the line," Rosalyn Chan asked, "and tell me the call was made in error?"

"I realized my mistake right away, I hung up so fast, I didn't think a connection had been made yet. That was stupid. I'm sorry, Rosalyn. I was calling 411."

"So you're all right?"

"I'm all right. It's just this crazy heat."

"Don't you have air conditioning?"

"I have it, but it conked out."

"That sucks."

"Totally."

The revolver lay on the desk. Billy picked it up. The freak was in the house.

"Hey, maybe I'll stop in the tavern around five," she said.

"Well, I won't be there. I'm feeling sort of punky, so I called in sick."

"I thought you said you were fine."

So easy to trip himself up. He needed to look for the intruder, but he needed to sound right to Rosalyn.

"I am fine. I'm okay. Nothing serious. Just a little stomach thing. Maybe it's a summer cold. I'm taking that nasal gel stuff."

"What stuff?"

"You know, that zinc gel, you squeeze it up your nose, it knocks the cold right out of you."

She said, "I think I heard about that."

"It's good. It works. Jackie O'Hara put me on to it. You should keep some on hand."

"So everything's okay there?" she asked.

"Except for the heat and me feeling punky, but you can't do much about that. Nine-one-one can't fix a cold or an air conditioner. I'm sorry, Rosalyn. I feel like an idiot."

"It's no big deal. Half the calls we get aren't emergencies."

"They aren't?"

"People call, their cat's in a tree, the neighbors are having a noisy party, things like that."

"That makes me feel better. At least I'm not the biggest idiot on the block."

"Just take care of yourself, Billy."

"I will. You too. You take care of yourself."

"Bye," she said.

He put down the phone and rose from his chair.

While Billy had been in the bathroom with the corpse, the freak had come back into the house. Or maybe he had already been inside, hiding in a closet or somewhere that Billy hadn't checked.

The guy had balls. Big brass ones. He knew about the .38, but he came back into the house and he called 911 while Billy was taking the vinyl cover off the computer.

The freak might still be here. Doing what? Doing something.

Billy crossed the study to the door, which he had left open. He went through fast, two hands on the revolver, sweeping it left, then right.

The freak wasn't in the hall. He was somewhere.

# 27

Although Billy Wiles wasn't wearing his wristwatch, he knew that time was running out as fast as water through a sieve.

In the bedroom, he slid aside one of the closet doors. No one.

The space under the bed was too tight. No one would choose to hide under there because squirming out quickly wasn't possible; that hiding place would be a trap. Besides, no overhanging spread curtained that low space.

Looking under the bed would be a waste of time. Billy started toward the door. He returned to the bed, dropped to one knee. A waste.

The freak was gone. He was crazy, but he wasn't crazy enough to stay here after calling 911 and hanging up on them.

In the hallway again, Billy hurried to the threshold of the bathroom. Cottle sat alone in there.

The shower curtain was drawn open. If it had been drawn shut, it would have been a prime place to look.

A large hall closet housed the oil-fired furnace. It offered no options.

The living room. An open space, easy to search with a sweep of the eyes.

The kitchen cabinetry featured a tall, narrow broom closet. No good.

He tore open the door to the walk-in pantry. Canned goods, boxes of pasta, bottles of hot sauce, household supplies. Nowhere to hide a grown man.

In the living room again, he shoved the revolver deep under a sofa cushion. It didn't leave a visible lump, but anyone who sat on the gun would feel it.

He had left the front door standing open. An invitation. Before hastening once more to the bathroom, he closed the door.

Cottle with his head tipped back and his mouth open, with his hands together in his lap as if clapping, might have been singing Western swing and keeping time.

The knife sawed against bone as Billy pulled it out of the wound. Blood smeared the blade.

With a few Kleenex plucked from a box beside the sink, he wiped the knife clean. He balled up the tissues and put them on top of the toilet tank.

He folded the blade into the yellow handle and put the knife beside the sink.

When Billy shifted the corpse sideways on the toilet, the head fell forward, and a gaseous sputter escaped the lips, as if Cottle had died on an inhalation, as if his last breath, until now, had been trapped in his throat.

He hooked his arms under the dead man's arms. Trying to avoid the blood-soaked part of the suit coat, Billy hauled him off the toilet.

Worn thin by a diet of spirits, Cottle weighed hardly more than an adolescent. Carrying him would be too difficult, however, because he was gangly, spindle-legged.

Fortunately, rigor mortis had not begun to set in. Cottle was limp, flexible.

Shuffling backward, Billy dragged the body out of the bathroom. The heels of the dead man's sneakers squeaked and stuttered along the ceramic-tile floor.

They protested against the polished Santos-mahogany floors of the hall and study, too, all the way around behind the desk, where he lowered the corpse to the hardwood.

Billy heard himself breathing hard, not so much from exertion as from high anxiety.

Time rushed away, rushed like a river over a falls.

After rolling the office chair aside, he shoved the corpse into the knee space. He had to bend the legs to make the dead man fit.

He swung the chair in front of the computer

again. He pushed it as far into the knee space as possible.

The desk was deep and had a privacy panel on the front. Anyone who came into the room would have to walk all the way behind the work station and peer purposefully into the kneehole to see the cadaver.

Even then, because of the chair and depending on the angle of view, a casual look might not reveal this grisly secret.

Shadows would be helpful. Billy switched off the overhead light. He left only the desk lamp aglow.

In the bathroom once more, he saw a smear of blood on the floor. None had been there before he'd moved Cottle.

His heart was a kicking horse battering the board walls of his chest.

One mistake. If he made one mistake here, it would finish him.

His time perception was whacked. He *knew* that only a few minutes had passed since he'd set out to search the house, but he felt as if ten minutes had fled, fifteen.

He wished that he had his wristwatch. He didn't dare take the time to retrieve it from the front-porch railing.

With a wad of toilet paper, he wiped the blood off the floor. The tiles came clean, but a faint discoloration remained in a section of grout. It

looked like rust, not like blood. That's what he wanted to believe.

Into the toilet he dropped the wad of paper as well as the Kleenex with which he had swabbed the blade of the knife. He flushed them away.

The murder weapon lay on the counter beside the sink. He buried it at the back of a vanity drawer, behind bottles of shaving lotion and suntan oil.

When he slammed the drawer shut so hastily, so hard, that it banged like a gunshot, he knew he needed to get a tighter grip on himself.

*Teach us to care and not to care. Teach us to sit still.*

He would remain calmer if he remembered his true purpose. His true purpose was not the endless cycle of idea and action, was not the preservation of his freedom or even his life. He must live that she could live, helpless but safe, helpless and sleeping and dreaming but subjected to no indignity, no evil.

He was a shallow man. He had often proved that truth to himself.

In the face of suffering, he had not possessed the strength of will to pursue his gift for the written word. He rejected the gift not just once but a damning number of times, for gifts conferred by the power that had conferred this one are perpetually offered and can come to nothing only if they are perpetually rejected.

In his suffering, he had been humbled by the

limitations of language, which he should have been. He had also been defeated by the limitations of language, which he should not have been.

He was a shallow man. He did not have within him the capacity to care deeply about multitudes, to accept every neighbor into his heart without qualification. The *power* of compassion was in him merely an *ability,* and its potentiality seemed to be fulfilled by caring for one woman.

Because of this shallowness, he believed himself to be a weak man, perhaps not as weak as Ralph Cottle, but not strong. He had been chilled but never surprised when the stewbum had said *I see the way you're a little like me.*

The sleeper, safe and dreaming, was his true purpose and also his only hope of redemption. For that, he must care and not care; he must be still.

Calmer than when he had slammed the drawer, Billy reviewed the bathroom one more time. He saw no evidence of the crime.

Time was still a river rushing, a spinning wheel.

Hurriedly but thoroughly, he retraced the route along which he had dragged the dead man, searching for additional smears of blood like the one in the bathroom. He discovered none.

Doubting himself, he quickly toured the bedroom, living room, and kitchen once more. He tried to see everything through the eyes of suspicious authority.

Only the situation on the front porch remained to be set right. He had left that task for last because it was less urgent than the need to conceal the corpse.

In case he didn't have time to address the porch, he took from a kitchen cabinet the bottle of bourbon with which he had spiked his Guinness stout on Monday night. He swigged directly from the bottle.

Instead of swallowing, he swished the whiskey between his teeth, around his mouth, as if it were mouthwash. The longer he held the alcohol, the more it burned his gums, tongue, cheeks.

He spat it in the sink before he remembered to gargle.

He rinsed his mouth with another swig but also let it churn in his throat for several seconds.

With a wheeze but not a choke, he spat this second mouthful in the sink just as the expected knock came at the front door, loud and protracted.

Perhaps four minutes had passed since he'd hung up the phone after his conversation with Rosalyn Chan. Maybe five. It felt like an hour; it felt like ten seconds.

As the knock sounded, Billy turned on the cold water to wash the reek of booze out of the sink. He left it streaming.

In the quiet after the knock, he capped the bourbon and returned it to the cabinet.

At the sink once more, he cranked off the water as the knocking came again.

Answering at once on the first knock might have made him seem anxious. Waiting for a third might make it appear as though he had considered not answering at all.

Crossing the living room, he thought to examine his hands. He did not see any blood.

# 28

When Billy Wiles opened the front door, he found a sheriff's deputy standing three cautious steps from the threshold and to one side. The cop's right hand rested on the pistol in the swivel holster at his hip, rested there not as if he were prepared to draw it, but as casually as anyone might stand with a hand on his hip.

Billy had hoped that he would know him. He didn't.

The officer's badge featured a nameplate: SGT. V. NAPOLITINO.

At forty-six, Lanny Olsen had held the same rank—deputy—at which he had entered service as a younger man.

In his early twenties, V. Napolitino had already been promoted to sergeant. He had the well-scrubbed, clear-eyed, intelligent, and diligent look of a man who would make lieutenant by twenty-

five, captain by thirty, commander by thirty-five, and chief before forty.

Billy's preference would have been a fat, rumpled, weary, and cynical specimen. Maybe this was one of those days when you should stay away from roulette because every bet on black would ensure a red number.

"Mr. Wiles?"

"Yeah. That's me."

"William Wiles?"

"Billy, yes."

Sergeant Napolitino shifted his attention back and forth between Billy and the living room behind him.

The sergeant's face remained expressionless. His eyes revealed neither apprehension nor even disquiet, nor as much as wariness, but were only watchful.

"Mr. Wiles, would you mind stepping out to my car with me?"

The sheriff's-department cruiser stood in the driveway.

"You want to come in?" Billy asked.

"Not necessarily, sir. Just to the car for a minute or two, if you don't mind."

This almost sounded like a request, but it wasn't.

"Sure," Billy said. "All right."

A second patrol car pulled off the county blacktop, into the driveway, and halted ten feet behind the first.

As Billy reached for the knob to pull the front door shut after him, Sergeant Napolitino said, "Why don't you leave it open, sir."

The deputy's tone of voice did not signify either a question or a suggestion. Billy left the door open.

Napolitino clearly expected him to lead the way.

Billy stepped over the pint bottle, past the spilled Seagram's.

Although the puddle was at least fifteen minutes old, less than half of it had evaporated in the heat. In the still air, the porch stank of whiskey.

Billy went down the steps and onto the lawn. He didn't pretend to be unsteady. He wasn't a good enough actor to play drunk, and any attempt to do so would call his sincerity into doubt.

He intended to rely on his potent breath to suggest functional inebriation and to give credence to the story that he intended to tell.

As a deputy got out of the second patrol car, Billy recognized him. Sam Sobieski. He also was a sergeant, and perhaps five years older than Sergeant Napolitino.

Sobieski visited the tavern once in a while, usually with a date. He came for the bar food more than to drink, and two beers were his limit.

Billy didn't know him well. They weren't friends, but knowing him at all was better than dealing with two strangers.

On the front lawn, Billy turned to look back at the house.

Napolitino was still on the porch. He managed to cross to the steps and begin to descend without fully turning his back on either the open door or the windows, yet appearing unconcerned all the while.

Now he took the lead and brought Billy around the patrol car, putting it between them and the house.

Sergeant Sobieski joined them. "Hi, Billy."

"Sergeant Sobieski. How're you doin'?"

Everybody called a bartender by his first name. In some cases, you knew familiarity was expected in return; in this case not.

"Yesterday was chili day, and I forgot," said Sobieski.

Billy said, "Ben makes the best chili."

"Ben is a chili god," Sobieski said.

The car was a lodestone to the sun, scorching the air around it and no doubt blistering to the touch.

First on the scene, Napolitino took charge: "Mr. Wiles, are you all right?"

"Sure. I'm okay. This is about my screw-up, I guess."

"You called 911," Napolitino said.

"I meant to call 411. I told Rosalyn Chan."

"You didn't tell her until she called you back."

"I hung up so fast I didn't realize a connection had been made."

"Mr. Wiles, are you to any degree under duress?"

"Duress? Hey, no. You mean was somebody holding a gun to my head when I was on the phone with Rosalyn? Wow. That's a pretty wild idea. No offense, I know that sort of thing happens, but not to me."

Billy cautioned himself to give short answers. Longer ones could sound like nervous babbling.

"You called in sick to work?" Napolitino asked.

"Yeah." Grimacing but not too dramatically, he put one hand on his abdomen. "I've got this stomach thing."

He hoped they could smell his breath. He himself could smell it. If they could smell his breath, they would think his claim of illness was a lame attempt to conceal the fact that he was on a little bit of a bender.

"Mr. Wiles, who else lives here?"

"No one. Just me. I live alone."

"Is anyone in the house right now?"

"No. No one."

"No friend or member of the family?"

"No. Not even a dog. Sometimes I think about getting a dog, but I never do."

Scalpels were not sharper than Sergeant Napolitino's dark eyes. "Sir, if there's a bad guy in there—"

"No bad guy," Billy assured him.

"If someone you care about is being held in there under duress, the best thing you could do is tell me."

"Of course. I know that. Who wouldn't know that?"

The intense heat coming off the sun-hammered car made Billy half sick. His face felt seared. Neither of the sergeants appeared to be bothered by the broiling air.

"Under stress, intimidated," Sobieski said, "people make bad decisions, Billy."

"Sweet Jesus," Billy said, "I *really* made an ass of myself this time, hanging up on 911, then what I said to Rosalyn."

"What did you say to her?" Napolitino asked.

Billy was certain they knew the essentials of what he had said, and he himself remembered every word with piercing clarity, but he hoped to convince them that he was too booze-confused to recall quite how he had gotten himself in this predicament.

"Whatever I said, it must have been stupid if I gave her the idea somebody might be giving me trouble. Duress. Man. This is way embarrassing."

He shook his head at his foolishness, found a dry laugh, and shook his head again.

The sergeants just watched him.

"No one's here but me. No one's come around here in days. No one's ever here but me. I pretty much keep to myself, it's the way I am."

That was enough. He was perilously close to babbling again.

If they knew about Barbara, they knew how he was. If they didn't know about her, Rosalyn would tell them.

He had taken a risk by saying that nobody had visited in days. Rightly or wrongly, he'd felt that he should make a point of his reclusive life.

If someone in the nearest houses down-slope had seen Ralph Cottle walking up this driveway or had noticed him sitting on the porch, and if the sergeants decided to have a word with the neighbors, Billy would be caught in a lie.

"What happened to your forehead?" Napolitino asked.

Until that moment, Billy had forgotten about the hook wounds in his brow, but a low throbbing pain arose in them when the sergeant asked the question.

# 29

"Isn't that a bandage?" Sergeant Napolitino persisted.

Although Billy's thick hair fell over his forehead, it did not entirely conceal the gauze pads and adhesive tape.

"I had a little table-saw accident," Billy said, pleasantly surprised by the swiftness with which a suitable lie occurred to him.

"Sounds serious," Sergeant Sobieski said.

"It's not. It's nothing. I have a woodworking shop in the garage. I built all the cabinetry in the house. Last night, I was working on something, cutting a walnut one-by-six, and there was a knot in it. The blade cracked the knot, and a few splinters shot into my forehead."

"You could lose an eye like that," Sobieski said.

"I wear safety goggles. I always wear goggles."

Napolitino said, "Did you go to a doctor?"

"Nah. No need. Just some splinters. I dug 'em

out with tweezers. Hell, the only reason I need a bandage is I did more damage with the tweezers, getting the splinters out, than they did going in."

"Be careful about infection."

"I soaked it with alcohol, hydrogen peroxide. Smeared Neosporin on it. I'll be all right. This kind of thing, it happens."

Billy felt that he had satisfied their concerns. To his ear, he didn't sound like a man under duress, with a life-or-death problem.

The sun was a furnace, a forge, and the heat coming off the car cooked him more effectively than a microwave oven might have done, but he was cool.

When the questioning took a negative and more aggressive turn, he didn't at once recognize the change.

"Mr. Wiles," said Napolitino, "did you then call information?"

"Did I what?"

"After you mistakenly dialed 911 and hung up, did you dial 411 as you had intended?"

"No, I just sat there for a minute thinking about what I'd done."

"You sat there for a minute thinking how you had mistakenly dialed 911?"

"Well, not a whole minute. However long it was. I didn't want to screw up again. I was feeling a little woozy. Like I said, my stomach. Then Rosalyn called me back."

"Before you could dial 411 for information, she called back."

"That's right."

"After your conversation with the 911 operator—"

"Rosalyn."

"Yes. After your conversation with her, did you then call 411?"

The telephone company imposed a 411 service charge for each call. If he had placed one, they would have a record of it.

"No," Billy said. "I felt like such a bonehead. I needed a drink."

The reference to a drink had come naturally, not as if he were trying to sell them on his supposed inebriation. He thought he had sounded smooth, convincing.

Napolitino said, "What number would you have asked for if you had called 411?"

Billy realized that these inquiries were no longer related to his welfare and safety. A veiled antagonism colored Napolitino's questions, subtle but unmistakable.

Billy wondered if he should openly acknowledge this development and question their intent. He didn't want to appear guilty.

"Steve," he said. "I needed Steve Zillis's number."

"He is . . . ?"

"He's a bartender at the tavern."

"He covers your shift when you're sick?" Napolitino asked.

"No. He works the shift after mine. Why's it matter?"

"Why did you need to call him?"

"I just wanted to warn him that I was out, and when he came on he'd have a mess to clean up because Jackie would have been tending bar alone."

"Jackie?" Napolitino asked.

"Jackie O'Hara. He's the owner. He's covering my shift. Jackie doesn't continually tidy the work bar, the lower bar, like he should. The clutter and spills just build up till the guy following him needs like a frantic fifteen minutes to get the set-up workable again."

Every time Billy had to give a longer, more explanatory answer, he heard a shakiness arise in his voice. He didn't think that he was imagining it; he believed that the sergeants could hear it, too.

Maybe everyone sounded this way when talking to on-duty cops for any substantial length of time. Maybe uneasiness was natural.

A lot of gesturing was not natural, however, especially not for Billy. During his longer answers, he found himself using his hands too much, and he couldn't control them.

Defensively, but trying to appear casual, he slipped his hands into the pockets of his chinos.

In each pocket, his fingers found three .38 cartridges, spare ammunition.

Napolitino said, "So you wanted to warn Steve Zillis he'd have a mess."

"That's right."

"You don't know Mr. Zillis's phone number?"

"I don't call him often."

They were not engaged in an innocent Q and A anymore. They had not descended to the level of an interrogation yet, but they were on the down escalator.

Billy did not quite understand why this should be the case—except that perhaps his answers and his demeanor had not been as exculpatory as he had thought.

"Isn't Mr. Zillis's number in the directory?"

"I guess so. But sometimes it's just easier to call 411."

"Unless you mistakenly dial 911," Napolitino said.

Billy decided that making no reply would be better than berating himself for idiocy, as he had done earlier.

If the situation deteriorated to the point where they decided to search him, even just to pat him down, they would find the cartridges in his pockets.

He wondered if he'd be able to explain the bullets with another facile and convincing lie. At the moment, he couldn't think of one.

But he couldn't believe it would ever come to that. The deputies were here because they had been concerned that he might be in danger. He had only to convince them that he was safe, and they would leave.

Something that he had said—or had not said—left them with lingering doubts. If he could only find the right words, the magic words, the sergeants would go away.

Now, here, he chafed again at the limitations of language.

As real as the change in Napolitino's attitude seemed, a part of Billy argued that he was imagining it. The strain of disguising his anxiety had bent his perceptions, had made him a little paranoid.

He counseled himself to be still, to have patience.

"Mr. Wiles," said Napolitino, "are you absolutely sure that you yourself dialed 911?"

Although Billy could parse that sentence, he couldn't quite make sense out of it. He couldn't grasp the intention behind the question, and considering everything that he had told them thus far, he didn't know what answer they expected from him.

"Is there any possibility whatsoever that someone else in your house placed that call to 911?" Napolitino pressed.

For an instant Billy thought somehow they

knew about the freak, but then he understood. He *understood.*

Sergeant Napolitino's question was phrased with an eye toward eventual legal challenges to police procedure. What he *wanted* to ask Billy was more direct: *Mr. Wiles, are you holding someone in your house under duress, and did she get free long enough to dial 911, and did you tear the phone out of her hand and hang up, hoping a connection had not been made?*

To ask the question more bluntly than he had done, Napolitino would first have had to inform Billy of his constitutional right to remain silent and to have an attorney present during questioning.

Billy Wiles had become a suspect.

They were on the brink. A precipice.

Never had Billy's mind calculated options and consequences so feverishly, aware that every second of hesitation made him appear guiltier.

Fortunately, he did not have to counterfeit a flabbergasted expression. His jaw must have looked unhinged.

Not trusting his ability to fake anger or even indignation with any conviction whatsoever, Billy instead played his genuine surprise: "Good Lord, you don't think . . . ? You *do* think I . . . Good Lord. I'm the last guy I'd expect to be mistaken for Hannibal Lecter."

Napolitino said nothing.

Neither did Sobieski.

Their eyes were as steady as the axis of a spinning gyroscope.

"Of course you'd have to consider the possibility," Billy said. "I understand. I do. It's all right. Go inside if you want. Have a look around."

"Mr. Wiles, are you inviting us to search your house for an intruder or others?"

His fingertips resting on the cartridges in his pockets, his mind's eye resting on the shadowy form of Cottle in the knee space of the desk . . .

"Search it for anything," he said affably, as if relieved to understand at last what was wanted of him. "Go ahead."

"Mr. Wiles, I am not *asking* to search your residence. You do see the situation?"

"Sure. I know. It's okay. Go to it."

If they were invited to enter, any evidence they found could be used in court. If instead they entered uninvited, without a warrant or without adequate reason to believe that someone inside might be in jeopardy, the court would throw out the same evidence.

The sergeants would regard Billy's cooperation, happily given, as highly suggestive of innocence.

He felt relaxed enough to take his hands out of his pockets.

If he was open, relaxed, sufficiently encouraging, they might decide that he had nothing to hide. They might go away without bothering to search the place.

Napolitino glanced at Sobieski, and Sobieski nodded.

"Mr. Wiles, since you would feel better if I did so, I'll take a quick look through the house."

Sergeant Napolitino rounded the front of the patrol car and headed toward the porch steps, leaving Billy with Sobieski.

# 30

*Guilt spills itself in fear of being spilt,* someone had said, perhaps Shakespeare, perhaps O. J. Simpson. Billy couldn't remember who had nailed that thought so well in words, but he realized the truth in the aphorism and felt it keenly now.

At the house, Sergeant Napolitino climbed the front steps and crossed the porch, stepping over the pint bottle and whatever spilled whiskey had not yet evaporated.

"Too Joe Friday," Sobieski said.

"Excuse me?"

"Vince. He's too deadpan. He gives you those flat eyes, that cast-concrete face, but he's not really the hardass you think."

By sharing Napolitino's first name, Sobieski seemed to be taking Billy into his confidence.

Astutely alert for deception and manipulation, Billy suspected that the sergeant was no more taking him into his confidence than a trapdoor

spider would greet an in-falling beetle with gentleness and brotherhood.

At the house, Vince Napolitino disappeared through the open front door.

"Vince has still got too much of the academy in him," Sobieski continued. "When he's seasoned a little more, he won't come on so strong."

"He's just doing his job," Billy said. "I understand that. No big deal."

Sobieski remained in the driveway because he still at least half suspected Billy of some crime. Otherwise the two deputies would have searched the house together. Sergeant Sobieski was here to grab Billy if he tried to run.

"How're you feeling?"

"I'm all right," Billy said. "I just feel stupid putting you to all this trouble."

"I meant your stomach," Sobieski said.

"I don't know. Maybe I ate something that was off."

"Couldn't have been Ben Vernon's chili," Sobieski said. "That stuff is so hot it *cures* just about any sickness known to science."

Realizing that an innocent man, with nothing to fear, would not stare anxiously at the house, waiting for Napolitino to finish the search, Billy turned away from it and gazed out across the valley, at vineyards dwindling in a golden glare, toward mountains rising in blue haze.

"Crab will do it," Sobieski said.

"What?"

"Crab, shrimp, lobster—if it's a little off, it'll cause true mayhem."

"I had lasagna last night."

"That sounds pretty safe."

"Maybe not *my* lasagna," Billy said, trying to match Sobieski's apparent nonchalance.

"Come on, Vince," the sergeant said with a trace of impatience. "I know you're thorough, *compadre.* You don't have to prove anything to me." Then of Billy he asked, "You have an attic?"

"Yeah."

The sergeant sighed. "He'll want to check the attic."

Out of the west came a flock of small birds, swooping low and then soaring, swooping low again. They were flickers, unusually active for this heat.

"Are you hunting for one of these?" Sobieski asked.

The deputy offered the open end of a roll of breath mints.

For an instant Billy was bewildered, until he realized that his hands were in his pockets again, fingering the bullets.

He took his hands out of his chinos. "I'm afraid it's a little late for this," he said, but accepted the mint.

"Occupational hazard, I guess," said Sobieski. "A bartender, you're around the stuff all day."

Sucking on the mint, Billy said, "Actually, I don't drink that much. I woke up at three in the morning, couldn't turn my mind off, worrying about things I can't control anyway, thought a shot or two would knock me out."

"We all have nights like that. I call it the blue willies. You can't drink them away, though. A mug of hot chocolate will cure just about any insomnia, but not even that works with the blue willies."

"When the hooch didn't do the job, it still seemed like a way to pass the night. Then the morning."

"You hold it well."

"Do I?"

"You don't seem blotto."

"I'm not. I've been tapering off the last few hours, trying to *ease* out of it to avoid a hangover."

"Is that the trick?"

"It's one of them."

Sergeant Sobieski was easy to talk to: far *too* easy.

The flickers swooped low in their direction again, abruptly banked and soared and banked again, thirty or forty individuals flying as if with a single mind.

"They're a real nuisance," Sobieski said of the birds.

With pointed bills, flickers sought preferred

houses and stables and churches of Napa County to drill elaborate lacelike patterns in wooden cornices, architraves, eaves, bargeboards, and corner boards.

"They never bother my place," Billy said. "It's cedar."

Many people found the flickers' destructive work so beautiful that damaged wood trim was not always replaced until time and weather brought it down.

"They don't like cedar?" Sobieski asked.

"I don't know. But they don't like mine."

Having drilled its lacework, the flicker plants acorns in many of the holes, high on the building where the sun can warm them. After a few days, the bird returns to listen to the acorns. Hearing noise in some, not in others, it pecks open the noisy acorns to eat the larvae that are living inside.

So much for the sanctity of the home.

Flickers and sergeants will do their work.

Slowly, relentlessly, they will do it.

"It's not such a big place," Billy said, allowing himself to sound slightly impatient, as he imagined that an innocent man would.

When Sergeant Napolitino returned, he did not come out of the front door. He appeared along the south side of the house, from the direction of the detached garage.

He did not approach with one hand resting casually on his gun. Maybe that was a good sign.

As if by the sight of Napolitino, the birds were chased to a far corner of the sky.

"That's a nice wood shop you've got," he told Billy. "You could do just about anything in there."

Somehow the young sergeant made it sound as if Billy might have used the power tools to dismember a body.

Looking out across the valley, Napolitino said, "You've got a pretty terrific view here."

"It's nice," Billy said.

"It's paradise."

"It is," Billy agreed.

"I'm surprised you keep all your window shades down."

Billy had relaxed too soon. He said only half coherently, "When it's this hot, I do, the sun."

"Even on the sides of the house where the sun doesn't hit."

"On a day this bright," Billy said, "dodging a whiskey headache, you want soothing gloom."

"He's been tapering off the booze all morning," Sobieski told Napolitino, "trying to ease his way sober and avoid a hangover."

"Is that the trick?" Napolitino asked.

Billy said, "It's one of them."

"It's nice and cool in there."

"Cool helps, too," Billy said.

"Rosalyn said you lost your air conditioning."

Billy had forgotten that little lie, such a small filament in his enormous patchwork web of deceit.

He said, "It conks out for a few hours, then it comes on, then it conks out again. I don't know if maybe it's a compressor problem."

"Tomorrow's supposed to be a scorcher," Napolitino said, still gazing out across the valley. "Better get a repairman if they aren't already booked till Christmas."

"I'm going to have a look at it myself a little later," Billy said. "I'm pretty handy with things."

"Don't go poking around in machinery until you're full sober."

"I won't. I'll wait."

"Especially not electrical equipment."

"I'm going to make something to eat. That'll help. Maybe it'll even help my stomach."

Napolitino finally looked at Billy. "I'm sorry to have kept you out here in the sun, with your headache and all."

The sergeant sounded sincere, conciliatory for the first time, but his eyes were as cold and dark and humbling as the muzzles of a pair of pistols.

"The whole thing's my fault," Billy said. "You guys were just doing your job. I've already said six ways I'm an idiot. There's no other way to say it. I'm really sorry to have wasted your time."

"We're here 'to serve and protect.'" Napolitino smiled thinly. "It even says so on the door of the car."

"I liked it better when it said 'the best deputies money can buy,'" said Sergeant Sobieski,

surprising a laugh from Billy but drawing only a vaguely annoyed look from Napolitino. "Billy, maybe it's time to stop the tapering off and switch to food."

Billy nodded. "You're right."

As he walked to the house, he felt they were watching him. He didn't look back.

His heart had been relatively calm. Now it pounded again.

He couldn't believe his luck. He feared that it wouldn't hold.

On the porch, he took his watch off the railing, put it on his wrist.

He bent down to pick up the pint bottle. He didn't see the cap. It must have rolled off the porch or under a rocker.

At the table beside his chair, he dropped the three crackers into the empty Ritz box, which for a while had held the .38 revolver. He picked up the glass of cola.

He expected to hear the engines of the patrol cars start up. They didn't.

Without glancing back, he carried the glass and the box and the bottle inside. He closed the door and leaned against it.

Outside, the day remained still, the engines silent.

# 31

Sudden superstition warned Billy that as long as he waited with his back against the door, Sergeants Napolitino and Sobieski would not leave.

Listening, he went into the kitchen. He dropped the Ritz box in the trash can.

Listening, he poured the last ounce of whiskey from the bottle into the sink, and then chased it with the cola in the glass. He put the bottle in the trash, the glass in the dishwasher.

When by this time Billy had still heard no engines starting up, curiosity gnawed at him with ratty persistence.

The blinded house grew increasingly claustrophobic. Perhaps because he knew that it contained a corpse, it seemed to be shrinking to the dimensions of a casket.

He went into the living room, sorely tempted to put up one of the pleated shades, all of them.

But he didn't want the sergeants to think that he raised the shades to watch them and that their continued presence worried him.

Cautiously, he bent the edge of one of the shades back from the window frame. He was not at an angle to see the driveway.

Billy moved to another window, tried again, and saw the two men standing at Napolitino's car, where he'd left them. Neither deputy directly faced the house.

They appeared to be deep in conversation. They weren't likely to be discussing baseball.

He wondered if Napolitino had thought to search the woodworking shop for the half-cut, one-by-six walnut plank with the knothole. The sergeant would not have found that length of lumber, of course, because it did not exist.

When Sobieski turned his head toward the house, Billy at once let go of the shade. He hoped that he had been quick enough.

Until they were gone, Billy could do nothing other than worry. With everything he had to fret about, however, it was odd that his all-enveloping fog of anxiety quickly condensed upon the bizarre idea that Ralph Cottle's body no longer lay under the desk in the study, where he had left it.

To have moved the cadaver, the killer would have had to return to the house while both of the deputies had been speaking with Billy in the driveway, before he himself had returned to the

house. The freak had proved his boldness; but this would have been recklessness if not the worst temerity.

If the corpse had been moved, however, he would have to find it. He couldn't afford to wait until it turned up by surprise in an inconvenient and incriminating moment.

Billy withdrew the .38 revolver from under the sofa cushion.

When he broke out the cylinder and checked to be certain all six rounds were whole and loaded, he assured himself that this was an act of healthy suspicion, not a sign of creeping paranoia.

He followed the hallway as the disquiet that rang softly along his nerves quickened and, by the time he crossed the threshold into the study, swelled into clamorous alarm.

He shoved the office chair out of the way.

Embraced on three sides by the knee space, in the soft folds of his baggy and rumpled suit, Ralph Cottle looked like the meat of a walnut snugged inside its shell.

Even minutes previously, Billy could not have imagined that he would ever be *relieved* to find a corpse in his house.

He suspected that several pieces of subtle but direct evidence tying him to Cottle had been planted on the man's body. Even if he took the time for a meticulous inspection of the cadaver, he would surely miss one incriminating bit or another.

The body must be destroyed or buried where it would never be found. Billy had not yet decided how to dispose of it; but even as he coped with the mounting developments of the current crisis, dark corners of his mind were composing gruesome scenarios.

Finding the body as he left it, he also discovered the computer screen aglow and waiting. He had loaded the diskette that he'd found in Cottle's dead hands, but before he had been able to review its contents, Rosalyn Chan had called to ask if he had just phoned 911.

He rolled the office chair in front of the desk once more. He sat before the computer, tucking his legs under the chair, away from the corpse.

The diskette contained three documents. The first was labeled WHY, without a question mark.

When he accessed the document, he found that it was short:

*Because I, too, am a fisher of men.*

Billy read the line three times. He didn't know what to make of it, but the hook wounds in his brow burned anew.

He recognized the religious reference. Christ had been called a fisher of men.

The easy inference was that the killer might be a religious fanatic who thought he heard divine voices urging him to kill, but easy inferences were

usually wrong. Sound inductive reasoning required more than one particular from which to generalize.

Besides, the freak possessed a knack for duplicity, a faculty for obfuscation, a talent for deception, and a genius for carefully crafted enigma. He preferred the oblique to the straightforward, the circuitous to the direct.

WHY.

*Because I, too, am a fisher of men.*

The true, full meaning of that statement could not be surmised let alone ascertained in a hundred readings, nor in the limited time that Billy currently could devote to its analysis.

The second document was labeled HOW. It proved to be no less mysterious than the first:

*Cruelty, violence, death.*
*Movement, velocity, impact.*
*Flesh, blood, bone.*

Although without rhyme or meter, that triad seemed almost to be a stanza of verse. As with the most recondite poetry, the meaning was not on the surface.

Billy had the strange feeling that those three lines were three answers and that if only he knew the questions, he would also know the identity of the killer.

Whether that impression might be reliable

intuition or delusion, he had no time just now to consider it. Lanny's body still awaited final disposition, as did Cottle's. Billy was half convinced that if he consulted his wristwatch, he would see the minute and hour hands spinning as if they were counting off mere seconds.

The third document on the diskette was labeled WHEN, and as Billy accessed it, the dead man in the knee space seized his foot.

If Billy could have breathed, he would have cried out. By the time the trapped exhalation exploded from his throat, however, he realized that the explanation was less supernatural than it had at first seemed.

The dead man had not seized him; in Billy's agitation, he had pressed his feet against the corpse. He tucked them under the chair once more.

On the screen, the document labeled WHEN offered a message that required less interpretation than WHY and HOW.

*My last killing: midnight Thursday.*
*Your suicide: soon thereafter.*

# 32

*My last killing: midnight Thursday.*

*Your suicide: soon thereafter.*

Billy Wiles consulted his wristwatch. A few minutes past noon, Wednesday.

If the freak meant what he said, this *performance,* or whatever it was, would conclude in thirty-six hours. Hell was eternal, but any hell on earth must be by definition finite.

The reference to a "last" killing did not necessarily mean that only one more murder lay ahead. In the past day and a half, the freak had killed three, and in the day and a half ahead, he might be no less murderous.

*Cruelty, violence, death. Movement, velocity, impact. Flesh, blood, bone.*

Of those nine words in the second document, one struck Billy as more pertinent than the others. *Velocity.*

The *movement* had begun when the first note had been left under the windshield wiper on the Explorer. The *impact* would come with the last killing, the one meant to make him consider suicide.

Meanwhile, at a steadily accelerating pace, new challenges were being thrown at Billy, keeping him off balance. The word *velocity* seemed to promise him that the longest plunges of this roller coaster were still ahead.

He neither disbelieved the promise of increasing velocity nor dismissed the confident assertion that he would commit suicide.

Suicide was a mortal sin, but Billy knew himself to be a shallow man, weak in some ways, flawed. At this point, he wasn't capable of self-destruction; but hearts and minds can both be broken.

He had little difficulty imagining what might drive him to such a brink. In fact, no difficulty at all.

Barbara Mandel's death alone would not drive him to suicide. For almost four years, he had prepared himself for her passing. He had hardened himself to the idea of living without even the hope of her recovery.

The manner of her murder, however, might cause a fatal stress crack in Billy's mental architecture. In her coma, she might not be aware of much that the killer did to her. Nevertheless, assuming that she would be subjected to pain, to

vile abuse, to gross indignities, Billy could imagine a weight of horror so great that he would break under it.

*This was a man who beat lovely young schoolteachers to death and peeled off women's faces.*

Furthermore, if the freak intended to engineer circumstances in which it would appear that Billy himself had killed not only Giselle Winslow, Lanny, and Ralph Cottle, but also Barbara, then Billy would not want to endure months of being a media sensation or the spotlight of the trial, or the abiding suspicion with which he'd be regarded even if found innocent in a court of law.

The freak killed for pleasure, but also with a purpose and a plan. Whatever the purpose, the plan might be to convince police that Billy committed the homicides leading to Barbara's murder in her bed at Whispering Pines, that his intent had been to establish that a brutal serial killer was at work in the county, thereby directing suspicion from himself to the nonexistent psychopath.

If the freak was clever—and he would be—the authorities would swallow that theory as if it were a spoonful of vanilla ice cream. After all, in their eyes, Billy had a strong motive to do away with Barbara.

Her medical care was covered by the investment income earned by a seven-million-dollar trust fund established with a legal settlement from

the corporation responsible for her coma. Billy was the primary of three trustees who managed the fund.

If Barbara died while in a coma, Billy was the sole heir to her estate.

He did not want the money, none of it, and would not keep it if it came to him. In that sad event, he had always intended to give the millions away.

No one, of course, would believe that was his intention.

Especially not after the freak was finished setting him up, if in fact that's what the freak was doing.

The call to 911 certainly seemed to signify that intention. It had drawn Billy to the attention of the sheriff's department in a context that they would remember . . . and wonder about.

Now Billy combined all three documents and printed them on a single sheet of paper:

*Because I, too, am a fisher of men.*
*Cruelty, violence, death.*
*Movement, velocity, impact.*
*Flesh, blood, bone.*
*My last killing: midnight Thursday.*
*Your suicide: soon thereafter.*

With scissors, Billy trimmed out the block of text, intending to fold it and put it in his wallet, where he would have it for easy review.

As he finished, he realized that this paper appeared identical to that on which he had received the first four messages from the killer. If the diskette in Cottle's hands had been prepared on this computer, perhaps the first four notes had been composed here as well.

He exited Microsoft Word, and then entered the software again. He called up the directory.

The list of documents was not long. He had used this program solely for writing fiction.

He recognized the key words of the titles of his single novel and of the short stories that he had completed, as well as those of stories never finished. Only one document was unfamiliar to him: DEATH.

When he loaded that document, he discovered the text of the first four messages from the freak.

He hesitated, remembering procedures. Then he rattled the keys, summoning the date when the document had been first composed, which turned out to be 10:09 A.M. the previous Friday.

Billy had left for work fifteen minutes earlier than usual that day. He had swung by the post office to mail some bills.

The two notes left on his windshield, the one taped over the Explorer's ignition, and even the one he'd found on his refrigerator this same morning had been prepared on this computer more than three days before the first had been delivered, before the nightmare had begun Monday evening.

If Lanny had not destroyed the first two notes to save his job, if Billy had offered them to the police as evidence, sooner or later the authorities would have checked this computer. They would have reached the inescapable conclusion that Billy himself had written the notes.

The freak had prepared for all contingencies. He was nothing if not thorough. And he had been confident his script would play out as he had intended.

Billy deleted the document titled DEATH, which might still be used as evidence against him, depending on how events unfolded from here on.

He suspected that deleting it from the directory did not remove it from the hard disk. He would have to find a way to ask someone who was a computer maven.

When he shut down the computer, he realized that he had still not heard the patrol-car engines start up.

# 33

Peeling the shade aside at a study window, Billy discovered the driveway empty in the streaming sunshine. He had become so absorbed with the diskette that he had not heard the car engines start. The sergeants had gone.

He had expected to discover another challenge on the diskette: a choice between two innocent victims, a short deadline for making a decision.

No doubt another one would come soon, but for now he was free to deal with other urgent business. He had plenty of it.

He went to the garage and returned with a length of rope and one of the polyurethane drop cloths with which he covered furniture when he had repainted the interior of the house in the spring. He unfolded this tarp on the study floor in front of the desk.

After wrestling Cottle's body out of the knee

space and dragging it around the desk, he rolled it onto the drop cloth.

The prospect of turning out the dead man's pockets disgusted him. He got on with it, anyway.

Billy wasn't looking for planted evidence that would incriminate him. If the freak had salted the corpse, he had been subtle about it; Billy would not find everything.

Besides, he intended to dispose of the body in a place where it would never be found. For that reason, he was unconcerned about leaving fingerprints on the plastic sheeting.

The suit coat had two inner pockets. In the first, Cottle had kept the pint of whiskey that he had spilled. From the second, Billy extracted a pint of rum, and returned it.

In the two outer pockets of the coat were cigarettes, a cheap butane lighter, and a roll of butterscotch Life Savers. In the front pants pockets, he found sixty-seven cents in coins, a deck of playing cards, and a whistle in the form of a plastic canary.

Cottle's wallet contained six one-dollar bills, a five, and fourteen ten-dollar bills. These last must have come from the freak.

*Ten dollars for each year of your innocence, Mr. Wiles.*

Basically frugal, Billy didn't want to bury the money with the body. He considered dropping it in the poor box at the church where he had parked—and been assaulted—the previous night.

Squeamishness trumped frugality. Billy left the money in the wallet. As dead pharaohs had been sent to the Other Side with salt, grain, wine, gold, and euthanized servants, so Ralph Cottle would travel across the Styx with spending money.

Among the few other items in the wallet were two of interest, the first a worn and creased snapshot of Cottle as a young man. He looked handsome, virile, radically different from the beaten man of his later years but recognizable. With him was a lovely young woman. They were smiling. They looked happy.

The second item was a 1983 membership card in the American Society of Skeptics. RALPH THURMAN COTTLE, MEMBER SINCE 1978.

Billy kept the snapshot and the membership card and returned everything else to Cottle's hip pocket.

He rolled the cadaver tightly in the tarp. He folded the ends down and secured the bundle with yards of strapping tape.

His expectation had been that, inside multiple layers of opaque polyurethane, the body might pass for a rug wrapped in protective plastic. It looked like a corpse in a tarp.

Using the rope, he fashioned a tightly knotted handle to one end of the packaged cadaver, by which it could be dragged.

He did not intend to dispose of Cottle until after dark. The cargo space in his Explorer was

encircled by windows. SUVs were useful vehicles, but if you were going to be transporting corpses in broad daylight, you better have a car with a roomy trunk.

Because he'd begun to feel that his house was being as freely traveled as a public bus terminal, Billy hauled the body out of the study, to the living room, where he left it behind the sofa. It could not be seen from the front door or from the doorway to the kitchen.

At the kitchen sink, he vigorously scrubbed his hands with multiple applications of liquid soap, in near-scalding water.

Then he made a ham sandwich. Ravenous, he wondered how he could have an appetite after the gruesome business he had just concluded.

He would not have thought that his will to survive had remained this strong during his years of retreat. He wondered what other qualities, good and bad, he would rediscover or discover in himself during the thirty-six hours ahead.

*There is one who remembers the way to your door: Life you may evade, but Death you shall not.*

# 34

As Billy finished the ham sandwich, the telephone rang.

He didn't want to answer it. He didn't receive a lot of calls from friends, and Lanny was dead. He knew who this must be. Enough was enough.

On the twelfth ring, he pushed his chair back from the table.

The freak had never said anything on the phone. He didn't want to reveal his voice. He would do nothing but listen to Billy in mocking silence.

On the sixteenth ring, Billy got up from the table.

These calls had no purpose but to intimidate. Taking them made no sense.

Billy stood by the phone, staring at it. On the twenty-sixth ring, he lifted the handset.

The digital readout revealed no caller ID.

Billy didn't say hello. He listened.

After a few seconds of silence on the other end, a mechanical click was followed by a hiss. Pops and scratches punctuated the hiss: the sound of blank audio tape passing over a playback head.

When the words came, they were in a series of voices, some men, some women. No individual spoke more than three words, often just one.

Judging by the inconstant volume levels and other tells, the freak had constructed the message by sampling existing audio, perhaps books on tape by different readers.

*"I will . . . kill a . . . pretty redhead. If you . . . say . . . waste the bitch . . . I will . . . kill . . . her . . . quickly. Otherwise . . . she will . . . suffer . . . much . . . torture. You . . . have . . . one minute . . . to . . . say . . . waste the bitch. The choice . . . is . . . yours."*

Again, the hiss and pop and scratch of blank tape . . .

The conundrum had been perfectly constructed. It allowed an evasive man no room for further evasion.

Previously, Billy had been morally co-opted only to the extent that the choice of the victims had been made because of his inaction, and in Cottle's case because of the refusal to act.

In the choice between a lovely schoolteacher and a charitable old woman, the deaths seemed equally tragic unless you were biased toward the beautiful and against the aged. Making an active

decision resulted in neither less nor greater tragedy than did inaction.

When the possible victims had been an unmarried man "who won't much be missed by the world" or a young mother of two, the greater tragedy had seemed to be the death of the mother. In that case, the choice had been constructed so that Billy's failure to go to the police ensured the mother's survival, rewarding inaction and playing to his weakness.

Once again, he was being asked to choose between two evils, and thereby become the freak's collaborator. But this time, inaction was not a viable option. By saying nothing, he would be sentencing the redhead to torture, to a protracted and hideous death. By responding, he would be granting her a degree of mercy.

He could not save her.

In either case, death.

But one death would be cleaner than the other.

The running audio tape produced two more words: *". . . thirty seconds . . ."*

Billy felt as though he couldn't breathe, but he could. He felt as though he would choke if he tried to swallow, but he didn't choke.

*". . . fifteen seconds . . ."*

His mouth was dry. His tongue grew thick. He didn't believe that he could speak, but he did: "Waste the bitch."

The freak hung up. So did Billy.

Collaborators.

The masticated ham and the bread and the mayonnaise turned in his stomach.

If he had suspected that the freak might actually communicate by telephone, he could have been prepared to record the message. Too late.

Such a recording of a recording wouldn't be persuasive to the cops, anyway, unless the body of a redhead turned up. And if such a corpse was found, planted evidence would most likely tie it to Billy.

The air conditioner worked well, yet the kitchen air seemed to be sweltering, stifling, and it cloyed in his throat, and lay heavy in his lungs.

*Waste the bitch.*

Without any memory of having left the house, Billy found himself descending the back-porch steps. He didn't know where he was going.

He sat on the steps.

He stared at the sky, at the trees, at the backyard.

He looked at his hands. He didn't recognize them.

# 35

He left town by a circuitous route and saw no one following.

With no corpse burrito in the Explorer, Billy risked exceeding the speed limit most of the way to the southern end of the county. A hot wind quarreled at the broken-out window in the driver's door as he crossed the Napa city limits at 1:52 P.M.

Napa is a quaint, rather picturesque town, for the most part naturally so, not by dint of politicians and corporations conspiring to reconceive it as a theme park on the model of Disneyland, a fate of many places in California.

Harry Avarkian, Billy's attorney, had offices downtown, not far from the courthouse, on a street lined with ancient olive trees. He was expecting Billy and greeted him with a bear hug.

Fiftyish, tall and solid, avuncular, with a rubbery face and quick smile, Harry looked like

the spokesman for a miracle hair restorer. He had a head of wiry black hair so thick that it looked as though a barber might have to tend to it daily, a walrus mustache, and such a thatch of crisp black hairs on the backs of his big hands that he looked as if he might be prone to hibernate in winter.

He worked at an antique partner's desk, so that when Billy sat opposite him, the relationship didn't seem like that of attorney and client but like that of friends engaged in a business enterprise.

After the usual how-ya-beens and talk of the heat, Harry said, "So what's so important that we couldn't do it by phone?"

"It's not that I didn't want to talk on the phone," Billy lied. The rest was true enough: "I had to come down here for a couple other things, so I figured I might as well sit down with you in person and ask about what's troubling me."

"So hit me with your questions, and let's see if I know any damn thing about the law."

"It's about the trust fund that takes care of Barbara."

Harry Avarkian and Gi Minh "George" Nguyen, Billy's accountant, were the other two trustees on the three-member board.

"Just two days ago, I reviewed the second quarter's financial statement," Harry said. "Return was fourteen percent. Excellent in this market.

Even after Barbara's expenses, the principal is growing steadily."

"We're smartly invested," Billy agreed. "But I'm lying awake at night worrying is there a way anyone could get at the pot?"

"The pot? You mean Barbara's money? If you've got to worry about something, worry about an asteroid hitting the earth."

"I worry. I can't help it."

"Billy, I drew up those trust documents, and they're tighter than a gnat's ass. Besides, with you guarding the vault for her, nobody's going to pinch a nickel."

"I mean if something happens to me."

"You're only thirty-four. From my perspective, you're barely past puberty."

"Mozart died younger than thirty-four."

"This isn't the eighteenth century, and you don't even play the piano," Harry said, "so the comparison makes no sense." He frowned. "Are you sick or something?"

"I've felt better," Billy admitted.

"What's that patch on your forehead?"

Billy gave him the story about a knothole in a walnut plank. "It's nothing serious."

"You're pale for summer."

"I haven't been fishing much. Look, Harry, I don't have cancer or anything, but a truck could always hit me."

"Have they been after you lately, these trucks?

Have you had to dodge a few? Since when were you baptized a pessimist?"

"What about Dardre?"

Dardre was Barbara's sister. They were twins, but fraternal, not identical. They looked nothing alike, and were radically different people, as well.

"The court not only pulled her plug," Harry said, "they cut it off and took out her batteries."

"I know, but—"

"She's an Energizer Bunny of Evil, all right, but she's as much history as the Lebne and string cheese I ate for lunch a week ago."

Barbara and Dardre's mother, Cicily, had been a drug addict. She had never identified their father, and on their birth certificates, the twins had their mother's maiden name.

Cicily wound up in a psychiatric ward when the girls were two, and they were removed from their mother's custody and placed in a foster home. Cicily died eleven months later.

Until they were five, the sisters had been shuffled through the same series of foster homes. Thereafter they were separated.

Barbara had never seen Dardre again. In fact when, at the age of twenty-one, she tracked down and tried to reestablish a relationship with her sister, she had been rebuffed.

While not as self-destructive as Cicily, Dardre had acquired her mother's taste for illegal chemical compounds and the party life. She found

her clean-and-sober sibling to be boring and uncool.

Eight years later, after extensive media attention to the case, when the insurance company settled millions on Barbara to pay for her long-term care, Dardre developed a deep emotional attachment to her sister. As Barbara's only known blood relative, she had brought legal action to be declared sole trustee.

Fortunately, at good Harry's urging, immediately following their engagement, Billy and Barbara had drawn and signed, in this office, simple wills naming each other as heirs and executors.

Dardre's history, tactics, and unconcealed avarice had earned her the judge's scorn. Her action had been dismissed with prejudice.

She had tried to get another court to reinstate her case. She had not been successful. They hadn't heard from her in two years.

Now Billy said, "But if I died—"

"You've selected contingent trustees to replace you. If you're run down by a truck, one of them will."

"I understand. Nevertheless—"

"If you and I and George Nguyen are run down by trucks," Harry said, "in fact if each of us is run down by three trucks, willing candidates for trustees, acceptable to the court, are standing by and ready to take over. Until they could be

installed, day-to-day trust affairs would be in the hands of a bonded trust-management firm."

"You've thought of everything."

His massive mustache lifting with his smile, Harry said, "Of all my accomplishments, I'm proudest of never having yet been disbarred."

"But if anything happened to me—"

"You're making me nuts."

"—is there anyone besides Dardre that we should worry about?"

"Like who?"

"Anyone."

"No."

"You're sure?"

"Yes."

"No one who could take Barbara's money?"

Leaning forward, arms on his desk, Harry said, "What's this all about?"

Billy shrugged. "I don't know. Lately I've just been . . . spooked."

After a silence, Harry said, "Maybe it's time for you to get a life again."

"I've got a life," Billy said, his voice too sharp considering that Harry was a friend and a decent guy.

"You can look after Barbara, be faithful to her memory, and still have a life."

"She's not just a memory. She's alive. Harry, you're the last person I want to have to punch in the mouth."

Harry sighed. "You're right. No one can tell you what your heart should feel."

"Hell, Harry, I'd never punch you in the mouth."

"Did I look scared?"

Laughing softly, Billy said, "You looked you. You looked like a Muppet."

The graceful shadows of sunlit olive trees moved on the window glass, and in the room.

After a silence, Harry Avarkian said, "There are cases in which people have come out of a botulism coma with most of their faculties intact."

"They're rare," Billy acknowledged.

"Rare isn't the same as never."

"I try to be realistic, but I don't really want to be."

"I used to like vichyssoise," Harry said. "Now if I even happen to see it on a shelf in a supermarket, I get sick to my stomach."

While Billy had been working at the tavern one Saturday, Barbara had opened a can of soup for dinner. Vichyssoise. She made a grilled-cheese sandwich as well.

When she didn't answer her phone Sunday morning, he went to her apartment, let himself in with his key. He found her unconscious on the bathroom floor.

At the hospital she had been treated with antitoxin promptly enough to spare her from death. And now she slept. And slept.

Until she woke, if she woke, the extent of brain damage could not accurately be determined.

The manufacturer of the soup, a reputable company, instantly pulled an entire run of vichyssoise off store shelves. Out of more than three thousand cans, only six were found to be contaminated.

None of the six showed telltale signs of swelling; therefore, in a way, Barbara's suffering had spared at least six other people from a similar fate.

Billy never managed to find any comfort in that fact.

"She's a lovely woman," Harry said.

"She's pale and thin, but she's still beautiful to me," Billy said. "And inside somewhere, she's alive. She says things. I've told you. She's alive in there, and thinking."

He watched the olive-tree shadows projected onto the desk by the lens of the window.

He did not look at Harry. He didn't want to see the pity in the attorney's eyes.

After a while, Harry talked about the weather some more, and then Billy said, "Did you hear, at Princeton—or maybe it's Harvard—scientists are trying to make a pig with a human brain?"

"They're doing crap like that everywhere," Harry said. "They never learn. The smarter they are, the dumber they get."

"The horror of it."

"They don't see the horror. Just the glory and the money."

"I don't see the glory."

"What glory could anyone have seen in Auschwitz? But some did."

Following a mutual silence, Billy met Harry's eyes. "Do I know how to cheer up a room, or what?"

"I haven't laughed so hard since Abbott and Costello."

# 36

At an electronics store in Napa, Billy bought a compact video camera and recorder. The equipment could be used in the usual fashion or could be set instead to compile a continuous series of snapshots taken at intervals of a few seconds.

In its second mode, loaded with the proper custom disk, the system was able to provide week-long recorded surveillance similar to that in the average convenience store.

Considering that the Explorer's broken window didn't allow him to lock any valuables in the vehicle, he paid for his purchases and arranged to return for them in half an hour.

From the electronics store, he went in search of a newspaper-vending machine. He found one in front of a pharmacy.

The lead story concerned Giselle Winslow. The schoolteacher had been murdered in the early hours of Tuesday morning, but her body had not

been found until late Tuesday afternoon, less than twenty-four hours previously.

The picture of her in the newspaper was different from the one tucked in the book on Lanny Olsen's lap, but they were photos of the same attractive woman.

Carrying the newspaper, Billy walked to the main branch of the county library. He had a computer at home but no longer had Internet access; the library offered both.

He was alone at the cluster of work stations. Other patrons were at reading tables and prowling the stacks. Maybe the embrace of "book alternatives" wasn't turning out to be the future of libraries, after all.

When he'd been writing fiction, he had used the World Wide Web for research. Later, it had provided distraction, escape. In the past two years, he hadn't surfed the Web at all.

Meanwhile, things had changed. Access was faster. Searches were faster, too, and easier.

Billy typed in a search string. When he got no hits, he modified the string, then modified it again.

Drinking-age laws varied state by state. In many jurisdictions, Steve Zillis hadn't been old enough to tend bar until he was twenty-one, so Billy dropped *bartender* from the search string.

Steve had been working at the tavern only five months. He and Billy had never swapped biographies.

Billy vaguely recalled that Steve had gone to college. He could not remember where. He added *student* to the string.

Perhaps the word *murder* was too limiting. He replaced it with *foul play.*

He got one hit. From the *Denver Post.*

The story dated back five years and eight months. Although Billy warned himself not to read into this discovery more than it actually contained, the information struck him as relevant.

That November, at the University of Colorado at Denver, a coed named Judith Sarah Kesselman, eighteen, had gone missing. Initially, at least, there were no signs of foul play.

In what appeared to be the first newspaper piece about the missing young woman, another UCD student, Steven Zillis, nineteen, was quoted as saying that Judith was "a wonderful girl, compassionate and concerned, a friend to everyone." He worried because "Judi is too responsible to just go off for a couple days without telling anyone her plans."

Another search string related to Judith Sarah Kesselman produced scores of hits. Billy steeled himself for the discovery that her dead body had been found without a face.

He went through the articles, reading closely at first. As the material became repetitive, he scanned.

Friends, relatives, and professors of Judith Kesselman were often quoted. Steven Zillis was not mentioned again.

Judging by the wealth of material available to Billy, no trace of Judith had ever been found. She vanished as completely as if she had stepped out of this universe into another.

The frequency of newspaper coverage declined steadily through Christmas of that year. It dropped sharply with the new year.

The media favors dead bodies over missing ones, blood over mystery. There is always new and exciting violence.

The last piece was dated on the fifth anniversary of Judith's disappearance. Her hometown was Laguna Beach, California, and the article appeared in the *Orange County Register.*

A columnist, sympathetic to the Kesselman family's unresolved grief, wrote movingly about their enduring hope that Judith was still alive. Somehow. Somewhere. And one day coming home.

She had been a music major. She played piano well, and guitar. She liked gospel music. And dogs. And long walks on the beach.

The press had been provided two photos of her. In both she looked impish, amused, and gentle.

Although Billy had never known Judith Kesselman, he could not bear the promise of her fresh face. He avoided looking at her photos.

He printed selected articles for review later. He folded them inside the newspaper that he'd gotten from the vending machine.

As he was leaving the library, passing the reading tables, a man said, "Billy Wiles. Long time no see."

In a chair at one of the tables, smiling broadly, sat Sheriff John Palmer.

# 37

Although he wore his uniform, without hat, the sheriff less resembled an officer of the law than he did a politician. Because his was an elected position, he was in fact both cop and pol.

Barbered to the point of affectation, shaved as smooth as a glass peach, teeth veneered to white perfection, features suitable for a Roman coin, he looked ten years younger than he was—and ready for the cameras.

Although Palmer sat at a reading table, neither a magazine nor a newspaper, nor a book, lay in front of him. He looked like he knew everything already.

Palmer did not get up. Billy remained standing.

"How're things up in Vineyard Hills?" Palmer asked.

"Lots of vineyards and hills," Billy said.

"You still tending bar?"

"There's always a need. It's the third oldest profession."

"What's second, after whores?" Palmer asked.

"Politicians."

The sheriff seemed to be amused. "Are you writing these days?"

"A little," Billy lied.

One of his published short stories had featured a character who was a thinly veiled portrait of John Palmer.

"Doing some research for your writing?" Palmer asked.

From where the sheriff sat, he had a direct view of the computer at which Billy had been working, although not of its screen.

Maybe Palmer had a way of finding out what Billy had been doing at the work station. A public computer might keep a record of a user's keystrokes.

No. Probably not. Besides, there were privacy laws.

"Yeah," Billy said. "Some research."

"Deputy of mine saw you parking in front of Harry Avarkian's office."

Billy said nothing.

"Three minutes after you left Harry's, the time on your parking meter ran out."

That might be true.

Palmer said, "I put two quarters in for you."

"Thanks."

"The window's busted out of your driver's door."

"A little accident," Billy said.

"It's not a code violation, but you ought to get it fixed."

"I've got an appointment on Friday," Billy lied.

"This doesn't bother you, does it?" the sheriff asked.

"What?"

"You and me talking like this." Palmer surveyed the library. No one was close to them. "Just the two of us."

"It doesn't bother me," Billy said.

He had every right and reason to walk away. Instead he stayed, determined not to give even the appearance of intimidation.

Twenty years ago, as a fourteen-year-old boy, Billy Wiles had endured interrogations conducted in such a way that they should have destroyed John Palmer's law-enforcement career.

Instead, Palmer had been promoted from lieutenant to captain, later to chief. Eventually he had campaigned for the office of sheriff and had been elected. Twice.

Harry Avarkian had a succinct explanation for Palmer's ascent and claimed that he had heard it from deputies in the department: Shit floats.

"How's Miss Mandel these days?" Palmer asked.

"The same."

He wondered if Palmer knew about the 911 call. Napolitino and Sobieski had no reason to file a report on it, especially since it had been a false alarm.

Besides, the two sergeants worked out of the

St. Helena substation. While Sheriff Palmer toured throughout his jurisdiction, his office was here in the county seat.

"What a sad thing that was," Palmer said.

Billy did not reply.

"At least for the rest of her life, she'll get the best care, with all that money."

"She's going to get well. She'll come out of it."

"Do you really think so?"

"Yes."

"All that money—I hope you're right."

"I am."

"She ought to have a chance to enjoy all that money."

Stone-faced, Billy gave no slightest sign that he understood Palmer's pointed implication.

Yawning, stretching, so relaxed and casual in his chair, Palmer probably saw himself as a cat toying with a mouse. "Well, people are going to be happy to hear that you're not burnt out, that you're writing a little."

"What people?"

"People who like your writing, of course."

"Do you know any of them?"

Palmer shrugged. "I don't move in those circles. But I'm pretty sure about one thing. . . ."

Because the sheriff wanted to be asked *What?*, Billy didn't ask.

Off Billy's silence, Palmer said, "I'm pretty sure your mom and dad would be so proud."

Billy walked away from him and out of the library.

After the air conditioning, the summer heat assaulted him. He felt as though he were suffocating when he inhaled, as if strangling when he exhaled. Or maybe it wasn't the heat, but the past.

# 38

Speeding north on Route 29, out of sun and into sun, with the famous and fertile valley narrowing imperceptibly at first and then perceptibly, Billy worried about protecting Barbara.

The trust fund could hire around-the-clock security for the duration, until Billy found the freak or until the freak finished him. Money was no issue.

But this wasn't a big city. The phone book didn't contain page after page of ads for private-security firms.

Explaining to the guards why they were needed would be risky. The whole truth would tie Billy to three murders for which he was most likely being set up to take the fall.

If he withheld too much of the truth, the guards wouldn't know what they were up against. He would be jeopardizing their lives.

Besides, most security guards around these parts

were former police officers or current cops who were moonlighting on their off hours. Many of them had worked—or still did work—for or with John Palmer.

Billy didn't want Palmer hearing about Barbara being watched over by hired bodyguards. The sheriff would wonder. He would have questions.

After a few years during which he had stayed under Palmer's radar, he was now on the scope again. He dared not draw more attention to himself.

He couldn't ask friends to help him stand watch over Barbara. They would be at great risk.

Anyway, he didn't have close friends whom he'd be comfortable approaching. The people in his life were largely *acquaintances.*

He had managed things that way. There is no life that is not in community. He knew this. He knew. Yet he had done no proper sowing and now had no harvest.

The wind at the broken window spoke chaos to him.

In the hours of Barbara's greatest danger, he alone would have to protect her. If he could.

She deserved better than him. With his history, no one in need of a guardian would turn to him first, or second, or at all.

*My last killing: midnight Thursday.*

If Billy read the freak correctly—and he was all but certain that he did—Barbara's murder

would be the climax on which the curtain of this cruel "performance" would be rung.

*Your suicide: soon thereafter.*

Tomorrow evening, long before midnight, he would station himself at her bedside.

This evening, he could not be with her. The urgent tasks on his agenda would probably keep him busy until dawn.

If he was wrong, if her murder was to be a second-act surprise, this sunny valley, for him, would become henceforth as dark as the vacant interstellar spaces.

Driving faster, borne forward by a longing for redemption, with sunlight slanting from his left and with the valley's great monument, Mount St. Helena, ahead and seeming never to grow nearer, Billy used his cell phone to call Whispering Pines, pressing 1 and holding to speed dial.

Because Barbara had a private room with an attached half-bath, the usual visiting-hour rules did not apply. With advance approval, a family member might even stay overnight.

He hoped to stop at Whispering Pines on his way home and arrange to stay with Barbara from Thursday evening at least through Friday morning. He had conceived a cover story that might be accepted without suspicion.

The receptionist who answered his call informed him that Mrs. Norlee, the manager, would be in meetings until five-thirty but would

be able to see him then. He took the appointment.

Shortly before four o'clock, he arrived home, half expecting to see patrol cars, a coroner's van, county deputies in number, and Sergeant Napolitino on the front porch, standing over a rocking chair in which Ralph Cottle's corpse sat, unwrapped. But all was quiet.

Instead of using the garage, Billy parked in the driveway, toward the back of the house.

He went inside and searched every room. He found no indications of an intruder having been here during his absence.

The corpse still lay cocooned behind the sofa.

# 39

Above the microwave oven, behind a pair of cabinet doors, a deep space contained baking sheets, two perforated pizza pans, and other narrow items stored vertically. Billy took the pans out—and the removable rack in which they stood—and put them in the pantry.

At the back of the now empty space was an electric outlet with two receptacles. A plug filled the bottom receptacle, and the cord disappeared through a cut-out in the rear wall of the cabinet.

The plug powered the microwave. Billy pulled it.

Standing on a stepladder, using a power drill, he bored a hole in the floor of the upper cabinet, through the ceiling of the oven. This ruined the microwave. He didn't care.

He used the drill bit as if it were a power file, simultaneously drawing it around the perimeter of the bore and pumping it up and down, widening the hole. The noise was horrendous.

A faint smell of scorched insulation arose, but he completed the job before the frictional heat grew to be a problem.

He cleaned the debris out of the microwave. He put the videocam inside.

After inserting the output jack of a video-transmission cable into the camera, he shoved the other end through the hole that he had drilled in the ceiling of the oven. He did the same with a pronged-at-both-ends power cord.

In the cabinet that previously held baking pans, Billy placed the video-disk recorder. Following printed instructions, he jacked the free end of the transmission cable into the recorder.

He plugged the camera power cord into the upper receptacle in the outlet at the back of the cabinet. The recorder took the lower receptacle into which the microwave had been plugged.

He loaded a seven-day disk. He set the system per instructions and switched it on.

When he closed the door of the microwave oven, the inner surface of the view window pressed against the rubber rim of the camera's lens hood. The videocam was aimed across the kitchen at the back door.

With the oven light off, Billy could see the camera inside only if he put his face very close to the view window. The freak would not discover it unless he decided to make microwave popcorn.

Because the window contained a fine screen

laminated between layers of glass, Billy didn't know if the camera would have a clear view. He needed to test it.

The pleated shades were drawn over all the kitchen windows. He raised them, and he turned on the overhead lights.

He stood just inside the back door for a moment. Then he crossed the room at an unhurried pace.

The recorder featured a mini screen for quick review. When Billy climbed the stepladder and replayed the time-lapse recording, he saw a darkish figure. As it crossed the room, resolution improved, and he could recognize himself.

He did not like watching himself. Ashen, sullen, and uncertain, full of determined action but with halting purpose.

In fairness to himself, the image was black-and-white, and a little grainy. His apparent lurch was merely the effect of time-lapse recording.

Allowing for all of that, he still saw an unconvincing figure: shape and shading, but no more substance than an apparition. He appeared to be a stranger in his own home.

He reset the machine. He closed the cabinet doors and put away the stepladder.

In the bathroom, he changed the dressing on his brow. The hook wounds were angry red, but no worse than before.

He changed into a black T-shirt, black jeans, black Rockports. Sunset was less than four hours

away, and when twilight passed, Billy would need to move as inconspicuously as possible in a hostile night.

# 40

Gretchen Norlee favored severe dark suits, wore no jewelry, combed her hair straight back from her forehead, regarded the world through steel-framed eyeglasses—and decorated her office with plush toys. A teddy bear, a toad, a duck, a Knuffle Bunny, and a midnight-blue kitten were arranged on shelves in a collection that consisted primarily of dogs that greeted visitors with a brightness of unfurled pink- and red-velvet tongues.

Gretchen managed the 102-bed Whispering Pines Convalescent Home with military efficiency and maximum compassion. Her warm manner belied the gruffness of her hard-edged voice.

She embodied no greater contradictions than any person who found temporary balance in this most temporary world. Hers were just more immediately visible, and more endearing.

Leaving her desk to signal that she viewed this as a personal consideration rather than as a

business matter, Gretchen sat in a wingback chair catercorner to the chair in which Billy sat.

She said, "Because Barbara occupies a private room, she may have company outside normal visiting hours without inconveniencing other patients. I see no problem, though family usually stay overnight only when a patient has just returned from a hospital transfer."

Although Gretchen had too much class to express her curiosity directly, Billy felt obliged to satisfy it with an explanation, even though every word he told her was a lie.

"My Bible-study group has been discussing what scripture says about the power of prayer."

"So you're in a Bible-study group," she said as if intrigued, as if he was not a man whom she could easily picture in such a pious pursuit.

"There was a major medical study that showed when friends and relatives actively pray for a sick loved one, the patient more often recovers, and recovers more quickly."

That controversial study had provided gas to inflate barroom debates when it had hit the newspapers. Recollection of all that boozy blather, not an earnest Bible-study group, had inspired Billy to concoct this cover story.

"I think I remember reading about it," Gretchen Norlee said.

"Of course I pray for Barbara every day."

"Of course."

"But I've come to see that prayer is more meaningful when it involves some sacrifice."

"Sacrifice," she said thoughtfully.

He smiled. "I don't mean to slaughter a lamb."

"Ah. That will please the janitorial staff."

"But a prayer before bed, however sincere, is no inconvenience."

"I see your point."

"Surely prayer will be more meaningful and effective if it comes at some personal cost—like at least the loss of a night's sleep."

"I've never thought of it that way," she said.

"From time to time," Billy said, "I'd like to sit with her all night in prayer. If it doesn't help her, it'll at least help me."

Listening to himself, he thought that he sounded as phony as a TV evangelist proclaiming the virtue of abstinence upon being caught naked with a hooker in the back of his limo.

Evidently, Gretchen Norlee heard him differently from how he heard himself. Behind her steel-rimmed spectacles, her eyes were moist with sympathy.

His newfound slickness dismayed Billy, and worried him. When a liar became too skilled at deception, he could lose the ability to discern truth, and could himself be more easily deceived.

He expected there might be a price for playing a nice woman like Gretchen Norlee for a fool, as there was a price for everything.

# 41

As Billy followed the main hall toward Barbara's room in the west wing, Dr. Jordan Ferrier, her physician, exited the room of another patient. They almost collided.

"Billy!"

"Hello, Dr. Ferrier."

"Billy, Billy, Billy."

"I sense a lecture coming on."

"You've been avoiding me."

"I've tried my best," Billy admitted.

Dr. Ferrier looked younger than forty-two. He was sandy-haired, green-eyed, perpetually cheerful, and a dedicated salesman for death.

"We're weeks overdue for our semiannual review."

"The semiannual review is your idea. I'm very happy with a once-every-decade review."

"Let's go see Barbara."

"No," Billy said. "I won't talk about this in front

of her."

"All right." Taking Billy by the arm, Dr. Ferrier steered him to the lounge where the staff took their breaks.

They were alone in the room. Vending machines for snacks and soft drinks hummed, ready to dispense high-calorie, high-fat, high-caffeine treats to medical workers who knew the consequences of their cravings but had the good sense to cut themselves some slack.

Ferrier drew a white plastic chair away from an orange Formica table. When Billy didn't follow suit, the doctor sighed, pushed the chair under the table, and remained on his feet.

"Three weeks ago I completed an evaluation of Barbara."

"I complete one every day."

"I'm not your enemy, Billy."

"It's hard to tell around this time of the year."

Ferrier was a hard-working physician, intelligent, talented, and well-meaning. Unfortunately, the university that turned him out had infected him with what they called "utilitarian ethics."

"She's gotten no better," said Dr. Ferrier.

"She's gotten no worse, either."

"Any chance of her regaining high cognitive function—"

"Sometimes she talks," Billy interrupted. "You know she does."

"Does she ever make sense? Is she coherent?"

"Once in a while," Billy said.

"Give me an example."

"I can't, offhand. I'd have to check my notebooks."

Ferrier had soulful eyes. He knew how to use them. "She was a wonderful woman, Billy. No one but you had more respect for her than I did. But now she has no meaningful quality of life."

"To me, it's very meaningful."

"You're not the one suffering. She is."

"She doesn't seem to be suffering," Billy said.

"We can't really know for sure, can we?"

"Exactly."

Barbara had liked Ferrier. That was one reason Billy did not replace him.

On some deep level she might perceive what was happening around her. In that event, she might feel safer knowing she was being cared for by Ferrier instead of by a strange doctor whom she'd never met.

Sometimes this irony was a grinding wheel that sharpened Billy's sense of injustice to a razor's edge.

Had she known about Ferrier's bioethics infection, had she known that he believed he possessed the wisdom and the right to determine whether a Down's Syndrome baby or a handicapped child, or a comatose woman, enjoyed a quality of life worth living, she might have changed physicians. But she had not known.

"She was such a vibrant, involved person," Ferrier said. "She wouldn't want to just hang on like this, year after year."

"She's not just hanging on," Billy said. "She's not lost at the bottom of a sea. She's floating near the surface. She's *right there.*"

"I understand your pain, Billy. Believe me, I do. But you don't have the medical knowledge to assess her condition. She's *not* right there. She never will be."

"I remember something she said just the other day. 'I want to know what it says . . . the sea, what it is that it keeps on saying.'"

Ferrier regarded him with equal measures of tenderness and frustration. "That's your best example of coherence?"

"'First do no harm,'" Billy said.

"Harm is done to other patients when we spend limited resources on hopeless cases."

"She's not hopeless. She laughs sometimes. She's *right there,* and she's got plenty of resources."

"Which could do so much good if properly applied."

"I don't want the money."

"I know. You're not the kind of guy who could ever spend a dime of it on yourself. But you could direct those resources to people who have a greater *potential* for an acceptable quality of life than she does, people who would be more likely to be helped."

Billy tolerated Ferrier also because the physician had been so effective in pre-trial depositions that the maker of the vichyssoise had chosen to settle long before getting near a courtroom.

"I'm only thinking of Barbara," Ferrier continued. "If I were in her condition, I wouldn't want to lie there like that, year after year."

"And I would respect your wishes," Billy said. "But we don't know what *her* wishes are."

"Letting her go doesn't require active steps," Ferrier reminded him. "We need only be passive. Remove the feeding tube."

In her coma, Barbara had no reliable gag reflex and could not properly swallow. Food would end up in her lungs.

"Remove the feeding tube and let nature take its course."

"Starvation."

"Just nature."

Billy kept her in Ferrier's care also because the physician was straightforward about his belief in utilitarian bioethics. Another doctor might believe the same but conceal it . . . and fancy himself an angel—or agent—of mercy.

Twice a year, Ferrier would make this argument, but he would not act without Billy's approval.

"No," Billy said. "No. We won't do that. We'll go on just the way we have been going."

"Four years is such a long time."

Billy said, "Death is longer."

# 42

Six o'clock sun on the vineyards filled the window with summer, life, and bounty.

Beneath her pale lids, Barbara Mandel's eyes followed the action of vivid dreams.

Sitting on the barstool by her bedside, Billy said, "I saw Harry today. He still smiles when he remembers you called him a Muppet. He says his greatest achievement is never having been disbarred."

He didn't tell her anything else about his day. The rest of it would not have lifted her spirits.

From the standpoint of defense, the two weak points of the room were the door to the hallway and the window. The adjoining bathroom was windowless.

The window featured a blind and a latch. The door could not be locked.

Like every hospital bed, Barbara's had wheels. Thursday evening, as midnight approached, Billy

could roll her out of here, where the killer expected to find her, and put her in another room, somewhere safer.

She wasn't tethered to life-support systems or to monitors. Her food supply and pump hung from a rack fixed to the bed frame.

From the nurses' station at midpoint of the long main corridor, no one could see around the corner to this west-wing room. With luck, he might be able to move Barbara at the penultimate moment without being seen, then return here to wait for the freak.

Assuming it came to that crisis point. Which was a safe if not happy assumption.

He left Barbara alone and walked the west wing, glancing in the rooms of other patients, checking a supply closet, a bathing chamber, reviewing possibilities.

When he returned to her room, she was talking: ". . . soaked in water . . . smothered in mud . . . lamed by stones . . ."

Her words suggested a bad dream, but her tone of voice did not. She spoke softly and as if enchanted.

". . . cut by flints . . . stung by nettles . . . torn by briars . . ."

Billy had forgotten his pocket notebook and his pen. Even if he had remembered them, he could not take the time to settle down and record these utterances.

"Quick!" she said.

Standing at her bedside, he put a comforting hand on Barbara's shoulder.

"Give it mouth!" she whispered urgently.

He half expected her eyes to open and to fix on him, but they did not.

When Barbara fell silent, Billy squatted to look for the cord that powered the bed's adjustable-mattress mechanism. If he needed to move her the following night, he would have to pull that plug.

On the floor, just under the high bed, lay a snapshot taken by a digital camera. Billy picked up the photo and stood to examine it in better light.

". . . creep and creep . . ." Barbara whispered.

He turned the snapshot three ways before he realized that it depicted a praying mantis, apparently dead, pale upon pale painted boards.

". . . creep and creep . . . and tear him open . . ."

Suddenly her whispering voice twitched like a dying mantis down through the spiraling chambers of Billy's ears, inspiring a shudder and a chill.

During normal visiting hours, family and friends of patients came through the front doors and went where they wished, without any requirement to sign a register.

". . . hands of the dead . . ." she whispered.

Because Barbara required less attention than

conscious patients with their myriad complaints and demands, nurses did not attend her as frequently as they did others.

"... great stones ... angry red ..."

A quiet visitor might stay here half an hour and never be seen at this bedside—or entering, or leaving.

He did not want to leave Barbara alone, talking to an empty room, though she must have done so on countless previous occasions. Billy's evening, already fully scheduled, had been complicated by the addition of one more urgent task.

"... chains hanging ... terrible ..."

Billy pocketed the snapshot.

He bent to Barbara and kissed her forehead. Her brow was cool, as always it was cool.

At the window, he drew down the blind.

Reluctant to leave, he stood in the open doorway, looking back at her.

She said something then that resonated with him, though he had no clue why.

"Mrs. Joe," she said. "Mrs. Joe."

He did not know a Mrs. Joe or Mrs. Joseph, or Mrs. Johanson, or Mrs. Jonas, or anyone by any name similar to the one that Barbara had spoken. And yet somehow ... he thought he did.

The phantom mantis twitched in his ears again. Along his spine.

With a prayer as real as any that he had lied

about to Gretchen Norlee, he left Barbara alone on this last night in which she might be safe.

Less than three hours of daylight remained in a sky too dry to support a wisp of a cloud, the sun a thermonuclear brilliance, the air gathered to a stillness as if in anticipation of a cataclysmic blast.

# 43

The picketed front yard contained no grass in need of mowing, but instead a lush carpet of baby's tears and, under the graceful boughs of pepper trees, lace flower.

Shading the front walk, an arbor tunnel was draped with trumpet vines. Orchestras of silent scarlet horns raised their flared bells to the sun.

The arched-lattice tunnel, a preview of twilight, led to a sunny front patio where pots were filled with red garnet, red valerian.

The house was a Spanish bungalow. Modest but graceful, it had been tenderly maintained.

The black silhouette of a bird had been painted on the red front door. The wings were on the upstroke, the bird in an angle of ascent.

Halfway through Billy's brief knock, the door opened, as though he had been expected and had been awaited with keen anticipation.

Ivy Elgin said, "Hi, Billy," without surprise, as

if she had seen him through a window in the door. It had no window.

Barefoot, she wore khaki shorts cut for comfort and a roomy red T-shirt that sold nothing. Hooded and cloaked, Ivy would still have been a lamp to every moth that flew.

"I wasn't sure you'd be here," he said.

"I'm off Wednesdays." She stepped back from the door.

Hesitating on the sun side of the threshold, Billy said, "Yeah. But you have a life."

"I'm shelling pistachios in the kitchen."

She turned and walked away into the house, leaving him to follow as if he had been here a thousand times. This was his first visit.

Heavily curtained sunlight and a floor lamp with a tasseled sapphire-silk shade accommodated shadows in the living room.

Billy glimpsed dark fir floors, midnight-blue mohair furniture, a Persian-style rug. The artwork seemed to be from the 1930s.

He made some noise on the hardwood floor, but Ivy did not. She crossed the room as if a slip of air always separated the soles of her feet from the fir planks, the way a sylph fly may choose to step across a pond without dimpling the surface tension of the water.

At the back of the house, the kitchen matched the size of the living room and contained a dining area.

Beadboard paneling, French-pane cabinet doors, a white tile floor with black-diamond inlays, and an ineffable quality made him think of the bayou and New Orleans charm.

Two windows between the kitchen and the back porch were open for ventilation. In one window sat a large black bird.

The creature's perfect stillness suggested taxidermy. Then it cocked its head.

Although Ivy said nothing, Billy felt invited to the table, and even as he sat, she put a glass of ice in front of him. She picked up a pitcher from the table and poured tea.

Also on the red-and-white-checkered oilcloth were another glass of tea, a dish of fresh cherries, a sheet-cake pan piled high with unshelled nuts, and a bowl half full of liberated pistachios.

"You've got a nice place," Billy said.

"It was my grandmother's house." She took three cherries from the dish. "She raised me."

Ivy spoke softly, as always. Even at the tavern, she never raised her voice, yet she never failed to make herself heard.

Not one to pry, Billy was surprised to hear himself ask, in a voice softened to match hers, "What happened to your mother?"

"She died in childbirth," Ivy said as she lined up the cherries on the window sill beside the bird. "My father just moved on."

The tea had been sweetened with peach nectar,

a hint of mint.

As Ivy returned to the table, sat, and continued shelling the nuts, the bird watched Billy and ignored the cherries.

"Is he a pet?" Billy asked.

"We own each other. He seldom comes farther than the window, and when he does, he respects my rules of cleanliness."

"What's his name?"

"He hasn't told me yet. Eventually he will."

Never in Billy's life, until now, had he felt entirely at ease and vaguely disoriented at the same time. Otherwise, he might not have found himself asking such an odd question: "Which came first, the real bird or the one on the front door?"

"They arrived together," she said, giving him an answer no less odd than his question.

"What is he—a crow?"

"He's more lordly than that," she said. "He's a raven, and wants us to believe he's nothing more."

Billy did not know what to say to that, so he said nothing. He felt comfortable with silence, and apparently so did she.

He realized that he had lost the sense of urgency with which he had left Whispering Pines. Time no longer seemed to be running out; in fact time seemed not to matter here.

Finally the bird turned to the cherries, using its bill to strip the meat from the pits with swift efficiency.

Ivy's long nimble fingers appeared to work slowly, yet she quickly added shelled pistachios to the bowl.

"This house is so quiet," Billy said.

"Because the walls haven't soaked up years of useless talk."

"They haven't?"

"My grandmother was deaf. We communicated by sign language and the written word."

Beyond the back porch lay a flower garden in which all blooms were red or deep blue, or royal purple. If one leaf stirred, if a cricket busied itself, if a bee circled a rose, no sound found its way through the open windows.

"You might like some music," Ivy said, "but I'd prefer none."

"You don't like music?"

"I get enough of it at the tavern."

"I like zydeco. And Western swing. The Texas Top Hands. Bob Wills and the Texas Playboys."

"Anyway, there's already music," she said, "if you're still enough to hear it."

He must not have been still enough.

Taking the photo of the dead mantis from his pocket and placing it on the table, Billy said, "I found this on the floor in Barbara's room at Whispering Pines."

"You can keep it if you want."

He didn't know what to make of that. "Were you visiting her?"

"I sit with her sometimes."

"I didn't know."

"She was kind to me."

"You didn't start to work at the tavern until a year after she was in a coma."

"I knew her before."

"Really."

"She was kind to me when Grandmother was dying in the hospital."

Barbara had been a nurse, a good one.

"How often do you visit her?" Billy asked.

"Once a month."

"Why have you never told me, Ivy?"

"Then we'd have to talk about her, wouldn't we?"

"Talk about her?"

"Talking about how she is, what she's suffered—does that give you peace?" Ivy asked.

"Peace? No. How could it?"

"Does remembering how she was, before the coma, give you peace?"

He considered. "Sometimes."

Her gaze rose from the pistachios, and her extraordinary brandy eyes met his eyes. "Then don't talk about now. Just remember when."

Finished with two cherries, the raven paused to stretch its wings. Silently they opened and silently closed.

When Billy looked at Ivy again, her attention had returned to her shelling hands.

He asked, "Why did you take this snapshot with you when you visited her?"

"I take them all with me everywhere, the most recent photos of dead things."

"But why?"

"Haruspicy," she reminded him. "I read them. They foretell."

He sipped his tea.

The raven watched him, beak open, as if it were shrieking. It made no sound.

"What do they foretell about Barbara?" Billy asked.

Ivy's serenity and fey quality concealed whether she calculated her answer or whether instead she hesitated only because her thoughts were divided between here and elsewhere. "Nothing."

"Nothing at all?"

She had given her answer. She didn't have another.

On the table, in the photo, the mantis said nothing to Billy.

"Where did you get this idea to read dead things?" he asked. "From your grandmother?"

"No. She disapproved. She was an old-fashioned devout Catholic. To her, believing in the occult is a sin. It puts the immortal soul in jeopardy."

"But you disagree."

"I do and I don't," Ivy said more softly than usual.

After the raven finished the third cherry, the naked pits were left side by side on the window sill, as if in acknowledgment of the household rules of neatness and order.

"I never heard my mother's voice," Ivy said.

Billy did not know what to make of that statement, and then he remembered that her mother had died in childbirth.

Ivy said, "Since I was very little, I've known my mother has something terribly important to say to me."

For the first time he noticed a wall clock. It had no second, minute, or hour hands.

"This house has always been so quiet," Ivy said. "So quiet. You learn to listen here."

Billy listened.

"The dead have things to tell us," Ivy said.

With polished-anthracite eyes, the raven regarded its mistress.

"The wall is thinner here," she said. "The wall between the worlds. A spirit might speak through if it wanted to badly enough."

Pushing the empty shells aside, dropping the nut meats in the bowl, she made the softest symphony of sounds, quieter even than the melting ice shifting in the tea glasses.

Ivy said, "Sometimes in the night or in a particularly still moment of an afternoon, or at twilight when the horizon swallows the sun and fully silences it, I know she's calling me. I can almost

hear the quality of her voice . . . but not the words. Not yet."

Billy thought of Barbara speaking from the abyss of unnatural sleep, her words meaningless to everyone else, yet fraught with enigmatic meaning to him.

He found Ivy Elgin as troubling as she was alluring. If her innocence sometimes seemed to approach the immaculate, Billy warned himself that in her heart, as in the heart of every man and woman, must be a chamber where light didn't reach, where a calming silence could not be achieved.

Nevertheless, regardless of whatever he himself might believe about life and death, and in spite of whatever impure motives Ivy entertained, if indeed she entertained any, Billy felt that she was sincere in her belief that her mother was trying to reach her, would continue trying, and would eventually succeed.

More important, she so impressed him, not by reason but by the judgment of his adaptive unconscious, that he was unable to write her off as a mere eccentric. In this house, the wall between worlds might well have been washed thin, rinsed by so many years of silence.

Her predictions based on haruspicy were seldom correct in any detail. She blamed this on her incompetence in reading signs, and would not abide suggestions that haruspicy itself was useless.

Billy now understood her obstinacy. If one

could not read the future in the unique conditions of each dead thing, it might also be true that the dead have nothing to tell us and that a child waiting to hear the voice of a lost mother might never hear it no matter how well she listened or how silent and attentive she remained.

And so she studied photos of possums broken along roadsides, of dead mantises, of birds fallen from the sky.

She silently walked her house, noiselessly shelled pistachios, softly spoke to the raven or did not speak at all, and at times the quiet became a perfect hush.

Such a hush had fallen over them now, but Billy broke it.

Interested less in Ivy's analysis than in her reaction, watching her more intently than ever the bird had done, Billy said, "Sometimes psychopathic killers keep souvenirs to remind them of their victims."

As though Billy's comment had been no stranger than a reference to the heat, Ivy paused for a sip of tea, then returned to shelling.

He suspected that nothing anyone said to Ivy ever elicited a reaction of surprise, as if she always knew what the words would be before they were spoken.

"I heard about this case," he continued, "where a serial killer cut off the face of a victim and kept it in a jar of formaldehyde."

Ivy scooped nut shells from the table and put

them in the waste can beside her chair. She didn't drop them, but *placed* them in the can in such a way that they did not rattle.

By watching Ivy, Billy could not tell if she had previously heard of the face thief or if instead this was news to her.

"If you came upon that faceless body, what would you read from it? Not about the future, but about *him*, the killer."

"Theater," she said without hesitation.

"I'm not sure what you mean."

"He likes theater."

"Why do you say that?"

"The drama of cutting off a face," she said.

"I don't make that connection."

From the shallow dish she took a cherry.

"The theater is deception," she said. "No actor plays himself."

Billy could only say, "All right," and wait.

She said, "In every role, an actor wears a false identity."

She put the cherry in her mouth. A moment later, she spit the pit into the palm of her hand, and swallowed the fruit.

Whether she meant to imply that the pit was the ultimate reality of the cherry, that was what he inferred.

Again, Ivy met his eyes. "He didn't want the face because it was a face. He wanted it because it was a mask."

Her eyes were more beautiful than readable, but he did not think that her insight chilled her as it did him. Maybe when you spent your life listening for the voices of the dead, you didn't chill easily.

He said, "Do you mean sometimes, when he's alone and in the mood, he takes it out of the jar and wears it?"

"Maybe he does. Or maybe he just wanted it because it reminded him of an important drama in his life, a favorite performance."

*Performance.*

That word had been impressed upon him by Ralph Cottle. Ivy might have repeated it knowingly, or in all innocence. He could not tell.

She continued to meet his eyes. "Do you think every face is a mask, Billy?"

"Do you?"

"My deaf grandmother, as gentle and kind as any saint, still had her secrets. They were innocent, even charming secrets. Her mask was almost as transparent as glass—but she still wore one."

He didn't know what she was telling him, what she meant for him to infer from what she had said. He did not believe that asking her directly would result in a more straightforward answer.

Not that she necessarily meant to deceive. Her conversation was frequently more allusive than straightforward, not by intention but because of her nature. Everything she said sounded as limpid

as a bell note to the ear—yet was sometimes semi-opaque to interpretation.

Often her silences seemed to say more than the words she spoke, as might make sense for a girl raised by the loving deaf.

If he read her half well, Ivy was not deceiving him in any way. But then why had she just suggested that every face, her own included, was a mask?

If Ivy visited Barbara only because Barbara had once been kind to her, and if she took photographs of dead things to Whispering Pines only because she took them everywhere, the photo of the mantis had no relationship to the trap in which Billy found himself, and she had no knowledge of the freak.

In which case, he could get up, go, and do what urgently needed to be done. Yet he remained at the table.

Her eyes had lowered once more to the pistachios, and her hands had returned to the quiet, useful work of shelling.

"My grandmother was deaf from birth," Ivy said. "She'd never heard a word spoken and didn't know how to form them."

Watching her nimble fingers, Billy suspected that Ivy's days were filled with useful work—tending to her garden, maintaining this fine house in its current state of spotless perfection, cooking—and that she avoided idleness at all costs.

"She'd never heard anyone laugh, either, but she knew how to do that, all right. She had a beautiful and infectious laugh. I never heard her cry until I was eight."

Billy understood Ivy's compulsive industry as a reflection of his own, and sympathized. Quite apart from the question of whether or not he could trust her, he liked her.

"When I was much younger," Ivy said, "I didn't fully understand what it meant that my mother had died in childbirth. I used to think that somehow I had killed her and was responsible."

In the window, the raven stretched its wings again, as silently as it had done before.

"I was eight when I realized I had no guilt," Ivy said. "When I signed my realization to my grandmother, I saw her cry for the first time. This sounds funny, but I had assumed when she cried, it would be the weeping of a perfect mute, nothing but tears and wrenching spasms of silence. But her sobs were as normal as her laugh. As far as those two sounds were concerned, she was not a woman apart from those who could hear and speak; she was one of their community."

Billy had thought that Ivy mesmerized men with her beauty and sexuality, but the spell she cast had a deeper source.

He knew what he intended to reveal only as he heard the words come forth: "When I was fourteen, I shot my mother and father."

Without looking up, she said, "I know."

"Dead."

"I know. Have you ever thought that one of them might want to speak to you through the wall?"

"No. I never have. And, God, I hope they never do."

She shelled, he watched, and in time she said, "You need to go."

By her tone, she meant that he could stay but understood that he needed to leave.

"Yes," he said, and rose from his chair.

"You're in trouble, aren't you, Billy?"

"No."

"That's a lie."

"Yes."

"And that's as much as you'll tell me."

He said nothing.

"You came here looking for something. Did you find it?"

"I'm not sure."

"Sometimes," she said, "you can listen so hard for the faintest of sounds that you don't even hear the louder ones."

He thought about that for a moment and then said, "Will you see me to the door?"

"You know the way now."

"You should lock up behind me."

"The door latches when you close it."

"That's not good enough. Before dark, you

should engage the deadbolts. And close those windows."

"I'm not afraid of anything," she said. "I never have been."

"I always have been."

"I know," she said. "For twenty years."

On his way out, Billy made less noise on the hardwood floors than he had done on his way in. He closed the front door, tested the latch, and followed the arbor-shaded walkway to the street, leaving Ivy Elgin with her tea and pistachios, with the watchful raven at her back, in the hush of the kitchen where the clock had no hands.

# 44

Steve Zillis rented a single-story house of no distinguishing architecture on a street where the bonding philosophy among the neighbors seemed to be neglect of property.

The only well-maintained residence was immediately north of Zillis's place. Jackie O'Hara's friend, Celia Reynolds, lived there.

She claimed to have seen Zillis in a rage chopping chairs, watermelons, and mannequins in his backyard.

The attached garage stood on the south side of his house, out of Celia Reynolds's line of sight. Having driven with frequent glances at his mirrors and having seen no tail, Billy parked boldly in the driveway.

Between Zillis and his southern neighbor rose a wall of eighty-foot, untrimmed eucalyptus trees that provided privacy.

When Billy got out of the Explorer, the extent

of his disguise was a blue baseball cap. He had pulled it low on his forehead.

His toolbox gave him legitimacy. A man with a toolbox, moving with purpose, is assumed to be a repairman, and excites no suspicion.

As a bartender, Billy had a well-known face in certain circles. But he didn't expect to be in the open for long.

He walked between the fragrant eucalyptus trees and the garage. As he hoped, he found a man-size side door.

In keeping with the property neglect and the cheap rent, only a simple lockset secured that entrance. No deadbolt.

Billy used his laminated driver's license to loid the latch bolt. He took his toolbox into the hot garage and turned on a light.

On his way from Whispering Pines to Ivy Elgin's house, he had driven past the tavern. Steve's car had been parked in the lot.

Zillis lived alone. The way was clear.

Billy opened the garage, drove the SUV inside, closed the door. He proceeded casually, not as if in a hurry to get out of sight.

Wednesday nights were usually busy at the tavern. Steve wouldn't be home until after two o'clock Thursday morning.

Nevertheless, Billy couldn't afford to take seven hours to get into the house and search it. Elsewhere, two dead bodies salted with evidence against him

needed to be disposed of long before dawn.

Festooned with webs and dust, the garage was free of clutter. In ten minutes, he found spiders but no spare key to the inner door.

He wanted to avoid signs of forced entry; however, picking a lock isn't as easy as it appears to be in movies. Neither is seducing a woman or killing a man, or anything else.

Having installed new locks in his house, Billy had not only learned to do the work correctly but also learned how often it is done badly. He hoped for sloppy workmanship—and found it.

Perhaps the door had been hung to swing from the wrong side. Rather than rehang it to match the lockset, they had installed the lockset in reverse, with the interior face turned to the garage.

Instead of an unremovable escutcheon, he was offered one with two spanner screws. The keyhole plug had a grip ring for extraction.

In less time than he had spent searching for a spare key, he opened the door. Before proceeding, he put the lock back together. He cleaned up all evidence of what he had done and wiped all his prints off the door hardware.

He returned the tools to the box—and took from it his revolver. To facilitate a hasty exit, he put the tools in the Explorer.

In addition to the toolbox, he had brought a box of disposable latex gloves. He slipped his hands into a pair.

Now, with an hour of daylight remaining, he toured the house, switching on lamps and ceiling fixtures as he went.

Many of the shelves in the pantry were bare. Steve's provisions were a cliché of bachelorhood: canned soups, canned stews, potato chips, corn chips, Cheez Doodles.

The dirty dishes and pots heaped in the sink outnumbered clean items in the cabinets, most of which were empty.

In a drawer, he found a collection of spare keys for a car, for padlocks, perhaps for the house. He tried a few in the back door and found one that worked. He pocketed that spare before returning the other keys to the drawer.

Steve Zillis scorned furniture. In the dinette off the kitchen, the single chair did not match the scarred Formica table.

The living room contained only a lumpy sofa, a cracked-leather ottoman, and a TV with DVD player on a wheeled stand. Magazines were stacked on the floor, and near them were a discarded pair of dirty socks.

Except for the lack of posters, the decor was that of a dorm room. Enduring adolescence was pathetic but not criminal.

If a woman ever visited, she wouldn't return—or sleep over. Being able to tie knots in a cherry stem with your tongue was not enough to ensure a life of torrid romance.

The spare bedroom contained no furniture, but four mannequins. They were all female, naked, wigless, bald. Three had been altered.

One lay on its back, on the floor, in the center of the room. It gripped two steak knives. Each knife had been driven into its throat, as if it had twice stabbed itself.

A hole had been drilled between its legs. Also between its legs was a spear-point stave from a wrought-iron fence. The sharp end of the stave had been inserted in the crudely formed vagina.

Instead of feet, the mannequin had another pair of hands at the ends of its legs. Both legs were bent to allow the additional hands to grip the iron stave.

A third pair of hands grew by the wrists from the breasts. They grasped at the air, seeking and eager, as though the mannequin were insatiable.

# 45

In more than a few houses, if you could prowl at leisure, you might discover evidence of perversity, kinky secrets.

Because such care had been taken in their alteration, so much time expended, these mannequins seemed to represent more than that. This was an expression not of desire but of a ravenous craving, of a rapacious *need* that could never be fully satisfied.

A second mannequin sat with its back to a wall, legs splayed. Its eyes had been cut out. Teeth had been inserted in their place.

These appeared to be animal teeth, perhaps those of reptiles and perhaps real. Hooked fangs and snaggled incisors.

Each tooth had been meticulously glued in the rim of the socket. Each cluster appeared to have been designed with much thought as to the most fearsome, bristling arrangement.

The mouth had been cut open, carved wide. Wicked, inhuman teeth filled the mannequin's maw.

Like the petals of a Venus flytrap, the ears were rimmed with poised teeth.

Teeth sprouted from the nipples and from the navel. A crafted vagina featured more fangs than the other orifices.

Whether this macabre figure represented a fear of all-devouring womanhood, whether instead it was being devoured by its own hunger, Billy didn't know, didn't care.

He just wanted to get out of here. He had seen enough. Yet he continued to look.

The third mannequin also sat with its back to a wall. Its hands rested in its lap, holding a bowl. The bowl was actually the top of its skull, which had been sawn off.

Photographs of male genitalia overflowed the bowl. Billy did not touch them, but he could see enough to suspect that every picture featured the same genitalia.

A bouquet of similar photos, scores of them, bloomed from the top of the open skull. Still more blossomed from the mannequin's mouth.

Evidently Steve Zillis had spent a lot of time taking snapshots of himself from various angles, in various states of arousal.

Billy's latex gloves served a purpose besides guarding against leaving fingerprints. Without

them, he would have been sickened by the need to touch doorknobs, light switches, anything in the house.

The fourth mannequin had not yet been mutilated. Zillis probably hungered to get at her.

During his shift at the tavern, drawing beers from the tap, telling jokes, doing his tricks, *these* were the thoughts behind the radiant smile.

Steve's bedroom proved to be as sparsely furnished as the rest of the house. The bed, a nightstand, a lamp, a clock. No art on the walls, no knickknacks, no memorabilia.

The bedclothes were in disarray. One pillow lay on the floor.

A corner of the room evidently served in place of a laundry hamper. Rumpled shirts, khakis, jeans, and dirty underwear were heaped as Steve had tossed them.

A search of the bedroom and closet turned up another disturbing discovery. Under the bed were a dozen pornographic videos, the covers of which depicted naked women in handcuffs, in chains, some gagged, some blindfolded, cowering women threatened by sadistic men.

These weren't homemade videos. They were professionally packaged and probably available in any adult-video shop, whether brick-and-mortar or on-line.

Billy put them back where he had found them, and he considered whether he had discovered

enough to warrant calling the police.

No. Neither the mannequins nor the pornography proved that Steve Zillis had ever harmed a real human being, only that he nurtured a sick and vivid fantasy life.

Meanwhile, a dead man was wrapped for disposal and stowed behind the sofa in Billy's house.

If he became a suspect in the murder of Giselle Winslow in Napa or if Lanny Olsen's body was found and Billy became a suspect in that murder, he would at the very least be put under surveillance. He would lose his freedom of action.

If they found Cottle's body, he would be arrested.

No one would understand or believe the threat against Barbara. They would not take his warnings seriously. When you were a prime suspect, what the police wanted to hear from you was what they *expected* to hear from you, which was a confession.

He knew how it worked. He knew exactly how it worked.

During the twenty-four hours or the forty-eight hours—or the week, the month, the year—that it took to establish his innocence, if he ever could establish it, Barbara would be vulnerable, without a guardian.

He had been drawn in too deep. Nobody could save him except he himself.

If he found the face in a jar of formaldehyde and other grisly souvenirs, he might be able to nail Zillis for the authorities. But nothing less would convince them.

Like most California houses, this one didn't have a basement, but it did have an attic. The hall ceiling featured a trapdoor with a dangling rope handle.

When he pulled the trap down, an accordion ladder unfolded from the back of it.

He heard something behind him. In his mind, he saw a mannequin with teeth in its eye sockets, reaching toward him.

He pivoted, clawing for the gun under his belt. He was alone. He had probably heard just a settling noise, an old house easing itself at the insistence of gravity.

At the top of the ladder, he found a light switch set in the frame of the trap. Two bare bulbs, dimmed by dust, illuminated a raftered space empty of everything except the smell of wood rot.

Evidently the freak was canny enough to keep his incriminating souvenirs elsewhere.

Billy suspected that Zillis stayed in this rental house but did not in the truest sense *live* here. With its minimum of furniture and utter lack of decorative items, the place had the feeling of a way station. Steve Zillis had no roots here. He was just passing through.

He had worked at the tavern for five months.

Where had he been between the University of Colorado at Denver, five and a half years ago, when Judith Kesselman had disappeared, and this place?

Across the World Wide Web, his name had been linked to only one disappearance, and to no murders at all. Googled, Billy himself would not appear that clean.

But if you had a list of the towns in which Steve Zillis had settled for a while, if you researched murders and disappearances that occurred in those communities, the truth might be clearer.

The most successful serial killers were the vagabonds, roamers who covered a lot of ground between their homicidal frenzies. When clusters of killings were separated by hundreds of miles and scores of jurisdictions, they were less likely to be connected; patterns in landscape, visible from an airplane, are seldom discernible to a man on foot.

An itinerant bartender who's a good mixologist, who's outgoing and able to charm the customers, can get work anywhere. If he applies to the right places, he won't often be asked for a formal employment history, only for a social-security card, a driver's license, and an all-clean report from the state liquor-control board. Jackie O'Hara, typical of his breed, didn't phone an applicant's former employers; he made hiring decisions based on gut instinct.

Billy turned out the lights as he left the house. He used the spare key to lock up after himself, and he pocketed it again because he expected to return.

# 46

The dying sun spilled fierce bloody light on the dimensional mural under construction across the highway from the tavern.

As Billy drove past on his way home to collect Cottle's body, this scintillant display seized his attention. It captured him so completely that he pulled to the shoulder of the road and stopped.

Outside the large yellow-and-purple tent in which the artists and artisans of the project regularly met for lunch, for progress meetings, and for receptions in honor of various art- and academic-world dignitaries, they assembled now to assess this fleeting work of nature.

Parked near the tent, the giant yellow-and-purple motor home, built on a bus chassis and emblazoned with the name *Valis*, offered much chrome and steel in which the sun could reveal a latent fire. The tinted windows glowed a crimson bronze, sullen and smoky, yet incandescent.

Neither the festive tent nor the rock-star motor home, nor the glamorous artists and artisans enjoying the effects of sunset were what brought Billy to a stop.

At first he would have said that the scarlet-and-gold brightness of the spectacle was the primary thing that arrested him. This self-conscious analysis, however, missed the truth.

The construction was pale gray, but reflections of the sun's fury blazed in the glossy enamel. This glistering glaze and the heat shimmering the air as it rose off the hot painted surfaces combined to create the illusion of the mural afire.

And briefly *this* seemed to be what pulled Billy to the side of the highway: this clairvoyant vision of the blazing construct, which would indeed be razed after it had been completed.

Here was an eerie foretelling by a fluke of seasonal light and atmospheric conditions. The fire to come. And even the ultimate ashes could be glimpsed as a grayness underlying the phantom flames.

As the intensity of these pyrotechnics increased simultaneously with the distillation of the sun's last light, a truer reason for the hypnotic power of the scene grew clear to Billy. What riveted him was the great figure caught in the stylized machinery, the man struggling to survive among the giant grinding wheels, the tearing gears, the hammering pistons.

During the weeks of construction, as the mural had been crafted and refined, the man in the machine had always appeared to be trapped by it, just as the artist intended. He had been a victim of forces larger than himself.

Now by the peculiar grace of the setting sun, the man didn't appear to be burning as did the machine shapes around him. He was luminous, yes, but uniquely so, luminous and solid and strong, not being consumed by the flames but impervious to them.

Nothing about the phantasmagoric machine made engineering sense. A mere assemblage of *symbols* of machines, it had no functional purpose.

A machine without productive function is without meaning. It can not serve even as a prison.

The man could step out of the machine whenever he wished. He was not trapped. He only *believed* himself to be imprisoned, a belief born of self-indulgent despair and herewith revealed as fallacious. The man must walk away from meaninglessness, find meaning, and from meaning at last take upon himself a worthwhile purpose.

Billy Wiles was not a man given to epiphanies. He had spent his life fleeing them. Insight and pain were all but synonymous to him.

He recognized this as an epiphany, however, and he did not flee from it. Instead, as he drove back onto the highway and continued homeward into the darkling twilight, he climbed a mental

stairway of ascending implications, came to a turning in the stair, and climbed, and came to another turning.

He could not foresee what he would make of this sudden intuitive perception. He might not be man enough to make anything worthwhile of it, but he knew that he would make *something.*

When he arrived home under an indigo sky with one thin smear of evidence remaining in the west, Billy drove off the driveway, onto the back lawn. He parked with the tailgate near the porch steps, to facilitate the loading of Ralph Cottle.

He could not be seen from the county road or from the property of the nearest neighbor. Getting out of the SUV, he heard the first hoot of a night owl. Only the owl would see him, and the stars.

Inside, he took the stepladder out of the pantry and checked the video-disk recorder in the cabinet above the microwave. Replayed at high speed in the review screen, the security recording revealed that no one had entered the house in Billy's absence, at least not through the kitchen.

He hadn't expected to see anyone. Steve Zillis was working at the tavern.

After putting away the stepladder, he dragged Cottle through the house, onto the back porch and down the steps, using the rope handle that he had fashioned around the tarp-wrapped corpse. Loading Cottle into the back of the Explorer

required more patience and muscle than Billy had expected.

He gazed across the dark yard at the black woods, the regimented ranks of sentinel trees. He did not have a sense of being watched. He felt deeply alone.

Although locking the house seemed pointless, he locked it and then drove the Explorer to the garage.

At the sight of his table saw and drill press and tools, Billy irrationally wanted to turn from the crisis at hand. He wanted to smell fresh-cut wood, experience the satisfaction of a well-made dove-tail joint.

In recent years, he had built so much for the house, for himself, all for himself. If now he were to build for others, with what would he begin except with what was needed: coffins. He had built for himself a career in coffins.

Grimly, he stowed another plastic tarp, a coil of sturdy rope, strapping tape, a flashlight, and other needed items in the Explorer. He added a few folded moving blankets and a couple of empty cardboard boxes atop and around the wrapped corpse to disguise its telltale shape.

Before Billy lay a long night of death and grave-yard work, and he was afraid not solely of the homicidal freak but of many things in the dark-ness ahead. Darkness conjures infinite terrors in the mind, but it is true—and he took hope from

this—it is true that darkness also reminds us of light. The light. Regardless of what waited in the hours immediately ahead, he did believe that he would live in the light again.

# 47

Four hours of sleep facilitated by Vicodin and Elephant beer had not been sufficient rest.

More than twelve active hours had passed since Billy had rolled out of bed. He still had physical resources, but the wheels of his mind, so long racing, were not spinning as fast as they had been, as fast as he needed them to spin.

Confident that the Explorer did not look like the death wagon that it was, he stopped at a convenience store. He bought Anacin for a swelling headache and a package of No-Doz caffeine tablets.

He'd eaten two English muffins for breakfast and later a ham sandwich. He was in a calorie deficit, and shaky.

The store offered vacuum-packaged sandwiches and a microwave in which to heat them. For some reason, just the thought of meat stirred a billowing sensation in his stomach.

He bought six Hershey's bars for sugar, six Planters Peanut Bars for protein, and a bottle of Pepsi to wash down the No-Doz.

Referring to all the candy, the cashier said, "Is it Valentine's Day in July or something?"

"Halloween," Billy said.

Sitting in the SUV, he took the Anacin and the No-Doz.

On the passenger's seat lay the newspaper he'd bought in Napa. He'd not yet found time to read the story about the Winslow murder.

With the newspaper were a few *Denver Post* articles downloaded from the library computer. Judith Kesselman, gone missing forever.

As he ate a Hershey's bar, a Planters, he read the printouts. University, public, and police officials were quoted. Everyone except the police expressed confidence that Judith would be found safe.

The cops were guarded in their statements. Unlike the academics, bureaucrats, and politicians, they avoided bullshit. They were the only ones who sounded as if they truly cared about the young woman.

The officer in charge of the investigation was Detective Ramsey Ozgard. Some of his colleagues called him Oz.

Ozgard had been forty-four at the time of the disappearance. At that point in his career, he'd received three citations for bravery.

At fifty, he was probably still on the force, a likelihood supported by the only other personal information about him in the articles. When he was thirty-eight, Ramsey Ozgard had been shot in the left leg. He had been approved for permanent disability. He had turned it down. He did not limp.

Billy wanted to talk to Ozgard. To do so, however, he could not use his real name or his phone.

As the candy, Pepsi, and No-Doz began to lubricate the flywheels of his mind, Billy drove to Lanny Olsen's place.

He did not park at the church and walk from there, as he'd done before. When he arrived at the isolated house at the end of the lane, he drove across the ascending backyard, past the pistol range with the hay-bale-and-hillside backstop.

Lawn gave way to wild grass, to brambles and sparse brush. The terrain grew stony and furrowed.

He stopped two-thirds of the way up the slope, put the Explorer in park, and engaged the emergency brake.

He could have benefited from the headlights. This high on the hillside, however, they could be seen from the residences down near the county road.

Worried about attracting attention and inspiring curiosity, he switched off the lights. He killed the engine.

On foot, using a flashlight, he quickly found the vent hole, twenty feet from the SUV.

Before vineyards, before the arrival of Europeans, before the ancestors of American Indians had crossed a land or ice bridge from Asia, volcanoes shaped this valley. They had defined its future.

The old Rossi winery, now the aging cellars for Heitz, and other buildings in the valley were built of rhyolite, the volcanic form of granite, quarried locally. The knoll on which the Olsen house stood was largely basalt, another volcanic stone, dark and dense.

When an eruption is exhausted, it sometimes leaves lava pipes, long tunnels through surrounding stone. Billy didn't know enough volcanology to conclude whether the dormant vent on this knoll was such a pipe or was a fumarole that had expelled fiery gases.

He knew, however, that the vent was four feet wide at the mouth—and immeasurably deep.

This property was intimately familiar to Billy, because when he had been fourteen and alone, Pearl Olsen had given him a home. She never feared him, as some had. She knew the truth when she heard it. Her good heart opened to him, and in spite of her recurring cancer, she raised him as if he were her son.

The twelve-year difference in Billy's age and Lanny's meant they were never like brothers,

although they lived in the same house. Besides, Lanny had always been self-contained and when not on duty with the sheriff's department had lost himself in his cartooning.

The two of them had been friendly enough. And occasionally Lanny could be an engaging honorary uncle.

On one such day, Lanny had involved Billy in an attempt to determine the depth of the vent.

Although no young children played on the brambly knoll, Pearl worried for the safety of even imaginary tykes. Years earlier, she'd had a redwood frame bolted to the stone rim of the vent. A redwood lid was screwed to the frame.

After removing the lid, Lanny and Billy began their research with a handheld police spotlight powered off a pickup-truck engine. The beam illuminated the walls to about three hundred feet but could not find the bottom.

Past the mouth, the shaft widened to between eight and ten feet. The walls were undulant, whorled, and strange.

They tied one pound of brass washers to the end of a length of binder twine and lowered them into the center of the hole, listening for the distinctive ring of the discs meeting the vent floor. They only had a thousand feet of twine, which proved inadequate.

Finally they dropped steel ball bearings into the abyss, timing their fall to a first impact, using text-

book formulae to calculate distance. No bearing ever hit short of fourteen hundred feet.

The bottom did not lie at fourteen hundred feet.

After that long vertical drop, the vent apparently descended further at an angle, perhaps more than once changing direction, too. After the hard *clack* of the initial strike, each bearing ricocheted from wall to wall, rattling on, the noise never suddenly coming to a stop but always fading, fading until it dwindled into silence.

Billy guessed that the lava pipe was miles long and descended at least a few thousand feet under the floor of the valley.

Now, by the glow of the flashlight, he used a battery-powered screwdriver to extract the twelve Phillips-head steel screws that held the redwood lid—a more recent one than they had removed almost twenty years ago. He slid the lid aside.

No draft rose out of the hole. Billy could smell nothing but a faint cindery scent, and under that the vaguest hint of salt, a whiff of lime.

Grunting with the effort, he hauled the dead man out of the SUV and dragged him to the vent.

He wasn't concerned about the trail he left through the brush or about the trail the Explorer had left. Nature was resilient. In a few days, the disturbance would not be obvious.

Although the dead man might not have approved, given his status as a former member of

the Society of Skeptics, Billy murmured a brief prayer for him before shoving his body into the hole.

Ralph Cottle made a lot more noise going down than had any of the ball bearings. The first few impacts sounded bone-shattering.

Then the slippery tarp produced an eerie whistling sound as the tunnel angled from the vertical and the plastic-wrapped mummy slid at increasing velocity into the depths, perhaps spiraling around the walls of the lava tube as a bullet spirals along the grooved barrel of a gun.

# 48

Billy parked the Explorer on the lawn behind the garage, where it could not be seen by any motorist who might use the dead end of the lane as a turnaround. He worked his hands into latex gloves.

With the spare key that he had taken from the hole in the oak stump little more than nineteen hours earlier, he let himself into the house through the back door.

He had with him the tarp, the strapping tape, the rope. And of course the .38 revolver.

As Billy moved forward through the ground floor, he turned on lights.

Wednesday and Thursday were Lanny's days off, so he might not be thought missing for another thirty-six hours. If a friend dropped by unannounced for a visit, however, saw lights in the house, but could not get an answer to the doorbell, trouble would follow.

Billy intended to do what needed to be done as quickly as possible and get out, turning the lights off after himself.

The cartoon hands, pointing the way to the corpse, were still taped to the walls. He would remove them later, as part of the cleanup.

If Lanny's body had been salted with evidence pointing to Billy, as Cottle said that Giselle Winslow's had been, none of it could be used in a court of law if Lanny lay forever at rest a mile or more under the earth.

Billy realized, as he eliminated planted evidence incriminating himself, he also would be destroying any evidence of the killer's guilt that the freak might unintentionally have left. He was doing cleanup for both of them.

The cunning with which this trap had been designed and the early choices that Billy had made as the *performance* unfolded had virtually ensured that he would come to this juncture and would have to proceed as he was proceeding now.

He didn't care. Nothing mattered but Barbara. He had to stay free to protect her, because no one else would.

If Billy came under suspicion in a homicide, John Palmer would lock him down fast and tight. The sheriff would seek vindication in the conviction of Billy for murder, and if he got that conviction, he would use it to try to rewrite history, as well.

They could hold him on suspicion alone. He

wasn't sure how long. Certainly for forty-eight hours.

By then Barbara would be dead. Or missing, gone, like Judith Kesselman, music student, dog fancier, walker on beaches.

The performance would be concluded. Maybe the freak would have another face in another jar.

Past, present, future, all time eternally present in the here and now, and *racing*—he swore he could hear the hands on his watch *whirring*—and so he hurried to the stairs and climbed.

Even before arriving at this house, he'd feared that he would not find Lanny's body in the bedroom armchair where he had last seen it. Another move in the game, one more twist in the performance.

When he reached the top of the stairs, he hesitated, stopped by that same dread. He hesitated again at the doorway to the master bedroom. Then he crossed the threshold and switched on the light.

Lanny sat in the chair with the book in his lap, the photograph of Giselle Winslow tucked in the book.

The corpse didn't look good. Perhaps delayed somewhat by the air conditioning, visible decomposition had not yet occurred, but blood vessels in his face had begun to be revealed as a faint green marbling.

Lanny's eyes shifted to follow Billy across the room, but that was just a trick of the light.

# 49

After spreading the polyurethane tarp on the floor but before proceeding further, Billy sat on the edge of the bed and picked up the phone. Careful not to make the error that he had claimed to have made earlier in the day, he keyed in 411. From directory assistance he obtained the area code for Denver.

Even if Ramsey Ozgard continued to serve as a detective with the Denver Police Department, he might not live within the city. He might be in one of several suburbs, in which case locating him would be too difficult. His home number might also be unlisted.

When Billy called directory assistance in Denver, he got lucky. He was overdue for some luck. They had a listing for Ozgard, Ramsey G., in the city.

It was 10:54 in Colorado, but the hour might make the call seem more urgent and therefore more credible.

A man answered on the second ring, and Billy said, "Detective Ozgard?"

"Speaking."

"Sir, this is Deputy Lanny Olsen of the Napa County Sheriff's Department, here in California. First, I want to apologize for disturbing you at this hour."

"I'm a lifelong insomniac, Deputy, and now I have like six hundred channels on the TV, so I'll be watching reruns of *Gilligan's Island* or some damn thing until three in the morning. What's up?"

"Sir, I'm calling you from my home about a case you handled some years back. You might want to ring the watch commander in our north-county substation to confirm that I'm with the department, and get my home number from them for call-back."

"I've got caller ID," Ozgard said. "I can see who you are good enough for now. If what you want from me seems at all sticky, then I'll do what you say. But right now let's go for it."

"Thank you, sir. There's a missing-person's case of yours that might have some pertinence to a situation here. About five and a half years ago—"

"Judith Kesselman," said Ozgard.

"You jumped right to it."

"Deputy, don't tell me you found her. At least don't tell me you found her dead."

"No, sir. Neither dead or alive."

"God help her, I don't expect *alive*," Ramsey said. "But it's going to be a miserable day when I know for sure she's dead. I love that girl."

Surprised, Billy said, "Sir?"

"I never met her, but I love her. Like a daughter. I've learned so much about Judi Kesselman that I know her better than a lot of people who're actually *in* my life."

"I see."

"She was a wonderful young woman."

"That's what I hear."

"I talked to so many of her friends and family. Not a bad word about her from anyone. The stories of things she did for others, her kindnesses . . . You know how sometimes a vic haunts you, how you can't be entirely objective?"

"Sure," Billy said.

"I'm haunted by this one," Ozgard said. "She was a great letter writer. Once someone entered her life, she held on to them, she didn't forget them, she stayed in touch. I read hundreds of Judi's letters, Deputy Olsen, hundreds."

"So you let her in."

"You can't help it with her, she walks right in. They were the letters of a woman who embraced people, who just gave her heart to everyone. *Luminous* letters."

Billy found himself staring at the bullet hole in Lanny Olsen's forehead. He looked toward the open door to the upstairs hall.

"We've got a situation here," he said. "I can't spell it out in detail at this time, because we're still working the evidence and we aren't ready to bring charges."

"I understand," Ozgard assured him.

"But there's a name I want to run by you, see if it rings three cherries with you."

"The hairs are up on the back of my neck," Ozgard said. "That's how bad I want this to be something."

"I Googled our guy, and the only thing I got was this one hit regarding the Kesselman disappearance, and even that was less than nothing."

"So Google *me*," said Ozgard.

"Steven Zillis."

In Denver, Ramsey Ozgard let out his pent-up breath with a hiss.

"You remember him," Billy said.

"Oh yeah."

"He was a suspect?"

"Not officially."

"But you personally felt . . ."

"He made me uneasy."

"Why?"

Ozgard was silent. Then: "Even a man you wouldn't want to share a beer with, wouldn't want to shake hands with—his reputation isn't to be taken lightly."

"This is background, off the record," Billy assured him. "You tell me as much as makes you

comfortable and just how big a spoonful of salt I should take with it."

"The thing is, for the entire day when Judi had to have been snatched—if she was snatched, and I believe she was—for that entire day, for the whole twenty-four-hour window and then some, Zillis had an alibi you couldn't crack with a nuke."

"You tried."

"Believe it. But even if he hadn't had an alibi, there wasn't any evidence pointing his way."

"Then why did he make you uneasy?"

"He was too forthcoming."

Billy didn't say anything, but he was disappointed. He was in the market for certainty, and Ozgard didn't have any to sell.

Sensing that disappointment, the detective expanded on what he had said. "He came to me before he was even on my scope. Fact is, he might *never* have been on my scope if he *hadn't* come to me. He wanted so much to help. He talked and talked. He cared about her too much, like she was a beloved sister, but *he had only known her a month.*"

"You said she was exceptional at relationships, she embraced people, they bonded with her."

"According to her best friends, she didn't even know Zillis that well. Only casually."

Reluctantly playing the devil's advocate, Billy said, "He could have felt closer to her than she

did to him. I mean, if she had that kind of magnetism, that appeal . . ."

"You would have had to see him, the way he was with me," Ozgard said. "It's like he *wanted* me to wonder about him, to check him out and find the airtight alibi. And after I did, there was this smugness about him."

Remarking on the quiet revulsion in Ozgard's voice, Billy said, "You're still hot."

"I *am* hot. Zillis—he's coming back to me, the way he was. For a while, before he finally faded away, he kept trying to help, calling up, dropping by, offering ideas, and you had this feeling it was all mockery, he was just performing."

"Performing. I have a feeling like that, too," Billy said, "but I really need more."

"He's a prick. That doesn't mean he's anything worse, but he is a self-satisfied prick. The little prick even started acting like we were pals, him and me. Potential suspects, they just never do that. It's not natural. Hell, you know. But he had this easy, jokey way about him."

"'How're they hangin', Kemosabe.'"

"Shit, does he still say that?" Ozgard asked.

"He still does."

"He's a prick. He covered it with this goofy charm, but he's a prick, all right."

"So he was all over you, and then he just faded away."

"The whole investigation faded away. Judi was

gone like she'd never existed. Zillis dropped out of school at the end of that year, his sophomore year. I never saw him again."

"Well, he's here now," Billy said.

"I wonder where he's been in between."

"Maybe we'll find out."

"I hope you find out."

"I'll be back to you," Billy said.

"Any hour on this one, anytime. You have tin in your blood, Deputy?"

Billy didn't get it for a moment, and then he almost forgot who he was supposed to be, but he came back with the right answer: "Yeah. My dad was a cop. He was buried in his uniform."

"My dad and my grandfather," Ozgard said. "I've got so much tin in my blood it rattles in my veins, I don't even need the badge for people to know what I am. But Judith Kesselman, she's in my blood as bad as the tin. I want her to be at rest with some respect, not just . . . not just dumped somewhere. Christ knows, there's not much justice, but there *has* to be some in this case."

After hanging up, Billy could not for a moment move from the edge of the bed. He sat staring at Lanny, and Lanny seemed to stare at him.

Ramsey Ozgard was *in* life, all the way in the tides, swimming, not treading carefully along the shore. *Immersed* in the life of his community, committed to it.

Billy had heard the detective's commitment coming down the line from Denver, as fresh to the senses as if the two of them had been in the same room. Hearing it, Billy had been stung by the realization of how complete his own withdrawal had been. And how dangerous.

Barbara had begun to reach him; then vichyssoise. Life packed a clever one-two punch: cruelty and absurdity.

He was in the tides now, but not by choice. Events had *thrown* him in deep, swift water.

The weight of twenty years of guarded emotions, of studied avoidance, of defensive reclusiveness, encumbered him. Now he was trying to learn to swim again, but a riptide seemed to be sweeping him farther from any community, toward greater isolation.

# 50

As though he knew where he would be going, down the lava tube without benefit of mourners or memorial, Lanny didn't want to be wrapped.

The shooting had not taken place in this room, so no blood or brains stained the walls or furniture. Because he wanted Lanny to vanish in such a way that would engender the most uncertainty and therefore would not instigate an immediate and intense homicide investigation, Billy hoped to keep everything clean.

From the linen closet, he fetched an armload of fluffy towels. Lanny still used the same detergent and fabric softener that Pearl had used. Billy recognized the distinctive, clean fragrance.

He draped the towels over the arms and the back of the chair in which the cadaver sat. If anything remained to be spilled from the exit wound in the back of the skull, the carefully layered towels would catch it.

He had brought from home a plastic bag used as a liner for small bathroom waste cans. Avoiding the filmy protuberant eyes, he pulled the bag over the dead man's head and with adhesive tape sealed it as best he could around the neck—further insurance against a spill.

Although he knew that no one could be driven mad by grisly work, knew that the horror came after the madness, not before, he wondered how much more he could traffic with the dead before his every dream, if not his waking hours, would be a howling bedlam.

Lanny came out of the chair onto the tarp readily enough, but then he became uncooperative. He lay on the floor in the position of a man sitting in a chair; and his legs couldn't be pulled straight.

Rigor mortis. The corpse was stiff and would largely remain so until decomposition advanced far enough to soften the tissues that rigor mortis made rigid.

Billy had no idea how long that would be. Six hours, twelve? He couldn't wait around to see.

He struggled to wrap Lanny in the tarp. At times the dead man's resistance seemed conscious and stubborn.

The final package was awkward but adequately sealed. He hoped the rope handle would hold.

The towels were spotless. He folded them and returned them to the linen closet.

They didn't seem to smell as good as they had earlier.

Lanny to the head of the stairs proved easy, but Lanny down the first flight was a hard thing to hear. In its half-fetal position, the body rapped and knocked step by step, managing to sound bony and gelatinous at the same time.

At the landing, Billy reminded himself that Lanny had betrayed him in an attempt to save a job and pension, and that they were *both* here because of that. This truth, while inescapable, didn't make the descent of the final flight of steps any less disturbing.

Getting the body along the lower hall, through the kitchen, and across the back porch was easy enough. Then more steps, just a short flight, and they were in the yard.

He considered loading the body in the Explorer and driving it as close to the ancient vent as possible. The distance was not great, however, and dragging Lanny all the way to his final resting place seemed to require no more exertion than to heave him into the SUV and wrestle him out again.

Like a banked furnace, the land now returned the stored heat of the day, but at last a faint breeze came down out of the stars.

En route, the sloping yard and the swath of tall grass and knee-high brush beyond proved longer than he had imagined it would be from

the foot of the porch steps. His arms began to ache, his shoulders, his neck.

The hook wounds, which had not recently bothered him, began to throb with new heat.

Somewhere along the way, he realized that he was crying. This scared him. He needed to remain tough.

He understood the source of the tears. The nearer that he drew to the lava pipe, the less Billy was able to regard his burden as an incriminating cadaver. Neither anointed nor eulogized, this was Lanny Olsen, the son of the good woman who had opened her heart and her home to an emotionally devastated fourteen-year-old boy.

Now in the starlight, to Billy's dark-adapted eyes, the knob of rock embracing the lava pipe looked increasingly like a skull.

No matter what lay ahead, whether a mountain of skulls or a vast plain of them, he could not go back, and he certainly could not bring Lanny to life again, for he was only Billy Wiles, a good bartender and a failed writer. There were no miracles in him, only a stubborn hope, and a capacity for blind perseverance.

So in the starlight and the hot breeze, he came to the place of the skull. There, he didn't delay, not even to catch his breath, but pushed the wrapped cadaver into the hole.

He lay against the redwood frame, peering into the bottomless blackness, listening to the long

descent of the body, the only way he could bear witness.

When silence came, he closed his eyes against the dark below and said, "It is finished."

Of course only this task was finished, and others lay ahead of him, perhaps some as bad, though surely none worse.

He had left the flashlight and the power screwdriver on the ground beside the lava pipe. He slid the redwood lid into place, fished the steel screws out of his pockets, and secured the cover.

Sweat had washed the last tears from his face by the time that he returned to the house.

Behind the garage, he left the screwdriver and the flashlight in the Explorer. The latex gloves were torn. He stripped them off, stuffed them into the SUV's litter bag, and drew on a fresh pair.

He returned to the house to inspect it from top to bottom. He dared leave nothing behind to indicate that either he or a dead body had been there.

In the kitchen, he could not decide what to do about the rum, cola, sliced lime, and other items on the table. He gave himself time to think about them.

Intending to start upstairs, in the master bedroom, he followed the rose-flowered runner along the hallway to the front of the house. As he approached the foyer, he grew aware of an unexpected brightness to his right, beyond the living-room archway.

The revolver in his hand suddenly became less a burdensome weight than an essential tool.

On his first pass through the house, on his way upstairs to see if Lanny's body remained in the bedroom armchair, Billy had switched on the overhead fixture in the living room, but only that. Now every lamp was aglow.

Sitting on a sofa, facing the archway, a testament to unreason and the durability of thrift-shop clothes, sat Ralph Cottle.

# 51

Ralph Cottle had incredibly shed his plastic shroud, improbably ascended from thousands of feet beneath the valley floor, impossibly let himself into the Olsen house, just forty minutes after whistling down the lava pipe, and all while remaining dead and a registered skeptic.

So disorienting was the sight of Cottle that for an instant Billy believed the man had to be alive, that somehow he had *never* been dead, but in the *next* instant he realized that the first body he had dropped into the volcanic vent had not been Cottle, that the filling of the corpse burrito had been replaced.

Billy heard himself say "Who?" by which he meant to ask who could have been in the tarp, and he began to turn toward the hallway behind him, intending to shoot anyone there, no questions asked.

A lead-shot sap, or something rather like it,

expertly rapped him at precisely the right point above the back of the neck, at the base of the skull, inducing less pain than color. Brilliant but brief electric-blue and magma-red coruscations fanned through his head and dazzled on the backs of his descending eyelids.

He never felt the floor come up to meet him. For what seemed like hours, he dropped in free fall through a lightless lava pipe, wondering how the dead amused themselves in the cold heart of an extinguished volcano.

The darkness seemed to want him more than the light, for he woke in fits and starts, repeatedly plucked back into the depths just as he floated to the surface of consciousness.

Twice, a demanding voice spoke to him, or twice that he heard. Both times he understood it, but only the second time was he able to respond.

Even dazed and confused, Billy warned himself to listen to the voice, to remember the pitch and the timbre, so he could identify it later. Identification would be difficult because it didn't sound much like a human voice; rough, strange, distorted, it insistently posed a question.

*"Are you prepared for your second wound?"*

Following the repetition, Billy discovered that he was able to answer: "No."

Finding his voice, worried that it sounded so wheezy, he also found the power to open his eyes.

Although his vision was blurred and clearing too slowly, he could see the man in the ski mask and dark clothes standing over him. The freak's hands were clad in supple black leather, and he needed both to hold a futuristic handgun.

"No," Billy said again.

He lay on his back, half on the rose-flowered runner, half on the dark wood floor, his right arm across his chest, his left flung out to his side, the revolver in neither hand.

As the last of the blur washed out of his vision, Billy saw that the handgun did not, after all, provide proof of a time traveler or of an extra-terrestrial visitor. It was just one of those portable nail guns not limited to the length of a compressor hose.

His left hand lay palm-up on the floor, and the man in the mask nailed it to the hardwood.

# PART THREE

# All You Have is How You Live

# 52

Pain and fear muddle reason, fog the mind.

Punctured flesh punched a scream from Billy. A paralytic haze of terror slowed his thoughts as he realized he was pinned to the floor, immobilized in the presence of the freak.

Pain can be endured and defeated only if it is embraced. Denied or feared, it grows in perception if not in reality.

The best response to terror is righteous anger, confidence in ultimate justice, a refusal to be intimidated.

Those thoughts didn't march now in orderly fashion through his mind. They were truths held in his adapted unconscious, based on hard experience, and he acted on them as if they were instincts born in blood and bone.

When he'd fallen, he dropped the revolver. The freak didn't appear to have it. The weapon might be within reach.

Billy rolled his head, searching the hallway. With his free hand, he felt the floor along his right side.

The freak threw something in Billy's face.

He flinched, expecting more pain. Just a photograph.

He couldn't see the image. He shook his head to cast the photo off his face.

The picture flipped onto his chest, where suddenly he thought the freak would spike it.

No. Carrying the nail gun, the killer walked away along the hall, toward the kitchen. One nail well placed. His work here was done.

Get an image of him. Freeze it in memory. Approximate height, weight. Big in the shoulders or not? Wide or narrow in the hips? Anything distinctive in the walk, graceful or not?

Pain, fear, swimming vision, but most of all the extreme angle of view—Billy flat on his back; the killer on his feet—defeated an attempt to build a physical profile of the man in the few seconds that he was in sight.

The freak disappeared into the kitchen. He moved around out there, making noise. Looking for something. Doing something.

Billy spotted the crisp shine of machined steel on the dark hardwood floor of the foyer—the revolver. The weapon lay behind him and beyond his reach.

Having been to the place of the skull, having

consigned Lanny to the lava pipe, Billy had exhausted his capacity for dread, or thought that he had until he realized that he must test the nail to see how securely it fixed him to the floor. He was loath to move his hand.

The pain was constant but tolerable, bad but not as terrible as he might have imagined. Trying to move the hand, however, trying to pry loose the spike, would be like chewing taffy with an abscessed tooth.

He wasn't only loath to move his hand, but also to look at it. Although he knew the image conjured in his mind had to be worse than the reality, his stomach clenched as he turned his head and focused on his wound.

Except for an excess of fingers, the white latex surgical glove made his hand look like Mickey Mouse's hand, like the cartoon hands taped to the walls and pointing the way to the chair where Lanny had been posed with one of his mother's books. The cuff of the glove even had a little roll to it.

A spidery crawling at his wrist proved to be a trickling thread of blood, which robbed the moment of even dark comedy.

He expected the bleeding to be much worse than this. The nail obstructed flow. When he extracted it . . .

Holding his breath, Billy listened. No noise in the kitchen. Apparently the killer had gone.

He didn't want the freak to hear him scream again, didn't want to give him that satisfaction.

The nail. The head had not been driven flat to the flesh. About three-quarters of an inch of shank separated the nailhead from his palm. He could see the gripper marks in the steel.

He had no way of knowing the length of the nail. Judging by its diameter, he estimated that it measured at least three inches from head to point.

Subtracting both the portion that stood above his palm and the portion that passed through it, as much as an inch and a half might be embedded in the floor. After it penetrated the surface hardwood and the subflooring, little of the nail would remain to grip a joist.

If it was *four* inches long, however, it might be securely wedged in a joist. Getting loose would be one inch nastier.

Houses were well put together in the days when this one had been built. Either two-by-fours or two-by-sixes, most likely set twelve inches center-to-center, supported the subfloor.

Nevertheless, his odds were good. In every fourteen inches of floor width, only four inches were underlaid by joists.

Hammer ten nails into the floor at random, and three would find joists. The other seven would penetrate the empty spaces between timbers.

When he tried to cup his left hand to test its

flexibility, he throttled an involuntary howl of pain into a snarl. He couldn't choke it off entirely.

No laughter came from the kitchen, supporting his suspicion that the freak had gone.

Suddenly Billy wondered if, before leaving, the killer had dialed 911.

# 53

As still and attentive as only a corpse can be, Ralph Cottle sat sentinel on the sofa.

The killer had crossed the dead man's right leg over his left and had arranged his hands in his lap to give him a casual posture. He seemed to be waiting patiently for his host to appear with a tray of cocktails—or for Sergeants Napolitino and Sobieski.

Although Cottle had not been mutilated or tricked up with props, Billy thought of the macabre mannequins arranged with such care in Steve Zillis's house.

Zillis was tending bar. Billy had seen his car there earlier, when he had stopped across the highway from the tavern to watch the setting sun blaze in the giant mural.

Cottle later. Zillis later. Now the nail.

Carefully, Billy turned on his left side to face the pierced hand.

With the thumb and forefinger of his right hand, he gripped the head of the nail. He tried gently to wiggle it back and forth, hoping to detect some play in it, but the nail felt rigid, deeply seated.

If the head had been small, he might have tried to slide his hand up the shank and pull it loose, leaving the nail in the floor.

The head was broad. Even if he could have tolerated the pain of twisting it backward through his hand, he would have done unthinkable damage in the process.

When he worked the nail more forcefully, pain tried to make a child of him. He ground the pain between his teeth, ground it so hard that his molars creaked in his jaws.

The nail did not creak in the wood, however, and it seemed that he would lose his teeth before extracting that spike. Then it moved.

Between his pinched thumb and finger, the nail loosened, not much but perceptibly. As it moved in the wood of the floor, it moved also in the flesh of his hand.

Pain was a light. Like chain lightning, it flared within him, flashed and flared.

He felt the shank grinding against bone. If the nail had cracked or chipped a bone, he would need medical attention sooner than later.

Although air-conditioned, the house had not previously seemed cold. Now sweat seemed to turn to ice on his skin.

Billy worked the nail, and the light of pain inside him grew brighter, brighter, until he thought that he must be translucent now, that the light would be visible, shining forth from him, if anyone but Cottle were there to see.

Although the odds were against a random nail finding a joist, this one had pierced not merely the flooring and the subflooring but also hard timber. The first grim truth of desperation roulette: You play the red, and the black comes up.

The nail came loose, and in a rush of triumph and rage, Billy almost threw it away from him, into the living room. Had he done so, he would have had to go find it because his blood was on the shank.

He put it on the floor beside the hole that it had made.

The blaze of pain darkened to throbbing embers, and he found that he could get to his feet.

His left hand bled from the entry and exit points, but not in a gush. He had been pierced, after all, not drilled, and the wound was not wide.

Cupping his right hand under his left to avoid dripping blood on the hallway runner and the flanking wood floor, he hurried into the kitchen.

The killer had left the back door open. He wasn't on the porch, probably not in the yard, either.

At the sink, Billy cranked a faucet and held his left hand under the spout until it grew half numb from the cold water.

Soon the stream of blood diminished to an ooze. Pulling paper towels off a dispenser, he wound several layers around his hand.

He stepped onto the back porch. He held his breath, listening not for the killer but for approaching sirens.

After a minute, he decided there had not been a 911 call this time. The freak, the *performer,* prided himself on his cleverness; he would not repeat a trick.

Billy returned to the front of the house. He saw the photograph, which the killer had thrown in his face and which he had forgotten, and he plucked it off the hallway floor.

She was a pretty redhead. Facing the camera. Terrified.

She would have had a nice smile.

He had never seen her before. That didn't matter. She was somebody's daughter. Somewhere people loved her.

*Waste the bitch.*

Those words, echoing in memory, nearly dropped Billy to his knees.

For twenty years, his emotions had not merely been restrained. Some of them had been denied. He had allowed himself to feel only what seemed safe to feel.

He had permitted himself anger only in moderation, and he had not indulged hatred whatsoever. He had been afraid that by admitting to one

drop of hatred, he might unleash furious torrents that would destroy him.

Restraint in the face of evil, however, was no virtue, and to hate this homicidal freak was no sin. This was a righteous passion, more vehement than abhorrence, brighter even than the pain that had seemed to make of him an incandescent lamp.

He picked up the revolver. Leaving Cottle to his own devices in the living room, Billy climbed the stairs, wondering if when he returned he would find the dead man still on the sofa.

# 54

In Lanny's bathroom medicine cabinet, Billy found alcohol, an unopened package of liquid bandage, and an array of pharmacy bottles with caps that all warned CAUTION! NOT CHILD RESISTANT.

The nail, having been clean, had not itself been an agent of infection. But it might have carried bacteria from the surface of the skin into the wound.

Billy poured alcohol in his cupped left hand, hoping it would seep into the puncture wound. After a moment, the stinging began.

Because he had been careful not to flex his hand more than necessary, the bleeding had already nearly stopped. The alcohol did not restart it.

This was imperfect sterilization. He had neither the time nor the resources to do a better job.

He painted liquid bandage on both the entrance

and exit wounds. This would help prevent filth from working into the puncture.

More important, the liquid bandage—which dried into a flexible rubbery seal—should inhibit further bleeding.

The plethora of pharmacy bottles each contained a few tablets or capsules. Evidently Lanny had been a bad patient who never quite finished a course of medication, but always reserved a portion with which to treat himself in the future.

Billy found two prescriptions for an antibiotic—Cipro, 500 mg. One bottle contained three tablets, the other five.

He combined all eight into one bottle. He peeled the label off and threw it in the waste can.

More than infection, he worried about inflammation. If his hand swelled and stiffened, he would be at a disadvantage in whatever confrontation might be coming.

Among the medications, he discovered Vicodin. It would not prevent inflammation but would relieve pain if that grew worse. Four tablets remained, and he added those to the Cipro.

Keeping time with his pulse, an ache throbbed in his wounded hand. And when he looked again at the photograph of the redhead, pain of a different character, emotional rather than physical, swelled too.

Pain is a gift. Humanity, without pain, would

know neither fear nor pity. Without fear, there could be no humility, and every man would be a monster. The recognition of pain and fear in others gives rise in us to pity, and in our pity is our humanity, our redemption.

In the redhead's eyes, pure terror. In her face, the wretched recognition of her fate.

He had not been able to save her. But if the freak had played the game according to his rules, she had not been tortured.

As Billy's attention shifted from her face to the room behind her, he recognized his bedroom. She had been held captive in Billy's house. She had been killed there.

# 55

Sitting on the edge of the tub in Lanny's bathroom, holding the photo of the redhead, Billy worked out the chronology of the murder.

The psychopath had called—when?—perhaps around twelve-thirty in the afternoon, earlier this same day, after the sergeants had left and after Cottle had been wrapped for disposal. For Billy, he had played the recording that offered two choices: the redhead tortured to death; the redhead murdered with a single shot or thrust.

Even at that time, the killer already held her captive. Almost surely he let her listen to the tape as he played it over the phone.

At one o'clock, Billy had left for Napa. Thereafter, the killer brought the woman into the house, took this snapshot, and killed her cleanly.

When the freak found Ralph Cottle wrapped in the tarp and stowed behind the sofa, his spirit

of fun had been engaged. He swapped them, the young woman for the stewbum.

Billy had unknowingly dropped the redhead down the lava pipe, thereby denying her family the little solace that might come from having a body to bury.

This switch of cadavers felt like Zillis: this adolescent humor, the casualness with which he could sometimes deliver a mean joke.

Steve had not gone to work until six o'clock. He would have been free to play.

But now the creep *was* at the tavern. He could not have propped Cottle on the sofa and fired the nail gun.

Billy glanced at his wristwatch. Eleven-forty-one.

He made himself look at the redhead again because he thought he was going to bundle the photo with other evidence and drop it down the volcanic vent. He wanted to remember her, felt obliged to fix her face in memory forever.

When the freak had played the recorded message over the phone, if this woman had been there, bound and gagged and listening, perhaps she had also heard Billy's reply: *Waste the bitch.*

Those words had spared her torture, but now they tortured Billy.

He could not throw away her photo. Keeping the snapshot was not a prudent act; it was

dangerous. Yet he folded it, being careful not to crease her face, and tucked it in his wallet.

Warily, he went out to the Explorer. He thought he would know if the freak was still nearby, watching. The night felt safe, and clean.

He put the punctured latex glove in the trash bag, and pulled on a fresh one. He unplugged his cell phone and took it with him.

In the house again, he went through all the rooms from top to bottom, gathering all evidence into a plastic garbage bag, including the photo of Giselle Winslow (which he would not keep), the cartoon hands, the nail. . . .

Finished, he put the bag by the back door.

He got a clean glass. From the jug on the table, he poured a few ounces of warm Coke.

With exercise, the ache in his hand had grown worse. He took one tablet of Cipro, one of Vicodin.

He decided to eradicate all evidence of his friend's drinking binge. The house should offer nothing unusual for the police to contemplate.

When Lanny went missing long enough, they would come here to knock, to look through the windows. They would come inside. If they saw that he'd been pouring down rum, they might infer depression and the possibility of suicide.

The sooner they leaped to dire conclusions, the sooner they would search the farther reaches of the property. The longer that the trampled brush had to recover, the less likely they would ever

focus on the securely covered lava pipe.

When all was neat and when the garbage bag of evidence was tied shut, when only Ralph Cottle remained to be attended, Billy used his cell phone to call the backbar number at the tavern.

Jackie O'Hara answered. "Tavern."

"How're the pigs with human brains?" Billy asked.

"They drink at some other joint."

"Because the tavern is a family bar."

"That's right. And always will be."

"Listen, Jackie—"

"I hate 'listen, Jackie.' It always means I'm going to be screwed."

"I'm going to have to take off tomorrow, too."

"I'm screwed."

"No, you're just melodramatic."

"You don't sound that sick."

"It's not a head cold. It's a stomach thing."

"Hold the phone to your gut, let me listen."

"Suddenly you're a hardass."

"It doesn't look right, the owner working the taps too much."

"The place is so busy, Steve can't handle a midnight crowd by himself?"

"Steve isn't here, just me."

Billy's hand tightened on the cell phone. "I drove past earlier. His car was parked out front."

"It's a day off for Steve, remember?"

Billy had forgotten.

"When I couldn't get a temp to fill your shift, Steve came in from three to nine to save my ass. What're you doing out driving around when you're sick?"

"I was going to a doctor's appointment. Steve could only give you six hours?"

"He had stuff to do before and after."

Like kill a redhead before, nail Billy's hand to a floor after.

"What did the doctor say?" Jackie asked.

"It's a virus."

"That's what they always say when they don't know what the hell it really is."

"No, I think it's really a forty-eight-hour virus."

"As if a virus knows from forty-eight hours," Jackie said. "You go in with a third eye growing out of your forehead, they'll say it's a virus."

"Sorry about this, Jackie."

"I'll survive. It's just the tavern business, after all. It's not war."

Pressing END to terminate the call, Billy Wiles felt very much at war.

On a kitchen counter lay Lanny Olsen's wallet, car keys, pocket change, cell phone, and 9-mm service pistol, where they had been since the previous night.

Billy took the wallet. When he left, he would also take the cell phone, the pistol, and the Wilson Combat holster.

From the items in the bread drawer, he selected

half a loaf of whole wheat in a tie-top plastic bag.

Outside, standing at the eastern end of the porch, he threw the slices of bread onto the lawn. The morning birds would feast.

In the house once more, he lined the empty plastic bag with a dishtowel.

A gun case with glass doors stood in the study. In drawers under the doors, Lanny kept boxes of ammunition, four-inch aerosol cans of chemical Mace, and a spare police utility belt.

On the belt were pouches for backup magazines, a Mace holder, a Taser sleeve, a handcuff case, a key holder, a pen holder, and a holster. It was all ready to go.

From the belt, Billy removed a loaded magazine. He also took the handcuffs, a can of Mace, and the Taser. He put those items in the bread bag.

# 56

Quick winged presences, perhaps bats feeding on moths in the first hour of Thursday morning, swooped low through the yard, past Billy, and climbed. When he followed the sound of what he could not see, his gaze rose to the thinnest silver shaving of a new moon.

Although it must have been there earlier, making its way west, he had not noticed this fragile crescent until now. Not surprising. Since night-fall, he'd had little time for the sky, his attention grimly earthbound.

Ralph Cottle, limbs stiffened at inconvenient angles by rigor mortis, wrapped in a blanket because no plastic drop cloth could be found, held in a bundle by Lanny's entire collection of neck-ties—three—did not drag easily across the sloped yard to the brush line.

Cottle had said that he was nobody's hero. And certainly he had died a coward's death.

He had wanted to live even his shabby existence because—*What else is there?*—he could not imagine that something better might be his to strive for, or to accept.

In the moment when the blade slipped between his ribs and stopped his heart, he would have realized that while life could be evaded, death could not.

Billy felt a certain solemn sympathy for even this man, whose despair had been deeper than Billy's and whose resources had been shallower.

And so when the brush and brambles snared the soft blanket and made dragging the body too difficult, he picked it up and hauled it across his shoulder, without revulsion or complaint. Under the burden, he staggered but didn't collapse.

He had returned minutes earlier to remove, once again, the lid from the redwood frame. The open vent waited.

Cottle had said there wasn't one world but a billion, that his was different from Billy's. Whether that had been true or not, here their worlds became one.

The bundled body dropped. And hit. And tumbled. And dropped. Into the dark, the vacant into the vacant.

When silence endured, suggesting that the skeptic had reached his deep rest with the good son and the unknown woman, Billy shoved the cover into place, used his flashlight to be sure the

holes were aligned, and screwed it down once more.

He hoped never to see this place again. He suspected, however, that he would have no choice but to return.

Driving away from the Olsen house, he did not know where to go. Eventually he must confront Steve Zillis, but not at once, not yet. First he needed to prepare himself.

In another age, men on the eve of battle had gone to churches to prepare themselves spiritually, intellectually, emotionally. To incense, to candlelight, to the humility that the shadow of the redeemer pressed upon them.

In those days, every church had been open all day and night, offering unconditional sanctuary.

Times had changed. Now some churches might remain open around the clock, but many operated according to posted hours and locked their doors long before midnight.

Some withheld perpetual sanctuary because of the costs of heat and electricity. Budgets trump mission.

Others were plagued by vandals with cans of spray paint and by the faithless who, in a mocking spirit, came to copulate and leave their condoms.

In previous ages of rampant hatred, such intolerance had been met with resolve, with teaching, and with the cultivation of remorse. Now the clerical consensus was that locks and

alarms worked better than the former, softer remedies.

Rather than travel from church to church, trying their doors and finding only sanctuary by prior appointment, Billy went where most modern men in need of a haven for contemplation were drawn in post-midnight hours: to a truck stop.

Because no interstate highways crossed the county, the available facility, along State Highway 29, was modest by the standards of the Little America chain that operated truck stops the size of small towns. But it featured banks of fuel pumps illuminated to rival daylight, a convenience store, free showers, Internet access, and a 24/7 diner that offered fried everything and coffee that would stand your hair on end.

Billy didn't want the coffee or cholesterol. He sought only the bustle of rational commerce to balance the irrationality with which he'd been dealing, and a place so public that he would not be at risk of attack.

He parked in a space outside the diner, under a lamppost of such wattage he could read by the light that fell through the windshield.

From the glove box, he took foil packets of moist towelettes. He used them to scrub his hands.

They had been invented to mop up after a Big Mac and fries in the car, not to sterilize the hands after disposing of corpses. But Billy wasn't in a position—or of a mind—to be fussy.

His left hand, nailed and unpaled, felt hot and slightly stiff. He flexed it slowly, gingerly.

Because of the Vicodin, he felt no pain. That might not be good. A growing problem with the hand, not sensed, might manifest in a sudden weakness of grip at the very moment in the evolving crisis when strength was needed.

With warm Pepsi, he washed down two more Anacin, which had some effect as an anti-inflammatory. Motrin would have been better, but what he had was Anacin.

The right dose of caffeine could compensate somewhat for too little sleep, but too much might fray the nerves and compel him to rash action. He took another No-Doz anyway.

Busy hours had passed since he had eaten the Hershey's and the Planters bars. He ate another of each.

While he ate, he considered Steve Zillis, his prime suspect. His only suspect.

The evidence against Zillis seemed overwhelming. Yet it was all circumstantial.

That did not mean the case was unsound. Half or more of the convictions obtained in criminal courts were based on convincing webs of circumstantial evidence, and far less than one percent of them were miscarriages of justice.

Murderers did not obligingly leave direct evidence at the scenes of their crimes. Especially in this age of DNA comparison, any felon with a

TV could catch the *CSI* shows and educate himself in the simple steps that he must take to avoid self-incrimination.

Everything from antibiotics to zydeco had its downside, however, and Billy knew too well the dangers of circumstantial evidence.

He reminded himself that the problem had not been the evidence. The problem had been John Palmer, now the sheriff, then an ambitious young lieutenant bucking for a promotion to captain.

The night that Billy had made an orphan of himself, the truth had been horrific but clear and easily determined.

# 57

From a dream erotic, fourteen-year-old Billy Wiles is awakened by raised voices, angry shouting.

At first he is confused. He seems to have rolled out of a fine dream into another that is less pleasing.

He pulls one pillow over his head and buries his face in a second, trying to press himself back into the silken fantasy.

Reality intrudes. Reality *insists.*

The voices are those of his mother and father, rising from downstairs, so loud that the intervening floor hardly muffles them.

Our myths are rich with enchanters and enchantresses: sea nymphs that sing sailors onto rocks, Circe turning men into swine, pipers playing children to their doom. They are metaphors for the sinister secret urge to self-destruction that has been with us since the first bite of the first apple.

Billy is his own piper, allowing himself to be drawn out of bed by the dissonant voices of his parents.

Arguments are not common in this house, but neither are they rare. Usually disagreements remain quiet, intense, and brief. If bitterness lingers, it is expressed in sullen silences that in time heal, or seem to.

Billy does not think of his parents as unhappy in marriage. They love each other. He knows they do.

Barefoot, barechested, in pajama bottoms, waking as he walks, Billy Wiles follows the hallway, descends the stairs. . . .

He does not doubt that his parents love him. In their way. His father expresses a stern affection. His mother oscillates between benign neglect and raptures of maternal love that are as genuine as they are overdone.

The nature of his mother's and father's frustrations with each other has always remained mysterious to Billy and seemed to be of no consequence. Until now.

By the time that he reaches the dining room, within sight of the kitchen door, Billy is immersed against his will—or is he?—in the cold truths and secret selves of those whom he thought he knew best in the world.

He has never imagined that his father could contain such fierce anger as this. Not just the

savage volume of the voice but also the lacerating tone and the viciousness of the language reveal a long-simmering resentment boiled down to a black tar that provides the ideal fuel for anger.

His father accuses his mother of sexual betrayal, of serial adultery. He calls her a whore, calls her worse, graduating from anger to rage.

In the dining room, where Billy is immobilized by revelation, his mind reels at the accusations hurled at his mother. His parents have seemed to him to be asexual, attractive but indifferent to such desires.

If he had ever wondered about his conception, he would have attributed it to marital duty and to a desire for family rather than to passion.

More shocking than the accusations are his mother's admission of their truth—and her counter-charges, which reveal his father to be both a man and also something less than a man. In language more withering than what is directed at her, she scorns her husband, and mocks him.

Her mockery puts the pedal to his rage and drives him into fury. The slap of flesh on flesh suggests hand to face with force.

She cries out in pain but at once says, "You don't scare me, you can't scare me!"

Things shatter, crack, clatter, ricochet—and then comes a more terrible sound, a brutal bludgeoning *ferociousness* of sound.

She screams in pain, in terror.

Without memory of leaving the dining room, Billy finds himself in the kitchen, shouting at his father to stop, but his father does not appear to hear him or even to recognize his presence.

His father is enthralled by, hypnotized by, *possessed* by the hideous power of the bludgeon that he wields. It is a long-handled lug wrench.

On the floor, Billy's devastated mother hitches along like a broken bug, no longer able to scream, making tortured noises.

Billy sees other weapons lying on the kitchen island. A hammer. A butcher knife. A revolver.

His father appears to have arranged these murderous instruments to intimidate his mother.

She must not have been intimidated, must have thought that he was a coward, fatuous and ineffectual. A coward he surely is, taking a lug wrench to a defenseless woman, but she has badly misjudged his capacity for evil.

Seizing the revolver, gripping it with both hands, Billy shouts at his father to stop, for God's sake stop, and when his warning goes unheeded, he fires a shot into the ceiling.

The unexpected recoil knocks back through his shoulders, and he staggers in surprise.

His father turns to Billy but not in a spirit of submission. The lug wrench is an avatar of darkness that controls the man at least as much as he controls it.

"Whose seed are you?" his father asks. "Whose

son have I been feeding all these years, whose little bastard?"

Impossibly, the terror escalates, and when he understands that he must kill or be killed, Billy squeezes the trigger once, squeezes twice, a third time, his arms jumping with the recoil.

Two misses and a chest wound.

His father is jolted, stumbles, falls backward as the bullet pins a boutonniere of blood to his breast.

Dropped, the lug wrench rings against—and cracks—the tile floor, and after it there is no more shouting, no more angry words, just Billy's breathing and his mother's muted expressions of misery.

And then she says, "Daddy?" Her voice is slurred, and cracked with pain. "Daddy Tom?"

Her father, a career Marine, had been killed in action when she was ten. Daddy Tom was her stepfather.

"Help me." Her voice grows thicker, distressingly changed. "Help me, Daddy Tom."

Daddy Tom, a juiceless man with hair the color of dust, has eyes the yellow-brown of sandstone. His lips are perpetually parched, and his atrophied laugh rasps any listener's nerves.

Only in the most extreme circumstances would anyone ask Daddy Tom for help, and no one would expect to receive it.

"Help me, Daddy Tom."

Besides, the old man lives in Massachusetts, a continent away from Napa County.

The urgency of the situation penetrates Billy's immobilizing shock, and terrified compassion now moves him toward his mother.

She seems to be paralyzed, the little finger on her right hand twitching, twitching, but nothing else moving from the neck down.

Like broken pottery poorly repaired, the shape of her skull and the planes of her face are wrong, all wrong.

Her one open eye, now her only eye, focuses on Billy, and she says, "Daddy Tom."

She does not recognize her son, her only child, and thinks that he is the old man from Massachusetts.

"Please," she says, her voice cracking with pain.

The broken face suggests irreparable brain damage of an extent that wrings from Billy a choking sob.

Her one-eyed gaze travels from his face to the gun in his hand. "Please, Daddy Tom. *Please.*"

He is only fourteen, a mere boy, so recently a child, and there are choices he should not be asked to make.

*"Please."*

This is a choice to humble any grown man, and he cannot choose, will not choose. But, oh, her pain. Her fear. Her *anguish.*

With a thickening tongue, she pleads, "Oh, Jesus, oh, Jesus, where is me? Who's you? Who's in here crawling, who is that? Who is you in here, scares me? *Scares me!*"

Sometimes the heart makes decisions that the mind cannot, and although we know that the heart is deceitful above all things, we also know that at rare moments of stress and profound loss it can be purged pure by suffering.

In the years to come, he will never know if trusting his heart at this moment is the right choice. But he does as it tells him.

"I love you," he says, and shoots his mother dead.

Lieutenant John Palmer is the first officer on the scene.

What initially appears to be the bold entrance of dependable authority will later seem, to Billy, like the eager rush of a vulture to carrion.

Waiting for the police, Billy has been unable to move out of the kitchen. He cannot bear to leave his mother alone.

He feels that she hasn't fully departed, that her spirit lingers and takes comfort from his presence. Or perhaps he feels nothing of the sort and only wishes this to be true.

Although he cannot look at her anymore, at what she has become, he stays nearby, eyes averted.

When Lieutenant Palmer enters, when Billy is no longer alone and no longer needs to be strong, his composure slips. Tremors nearly shake the boy to his knees.

Lieutenant Palmer asks, "What happened here, son?"

With these two deaths, Billy is no one's child, and he feels his isolation in his bones, bleakness at the core, fear of the future.

When he hears the word *son,* therefore, it seems to be more than a mere word, seems to be a hand extended, hope offered.

Billy moves toward John Palmer.

Because the lieutenant is calculating or only because he is human, after all, he opens his arms.

Shaking, Billy leans into those arms, and John Palmer holds him close. "Son? What happened here?"

"He beat her. I shot him. He beat her with the wrench."

"You shot him?"

"He beat her with the lug wrench. I shot him. I shot her."

Another man might allow for the emotional turmoil of this young witness, but the lieutenant's primary consideration is that he has not yet made captain. He is an ambitious man. And impatient.

Two years previous, a seventeen-year-old boy in Los Angeles County, far south of Napa, had shot his parents to death. He pleaded innocent by reason of long-term sexual abuse.

That trial, having concluded only two weeks before this pivotal night in Billy Wiles's life, had resulted in conviction. The pundits predicted the

boy would go free, but the detective in charge of the case had been diligent, accumulating a convincing mass of evidence, catching the perpetrator in lie after lie.

For the past two weeks, that indefatigable detective had been a media hero. He received lots of face time on TV. His name was better known than that of the mayor of Los Angeles.

With Billy's admission, John Palmer does not see an opportunity to pursue the truth but instead sees an *opportunity.*

"Who did you shoot, son? Him or her?"

"I s-shot him. I shot her. He beat her so bad with the wrench, I had to s-shoot them both."

As other sirens swell in the distance, Lieutenant Palmer leads Billy out of the kitchen, into the living room. He directs the boy to sit on the sofa.

His question no longer is *What happened here, son?* His question now is, "What have you done, boy? What have you done?"

For too long, young Billy Wiles does not hear the difference.

Thus begins sixty hours of hell.

At fourteen, he cannot be made to stand trial as an adult. With the death penalty and life imprisonment off the table, the pressures of interrogation should be less than with an adult offender.

John Palmer, however, is determined to break Billy, to wring from him a confession that he himself beat his mother with the lug wrench, shot

his father when his father tried to protect her, then finished her, too, with a bullet.

Because the punishment for juvenile offenders is so much less severe than for adults, the system sometimes guards their rights less assiduously than it should. For one thing, if the suspect does not know he should demand an attorney, he might not be informed of that right on as timely a basis as would be ideal.

If the suspect's lack of resources requires a public defender, there is always the chance that the one assigned will be feckless. Or foolish. Or badly hungover.

Not every lawyer is as noble as those who champion the oppressed in TV dramas, just as the oppressed themselves are seldom as noble in real life.

An experienced officer like John Palmer, with the cooperation of selected superiors, guided by reckless ambition and willing to put his career at risk, has a sleeve full of tricks to keep a suspect away from legal counsel and available for unrestricted interrogation in the hours immediately after taking him into custody.

One of the most effective of these ploys is to make Billy into a "busboy." A public defender arrives at the holding facility in Napa only to discover that because of limited cell space or for other bogus reasons, his client has been moved to the Calistoga substation. On arriving in

Calistoga, he hears that a regrettable mistake has been made: The boy has actually been taken to St. Helena. In St. Helena, they send the attorney chasing back to Napa.

Furthermore, while transporting a suspect, a vehicle sometimes has mechanical problems. An hour's drive becomes three hours or four depending on the required repairs.

During these two and a half days, Billy passes through a blur of drab offices, interrogation rooms, and cells. Always, his emotions are raw, and his fears are as constant as his meals are irregular, but the worst moments occur in the patrol car, on the road.

Billy rides in back, behind the security barrier. His hands are cuffed, and a chain shackles his cuffs to a ring bolt in the floor.

There is a driver who never has a thing to say. In spite of regulations forbidding this arrangement, John Palmer shares the backseat with his suspect.

The lieutenant is a big man, and his suspect is a fourteen-year-old boy. In these close quarters, the disparity in their sizes is of itself disturbing to Billy.

In addition, Palmer is an expert at intimidation. Ceaseless talk and questions are punctuated only by accusing silences. By calculated looks, by carefully chosen words, by ominous mood shifts, he wears on the spirit as effectively as a power sander wears on wood.

The touching is the worst.

Palmer sits closer some times than others. Occasionally he sits as close as a boy might want to sit to a girl, his left side pressed to Billy's right.

He ruffles Billy's hair with patently false affection. He rests one big hand on Billy's shoulder, now on his knee, now on his thigh.

"Killing them isn't a crime if you had a good reason, Billy. If your father molested you for years and your mother knew, no one could blame you."

"My father never touched me like that. Why do you keep saying he did?"

"I'm not saying, Billy. I'm asking. You've nothing to be ashamed about if he's been poking you since you were little. That makes you a *victim*, don't you see? And even if you liked it—"

"I wouldn't like it."

"Even if you did like it, you've no reason to be ashamed." The hand on the shoulder. "You're still a victim."

"I'm not. I wasn't. Don't say that."

"Some men, they do awful things to defenseless boys, and some of the boys get to like it." The hand on the thigh. "But that makes the boy no less innocent, Billy. The sweet boy is still innocent."

Billy almost wishes that Palmer would hit him. The touching, the gentle touching and the insinuation are worse than a blow because it seems that the fist might come anyway when the touching fails.

On more than one occasion, Billy nearly confesses just to escape the maddening rhythms of Lieutenant John Palmer's voice, to be free from the touching.

He begins to wonder why . . . After he put an end to his mother's suffering, why had he called the police instead of jamming the muzzle of the revolver in his mouth?

Billy is saved at last by the good work of the medical examiner and the CSI technicians, and by the second thoughts of other officers who have let Palmer whip the case as he wishes. The evidence indicts the father; none points to the son.

The only print on the revolver is one of Billy's, but one clear fingerprint and a partial palm on the long handle of the polished-steel wrench belong to Billy's father.

The killer swung the lug wrench with his left hand. Unlike his father, Billy is right-handed.

Billy's clothes were marked by a small amount of blood but not a liberal spattering. A back-spray of blood stippled the sleeves of his father's shirt.

Clawing, she had tried to fend off her husband. His blood and skin, not Billy's, were under her fingernails.

In time, two members of the department are forced to resign, and another is fired. When the smoke dissipates, Lieutenant John Palmer somehow remains standing without sear or singe.

Billy considers accusing the lieutenant, but fears testifying and, most of all, fears the consequences of not prevailing in court. Prudence suggests withdrawal.

Stay low, stay quiet, keep it simple, don't expect much, enjoy what you have. Move on.

Amazingly, moving on eventually means moving in with Pearl Olsen, the widow of one deputy and the mother of another.

She makes the offer to rescue Billy from the limbo of child-service custody, and in their first meeting, he knows instinctively that she will always be no more and no less than she *appears* to be. Although he is only fourteen, he has learned that harmony between reality and appearance may be more rare than any child imagines, and is a quality he may hope to foster in himself.

# 58

Parked in the bright lights of the truck stop, outside the diner, Billy Wiles ate Hershey's, ate Planters, and brooded about Steve Zillis.

The evidence against Zillis, while circumstantial, seemed to support suspicion far more than anything that John Palmer had used to justify targeting Billy.

Nevertheless, he worried that he might be about to move against an innocent man. The mannequins, the bondage pornography, and the general condition of Zillis's house proved he was a creep and perhaps even deranged, but none of it proved he had killed anyone.

Billy's experience at the hands of Palmer left him yearning for certainty.

Hoping to turn up one case-fortifying fact, even something as thin as the wisp of crescent moon above the diner, Billy picked up the paper that he had bought in Napa and had heretofore had

no time to read. The front-page story about Giselle Winslow's murder.

Crazily, he hoped that the cops had found a cherry stem tied in a knot near the corpse.

Instead, what leaped at him from the article, what *flew* at him as quick as a bat to a moth, was the fact that Winslow's left hand had been cut off. The freak had taken a souvenir, not a face this time, but a hand.

Lanny had not mentioned this. But when Lanny had driven into the tavern parking lot as Billy took the second note off the Explorer's windshield, Winslow's body had only recently been found. Not all of the details had yet been shared on the sheriff's-department hotline.

Inevitably, Billy remembered the note that had been taped to his refrigerator seventeen hours earlier and that he had secreted in his copy of *In Our Time*. The message warned him that "An associate of mine will come to see you at 11:00. Wait for him on the front porch."

In memory, he could see the last two lines of that note, which had been baffling at the time, but were less so now.

*You seem so angry. Have I not extended to you the hand of friendship? Yes, I have.*

Even on first reading, those lines had seemed to be mocking, taunting. Now they jeered him,

challenged him to accept that he was hopelessly outclassed.

Somewhere in his house, the severed hand awaited discovery by the police.

# 59

A man and woman, a trucker couple in jeans and T-shirts and baseball caps—his said PETERBILT; hers said ROAD GODDESS—came out of the diner. The man probed his incisors with a toothpick, while the woman yawned, rolled her shoulders, and stretched her arms.

From behind the wheel of the Explorer, Billy found himself staring at the woman's hands, thinking how small they were, how easily one of them could be hidden.

In the attic. Under a floorboard. Behind the furnace. In the back of a closet. In the crawlspace under one of the porches, front or back. Perhaps in the garage, in a workshop drawer. Preserved in formaldehyde or not.

If one victim's hand had been secreted on his property, why not a part of another victim, too? What had the freak harvested from the redhead, and where had he put it?

Billy was tempted to drive home at once, to search the house thoroughly from top to bottom. He might need the rest of the night and all of the morning to find these incriminating horrors.

And if he did not find them, would he spend the coming afternoon in the search, as well? How could he not?

Once the quest had begun, he would be compelled, obsessed to continue until he discovered the grisly grail.

According to his wristwatch, it was 1:36 A.M., Thursday morning. The pertinent midnight lay little more than twenty-two hours away.

*My last killing: midnight Thursday.*

Already Billy was functioning on caffeine and chocolate, Anacin and Vicodin. If he spent his day in a frantic search for body parts, if by twilight he had neither identified the freak nor gotten any rest, he would be physically, mentally, and emotionally exhausted; in that condition, he would not be a reliable guardian for Barbara.

He must not waste time searching for the hand.

Besides, as he read about it in the newspaper for the second time, he was reminded of something other than the note taped to his refrigerator. The mannequin with six hands.

With the fists at the ends of its arms, it had held steak knives that were rammed into its throat.

Its feet had been replaced with hands, the better

to grip the spear-point iron stave with which it abused itself.

A third pair of hands had been *severed* from a donor mannequin. They sprouted from the breasts of the six-handed specimen as if it were an obscene depiction of the Hindu goddess Kali.

Although the three other mannequins in that room had featured the usual number of hands, the one with six suggested Zillis might have a hand fetish.

In the photos on the covers of those pornographic videos, the women's hands had often been restrained. With handcuffs. With rope. With tightly cinched leather straps.

The fact that a hand had been harvested from Giselle Winslow seemed meaningful if not damning.

Billy was reaching. Stretching. He didn't have enough rope to fashion a legitimate noose for Steve Zillis.

*Have I not extended to you the hand of friendship? Yes, I have.*

Gross, juvenile humor. Billy could see Zillis smirking, could hear him saying those very words. He could hear them said in that cocky, jokey, performing-bartender voice.

Suddenly it seemed that so much of Zillis's act at the tavern involved his hands. He was unusually dexterous. He juggled the olives and other items. He knew card tricks, all sleight-of-hand.

He could "walk" a coin across his knuckles, make it disappear.

None of this helped Billy tie a better noose.

Soon it would be two o'clock. If he was going after Zillis, he preferred to do it under the cover of darkness.

The liquid bandage on the puncture wounds in his hand had been put to a thorough test. It had cracked at the edges, frayed.

He opened the bottle and painted another layer over the first, wondering if it was significant that the promised second wound had been a nail through his *hand.*

If he went after Zillis, he would first have a conversation with him. Nothing more. Nothing worse. Just a serious talk.

In case Zillis was the freak, the questions would have to be asked at the point of a gun.

Of course, if Zillis proved to be just a sick creep but not a killer, he would not be understanding; he would be pissed. He might want to press charges for forced entry, whatever.

The only way to keep him quiet might be to intimidate him. He wouldn't likely be intimidated unless Billy hurt him seriously enough to get his attention and unless he believed that he would be hurt even worse if he called the police.

Before he went after Zillis, Billy had to be sure that he had the capacity to assault an innocent man and brutalize him to keep him silent.

He flexed and opened his slightly stiff left hand. Flexed and opened.

Here was a choice not entirely forced upon him: He could put himself in a position where he might have to hurt and intimidate an innocent man—or delay, think, wait for events to unfold, and thereby possibly place Barbara in greater danger.

*The choice is yours.*

It always had been. It always would be. To act or not to act. To wait or to go. To close a door or open one. To retreat from life or to enter it.

He did not have hours or days to analyze the quandary. Anyway, given time, he would only get lost in the analysis.

He sought wisdom learned from hard experience and applicable to this situation, but he found none. The only wisdom is the wisdom of humility.

In the end, he could make his decision based on nothing more than the purity of his motive. And even the full truth of motive might not be known.

He started the engine. He drove away from the truck stop.

He couldn't find the moon, that thinnest palest sliver of a moon. It must have been at his back.

# 60

At 2:09 a.m., Billy parked on a quiet residential street, two and a half blocks from Steve Zillis's house.

The lower limbs of Indian laurels hung under the streetlights, and across the lamp-yellowed sidewalks, leaf shadows spilled like a treasure of black coins.

He walked unhurriedly, as if he were a lifelong insomniac who regularly went strolling in these dead hours.

The windows of the houses were dark, the porch lights off. No traffic passed him.

By now the earth had given back a lot of the stored heat from the day. The night was neither hot nor cool.

The twisted neck of the bread bag was looped around his belt, and the bag, lined with a dishtowel, hung at his left side. In it were the handcuffs, the small can of Mace, and the Taser.

Depending from his belt at his right hip: the Wilson Combat holster. The loaded pistol filled it.

He had pulled his T-shirt out of his jeans, to wear it loose. The T-shirt somewhat concealed the pistol. From a distance of more than a few feet, at night, no one would recognize the telltale outline of the weapon.

When he reached Zillis's place, he left the sidewalk for the driveway and then followed the wall of eucalyptus trees past the garage.

At the front, the house had been dark behind the drawn blinds; but lights shone softly at some rear windows. Zillis's bedroom, his bathroom.

Billy stood in the backyard, studying the property, alert to every nuance of the night. He let his eyes forget the streetlamps and adapt more completely to the darkness.

He tucked his T-shirt into his jeans once more, to make the holstered pistol accessible.

From a pocket he took a pair of latex gloves, slipped his hands into them.

The neighborhood was quiet. The houses were not far apart. He would need to be careful about noise when he got inside. Screams would be heard, as would gunfire not well muffled by a pillow.

He left the yard for the covered patio, on which stood a single aluminum chair. No table, no barbecue, no potted plants.

Through the panes in the back door, he could see the kitchen lighted only by two digital clocks,

one on the oven and one on the microwave.

He pulled the bread bag loose from his belt and withdrew from it the can of Mace. The dishtowel liner softened the sound of the shifting handcuffs. He twisted the neck of the bag and looped it securely around his belt again.

On his first visit, he had stolen a spare key from a kitchen drawer. He inserted the key cautiously, turned it slowly, concerned that the lock might be noisy and that sound might carry too well in the small house.

The door eased open. The hinges whispered with corrosion but did not squeak.

He stepped inside and shut the door behind him.

For a minute he did not move. His eyes were well accustomed to the dark, but he still needed to orient himself.

His heart raced. Maybe that was partly the caffeine tablets at work.

As he crossed the kitchen, the rubber soles of his Rockports squeaked slightly on the vinyl flooring. He winced but kept going.

The living room was carpeted. He took two silent steps into it before stopping again to orient himself.

Zillis's scorn for furniture was a blessing. There weren't many obstructions to worry about in the dark.

Billy heard faint voices. Alarmed, he listened.

He couldn't make out what they were saying.

Having expected to find Zillis alone, he considered retreating. But he had to know more.

A dim glow marked the entrance to the hallway that led off the living room to the two bedrooms and bath. The hall fixture was off, but soft light entered the far end from the open doors of the last two rooms.

Those rooms faced each other across the hall. As Billy recalled, the one on the left was the bathroom, Zillis's bedroom on the right.

Judging by pitch and timbre, not by content, he thought there were two voices, one male and one female.

He held the Mace in his right hand, thumb under the safeguard, squarely on the button trigger.

Instinct whispered that he should trade the Mace for the pistol. Not every instinct was more reliable than reason.

If he started by shooting Zillis, he had nowhere to go. He must first disable him, not wound him.

Moving along the hall, he passed the make-believe abattoir where the mannequins sat in bloodless mutilation.

The better he could hear them, the more the voices had a make-believe quality, too. They were actors sharing a bad performance. A vaguely tinny quality suggested they issued from the speakers of a cheap TV.

The woman suddenly cried out in pain, but sensuously, as if her pain were also her pleasure.

Billy had nearly reached the end of the hall when Steve Zillis exited the bathroom, to the left.

Barefoot, barechested, wearing pajama bottoms, he was scrubbing his teeth with a brush, hurrying to see what was on the television in the bedroom.

His eyes widened when he spotted Billy. He spoke around the toothbrush: "What the fuh—"

Billy Maced him.

Police Mace is highly effective up to a distance of twenty feet, although fifteen is ideal. Steve Zillis stood seven feet from Billy.

Mace in the mouth and in the nose will somewhat inhibit an attacker. You can stop him hard and fast only if you squirt him liberally in the eyes.

The stream doused both eyes, point-blank, and also hosed his nostrils.

Zillis dropped the toothbrush, covered his eyes with his hands, too late, and turned blindly away from Billy. He collided at once with the end wall of the hallway. Making a desperate wheezing sound, he bent over, retching, and spewed gobs of toothpaste foam as if he were a rabid dog.

The burning in his eyes was hellacious, his pupils open so wide that he could see only a fierce blurred brightness, not even the form of his assailant, not even a shadow. His throat also

burned with the chemical that had gone down by way of his nose, and his lungs tried to reject every tainted breath that he drew.

Billy went in low, grabbed the cuff of a pajama leg, and jerked the man's left foot out from under him.

Clawing the air in search of a wall, a doorway, something that would offer support, finding nothing, Zillis dropped hard enough to make the floorboards vibrate.

Between gasps and wheezes, between fits of choking, he shrieked about his eyes, the pain, the stinging brightness.

Billy drew the 9-mm pistol and rapped him along the side of the head with the barrel, just hard enough to hurt.

Zillis howled, and Billy warned, "Quiet down, or I'll hit you again, harder."

When Zillis cursed him, Billy rapped him with the gun once more, not as hard as promised, but that got the idea across.

"All right," Billy said. "Okay. You're not going to see well for twenty minutes, half an hour—"

Still inhaling in rapid shallow pants, exhaling in shudders, Zillis interrupted Billy: "Jesus, I'm blind, I'm—"

"It was just Mace."

"What're you *nuts*?"

"Mace. No permanent damage."

"I'm blind," Zillis insisted.

"You stay there."

"I'm blind."

"You're not blind. Don't move."

"Shit. It *HURTS*!"

A thread of blood unraveled from Zillis's scalp. Billy hadn't hit him hard, but the skin had broken.

"Don't move, listen to me," Billy said, "co-operate, and we'll get through this, it'll be all right."

He realized that he was already comforting Zillis as if the man's innocence were a foregone conclusion.

Until now, there had seemed to be a way to do this. A way to do it even if Steve Zillis turned out not to be the freak, and to walk away with minimal consequences.

In his imagination, however, the opening encounter had not been this violent. A spritz of Mace. Zillis at once disabled, obedient. So easy in the planning.

They had hardly begun, and the situation seemed out of control.

Striving to sound confident, Billy said, "You don't want to be hurt, then just lie there till I tell you what to do next."

Zillis wheezed.

"You hear me?" Billy asked.

"Shit, yeah, how could I not hear you?"

"You understand me?"

"I'm blind here, I'm not deaf."

Billy stepped into the bathroom, switched off the water running in the sink, and looked around.

He did not see what he needed, but he saw something that he did not want to see: his reflection in the mirror. He might have expected to look frantic, even dangerous, and he did. He might have expected to look scared, and he did. He would not have expected to see the potential for evil, but he did.

# 61

On the bedroom TV, a naked man in a black mask lashed a woman's breasts with a cluster of leather straps.

Billy switched off the TV. "I'm thinking about you handling the lemons and limes you slice for drinks, and I want to puke."

Lying disabled in the hall past the open door, Zillis either didn't hear him or pretended that he didn't.

The bed did not have a headboard or a footboard. The mattress and box springs sat on a wheeled metal frame.

Because Zillis didn't bother with such niceties as bedspreads and dust ruffles, the frame of the bed was exposed.

Billy took the handcuffs from the bread bag. He locked one of the bracelets to the bottom rail of the bed frame.

"Get up on your hands and knees," he said. "Crawl toward my voice."

Remaining on the hall floor, breathing easier but still noisily, Zillis spat vigorously on the carpet. His flooding tears had carried the Mace to his lips, and the bitter taste had gotten in his mouth.

Billy went to him and pressed the muzzle of the pistol to the nape of his neck.

Zillis became very still, wheezing softly.

Billy said, "You know what this is?"

"Man."

"I want you to crawl into the bedroom."

"Shit."

"I mean it."

"All right."

"To the bottom of the bed."

Although the only light in the room issued from a dim bedside lamp, Zillis squinted against a stinging, blinding brightness as he crawled to the bed.

Billy had to redirect him twice. Then: "Sit on the floor with your back against the foot of the bed. That's good. With your left hand, feel beside you. A set of handcuffs is hanging from the bed rail. There you go."

"Don't do this to me, man." Zillis's eyes watered copiously. Fluid bubbled in his nostrils. "Why? What is this?"

"Put your left wrist in the empty bracelet."

"I don't like this," Zillis said.

"You don't have to."

"What're you going to do to me?"

"That depends. Put it on now."

After Zillis fumbled with the cuff, Billy leaned in to test the double lock, which was secure. Zillis still couldn't see well enough to strike out or to make a play for the gun.

Steve could drag the bed around the room if he wanted. He could overturn it with effort, dump the mattress and the box springs, and patiently dismantle the bolted frame until he could slide the cuff free. But he couldn't move fast.

The carpet looked filthy. Billy wouldn't sit or kneel on it.

He went to the dinette alcove off the kitchen and returned with the only straight-backed chair in the house. He stood it in front of Zillis, out of his reach, and sat down.

"Billy, I'm dying here."

"You aren't dying."

"I'm scared about my eyes. I still can't see."

"I want to ask you some questions."

"Questions? Are you crazy?"

"I half feel like it," Billy admitted.

Zillis coughed. The single cough became a fit of coughing, which became a fearsome choking. He wasn't faking any of it.

Billy waited.

When Zillis could speak, his voice was hoarse, and it shook: "You're scaring the shit out of me, Billy."

"Good. Now I want you to tell me where you keep your gun."

"Gun? What do I need with a gun?"

"The one you shot him with."

"Shot him? Shot who? I didn't shoot anybody. Jesus, Billy."

"You shot him in the forehead."

"No. No way. Not me, man." His eyes swam with tears induced by the Mace, so they could not be read for deception. He blinked and blinked, trying to see. "Man, if this is some half-assed joke—"

"You're the joker," Billy said. "Not me. You're the performer."

Zillis didn't react to the word.

Billy went to the nightstand and opened the drawer.

"What're you doing?" Zillis asked.

"Looking for the gun."

"There *isn't* a gun."

"There wasn't one earlier, when you weren't here, but there will be now. You'll keep it close to you."

"You were here earlier?"

"You wallow in every kind of filth, don't you, Steve? I wanted to shower in boiling water after I left."

Billy opened the door on the bottom of the nightstand, rummaged inside.

"What're you going to do if you don't find a gun?"

"Maybe I'll nail your hand to the floor and cut your fingers off one by one."

Zillis sounded as if he was about to start crying for real. "Oh, man, don't say crazy shit like that. What did I do to you? I didn't do anything to you."

Sliding open the closet door, Billy said, "When you were at my place, Stevie, where did you hide the severed hand?"

A groan escaped Zillis, and he began to shake his head: no, no, no, no.

The closet shelf over the hanging clothes lay just above eye level. As Billy felt along the shelf for the gun, he said, "And what else did you hide in my place? What did you cut off the redhead? An ear? A breast?"

"This doesn't compute," Zillis said shakily.

"Doesn't it?"

"You're Billy Wiles, for God's sake."

Returning to the bed, searching for the gun, Billy felt between the mattress and the box springs, which he wouldn't have had the stomach to do if he hadn't been wearing the gloves.

"You're *Billy Wiles,*" Zillis repeated.

"Which means what—that you didn't think I'd know how to take care of myself?"

"I didn't *do* anything, Billy. I *didn't.*"

Going around to the other side of the bed, Billy said, "Well, I know how to take care of myself, all right, even if I don't exactly ring the bell on the *zing* meter."

Recognizing his own words, Zillis said, "I didn't mean anything by that. You think that was an insult? I didn't mean it that way."

Billy searched between mattress and box springs again. Nothing.

"I say things, Billy. You know how I am. I'm always joking. You know me. Hell, Billy, I'm an asshole. You *know* I'm an asshole, all the time talking, half the time not listening to myself."

Billy returned to the chair and sat again. "Can you see me better, Stevie?"

"Not much, no. I need some Kleenex."

"Use the bed sheet."

With his free hand, Zillis pawed loose the thin blanket tucked into the foot of the bed. He freed a corner of the sheet, mopped his face with it, blew his nose.

Billy said, "Do you have an ax?"

"Oh, God."

"Do you own an ax, Stevie?"

"No."

"Be truthful with me, Stevie."

"Billy, don't."

"Do you own an ax?"

"Don't do this."

"Do you own an ax, Stevie?"

"Yes," Zillis admitted, and a sob of dread escaped him.

"You're either one hell of an actor or you're

really just poor dumb Steve Zillis," Billy said, and it was the latter possibility that had begun to worry him.

# 62

"When you're chopping the mannequins in the backyard," Billy asked, "do you dream that they're real women?"

"They're just mannequins."

"Do you like to chop watermelons because they're red inside? Do you like to see the red meat explode, Stevie?"

Zillis seemed astonished. "What? She told you about that? What'd she tell you?"

"Who is 'she,' Stevie?"

"The old bitch next door. Celia Reynolds."

"You're in no position to call anyone an old bitch," Billy said. "You're in no position at all."

Zillis looked chastened. He nodded in eager agreement. "You're right. I'm sorry. She's just lonely. I know. But Billy, she's a *nosy* old lady. She just can't mind her own business. She's always at her windows, watching from behind the blinds. You can't go out in the yard, she isn't watching you."

"And there's a lot of things you do that you can't afford for people to see, aren't there, Stevie?"

"No. I don't do anything. I just want some privacy. So a couple times I gave her a show with the ax. Played crazy. Just to spook her off."

"Spook her off."

"Just to make her mind her own business. I only did it three times, and the third time I let her *know* it was a show, let her know I could see her watching."

"How did you let her know?"

"I'm not proud of this now."

"I'm sure there's a lot you're not proud of, Stevie."

"I gave her the finger," Zillis said. "The third time, I chopped a mannequin and a watermelon—which I don't *dream* are anything but what they are—and I walked over to the fence, and I gave her the finger big time."

"You chopped up a chair once."

"Yeah. I chopped up a chair. So what?"

"The one I'm sitting on is the only chair you have."

"I used to have two. I only needed one. It was just a *chair.*"

"You like to see women being hurt," Billy said.

"No."

"Did you just this evening *find* the porno under the bed? Did some gremlin put it there, Stevie?

Should we call Orkin and have them send a gremlin exterminator?"

"Those aren't real women."

"They're not mannequins."

"I mean, they're not really being hurt. They're acting."

"But you like to watch."

Zillis said nothing. He hung his head.

In some ways, this was easier than Billy had expected it to be. He had thought that asking deeply unpleasant questions and listening to another human being grovel in despondent self-justification would be so distressing that he would not be able to sustain a productive interrogation. Instead, he had a sense of power from which he drew confidence. And satisfaction. The ease of it surprised him. The ease of it scared him.

"They're very nasty videos, Stevie. They're very sick."

"Yes," Zillis said softly. "They are. I know."

"Have you ever made any videos of yourself hurting women that way?"

"No. God, no."

"You're whispering, Stevie."

He raised his chin from his chest, but he wouldn't look toward Billy. "I've never hurt a woman that way."

"Never? You've never hurt a woman that way?"

"No. I swear."

"How *have* you hurt them, Stevie?"

"I never have. I couldn't."

"You're such a choirboy, is that it?"

"I like to . . . watch it."

"Watch women being hurt?"

"I like to watch, all right? But I'm ashamed."

"I don't think you're ashamed at all."

"I am. I am ashamed. Not always during, but always after."

"After what?"

"After . . . watching. This isn't . . . Oh, man. This isn't what I want to be."

"Who would want to be what you are, Stevie?"

"I don't know."

"Name me one person. One person who would want to be what you are."

"Maybe nobody," Zillis said.

"How ashamed are you?" Billy persisted.

"I've thrown the videos away. Lots of times. I've even destroyed them. But then, you know . . . after a while, I buy new ones. I need help to stop."

"Have you ever sought help, Stevie?"

Zillis didn't respond.

"Have you ever sought help?" Billy pressed.

"No."

"If you really want to stop, why haven't you sought help?"

"I thought I could stop on my own. I thought I could."

Zillis began to cry. His eyes were still glazed from the Mace, but these were real tears.

"Why have you done those things to the mannequins in the other room, Stevie?"

"You can't understand."

"Yeah, I'm just stodgy old Billy Wiles, got no zing, but give me a try anyway."

"That doesn't mean anything, what I did to them."

"For something that doesn't mean anything, you sure put a lot of time and energy into it."

"I won't talk about this. Not this." He wasn't refusing as much as pleading. "I won't."

"Does it make you blush? Stevie? Does it offend your tender sensibilities?"

Zillis cried continuously now. Not wrenching sobs. The steady, scalding tears of humiliation, of abashment.

He said, "Doing it isn't the same as talking about it."

"You mean what you do to the mannequins," Billy clarified.

"You can . . . you can blow my brains out, but I won't talk about it. I *can't*."

"When you mutilate the mannequins, are you excited, Stevie? Are you *huge* with excitement?"

Zillis shook his head, hung his head.

"Doing it to them and talking about it are so different?" Billy asked.

"Billy. Billy, *please.* I don't want to hear myself, hear myself talking about it."

"Because when you're doing it, then it's just something you do. But if you talk about it, then it's something you *are.*"

Zillis's expression confirmed that Billy had gotten to the quick of it.

Not much could be gained by harping on the mannequins. They were what they were. Rubbing Steve Zillis's face in his perversion could be counterproductive.

Billy had not yet gotten what he needed, what he had come here to prove.

He was simultaneously tired and wired, in need of sleep but strung out on caffeine. At times, his pierced hand ached; the Vicodin had begun to wear off.

Because of exhaustion staved off with chemicals, he might not be conducting the interrogation cleverly enough.

If Zillis was the freak, he was a genius of emotional fakery.

But then that's what sociopaths *were*: voracious spiders with an uncanny talent for projecting a convincing image of a complex human being that obscured the insectile reality of icy calculation and ravenous intent.

Billy said, "When you do what you do to the mannequins, when you watch those sick videos, do you ever think of Judith Kesselman?"

In the course of this encounter, Zillis had been surprised more than once, but this question shocked him. Bloodshot from the residual effect of the Mace, his eyes widened. His face paled and went loose, as if he had taken a blow.

# 63

Zillis shackled to the bed. Billy free on the chair but with a growing sense of being trammeled by his prisoner's evasiveness.

"Stevie? I asked you a question."

"What *is* this?" Zillis said with apparent earnestness and even the merest trace of righteous affront.

"What is what?"

"Why did you come here? Billy, I don't understand what you're *doing* here."

"Do you think of Judith Kesselman?" Billy persisted.

"How do you know about her?"

"How do you think I know?"

"You answer questions with questions, but *I'm* supposed to have real answers to everything."

"Poor Stevie. What about Judi Kesselman?"

"Something happened to her."

"What happened to her, Stevie?"

"It was in college. Five, five and a half years ago."

"Do you know what happened to her, Stevie?"

"Nobody knows."

"Somebody does," Billy said.

"She disappeared."

"Like in a magic show?"

"She was just gone."

"She was such a lovely girl, wasn't she?"

"Everybody liked her," Zillis said.

"Such a lovely girl, so innocent. The innocent are the most delicious, aren't they, Stevie?"

Frowning, Zillis said, "Delicious?"

"The innocent—they're the most succulent, the most satisfying. I know what happened to her," Billy said, meaning to imply that he knew Zillis had kidnapped and killed her.

Such a full-body shudder passed through Steve Zillis that the handcuffs rattled protractedly against the metal bed frame.

Pleased with that reaction, Billy said, "I know, Stevie."

"What? What do you know?"

"Everything."

"What happened to her?"

"Yes. Everything."

Zillis had been sitting with his back against the bed, his legs splayed on the floor in front of him. Now he suddenly drew his knees up to his chest. "Oh, God." A groan of abject misery escaped him.

"Precisely everything," Billy said.

Zillis's mouth softened and his voice grew tremulous. "Don't hurt me."

"What do you think I might do to you, Stevie?"

"I don't know. I don't want to think."

"You're so imaginative, so *talented* when it comes to dreaming up ways to hurt women, but suddenly you don't want to *think*?"

Shivering continuously now, Zillis said, "What do you want from me, what can I do?"

"I want to talk about what happened to Judith Kesselman."

When Zillis began to sob like a young boy, Billy got up from the chair. He sensed that a breakthrough was coming.

"Stevie?"

"Go away."

"You know I'm not going to. Let's talk about Judi Kesselman."

"I don't want to."

"I think you do." Billy didn't go closer to Zillis, but he squatted in front of him, coming down almost to his level. "I think you want very much to talk about it."

Zillis shook his head violently. "I don't. I don't. If we talk about it, you'll kill me for sure."

"Why do you say that, Stevie?"

"You know."

"Why do you say I'll kill you?"

"Because then I'll know too much, won't I?"

Billy stared at his prisoner, trying to read him.

"You did her," Zillis said with a groan.

"Did what?"

"You killed her, and I don't know why, I don't understand, but now you're going to kill me."

Billy took a deep breath and grimaced. "What've you done?"

For an answer, Zillis only sobbed.

"Stevie, what've you done to yourself?"

Zillis had drawn his knees to his chest. Now he stretched out his legs again.

"Stevie?"

The crotch of the man's pajamas was dark with urine. He had wet himself.

# 64

Some monsters are pathetic rather than murderous. Their lairs are not lairs in the fullest sense because they do not lie in wait. They take to ill-kept burrows, with minimal furniture and the objects of their misshapen sense of beauty. They hope only to indulge their mutant fantasies and live their monstrous lives in as much peace as they can find, which is precious little, for they torment themselves even when the rest of the world leaves them unmolested.

Billy resisted the conclusion that Steve Zillis was one of this pathetic breed.

To admit that Zillis was not a homicidal sociopath, Billy must accept that much precious time had been wasted in the pursuit of a wolf, presumed fierce, that was in fact a meek dog.

Worse, if Zillis was not the freak, Billy had no idea where to go from here. All the evidence had

seemed to funnel him to a single conclusion. The circumstantial evidence.

Worst of all, if the killer was not before him now, then he had stooped to this brutality without profit.

Consequently, for a while he continued to question and harass his captive, but by the minute, the contest between them seemed to be less a contest than an act of oppression. A matador can find no glory when the bull, bristling with banderillas and lanced by the picador, loses all spirit and will pass not even listlessly at the red muleta.

Sooner than later, concealing his growing despair, Billy sat on the chair once more and raised his final issue, hoping that a trap might spring when he least expected.

"Where were you earlier tonight, Steve?"

"You know. Don't you know? I was at the bar, working your shift."

"Only until nine o'clock. Jackie says you worked between three and nine because you had stuff to do before and after."

"I did. I had stuff."

"Where were you between nine o'clock and midnight?"

"What does it matter?"

"It matters," Billy assured him. "Where were you?"

"You're gonna hurt . . . you're gonna kill me anyway."

"I'm not going to kill you, and I didn't kill Judith Kesselman. I'm pretty sure you killed her."

*"Me?"* His amazement rang as true as any reaction he'd had since this had started.

"You're really good at this," Billy told him.

"Good at what? Killing people? You're bugshit crazy! I never killed anyone."

"Steve, if you can convince me you have a solid alibi for nine to midnight, then this is over. I'm out of here, and you're free."

Zillis looked dubious. "That easy?"

"Yes."

"After all this—it's over that easy?"

"It could be. Depending on the alibi."

Zillis worried over his answer.

Billy began to think he was concocting it from scratch.

Then Zillis said, "What if I tell you where I was, and it turns out *that's* why you're here, because you already know where I was, and you want to hear me say it so you can beat the shit out of me."

"I'm not following you," Billy told him.

"All right. Okay. I was with someone. I never heard her mention you, but if you have a thing for her, what're you going to do to me?"

Billy regarded him with disbelief. "You were with a woman?"

"I wasn't *with* her, not like in bed. It was just a date. A late dinner, which had to be later 'cause

I covered for you. This was our second date."

"Who?"

Steeling himself against Billy's jealous outrage, Zillis said, "Amanda Pollard."

"Mandy Pollard? I know her. She's a nice girl."

Warily, Zillis said, "That's it—'She's a nice girl'?"

The Pollards owned a successful vineyard. They grew grapes on contract for one of the valley's finest vintners. Mandy was about twenty, pretty, friendly. She worked in the family business. Judging by all evidence, she was wholesome enough to have come from an era better than this one.

Billy let his gaze travel the sleazy bedroom, from the porno-tape package lying on the floor beside the TV to the pile of dirty laundry in one corner.

"She's never been here," Zillis said. "We've only had two dates. I'm looking for a better place, a nice apartment. I want to get rid of all this stuff. Make a clean start."

"She's a decent girl."

"She is," Zillis eagerly agreed. "I think with her in my corner, I could clean up my act, start over, do the right thing for once."

"She ought to see this place."

"No, no. Billy, no, for God's sake. This isn't the me I want to be. I want to be better for her."

"Where did you go to dinner?"

Zillis named a restaurant. Then: "We got there

about twenty past nine. We left at about a quarter past eleven because we were the only people in the place by then."

"After that?"

"We went for a drive. A nice drive. I don't mean we parked. She isn't like that. We just drove around, talking, listening to music."

"Until when?"

"I took her home a little after one o'clock."

"And came back here."

"Yeah."

"And put on a porno flick of a guy whipping a woman."

"All right. I know what I am, but I also know what I can be."

Billy went to the nightstand and picked up the phone. It had a long cord. He brought it to Zillis. "Call her."

"What, *now*? Billy, it's after three in the morning."

"Call her. Tell her how much you enjoyed the evening, how very special she is. She won't mind if you wake her up for that."

"We don't have that kind of relationship yet," Zillis worried. "She's gonna think this is weird."

"You call her and let me listen in," Billy said, "or I jam this pistol in your ear and blow your brains out. What do you think?"

Zillis's hands shook so badly that he misdialed twice. He got it right the third time.

Hunkering beside his captive, the muzzle of the pistol pressed against Zillis's side so he wouldn't get a half-wise idea, Billy listened to Mandy Pollard answer the phone and express surprise at hearing from her new beau at that hour.

"Don't worry about it," Mandy told Zillis. "You didn't wake me. I was just lying here staring at the ceiling."

Zillis's voice had a tremor, but Mandy might easily have assumed he was nervous about calling at this late hour and about expressing his affection more directly than perhaps he had done previously.

For a few minutes, Billy listened to them recap the night—their dinner, the drive—and then he gestured at Zillis to wrap it up.

Mandy Pollard had spent the evening with this man, and she was not some half-cracked thrill seeker who knowingly hung out with bad boys.

Having dinner with Mandy, Steve Zillis could not have been the freak who propped Ralph Cottle's corpse on Lanny's living-room sofa and nailed Billy's hand to the hallway floor.

# 65

Slipping the pistol into the holster at his hip, Billy said, "I'm going to leave you handcuffed to the bed."

Steve Zillis looked relieved at the holstering of the weapon, but remained wary.

Billy tore the phone cord out of the wall and out of the phone, knotted it, and put it in his bread bag. "I don't want you calling anyone until you've had plenty of time to cool down and to think about what I'm going to say."

"You're really not gonna kill me?"

"I'm really not. I'll leave the handcuff key on a counter in the kitchen."

"All right. The kitchen. But how's that gonna help me?"

"After I'm gone, you can work the mattress and the box springs off the frame. It's held together by nuts and bolts, isn't it?"

"Yeah. But—"

"You can work the nuts with your fingers."

"Maybe they're rusted—"

"You only moved in six months ago. They haven't rusted in six months. If they're tight, torque the sections of the frame, try to wrench a little play into the connections. You'll figure it out."

"I can figure that out, sure, but I still can't figure why the *hell* you did this. You can't believe I killed Judith Kesselman, like you said. I know you can't believe that. What *was* this?"

Putting the can of Mace in the bread bag, Billy said, "I'm not going to explain, and you don't want to know. Believe me, you don't."

"Look at me here," Zillis whined. "My eyes still sting. I'm sitting in a puddle, for God's sake. This is humiliating. You hit me with that gun, you cut my scalp, you *hurt* me, Billy."

"It could have been worse," Billy assured him. "It could have been a whole lot worse."

Choosing to interpret those words as a threat, Zillis became placating. "All right. Okay. I hear you. I'm cool."

"Depending on how tight the bolts are, you'll need at least an hour, probably two, to get loose of the bed. The cuff key will be in the kitchen. After you use it, start packing."

Zillis blinked. "What?"

"Call Jackie, tell him you're quitting."

"I don't want to quit."

"Get real, Steve. We aren't going to see each other every day. Not with what I know about you and not with what you know about me. You're going to move on."

"Where?"

"I don't care where. Just not in Napa County."

"I like it here. Besides, I can't afford to move right now."

"Go to the tavern Friday night to get your last paycheck," Billy said. "I'll leave an envelope for you with Jackie. It'll contain ten thousand in cash. That'll get you started somewhere."

"I did nothing, but my whole *life* gets turned upside down? This isn't fair."

"You're right. It isn't fair. But it's the way it is. Your furniture isn't worth crap. You can junk it. Pack the personal stuff and be out of town by Friday night."

"I could call the cops, I could press charges."

"Really? You'd want the cops to see the scene of the crime, have them tramping through here, with the bondage pornos, those mannequins in the next room?"

Although still scared, Zillis found sufficient self-pity to pout. "Who died and made *you* God?"

Billy shook his head. "Steve, you're pathetic. You'll take the ten thousand, be glad you're alive, and get out. Plus one more thing—don't ever call Mandy Pollard again."

"Wait a minute. You can't—"

"Don't call her, don't see her. Not ever."

"Billy, she could make all the difference for me."

"She's a nice girl. She's a decent girl."

"That's what I mean. I know I could clean up my act if she—"

"A good woman can turn a man around," Billy said. "But not a man who's as far down the rathole as you are. If you call her or see her, even just once, I'll know. And I'll find you. You believe that?"

Zillis said nothing.

"And if you *touch* her," Billy said, "so help me God, I'll kill you, Steve."

"This is *so* not right," Zillis said.

"Do you believe me? You better believe me, Steve."

When Billy put his hand on the grip of the holstered pistol, Zillis said, "Hey. All right. I hear you."

"Good. I'm leaving now."

"This place sucks anyway," Zillis said. "*Wine country* is just another word for *farm*. I'm not a farm boy."

"No, you're not," Billy said from the doorway.

"There's no action around here."

"There's no *zing*," Billy agreed.

"Screw you."

Billy said, "Happy trails, Kemosabe."

# 66

By the time that he'd driven only half a mile from Zillis's place, Billy had the shakes so bad that he had to pull to the curb, put the Explorer in park, and get control of himself.

Under pressure, he had become the thing he most despised. For a while, he had become John Palmer.

Paying Zillis ten thousand bucks didn't make Billy any less like Palmer, either.

When the shakes subsided, he didn't put the SUV in gear because he didn't know where to go from here. He felt that he was at a brink. You don't drive over a brink.

He wanted to go home, but nothing there would help him work out a solution to this puzzle.

He wanted to go home just to *be* home. He recognized the familiar reclusive urge. Once home, he could sit at his carving bench with the blocks of oak, and the world could go to Hell.

Except this time, he would go to Hell with it. He could not take Barbara home with him, and if he left her alone and in jeopardy, he would have trashed his only excuse for living.

Events had thrust him into action, into the rush of life, yet he felt isolated and beyond desperation.

For too long he'd done no proper sowing and now had no harvest. His friends were all acquaintances. Though life is community, he had no community.

In fact, his situation was worse than isolation. The friends who were no more than acquaintances were now not even acquaintances as much as they were suspects. He had carpentered for himself a loneliness of exquisite paranoia.

Pulling away from the curb, Billy drove with no destination in mind, as far as he was aware. Like a bird, he rode the currents of the night, intent only upon staying aloft and not falling into absolute despair before some gleam of hope appeared.

He had learned more about Ivy Elgin in one brief visit to her house than he had troubled himself to know about her during the years they had worked together. And though he liked Ivy, he found her more mysterious now than when he had known so much less about her.

He did not think that she could have any connection to the freak committing these murders.

But his experience with his own mother and father reminded him that he could not be sure of anyone.

Harry Avarkian was a kind man and a fine attorney—but also one of three trustees overseeing seven million dollars, a temptation that could not be discounted. Before Barbara, Billy had been to Harry's house only once. Barbara socialized him. They had gone to Harry's for dinner half a dozen times in a year—but since the coma, Billy had not visited Harry anywhere but at his office.

He knew Harry Avarkian. But he didn't *know* him.

Billy's mind circled to Dr. Ferrier. Which was crazy. Prominent physicians in the community didn't go around killing people.

Except Dr. Ferrier wanted Billy to cooperate with him in the killing of Barbara Mandel. Remove the feeding tube in her stomach. Let her die. Let her starve to death in her coma.

If you were willing to decide for another—for someone in no obvious pain—that her quality of life was insufficient to warrant the expenditure of resources on her behalf, how easy was it to make a step from pulling a plug to pulling a trigger?

Ridiculous. Yet he didn't know Ferrier a fraction as well as he had known his father; and in violation of all Billy *thought* he had known, his father had swung that polished-steel lug wrench with something like vicious *glee.*

John Palmer. He was a man whose love of power was clear for all to see, but whose internal landscape remained as enigmatic as an alien planet.

The more Billy considered the people he knew, the more he brooded on the possibility that the killer might be a perfect stranger, the more he became agitated to no purpose.

He told himself to care and not to care, to be still.

*In order to possess what you do not possess, you must go by way of dispossession.*

*And what you do not know is the only thing you know.*

Driving and yet giving himself to that inner stillness, he came in a short while, without conscious intention, to the truck stop. He parked where he had parked before, in front of the diner.

His left hand ached. When he fisted and opened it, he could feel that it had begun to swell. The Vicodin had worn off. He didn't know whether or not he should take another, but he should get some Motrin.

He was hungry, but the thought of another candy bar curdled his appetite. He needed a caffeine jolt, but he wanted more than pills.

After stowing the pistol and the revolver under the front seat, in spite of the broken-out window that left the vehicle unsecured, he went inside.

At 3:40 in the morning, he had his choice of empty booths.

Four truckers sat on stools at the counter, drinking coffee and eating pie.

They were attended by a beefy waitress with the neck of an NFL fullback and the face of an angel. In her masses of hair, dyed shoe-polish black, she wore yellow butterfly bows.

Billy sat at the counter.

# 67

According to the tag on her uniform, the waitress's name was Jasmine. She called Billy "honey," and served the black coffee and lemon pie that he ordered.

Jasmine and the truckers were in a lively conversation when Billy settled on a stool among them. From their exchanges, he learned that one of the men was named Curly, another Arvin. No one addressed the third man as anything but "you," and the fourth had an upper gold tooth in the front of his mouth.

At first they were talking about the lost continent of Atlantis. Arvin proposed that the destruction of that fabled civilization had come to pass because the Atlanteans had gotten involved in genetic engineering and had bred monsters that destroyed them.

This quickly turned the subject from Atlantis to cloning and DNA research, soon after which

Curly mentioned the fact that at Princeton or Harvard, or Yale, at one of those hellholes or another, scientists were trying to create a pig with a human brain.

"I'm not sure that's so new," Jasmine said. "Over the years, let me tell you, I've met my share of human pigs."

"What would be the purpose of a humanized pig?" Arvin wondered.

"Just because it's there," said You.

"It's where?"

"Like a mountain is just there," You clarified. "So some people have to climb it. Other people, they've got to make a humanized pig just because maybe they can."

"What work would it do?" Gold Tooth asked.

"I don't think they mean for it to have a job," Curly said.

"They mean for it to do *something,*" Gold Tooth said.

"One thing's for sure," Jasmine declared, "the activists will go nuts."

"What activists?" Arvin asked.

"One kind of activist or another," she said. "Once you've got pigs with human brains, that's the end of anyone allowed to eat ham or bacon."

"I don't see why," said Curly. "The ham and bacon will still come from the pigs that haven't been humanized."

"It'll be a sympathy thing," Jasmine predicted.

"How're you going to justify eating ham and bacon when your kids go to school with smart pigs and ask them home for sleepovers?"

"That'll never happen," You said.

"Never," Arvin agreed.

"What'll happen," Jasmine said, "is these fools playing around with human genes, they'll do something stupid and kill us all."

Not one of the four truckers disagreed. Neither did Billy.

Gold Tooth still felt the scientists had in mind some kind of work for a humanized pig. "They don't spend millions of dollars on something like this just for the fun of it, not those people."

"Oh, they do," Jasmine disagreed. "Money means nothing to them. It isn't theirs."

"It's taxpayer money," said Curly. "Yours and mine."

Billy offered a comment or two, but he mostly listened, familiar with these conversational rhythms, and curiously warmed by them.

The coffee was rich. The pie tasted wonderfully lemony and was topped with toasted meringue.

He was surprised by how calm he felt. Just sitting at the counter, just listening.

"You want to talk about a total waste of money," said Gold Tooth, "look at this damn fool monstrosity they're building out by the highway."

"What—you mean across from the tavern, the

thing they're gonna burn when they no sooner finish it?" Arvin asked.

"Oh, but it's *art,*" Jasmine archly reminded them.

"I don't see how it's art," You said. "Doesn't what's art have to *last*?"

"The guy's going to make millions selling his drawings of it," Curly told them. "He's got a hundred merchandising angles."

"Can anyone just call himself an artist?" Gold Tooth asked. "Don't they have to pass a test or something?"

"He calls himself a special kind of artist," Curly said.

"Special my ass," said Arvin.

"Honey," Jasmine told him, "no offense, but your dumpy backside doesn't look so special to me."

"What he calls himself," Curly said, "is a *performance* artist."

"What's that mean?"

"What I take it to mean," Curly said, "is art that doesn't last. It's made to do something, and when it does something, it's over."

"What are museums gonna be filled with in a hundred years?" You wondered. "Empty space?"

"There won't be museums anymore," Jasmine said. "Museums are for people. There won't be any people. Just humanized pigs."

Billy had grown very still. He sat with the

coffee cup to his lips, his mouth open, but unable to take a drink.

"Honey, something wrong with the brew?" Jasmine asked.

"No. No, it's fine. In fact, I'd like another cup. Do you serve it in mugs?"

"We have a triple cup in a plastic container. We call it the Big Shot."

"Give me one of those," Billy said.

# 68

An alcove off the diner served as an Internet café. Six work stations offered links to the World Wide Web.

A trucker sat at one computer, working the keyboard and the mouse, fixated on the screen. Maybe he was checking out his company's shipping schedules or playing an Internet game, or browsing a porn site.

The computer was bolted to a table that provided room for food. A cut-out in the table held Billy's Big Shot.

He didn't know the name of Valis's site, so he started with sites about performance art in general and linked his way to www.valisvalisvalis.com.

The artist maintained an elaborate and inviting site. Billy streamed colorful video of the Australian bridge to which Valis had fixed twenty thousand red balloons. He watched them pop all at once.

He sampled artist statements about individual

projects. They were overblown and semicoherent, slathered with the unmusical jargon of modern art.

In a windy interview, Valis said that every great artist was "a fisher of men," because they wanted to "touch the souls, even *capture* the souls" of those who saw their work.

Valis helped aficionados better understand the intention of each of his projects by providing three lines of "spiritual guidance." Each line contained three words. Billy pored over several of them.

From his wallet, he extracted the paper on which were printed the six lines that had been contained in three documents on the red diskette that he'd found in Ralph Cottle's clasped hands. He unfolded it and smoothed it flat on the table.

The first line—*Because I, too, am a fisher of men.*

The fifth line—*My last killing: midnight Thursday.*

The sixth line—*Your suicide: soon thereafter.*

The second, third, and fourth lines were chillingly similar to the "spiritual guidance" that Valis provided to assist his admirers in reaching a fuller appreciation of his works.

The first line of these guides always referred to the *style* of the project, of the *performance*. In this case, the style was *Cruelty, violence, death.*

The second line summarized the *techniques* by which the artist intended to execute the work of

art. With Billy, the technique was *Movement, velocity, impact.*

The third line described the *medium or media* in which Valis proposed to create. In this current performance, the media were *Flesh, blood, bone.*

Sometimes the most successful serial killers are vagabonds, footloose roamers who cover a lot of ground between their homicidal activities.

The freak didn't look at killing as a game. Only in part did he view it as a performance. For him, the essence was the *art* of it.

From the performance-art Web sites, Billy had learned that this artist of death had always been camera-shy. Valis claimed to believe that the art should be more important than the artist. He'd seldom been photographed.

Such a philosophy allowed him celebrity and wealth—and yet a degree of anonymity.

www.valisvalisvalis.com offered an official portrait. This proved to be not a photo but a realistic and detailed pencil drawing that the artist himself had done.

Perhaps intentionally, the portrait was not entirely faithful to Valis's actual appearance, but Billy at once recognized him. He was the Heineken drinker who, on Monday afternoon, had sat in patient amusement as Ned Pearsall had regaled him with the story of Henry Friddle's death by garden gnome.

*You're an interesting guy, Billy Barkeep.*

Even then, the freak had known Billy's last name, although he had pretended ignorance of it. He must have known almost everything about him. For reasons only Valis might ever understand, Billy Wiles had been identified, researched, and chosen for this *performance.*

Now, in addition to the other selections under the portrait, Billy noticed one titled HELLO, BILLY.

Although he no longer had much capacity for surprise, he stared at it for a minute.

At last he moved the mouse and clicked.

The portrait vanished, and on the screen appeared instructions: PRIVATE LEVEL—ENTER CODE-WORD.

Billy drank coffee. Then he typed WILES and pressed ENTER.

At once he received a reply: YOU ARE WORTHY.

Those three words remained before him for ten seconds, and then the screen went blank.

Only that and nothing more.

The pencil portrait returned. The selections under it no longer included HELLO, BILLY.

# 69

No lights brightened the massive dimensional mural. The wheels, flywheels, gears, crank-shafts, connecting rods, pipes, and strange armatures dwindled into the darkness.

Tormented, besieged, the giant human figure was dark-shrouded in its silent struggle.

The yellow-and-purple tent stood in shadowed swags, but inviting amber light shone at the windows of the big motor home.

Billy first pulled to a stop on the shoulder of the highway and studied the vehicle from a distance.

The sixteen artists and artisans who were building the mural under Valis's direction did not live on site. They were block-booked for six months at the Vineyard Hills Inn.

Valis, however, lived here for the duration. The motor home had electrical and water hookups.

Its waste-water holding tanks were pumped out

twice a week by Glen's Reliable Septic Service. Glen Gortner was proud of his fame by association, even though he thought the mural was "something I ought to be pumping away, too."

Not sure if he would stop or just cruise past, Billy drove the Explorer off the shoulder of the road, down a gentle embankment, into the meadow. He swung around to the far side of the motor home.

The door to the driver's compartment stood open. Light angled down the steps and painted a welcome mat on the ground.

He stopped. For a while he sat with the engine running, one foot on the brake, one poised above the accelerator.

Most of the windows were not covered. He couldn't see anyone in the spaces beyond.

Only the windows toward the rear, which were probably in the bedroom, featured curtains. Lamps glowed there, too, filtered by a golden material.

Inescapably, Billy concluded that he was expected.

He was loath to accept this invitation. He wanted to drive away. He had nowhere to go.

Less than twenty hours remained until midnight, when as foretold the "last killing" would occur. Barbara, still in jeopardy.

Because of evidence that Valis might have planted in addition to what had been on the cadavers, Billy remained a potential suspect in the

disappearances that would soon become known to the police: Lanny, Ralph Cottle, the redheaded young woman.

Somewhere in his house or garage, or buried in his yard, was the hand of Giselle Winslow. Surely other souvenirs, as well.

He put the Explorer in park, doused the headlights, but did not switch off the engine.

Near the dark tent stood a Lincoln Navigator. Evidently it was what Valis used for local travel.

*You are worthy.*

Billy pulled on a fresh pair of latex gloves.

Some stiffness but no pain troubled his left hand.

He wished he had not taken a Vicodin at Lanny's. Unlike most painkillers, Vicodin left the mind clear, but he worried that if his perceptions and reflexes were dulled even half a percent, that lost edge might be the death of him.

Maybe the caffeine tablets and the coffee would compensate. And the lemon pie.

He switched off the engine. In the first instant thereafter, the night seemed as silent as any house of the deaf.

In consideration of the unpredictability of this adversary, he prepared for action both lethal and otherwise.

As to the choice of a deadlier weapon, he preferred the .38 revolver because of its familiarity. He had killed with it before.

He got out of the Explorer.

Songs of crickets rose to dispel the silence, and the throat-clearing of toads. Pennants on the tent whispered in the barest breath of a breeze.

Billy walked to the open door of the motor home. He stood in the light but hesitated to ascend the steps.

From inside, all edges smoothed off by the high-quality speakers of the motor-home sound system, which apparently doubled as intercom, a voice said, "Barbara could be allowed to live."

Billy climbed the steps.

The cockpit featured two stylish swiveling armchairs for the driver and co-pilot. They were upholstered in what might have been ostrich skin.

Remotely operated, the door closed behind Billy. He assumed that it locked, as well.

In this highly customized vehicle, a bulkhead separated the cockpit from the living quarters. Another open door awaited him.

Billy stepped into a dazzling kitchen. Everything in shades of cream and honey. Marble floor, bird's-eye maple cabinets with the sinuous rounded contours of ship's cabinetry. The exceptions were black-granite countertops and stainless-steel appliances.

From the in-ceiling speakers, Valis's mellow and compelling voice made a proposal: "I could whip up an early breakfast if you'd like."

The marble floor continued into a built-in

dining area that could comfortably seat six, eight in a pinch.

The top of the maple table had been inlaid with ebonized wenge, carnelian, and holly wood as white as bone, in an intertwining ribbon motif—spectacular and expensive craftsmanship.

Through an archway in another bulkhead, Billy entered a large living room.

None of the fabrics cost less than five hundred a square yard, the carpet twice as much. The custom furniture was contemporary, but the numerous Japanese bronzes were priceless examples of the finest Meiji-period work.

According to some of the tavern regulars, who'd read about this motor home on the Internet, it had cost over a million and a half. That would not include the bronzes.

Sometimes vehicles like this were called "land yachts." The term wasn't hyperbole.

The closed door at the farther end of the living room no doubt led to a bedroom and bath. It would be locked.

Valis must be in that final redoubt. Listening, watching, and well armed.

Billy swiveled toward a soft noise behind him.

On the living-room side, the dining-area bulkhead had been finished with beautiful narrow-reed bamboo tambour. These panels slowly rolled up and out of sight, revealing secret display cases.

And now blinds of brushed stainless steel

descended to cover all the windows, but with a sudden pneumatic *snap* that startled.

Billy didn't think those blinds were solely decorative. Getting through them and out a window would be difficult if not impossible.

During the design and installation phase, they had most likely been called "security" devices.

As the ascending tambour panels continued to reveal more display cases, the voice of Valis came from the speakers again: "You may see my collection, as few ever have. Uniquely, you will be given the chance to leave here alive after seeing it. Enjoy."

# 70

The padded interiors of the cabinets behind the tambour panels were upholstered in black silk. Clear glass jars of two sizes held the collection.

The base of each jar nestled in a niche in its shelf. A black-enameled clamp held the lidded top, fixing it to the underside of the shelf above.

These containers would not move whatsoever when the motor home was in motion. They wouldn't make one clink.

Each jar was lighted by fiber-optic filaments under it, so the contents glowed against the backdrop of black silk. As the lamplight in the living room now dimmed to enhance the effect of the display, Billy thought of aquariums.

Each of these small glass worlds contained not fish but a memory of murder. In a preservative fluid floated faces and hands.

Every face was ghostly, each like a pale mantis

perpetually swimming, the features of one hardly distinguishable from those of the others.

The hands were different from one another, said more about each victim than did the faces, and were less grisly than he would have assumed, ethereal and strange.

"Aren't they beautiful?" Valis said, and sounded somewhat like HAL 9000 in *2001: A Space Odyssey*.

"They're sad," Billy said.

"What an odd word to choose," Valis said. "They delight me."

"They fill me with despair."

"Despair," Valis said, "is good. Despair can be the nadir of one life and the starting point of an ascent into another, better one."

Billy didn't turn away from the collection in fear or revulsion. He assumed that he was being watched by closed-circuit cameras. His reaction seemed to be important to Valis.

Besides, as despair-inspiring as this display might be, it had a hideous elegance, and exerted a certain fascination.

The collector had not been so coarse as to include genitalia or breasts.

Billy suspected that Valis did not kill for any kind of sexual gratification, did not rape his female victims, perhaps because to do so would be to acknowledge at least that single aspect of shared humanity. He seemed to want to think of himself as a creature apart.

Neither did the artist deform his collection with the gaudy and grotesque. No eyeballs, no internal organs.

Faces and hands, faces and hands.

Staring at the illuminated jars, Billy thought of mimes dressed all in black with white-powdered faces and white-gloved hands.

Although perverse, here was an aesthetic mind at work.

"A sense of balance," Billy said, describing the vivid display, "a harmony of line, a sensitivity to form. Perhaps most important, a restraint that is chaste but not fastidious."

Valis said nothing.

Curiously, by standing face to face with Death and not letting fear control, Billy was at last no longer evading life to any degree, but embracing it.

"I have read your book of short stories," Valis said.

"In critiquing your work," Billy told him, "I wasn't inviting criticism of my own."

A short surprised laugh escaped Valis, a warm laugh as the speakers translated it. "Actually, I found your fiction to be fascinating, and strong."

Billy did not reply.

"They are the stories of a seeker," Valis said. "You know the truth of life, but you circle around that fruit, circle and circle, reluctant to admit it, to taste it."

Turning from the collection, Billy moved to the nearest Meiji bronzes, a pair of fish, sinuous, simply but exquisitely detailed, the bronze meticulously finished to mimic the tone and texture of rusted iron.

"Power," Billy said. "Power is part of the truth of life."

Behind the locked door, Valis waited.

"And emptiness," Billy said. "The void. The abyss."

He moved to another bronze: a robed scholar and a deer sitting side by side, the scholar bearded and smiling, his robe embroidered with gold inlay.

"The choice," Billy said, "is chaos or control. With power, we can create. With power and chaste intent, we create art. And art is the only answer to chaos and the void."

After a silence, Valis said, "Only one thing holds you to the past. I can release you from it."

"By one more murder?" Billy asked.

"No. She can live, and you can move on to a new life . . . when you know."

"And what is it you know that I don't?"

"Barbara," Valis said, "lives in Dickens."

Billy heard a sharp intake of breath, his own, an expression of surprise and recognition.

"While in your house, Billy, I reviewed the pocket notebooks you've filled with things she said in coma."

"Have you?"

"Certain phrases, certain constructions resonated with me. On your living-room shelves, the complete set of Dickens—that belonged to her."

"Yes."

"She had a passion for Dickens."

"She'd read all the novels, several times each."

"But not you."

"Two or three," Billy said. "Dickens never clicked with me."

"Too full of life, I suspect," Valis said. "Too full of faith and exuberance for you."

"Perhaps."

"She knows those stories so well, she's *living* them in dreams. The words she speaks in coma come sequentially in certain chapters."

"Mrs. Joe," Billy said, recalling his most recent visit to Barbara. "I've read that one. Joe Gargery's wife, Pip's sister, the bullying shrew. Pip calls her 'Mrs. Joe.'"

"*Great Expectations,*" Valis confirmed. "Barbara lives all the books, but more often the lighter adventures, seldom the horrors of *A Tale of Two Cities.*"

"I didn't realize. . . ."

"She's more likely to dream *A Christmas Carol* than the bloodiest moments of the French Revolution," Valis assured him.

"I didn't realize, but you did."

"In any case, she knows no fear or pain because

each adventure is a well-known road, a pleasure and a comfort."

Billy moved through the living room, to another bronze, then past it.

"She needs nothing you can give her," Valis said, "and nothing more than what she has. She lives in Dickens, and she knows no fear."

Intuiting what was wanted to bring the artist forth, Billy put down the revolver on an antique Shinto altar table to the left of the bedroom door. Then he retraced his steps to the middle of the living room and sat in an armchair.

# 71

Handsomer than the self-portrait in pencil that could be viewed on his Web site, Valis entered.

Smiling, he picked up the revolver from the altar table and examined it.

Beside the armchair in which Billy sat, on a small table, stood another Japanese bronze from the Meiji period: a plump smiling dog held a turtle on a leash.

Valis approached with the handgun. Not unlike Ivy Elgin, he walked with a dancer's grace and as if gravity were not quite able to force the soles of his shoes flat to the floor.

His thick, soot-black hair, dusted with ashes at the temples. His smile so engaging. His gray eyes luminous, pellucid, and direct.

He had the presence of a movie star. The self-assurance of a king. The serenity of a monk.

Standing in front of the armchair, he aimed the revolver at Billy's face. "This is the gun."

"Yes," Billy said.

"You shot your father with it."

"Yes."

"How did that feel?"

Staring into the muzzle, Billy said, "Terrifying."

"And your mother, Billy?"

"Right."

"It felt right to shoot her?"

"At the time, in the instant," Billy said.

"And later?"

"I wasn't sure."

"Wrong is right. Right is wrong. It's all perspective, Billy."

Billy said nothing.

*In order to arrive at what you are not, you must go through the way in which you are not.*

Peering at him along the barrel of the gun, Valis said, "Who do you hate, Billy?"

"I don't think anyone."

"That's good. That's healthy. Hate and love exhaust the mind, inhibit clear thinking."

"I like these bronzes very much," Billy said.

"Aren't they wonderful? You can enjoy the form, the texture, the immense skill of the artist, and yet not care a damn thing about the philosophy behind them."

"Especially the fish," Billy said.

"Why the fish in particular?"

"The illusion of movement. The appearance of speed. They look so free."

"You've led a slow life, Billy. Maybe you're ready for some movement. Are you ready for speed?"

"I don't know."

"I suspect you do."

"I'm ready for something."

"You came here intending violence," Valis said.

Billy raised his hands from the arms of the chair and stared at the latex gloves. He stripped them off.

"Does this feel strange to you, Billy?"

"Totally."

"Can you imagine what might happen next?"

"Not clearly."

"Do you care, Billy?"

"Not as much as I thought I would."

Valis squeezed off a shot. The bullet punched into the broad back of the armchair, two inches from Billy's shoulder.

Unconsciously, he must have known the shot was coming. He saw in his mind's eye the raven on the window, the still and silent and watchful raven. Then the bang came, and he did not fly or even flinch, but sat in a Zen indifference.

Valis lowered the gun. He settled into an armchair that faced Billy's.

Billy closed his eyes and leaned his head back.

"I could have killed you two ways without leaving the bedroom," Valis said.

This was surely true. Billy didn't ask how.

"You must be very tired," Valis said.

"Very."

"How's your hand?"

"Okay. Vicodin."

"And your forehead?"

"Noble."

Billy wondered if his eyes were moving under his lids, the way Barbara's sometimes did in her dreams. They felt still.

"I had a third wound planned for you," Valis said.

"Can it wait until next week?"

"You're a funny guy, Billy."

"I don't feel that funny."

"Do you feel relieved?"

"Mmmmmm."

"Are you surprised by that?"

"Yeah." Billy opened his eyes. "Are *you* surprised?"

"No," the artist said. "I saw the potential in you."

"When?"

"In your short stories. Before I ever met you." Valis put the revolver on a table beside his chair. "Your potential so explicit on the page. As I researched your life, the potential became clearer."

"Shooting my parents."

"Not that so much. The loss of trust."

"I see."

"Without trust, there can be no tranquil resting of the mind."

"No rest," Billy said. "No real peace."

"Without trust, there can be no belief. No belief in kindness. Or integrity. In anything."

"You have more insight into me than I do."

"Well, I'm older," Valis said. "And more experienced."

"Way more experienced," Billy said. "How long have you planned this performance? Not just since Monday in the bar."

"Weeks and weeks," said Valis. "Great art requires preparation."

"Did you take the commission for the mural because I was here, or did the commission come first?"

"Together," Valis said. "It was quite serendipitous. Things often are."

"Amazing. And here we are."

"Yes, here we are."

"'Movement, velocity, impact,'" Billy said, quoting Valis's summary for the style of this production.

"In light of how the performance is turning out, I think I would edit that to 'Movement, velocity, freedom.'"

"Like the fish."

"Yes. Like the fish. Do you want freedom, Billy?"

"Yes."

"I am entirely free."

Billy said, "How long have you been . . . ?"

"Thirty-two years. Since I was sixteen. The first few were embarrassments. Crude hacking. No control. No technique. No *style.*"

"But now . . ."

"Now, I have become who I am. Do you know my name?"

Billy met those gray and lustrous eyes.

"Yes," Valis answered for him. "I see you do. You know my name."

A thought occurred to Billy, and he leaned forward slightly in his chair, curious. "Are the others on your project crew . . ."

"Are they what?"

"Are they . . . previous successes of yours?"

Valis smiled. "Oh, no. None of them has ever seen my collection. Men like you and I . . . we're rare, Billy."

"I suppose so."

"You're probably full of questions about all this."

"Maybe when I've gotten some sleep."

"I was out to Deputy Olsen's house a little while ago. You left it clean as a whistle."

Billy grimaced. "You didn't plant something else out there, did you?"

"No, no. I knew we were getting close to this moment, no need to torment you further. I just walked the house, admiring how your mind worked, how *thorough* you were."

Billy yawned. "Circumstantial evidence. I have this fear of it."

"You must be very tired."

"I'm whacked."

"I've only one bedroom, but you're welcome to a sofa."

Billy shook his head. "This amazes me."

"That I'm hospitable?"

"No. That I'm *here*."

"Art transforms, Billy."

"Will I feel different when I wake up?"

"No," Valis said. "You've made your choice."

"They were something, those choices."

"They gave you an opportunity to understand your potential."

"Those sofas look so clean, and I'm a mess."

"You're fine," Valis said. "They're Scotchgarded."

As they rose simultaneously from their chairs, Billy pulled the Mace from under his T-shirt.

Apparently surprised, Valis tried to turn his face away.

They were only ten feet apart, and Billy sprayed him in the eyes.

Blinded, Valis pawed for the revolver on the table but knocked it to the floor.

Billy ducked past him, scooped up the gun, and Valis clawed at the air, trying to find him.

Coming around behind the freak, Billy hammered the back of his skull with the butt of the revolver, then hit him again.

With none of his usual grace, Valis crashed to

the floor on his face. Billy went to his knees to be sure the freak was out. He was.

Valis wore his shirt tucked in his pants. Billy tugged it loose and pulled it over the man's head, forming a tight hood by tying the tails together.

His purpose was not to blindfold Valis but to form a bandage in case his scalp began bleeding where the gun clipped it. Billy wanted to avoid getting bloodstains on the carpet.

# 72

Billy stretched his hands into the latex gloves. He got to work.

The bedroom was even more sumptuous than the rest of the motor home. The bathroom glowed and lustered, a jewel box of marble, glass, beveled mirrors, and gold-plated fixtures.

Embedded at a slant in the top of a ribbon-maple bedroom desk, a touch-sensitive screen provided control of the electronic systems from music to security.

Apparently, these controls had to be accessed by entering a code. Fortunately, Valis had left the system open after using it to put up the tambour panels and put down the steel blinds at the windows.

All controls featured idiot-proof labels. Billy unlocked the front door.

In the living room, Valis was still limp and unconscious, his head hooded by his shirt.

Billy dragged Valis out of the living room, through the dining area and kitchen, into the cockpit. He tumbled him down the steps and out of the motor home.

No more than an hour of darkness remained. The slim sickle moon now harvested stars beyond the western horizon.

He had parked the Explorer between the tent and the motor home, out of sight from the highway. No traffic passed.

He dragged Valis to the SUV.

No one lived nearby. The tavern across the highway would be deserted for hours yet.

When Valis had fired the shot into the armchair, there had been no one to hear.

Billy opened the tailgate. He unfolded one of the quilted moving blankets with which he had disguised poor Ralph Cottle's tarp-wrapped body. He smoothed it across the floor of the cargo area.

On the ground, Valis twitched. He began to moan.

Billy suddenly felt weak, less with physical fatigue than with an exhaustion of the mind and heart.

*The world turns and the world changes, but one thing does not change. However you disguise it, this thing does not change: the perpetual struggle of Good and Evil.*

With another blanket, Billy knelt beside the renowned artist. Thrusting the revolver into those

quilted folds, using them as sound suppression, he expended the five remaining rounds in the freak's chest.

He dared not wait to see if this time the gun had been heard. Immediately, he unfolded the smoking blanket on the ground and rolled the dead man in it.

Getting the corpse into the Explorer proved more difficult than he expected. Valis was heavier than scrawny Ralph Cottle.

If someone had been filming Billy, he would have had in camera a classic piece of macabre comedy. This was one of those moments when he wondered about God; didn't doubt His existence, just wondered about Him.

With Valis wrapped and loaded, Billy slammed the tailgate and returned to the motor home.

The bullet Valis fired had passed through the padded armchair and out the back. By ricochet, it had damaged the wall paneling. Billy tried to track it from there.

Because his father and mother had been shot with the .38, forensic profiles of the revolver existed. He didn't think there was a high likelihood that a match would be made, but he didn't intend to take any chances.

In a few minutes, he found the spent slug under a coffee table. He pocketed it.

Police would recognize the hole in the armchair as damage from gunfire. They would know that

a weapon had been discharged; and there was nothing to be done about that.

They would not know, however, whether it had been fired at Valis or *by* him. Without blood, they would not be able to deduce to whom, if anyone, violence had been committed.

Turning slowly in a full circle, casting his mind back to the moment, Billy tried to remember if, during the short time he'd been without gloves, he'd touched any surface that could be finger-printed. No. The place was clean.

He left the steel blinds shut. He left the tambour panels raised to expose the collection of faces and hands.

He did not close the door when he stepped out of the motor home. Open, it invited.

What a surprise for the glamorous crew of artists and artisans.

No traffic appeared on the highway during the time that he drove away from the motor home, out of the meadow, and onto the pavement.

What patterns his tires had imprinted in the dust, if they had imprinted any, would be oblit-erated when the crew arrived in a few hours.

# 73

Once more to the lava pipe, this time by a different route to avoid trampling the same brush as before.

While Billy removed the redwood lid, the narrow ragged wound of an appropriately bloody dawn opened along the contours of the mountains in the east.

A prayer didn't feel appropriate.

As though his specific gravity were greater than those of the other three cadavers, Valis seemed to drop faster into the hungry shaft than had the dead who preceded him.

When the sounds of the body's descent faded into silence, Billy said, "Older and more experienced, my ass." Then he remembered to drop Lanny's wallet into the pipe, and he replaced the lid.

As the night futilely resisted the early purple light, Billy parked the Explorer on the yard behind Lanny's garage. He let himself into the house.

This was Thursday, only the second of Lanny's two days off. No one was likely to wonder about him or to come around looking for him until sometime Friday.

Although Valis had denied planting any additional evidence in the wake of Billy's previous visit, Billy decided to search the house once more. You just couldn't trust some people.

He began upstairs, moving with the deliberateness of extreme fatigue, and by the time that he returned to the kitchen, he had not found anything incriminating.

Thirsty, he took a glass from a cabinet and drew cold tap water. Still wearing gloves, he was unconcerned about leaving prints.

Thirst quenched, he rinsed the glass, dried it on a dishtowel, and returned it to the cabinet from which he'd taken it.

Something didn't feel right.

He suspected that he had missed a detail that had the power to undo him. Dulled by weariness, his gaze had traveled over some damning evidence without recognizing its importance.

In the living room once more, he circled the sofa on which Valis had propped Ralph Cottle's corpse. No stains marred the furniture or the carpet around it.

Billy took up the cushions to see if anything from Cottle's pockets might have fallen between them. When he found nothing, he replaced the cushions.

Still plagued by a disquieting feeling that he had overlooked something, he sat down to brood. Because he was a mess, he didn't risk soiling a chair but with a sigh of weariness sat cross-legged on the floor.

He had just killed a man, or something rather like a man, but he could still be concerned about the parlor upholstery. He remained a polite boy. A considerate little savage.

This contradiction struck him as funny, and he laughed out loud. The more he laughed, the funnier his fussiness about the upholstery seemed to be, and then he was laughing at his own laughter, amused by his inappropriate giddiness.

He knew this was dangerous laughter, that it could unravel the carefully tied knot of his equilibrium. He stretched out on the carpet, flat on his back, and took long deep breaths to calm himself.

The laughter relented, he breathed less deeply, and somehow he allowed himself to fall into sleep.

# 74

Billy woke disoriented. For a moment, blinking at the legs of chairs and sofas all around him, he thought that he had fallen asleep in a hotel lobby, and he marveled at how considerate the management had been to leave him undisturbed.

Then memory tweaked him fully awake.

Getting to his feet, he gripped the arm of the sofa with his left hand. That was a mistake. The nail wound was inflamed. He cried out and almost fell, but didn't.

The day beyond the curtained windows looked fiercely bright and well advanced.

When he consulted his wristwatch, he saw that it was 5:02 in the afternoon. He had slept almost ten hours.

Panic flew, and his heart drummed like frantic wings. He thought his unexplained absence must have made him the primary suspect in the disappearance of Valis.

Then he remembered that he had called in sick for a second day. No one was expecting him to be anywhere. And no one knew he had any connection whatsoever to the dead artist.

If the police were eager to find anyone, they were searching for Valis himself, to ask him pointed questions about the contents of the jars in his living room.

In the kitchen, Billy took a drinking glass out of the cabinet. He filled it from the tap.

Digging in the pockets of his jeans, he found two Anacins and took them with a long drink. He also swallowed one tablet of Cipro and a Vicodin.

For a moment he felt nauseated, but the feeling passed. Maybe all these medications would interact in a mortal fashion and drop him dead between one step and another, but at least he wouldn't puke.

He was no longer troubled by the feeling that he might have left incriminating evidence in this house. That fear had been a symptom of exhaustion. Rested now, reviewing his precautions, he knew that he had not missed anything.

After locking the house, he returned the spare key to the hole in the tree stump.

With the advantage of daylight, he opened the tailgate of the Explorer and checked the floor of the cargo space for Valis's blood. None had soaked through the moving blankets, and the blankets had gone into the lava pipe with the corpse.

He drove away from the Olsen house with relief, with a cautious optimism, with a growing sense of triumph.

The site of the Valis project looked like an auto dealership that sold only police vehicles.

Lots of uniforms milled around the motor home, the tent, the mural. Sheriff John Palmer would be one of them because there were also TV-news vans standing bumper-to-bumper along the shoulder of the highway.

Billy realized that he was still wearing latex gloves. All right. No problem. No one could see and wonder why.

Not a single available space remained in the parking lot at the tavern. The news of Valis and his grisly collection would bring out all the regulars as well as new customers, with something more to talk about than pigs with human brains. Good for Jackie.

When Billy's house came into view, the sight of it warmed him. Home. With the artist dead, the locks would not have to be rekeyed. Security was his again, and privacy.

In the garage, he cleaned out the Explorer, bagged the trash, put away the power screwdriver and other tools.

Somewhere on this property were incriminating souvenirs, a last bit of cleanup to be done.

When he stepped across the kitchen threshold, he allowed his instinct to guide him. Valis wouldn't

have brought Giselle Winslow's hand here in a jar full of formaldehyde. Such a container would have been too awkward and fragile to allow quick work on the sly. Instinct suggested the simplest solution.

He went to the refrigerator and opened the freezer drawer at the bottom. Among the containers of ice cream and packages of leftovers were two foil-wrapped objects that he did not recognize.

He opened them on the floor. Two hands, each from a different woman. One of them had probably belonged to the redhead.

Valis had used the new non-stick foil. The manufacturer would be pleased to hear that it worked as advertised.

Billy couldn't stop trembling as he rewrapped the hands. For a while, he had thought that he had become inured to horror. He had not.

Before the day was done, he would have to throw out all the contents of the freezer. No contamination could have occurred, but the *thought* of contamination sickened him. He might have to trash the refrigerator itself.

He wanted the hands out of the house. He didn't expect the police to knock on the door with a search warrant, but he wanted the hands gone, anyway.

Burying them somewhere on the property seemed like a bad idea. At the very least, he

would have dreams about them clawing out of their small graves and creeping into the house at night.

Until he could decide what to do with them, he put the frozen hands in a small picnic cooler.

From his wallet, he thought to extract the folded snapshot of Ralph Cottle as a young man, Cottle's membership card in the American Society of Skeptics, and the photo of the redhead. He had kept these with the vague idea of turning the tables on the freak and planting bits of evidence on *him*. He tossed them in the cooler with the hands.

He had Lanny's cell phone, which he hesitated to add to the cooler. As if the hands would strip off their foil shrouds and call 911. He put the cell phone on the kitchen table.

To get the hands out of the house, he took the cooler to the garage and put it in the Explorer, on the floor in front of the passenger's seat. He locked the garage after himself.

The hot afternoon had waned. Six-thirty-six.

High overhead, a hawk conducted its last hunt of the day.

Billy stood watching as the bird described a widening gyre.

Then he went inside, eager to take a long shower as hot as he could tolerate.

The business with the women's hands had suppressed his appetite. He didn't think he would feel comfortable eating at home.

Maybe he would return to the truck stop for dinner. He felt as if he owed the waitress, Jasmine, even a bigger tip than the one he had previously left her.

In the hallway, heading for the bathroom, Billy saw a light in his office. When he looked through the doorway, he found the shades drawn, as he had left them.

He didn't remember leaving the desk lamp on, but he had split in a hurry, eager to dispose of Cottle. Without going around the desk, he switched off the lamp.

Although Cottle was no longer sitting on the toilet, Billy could too easily remember him there. This was his only bathroom, however, and his desire for a shower proved greater than his squeamishness.

The hot water gradually melted the aches from his muscles. The soap smelled glorious.

A couple of times, he grew claustrophobic behind the shower curtain and became half convinced that he had been cast in the Janet Leigh role in a gender-reversal version of *Psycho*.

Happily, he managed not to embarrass himself by whipping the curtain open. He concluded his shower without being knifed.

He wondered how much time would have to pass before he got over the heebie-jeebies. Most likely, the rest of his life.

After toweling off and dressing, he applied a

fresh bandage to the hook wounds in his forehead.

He went into the kitchen, opened an Elephant beer, and used it to chase a pair of Motrin. The inflammation in his left hand worried him a little.

At the table with the beer, and with a few first-aid items, he tried to introduce iodine into the nail wound, then applied a fresh liquid bandage.

Beyond the windows, twilight approached.

He intended to go to Whispering Pines and spend a few hours. He had arranged to stay throughout the night in a prayer vigil; but in spite of his ten-hour sleep, he didn't think he would be able to stay that long. With Valis dead, midnight had no meaning.

When Billy had tended to the nail wound, as he sat at the table finishing the beer, his attention fell on the microwave. The security video.

All this while, he'd been recording himself at the table. Then he realized that he had caught himself taking the hands out of the freezer. The camera had a wide-angle lens, but he didn't believe that it could have captured his gruesome work well enough to serve as evidence.

Nevertheless . . .

He got the stepladder from the pantry. He climbed it and opened the cabinet above the microwave.

Using the reverse-scan mode, he studied the small review screen, watching himself walk

backward around the kitchen. The angle had not revealed the severed hands.

Suddenly wondering whether Valis might have visited the house for some purpose between the time Billy had left the previous day and their meeting in the motor home before dawn, he continued the reverse scan beyond his entrance shortly after six o'clock.

He didn't have to go all the way to the previous day. At 3:07 this *same* day, while Billy had still been asleep at the Olsen place, a man walked backward out of the living room, across the kitchen to the door, and reversed out of the house.

The intruder was not Valis, of course, because Valis was dead.

# 75

Billy couldn't remember the number. Using Lanny's cell phone, he called directory assistance in Denver, and they put him through to Detective Ramsey Ozgard.

Billy paced while the phone rang out there in the shadow of the Rockies.

Maybe Valis had been confident of Billy's conversion because he had previously bent someone else instead of destroying him. None of the sixteen members of his crew was like him, but that didn't mean the artist was a lone hunter.

Ramsey Ozgard answered on the fifth ring, and Billy identified himself as Lanny Olsen, and Ozgard said, "I hear blood in your voice, Deputy. Tell me you've got your man."

"I think I will have shortly," Billy said. "I've got an urgent situation here. I need to know—the year Judith Kesselman vanished, was there a professor at the university, calling himself Valis?"

"Not a professor," Ozgard said. "He was the artist in residence for six months. At the end of his time, he did this ridiculous thing he called performance art, wrapped two campus buildings in thousands of yards of blue silk and hung them with—"

Billy interrupted. "Steve Zillis had a perfect alibi."

"It was watertight," Ozgard assured him. "I can walk you through it if you have ten minutes."

"I don't. But tell me—do you remember—at the university, what was Zillis's major?"

"He was an art major."

"Sonofabitch."

No wonder Zillis hadn't wanted to talk about the mannequins. They weren't just expressions of the sick dreams of a sociopathic killer—they were his *art.*

At that point, Billy hadn't yet discovered the key words that would reveal the identity of the freak—*performance art.* He'd had only *performance,* and Zillis instinctively hadn't wanted to give him the rest of it, not when he was doing so well playing a harmless, put-upon pervert.

"The son of a bitch deserves an Oscar," Billy said. "I left his place feeling like the world's worst shit, the way I treated him."

"Deputy?"

"The famous and respected Valis vouched for Steve Zillis—didn't he?—said that Steve was with

him on a retreat or something on the day Judith Kesselman disappeared."

"You're right. But you'd only jump to that if—"

"Turn on your evening news, Detective Ozgard. By the time Judi Kesselman vanished, Steve and Valis were working together. They were *each other's* alibi. Gotta go."

Billy remembered to press END before dropping Lanny's phone.

He still had Lanny's pistol and Taser. He threaded the Wilson Combat holster onto his belt.

From the closet in his bedroom, he snared a sport coat, shrugged into it to conceal the pistol as best he could.

He slipped the Taser in an inner coat pocket.

What had Steve been doing here in the afternoon? By then he would have known that his mentor had been outed, the collection of hands and faces discovered. He might even suspect that Valis was dead.

Billy remembered finding the light on in the study. He went in there, all the way behind the desk this time, and found the computer in sleep mode. He hadn't left it on.

When he moved the mouse, a document appeared.

*Can torture wake the comatose?*
*Her blood, her mutilation will be*
*your third wound.*

Billy flew through the house. He leaped off the back-porch steps, stumbled when he landed, and ran.

Night had fallen. An owl hooted. Wings against the stars.

# 76

At 9:06 the guest parking lot in front of Whispering Pines contained only one car. Visiting hours ended at nine.

They hadn't locked the front door yet. Billy pushed inside, crossed to the main nurses' station.

Two nurses were behind the counter. He knew them both. He said, "I made arrangements to stay—"

The overhead lights went out. The parking-lot lights died, too. The main hall was almost as black as a lava pipe.

He left the nurses in confusion and followed the corridor toward the west wing.

At first he hurried, but within a dozen steps, in the dark, he collided with a wheelchair, grabbed at it, felt the shape of it.

From the chair, a frightened old woman said, "What's happening, what're you doing?"

"It's all right, you'll be okay," he assured her, and went on.

He didn't move as fast now, arms in front of him like a blind man feeling for obstructions.

Wall-mounted emergency lights flickered on, then off, pulsed again and died.

An authoritative male voice calmly called out, "Please stay in your rooms. We will come to you. Please stay in your rooms."

The emergency sconces tried to function again. But they pulsed at one-third brightness, and erratically.

These flares and leaping shadows were disorienting, but Billy could see well enough to avoid the people in the halls. Another nurse, an orderly, an elderly man in pajamas, looking bewildered . . .

A fire alarm issued an electronic ululation. A recorded voice began to give evacuation instructions.

A woman in a walker intercepted Billy as he approached her, plucked at his sleeve, seeking information.

"They've got it under control," he assured her as he hurried past.

He turned the corner into the west wing. Just ahead, on the right. The door stood open.

The room was dark. No auxiliary sconce in here. His own body blocked what little light pulsed in from the west hall.

Slamming doors, a cacophony of slamming

doors, which weren't doors at all, but his heart.

He felt his way toward the bed. He should have reached it. He went two steps farther. The bed wasn't here.

He pirouetted blindly, sweeping his arms through the air. All he found was the barstool.

Her bed was on wheels. Someone had moved her.

In the hallway again, he looked left, looked right. A few of the ambulatory patients had come out of their rooms. A nurse was marshaling them for an orderly exit.

Through the dance of light and shadow, Billy saw a man pushing a bed at the far end of the hall, moving fast toward a flashing red EXIT sign.

Dodging patients, nurses, phantoms of shadow, Billy ran.

The door at the end of the hall banged open as the man slammed the bed through it.

A nurse grabbed Billy by the arm, halting him. He tried to pull loose, but she had a grip.

"Help me roll some of the bedridden out of here," she said.

"There's no fire."

"There must be. We've got to evacuate them."

"My wife," he declared, though he and Barbara had never married, "my wife needs help."

He tore loose of the nurse, nearly knocking her off her feet, and hurried toward the flashing EXIT sign.

He shoved through the door, into the night. Dumpsters, cars and SUVs in a staff parking lot.

For a moment, he didn't see the man, the bed.

*There.* An ambulance waited thirty feet away, to the left, its engine running. The wide rear door stood open. The guy with the bed had almost reached it.

Billy drew the 9-mm pistol but didn't dare use it. He might hit Barbara.

Crossing the blacktop, he holstered the pistol, fumbled the Taser out of an inner coat pocket.

At the last instant, Steve heard Billy coming. The freak had a pistol. He fired twice as he turned.

Billy was already coming in under Steve's arm. The gun boomed over his head.

He jammed the business end of the Taser into Steve's abdomen and clicked the trigger. He knew it would work through thin clothing, a shirt, but he had never checked to be sure that it contained fresh batteries.

Zillis spasmed as the electric charge cried havoc along the wires of his nervous system. He didn't merely drop his gun but *flung* it away. His knees buckled. He rapped his head on the bumper of the ambulance as he fell.

Billy kicked him. He tried to kick him in the head. He kicked him again.

The fire department would be coming. The police. Sheriff John Palmer, sooner or later.

He put his hand to Barbara's face. Her breath

feathered his palm. She seemed to be all right. He could feel her eyes moving under her lids, dreaming Dickens.

Glancing back at Whispering Pines, he saw that no one had yet evacuated through the west-wing exit.

He rolled Barbara's bed aside.

On the ground, Steve was twitching, saying, "Unnn, unnn, unnn," in a bad imitation of an epileptic fit.

Billy zapped him again with the Taser, then pocketed it.

He grabbed the freak by his belt, by the collar of his shirt, hauled him off the blacktop. He didn't think he had the strength to lift and shove Zillis into the back of the ambulance, but panic flushed him with adrenaline.

The knuckles of the freak's right hand rapped uncontrollably against the floor of the ambulance, as did the back of his skull.

Billy slammed the door, seized the foot rail of Barbara's bed, and pushed her toward Whispering Pines.

When he was less than ten feet from the door, it opened, and an orderly appeared, leading a patient in a walker.

"This is my wife," Billy said. "I got her out. Will you look after her while I help some others?"

"It's covered," the orderly assured him. "I better get her a safe distance if there's fire."

Urging the man in the walker to keep pace with him, the orderly pushed Barbara away from the building but also away from the waiting ambulance.

When Billy got behind the wheel and pulled the driver's door shut, he heard the freak drumming his heels against something and making strangled noises that might have been fractured curses.

Billy didn't know how long the effect of a Tasering lasted. Maybe he was wrong to pray for convulsions, but he did.

He found the brake release, the gear shift, and he pulled around to the front of the building. He parked beside his Explorer.

People were coming out of the building, into the parking lot. They were too busy to wonder about him.

He transferred the cooler with the severed hands to the ambulance and then got away from there. He went two blocks before he could locate the switch for the emergency beacons and the siren.

By the time he passed the fire trucks, coming out from Vineyard Hills, the ambulance was in full flash and voice.

He figured the more he called attention to himself, the less suspicious he appeared. He broke every speed limit going through the northeast end of town, and turned due east on the state route that led to the Olsen house.

When he was two miles out of town, with vineyards to both sides of the road, he heard the freak muttering more coherently and banging around back there, evidently trying to get up.

Billy pulled to the shoulder of the road, parked, but left the beacons flashing. He climbed between the seats, into the back.

On his knees, clutching the bracketed oxygen cylinder, Zillis wanted badly to get to his feet. His eyes were bright, like those of a coyote at night.

Billy zapped him again, and Zillis flopped, twitched, but a Taser wasn't a deadly weapon.

If he shot the freak, blood might spray over all the life-support equipment, an ungodly mess. And evidence.

On the wheeled stretcher were two thin foam pillows. Billy grabbed both.

Flat on his back, rolling his head from side to side, Zillis had no muscle control whatsoever.

Billy dropped on his chest with both knees, driving the breath out of him, cracking more than one of his ribs, and shoved the pillows over his face.

Although the freak fought for life, he fought ineffectively.

Billy almost couldn't finish it. He made himself think about Judith Kesselman, her lively eyes, her elfin smile, and he wondered if Zillis had shoved a spear-point iron stave into her, whether he had cut off the top of her skull while she was alive and handed it to her as a drinking cup.

Then it was over.

Sobbing but not for Zillis, he climbed once more behind the steering wheel. He drove onto the highway.

Two miles from the turnoff to the Olsen place, Billy killed the emergency beacons and the siren. He slowed below the speed limit.

Because the alarm at Whispering Pines had been false, the fire-department crew would not linger. By the time he eventually returned the ambulance, the staff parking lot would be deserted again.

He had left his power screwdriver at home. He was pretty sure that Lanny owned one. He would borrow it. Lanny wouldn't care.

As he reached the house, he saw the sickle moon, a little thicker this night than last, and the silver blade perhaps somewhat sharper.

# 77

All year, the valley is home to rock doves and to band-tailed pigeons, to the song sparrow and to the even more musical dark-eyed junco.

The long-winged, long-tailed falcons known as American kestrels also stay the year. Their distinctive plumage is bright and cheerful. Their shrill, clear call sounds like *killy-killy-killy-killy,* which should not be pleasing to the ear, but is.

Billy bought a new refrigerator. And a microwave.

He knocked down a wall, combining his study with the living room because he had plans to use the space differently from the way it had been used before.

After choosing a cheerful butter-yellow color, he repainted every room.

He threw out the carpets and furniture, and purchased everything new, because he didn't know where the redhead might have been sitting

or lying when she had been strangled or otherwise dispatched.

He considered razing the house and rebuilding, but he realized that houses are not haunted. *We* are haunted, and regardless of the architecture with which we surround ourselves, our ghosts stay with us until we ourselves are ghosts.

When he was not at work on the house or behind the bar at the tavern, he sat in the room at Whispering Pines or on his front porch, reading the novels of Charles Dickens, the better to know where Barbara lived.

With the coming of autumn, the wood-pewees move on from the valley, and their *pee-didip, pee-didip* is not heard until spring. Most of the willow flycatchers migrate as well, although a few may adapt and linger.

By autumn, Valis remained big news, especially in the tabloids and on those TV shows that tricked up carnival-freakshow huckstering to pass for investigative journalism. They would feed on him for a year at least, like flickers feed on the larvae in noisy acorns, though Nature had not given them the imperative that she had given to the flickers.

Steve Zillis had been linked to Valis. Sightings of the pair—disguised but recognizable—were reported in South America, in Asia, in the more ominous regions of the former Soviet Union.

Lanny Olsen was assumed to be dead but also

in some mysterious way a hero. He had not been a detective, merely a deputy, and never before had he been a *motivated* officer; however, his calls to Ramsey Ozgard, of the Denver PD, indicated that he had reason to suspect Zillis and, in the end, Valis as well.

No one could explain why Lanny had not taken his suspicions to a superior. Sheriff Palmer said only that Lanny always had been "a lone wolf who did some of his best work outside the usual channels," and for some reason no one laughed or asked the sheriff what the hell he was talking about.

One theory—popular at the bar—held that Lanny had shot and wounded Valis, but that Steve Zillis had come on scene and murdered Lanny. Then Steve had driven away with Lanny's body to dispose of it, and with the wounded artist, as well, to nurse him to health in some hideaway, since all legitimate doctors are required to report gunshot wounds.

No one knew in what vehicle Steve had fled, as his own car was in the garage at his house; but obviously he had stolen wheels from someone. He hadn't taken the motor home because he had never before driven it, and no doubt because he feared that it would attract too much attention once Valis had been reported missing.

Psychologists and criminologists with knowledge of sociopathic behavior argued against the

idea that one homicidal psychopath would be inclined selflessly to nurse another homicidal psychopath back to health. The notion of these two monsters behaving with tender-hearted concern toward each other appealed to the press, however, and to the public. If Count Dracula and the Frankenstein monster could be good friends, as they had been in a couple of old films, Zillis might be stirred to minister to his grievously wounded artist mentor.

No one ever noticed that Ralph Cottle had vanished.

Surely the young redhead had been missed, but perhaps she had come from a distant part of the nation and had been snatched on the road while passing through the wine country. If there were stories in some other state about her disappearance, she was never connected to the Valis affair, and Billy never learned her name.

People go missing every day. The national news media don't have sufficient space or time to report upon the fall of every sparrow.

Although wood-pewees and most willow flycatchers leave with the summer, the common snipe appears when autumn trends toward winter, as does the ruby-crowned kinglet, which has a high, clear, lively song of many phrases.

In those rarefied circles where the simplest thoughts are deep and where even gray has shades of gray, a movement arose to complete the unfin-

ished mural. And burn it as planned. Valis might have been insane, the argument went; but art is art nonetheless, and must be respected.

The burning drew such an enthusiastic crowd of Hells Angels, organized anarchists, and sincere nihilists that Jackie O'Hara closed his doors that weekend. He didn't want their trade at a family tavern.

By late autumn, Billy quit his bartending job and brought Barbara home. One end of the expanded living room served as both her bedroom and his office. With her quiet company, he found that he could write again.

Although Barbara did not require life-support machines, only a pump to supply a steady food drip through the tube in her stomach, Billy initially depended on continuous help from registered nurses. He learned to care for her, however, and after several weeks, he seldom needed a nurse other than at night, when he slept.

He emptied her catheter bag, changed her diapers, cleaned her, bathed her, and was never repulsed. He felt better doing these things for her than he felt when he let strangers do them. In truth, he did not expect that tending to her in this fashion would make her seem more beautiful to him, but that was what happened.

She had saved him once, before she'd been taken from him, and now she saved him again. After the terror, the brutal violence, the murder,

she gave him the opportunity to become reacquainted with compassion and to find in himself a gentleness that otherwise he might have lost forever.

Strange, how the friends began to visit. Jackie, Ivy, the cooks Ramon and Ben, and Shirley Trueblood. Harry Avarkian often drove up from Napa. They sometimes brought members of their families, as well as friends of theirs who became Billy's friends. Increasingly, people seemed to enjoy hanging around the Wiles place. They had a crowd on Christmas Day.

By spring, when the wood-pewees and willow flycatchers returned in numbers, Billy had widened the front door and ramped the threshold to accommodate Barbara's bed on the porch. With an extension cord to keep her food pump working and to allow adjustment of the mattress, she was able to lie in an elevated position, her face to the warm spring breezes.

On the porch, he read, sometimes aloud. And listened to the bird songs. And watched her dreaming *A Christmas Carol.*

That was a good spring, a better summer, a fine autumn, a lovely winter. That was the year when people began to call him Bill instead of Billy, and somehow he didn't notice until the new name was the common usage.

In the spring of the following year, one day when he and Barbara were together on the porch,

Bill was reading to himself when she said, "Barn swallows."

He no longer kept a notebook of the things that she said, for he no longer worried that she was afraid and lost and suffering. She was not lost.

When he looked up from his book, he discovered a flock of that very bird, moving as one, describing graceful patterns over the yard beyond the porch.

He looked at her and saw that her eyes were open and that she seemed to be watching the swallows.

"They're more graceful than other swallows," he said.

"I like them," she said.

The birds were elegant with their long, slender, pointed wings and their long, deeply forked tails. Their backs were dark blue, their breasts orange.

"I like them very much," she said, and closed her eyes.

After holding his breath for a while, he said, "Barbara?"

She did not answer.

*I said to my soul, be still, and wait without hope, for hope would be hope for the wrong thing.*

Hope, love, and faith are all in the waiting. Power is not the truth of life; the love of power is the love of death.

The barn swallows flew elsewhere. Bill returned to the book that he had been reading.

What will happen will happen. There is time for miracles until there is no more time, but time has no end.

# Note

In moments of stress and indecision, words of wisdom enter Billy Wiles's mind, and he is guided by them. Although Billy does not make an attribution, these words are from the work of T. S. Eliot.

Chapter 9: *Preserve me from the enemy who has something to gain, and from the friend who has something to lose.* Also in that chapter: *Teach us to care and not to care. Teach us to sit still.*

Chapter 13: *The only wisdom we can hope to acquire is the wisdom of humility.*

Chapter 17: *May the judgment not be too heavy upon us.*

Chapter 33: *There is one who remembers the way to your door: Life you may evade, but Death you shall not.*

Chapter 66: *In order to possess what you do not possess, you must go by way of dispossession. And what you do not know is the only thing you know.*

Chapter 71: *In order to arrive at what you are not, you must go through the way in which you are not.*

Chapter 72: *The world turns and the world changes, but one thing does not change. However you disguise it, this thing does not change: the perpetual struggle of Good and Evil.*

Chapter 77: *I said to my soul, be still, and wait without hope, for hope would be hope for the wrong thing.*

The Napa County Sheriff's Department in this fiction bears no resemblance to the superlative law-enforcement agency of the same name in the real world, nor is any person in this story based in any way whatsoever on any real person in Napa County, California.

Barbara's most mysterious statement—*I want to know what it says, the sea. What it is that it keeps on saying*—is from *Dombey & Son.*

Correspondence for the author should be addressed to:


Dean Koontz
P.O. Box 9529
Newport Beach, California 92658, USA